Wizard Pox

David G. Cox

ISBN: 0615554369
ISBN-13: 978-0615554365
LCCN: 2011941041

Wizard Pox

DEDICATION

For my super fantastic intelligent smart-mouthed daughter who is usually my first critic of everything I write, this ones for you Deva.

CONTENTS

SECTION 1

1

Wendell Glasswright awoke feeling as if his insides were being clawed upon by Dragons and his head was on fire. His face had broken out in green bumps which looked like tiny mole hills oozing nasty yellow puss. His eyes were puffy, dry as a desert, and painfully bloodshot. Wendell didn't have the strength to get out of bed so he croaked for his mother after his futile attempt to rise failed.

"What is it, hon…Power's preserve us!" Wendell's plump little mother began but stopped dead in her tacks at the doorway and made a sign to ward away evil spirits as soon as she saw her son's condition.

"May I have some water mother?" Wendell croaked as if the mere act of speech was wearing him out.

Wendell's mother clapped a pudgy hand over her mouth and said something that could have been 'Yes, Dear' as she quickly backed out of the room. All color had drained out of Mrs. Glasswright's face before she slammed the door shut.

Wendell sank back into straw-filled mattress and half-dozed for a few moments before he heard his mother and father's voices in the next room of their humble cottage. The conversation made little sense through the boy's fevered delirium, but he did catch the word 'Plague' amidst their hushed whispers. Wendell couldn't make out the rest for at that moment he was distracted by a tiny visitor.

Across the small bedroom from under Wendell's dresser crept a tiny humanoid creature no bigger than Wendell's thumb. It was dressed in bright red and yellow garb that would have likely made a Jester puke, and it's pointed-toed boots were nearly twice again as long as its diminutive size required. This strange little creature had wild unkempt long white hair that completely concealed its features except for its large protruding nose. It paused just below the dresser's edge and sniffed the air cautiously like a wary animal then raced out towards one of Wendell's red and white striped stockings that he'd left in the middle of the floor.

"Your mother tells me you aren't feeling...Oh my Heavens, run and get the Leech, Maggie!" Wendell's father started to enter the room but stopped dead in his tracks still gripping the doorknob. His eyes boggled in his balding head at the sight of Wendell but the boy was too enthralled with the little creature to notice.

The tiny man-like thing which Wendell assumed was some type of Fairy had begun heaving the discarded stocking back towards the dresser with all its diminutive might. Despite its great efforts, the stocking was only moving about and inch at a time.

"Don't worry son, your going to be just fine," Mr. Glasswright told Wendell even though it sounded suspiciously like he was trying to convince himself of the truth of his words.

"Stop! You'll step on it!" Wendell croaked as his father began to step into the room. Both his father and the creature stopped dead in their tracks. Mr. Glasswright looked down as the creature looked up and sniffed the air warily.

"If you're not going to clean your room you can hardly blame others when they step on your clothes, Son," Mr. Glasswright stated after glancing down at the stocking before him. Wendell's exclamation did seem to be the excuse his father needed to remain at a distance however, and he stayed in the doorway.

"Don't you see it?" Wendell asked pointing down at the diminutive creature that was now sniffing the air towards Wendell. "It's right in front of you."

"See what, your stocking?" Wendell's father asked with a perplexed expression.

"Never mind father, it must be my fever," Wendell sighed and sank back into bed, while continuing to watch the creature. He had heard of fevered hallucinations before but had never expected them to be so vivid. The creature finished sniffing the air, shrugged, then continued to drag the stocking beneath the dresser.

"Try to get some rest, Son; your mother should be back with the Leech in a few minutes," Mr. Glasswright stated as he began to withdraw.

"May I have some water please, Father?" Wendell asked before his father could shut the door.

"Of course, Son," Mr. Glasswright nodded before withdrawing.

Wendell watched the creature and his stocking disappear beneath the dresser and wondered if he was going to die. It was a sobering question for the sickly twelve year old who had never given much thought to his mortality. He took stock of his life as he listened to his father filling a bucket at the hand pump in front of their cottage.

Wendell was the youngest of the Glasswright's five children, though his siblings had moved out while he was still very young so that he'd always felt more or less like an only child. His brothers and sister all lived within their village and saw him almost daily, but paid him little mind. Everyone seemed to pay Wendell little mind. He was just one of those people that was easily overlooked and forgotten. Often even his own parents would seem surprised that he was there when he spoke up at the supper table. It was something Wendell had learned to live with.

Wendell was small for his age and thin as a rail. His hair was a drab brown and hung limply around his head in the plain bowl cut his mother had given him. His features were pleasant though unremarkable, resembling none in his family save for the freckly skin that his mother and sister shared across the bridge of their noses. He was normally quite healthy despite his delicate appearance and his current state, but his mother always worried that he wasn't eating enough for rarely did Wendell have much of an appetite. His tastes ran more towards exploring the world around him in a cautious and speculative way.

Wendell was curious about all things large and small as most children are but unlike them he rarely voiced the questions rolling around his head. Instead Wendell was content to observe and digest his surroundings in a quiet and unobtrusive manner. After his chores were complete Wendell could often be found sitting and watching spiders build their webs, or the village tradesmen about their work. He liked to watch all and form his own conclusions about what he saw, and most of these conclusions were fairly accurate despite his lack of years.

So it was that when Wendell contemplated the possibility he might be dying he didn't look upon it with fear but more of a resigned curiosity. Good or ill, death would certainly be a new experience and new experiences were always interesting to Wendell's eyes. He was definitely curious about death though not eager. He just wished that it didn't have to be such a miserable and painful experience as he lay feeling every ache and itchy sensation of his illness.

Wendell's father returned with a bucket of water and a wooden ladle which he placed beside his son's bed. He was about to withdraw when the sounds of Mrs. Glasswright and Nicolas the Leech entering the cottage gave him pause. Mr. Glasswright greeted the Leech in the doorway warmly shaking his hand then stepped aside so that the elder physician could see Wendell in his bed.

"Eeeh…" Nicolas shivered and turned a shade paler as he crossed the threshold into the small bedroom. He immediately removed a handkerchief from his coat pocket and covered his nose and mouth with it. "How are you feeling, Wendell?"

"Not very well, Sir," Wendell croaked as he ladled some water out of the bucket to drink. Wendell had a sinking feeling that his condition was quiet severe simply from the fact that Nicolas seemed very reluctant to close the distance between them.

Nicolas set down his large leather satchel and squatted over it until his long graying black beard dropped within. He started to rummage through the satchel's contents but stopped to shoot a look of annoyance over his shoulder towards Wendell's parents who had both been leaning over the Leech in an attempt to spy on the secrets the satchel contained. Mr. and Mrs. Glasswright stammered their apologies as they stepped back outside the room to give Nicolas space. The physician continued his search with half-uttered grumbles of annoyance until he found what he was looking for in the shape of a small ear horn made of copper.

"Now relax boy and let me examine you," Nicolas ordered through his handkerchief as he pulled the thick quilt off of Wendell's feet. He paused long enough to tie his handkerchief around his head then lifted Wendell's left foot to listen to the soul with the ear horn.

"Hmmm...yes, yes," Nicolas muttered behind his handkerchief mask before repeating the procedure to Wendell's right foot. Wendell was at a loss as to what the Leech could be listening to but then medicine was a fairly new and secretive science so he merely observed quietly. "Interesting," Nicolas muttered as he set down Wendell's foot and returned to his satchel.

The next instrument that Nicolas removed from his satchel resembled the tongs used in blacksmithing but on a much smaller scale. Unlike those tongs, however, the ends of these tapered down to hook-like points that touched at the ends.

"Now hold still boy, this shouldn't hurt much," Nicolas grunted from behind his thick spectacles as he came to Wendell's side.

Wendell was beginning to become afraid. After shooting his parents a hopeful look, he knew that no help was coming from that quarter. Both his parents appeared to be holding their breath with anticipation as they leaned in the doorway completely enthralled by the Leech's trade. Wendell gulped deep in his irritated and scratchy throat as he did his very best to hold still for the physician. He became cross-eyed as he tried to watch Nicolas as the Leech fasten the tool onto one of the green bumps on his nose and gave it a gentle squeeze. Yellow puss instantly spouted forth and sprayed a slimy blob of the stuff across one of the Leech's thick glass lenses.

Nicolas jumped a foot straight back and very nearly vomited with disgust. Green around the gills, he took the time to wipe clean his lenses with yet another handkerchief from his pocket before retreating back to his satchel. He had just removed an instrument that appeared to be part saw and part vise-clamp that filled Wendell with no small amount of dread when the boy wrinkled his green-bumped and puss-covered nose and drew in breath for a sneeze.

In the instant before Wendell sneezed he saw a look of shear terror cross the old Leech's face as he apparently realized he was about to get sprayed with yet another disgusting and slimy substance. Wendell was more than a little tempted to blast the frightening physician but his well-learned manners wouldn't allow it, so at the last second he turned his head to the side. This was indeed fortunate for the blast of Wendell's great sneeze released a rather loud honk and transformed his bedside candle into a large white rabbit.

"Eeek!" Nicolas released a feminine shriek as he launched himself through the bedroom door, colliding with both of Wendell's parents. It took a few moments for the Leech and the Glasswrights to untangle themselves during which Wendell and the rabbit contemplated each other in mutual states of shock.

"Heavens protect us from the vile spirits which have invaded our home!" Mrs. Glasswright invoked as she traced one of her most powerful wards against evil in the air before her. The rabbit twitched its nose, hopped off Wendell's nightstand, and sought refuge under the boy's bed.

Nicolas licked his dry lips under his handkerchief mask as he leaned just far enough into the room to snatch up his satchel. Once the bag was retrieved, he withdrew with all the speed his old bones could muster and began to speak quickly.

"I'm afraid that your son's condition is not physical but metaphysical in nature, and as such there is nothing I can do," Nicolas stated loud enough for Wendell to hear from the safety of the next room. "Now that will be five chickens or a plump calf for the house call."

"What? But you didn't do anything!" Mr. Glasswright angrily accused. Even in his current state Wendell's father was a shrewd fellow and countered almost instantly. "One chicken and a half-dozen eggs."

"But what should we do?" Wendell's mother interrupted their haggling on the edge of panic.

"In my opinion you should consult a Wizard or if you wish to save money simply isolate the boy and start working on his gravestone. Two chickens and a half-dozen eggs," Nicolas answered after a moment's thought.

"That's outrageous; my boy isn't going to die!" Mr. Glasswright growled as if the matter had been decided by the shear force of his will. "One chicken and my restraint from punching you in the nose."

"Err, um, deal, Sir. Always a pleasure Mrs. Glasswright. I'll just go out and chase down one of those hens and be on my way," the Leech sputtered as he left the cottage hastily.

"Where are you going dear?" Wendell's mother broke the few moments of silence that followed the Leech's retreat.

"I'm going to fetch a Wizard," Wendell's father stated as the boy started to drift back to sleep.

"Can we afford one dear?" Wendell's mother asked anxiously.

"We'll find a way. That Bergstrom seems like a decent enough fellow. Maybe we can find a way to pay him back over time. I'm certain he'd be interested in a portion of our vegetables or some new windows for his tower, Wizards never seem to keen on manual labor," Wendell would have liked to have listened more to his parent's conversation but he couldn't stay awake any longer. Sleep overtook him nearly instantly.

2

Now as it happens, two Wizards had chosen to make their home in Wendell's village. The first went by the name of Scott Garroph, and had moved to the village thirty two winters ago. Little was known about Mr. Garroph for once construction of his great tower was completed the villagers rarely saw him. What few times he did appear in the village he conducted himself politely if very sternly, seeing to his business then was away again disappearing just as quickly as he'd arrived. It had actually been so many years now since the reclusive Mr. Garroph had been seen that the villagers might have doubted he still lived if it weren't for the strange lights that occasionally could be seen illuminating his towers windows in the dead of night when most honest men were in their beds. Rumors abounded about Mr. Garroph and any unexplained event within the village would be blamed upon him, though never directly and most often in hushed conspiratorial tones with a wary eye towards his tall square stone tower as if to do more would risk provoking the Wizard's wrath.

The second Wizard was of an entirely different breed and well known to almost everyone in the village. Bergstrom Weatherbee was his name and he was often found chatting with the villagers every other morning as he went about his grocery shopping. Mr. Weatherbee had moved to the village ten summers ago and like Mr. Garroph before him had a tower built on the opposite side of the village. He was a friendly good-humored fellow who would always make time to greet his neighbors and make more time should they wish to chat. He appeared very knowledgeable in most subjects and possessed a great wisdom that was often sought out to solve any of the villager's more difficult problems. He did, however, have some strange habits like talking to inanimate objects or activities that defied all reason. The latest example of Mr. Weatherbee's strange doings was when a farmer named Gregory Holts found him at the back of his property fishing down a hollowed out rotted stump with an apple attached to his fishing pole's line. It was widely believed that Mr. Weatherbee had lost more than a few of his marbles, but his strange antics were tolerated for he was always helpful and friendly to everyone despite his abnormal behavior.

So it was that when Mr. Glasswright set out to get a Wizard, he headed strait for Mr. Weatherbee's tower perched on a hill just above the west side of the village. He found the Wizard tending to his small vegetable garden below the large round tower and talking to the Bees he kept there. Mr. Glasswright was more than a bit apprehensive about approaching the tall clay hives and their busy little occupants and the Wizard seemed to sense this. So Mr. Weatherbee accomodated and cast a spell that finished the weeding of his garden in a matter of moments and walked out to meet Wendell's father at the gate.

"Hello there Mr. Glasswright and a fine morning to you. Is there something I can help you with?" The Wizard greeted him as he approached while brushing the soil from his dark tan robes.

"It's my son, Wendell, Mr. Weatherbee. He's caught some type of magical illness that the Leech could do nothing about." Mr. Glasswright informed the Wizard as he wiped the sweat from his brow and tried to regain his wind. The glass blower wasn't in the habit of jogging up hill and the summer morning was growing quite warm.

"Please lead the way, Sir, and I will see him at once," Mr. Weatherbee told him after handing the worried man his water skin. Mr. Glasswright couldn't remember the Wizard having the water skin a moment ago but his thirst outweighed his normal apprehension of the supernatural as he drank down the cool refreshing water. "You say the Leech could do nothing? That seems very fortunate for your son's continued state of health. You should count yourself lucky," The Wizard smirked with a wink.

"We haven't much in the way of payment, but perhaps we can come to some sort of long term arrangement for your services?" Mr. Glasswright asked sheepishly as he handed back the water skin with a nod of thanks.

"Well, let's see what sort of treatment your son requires before we speak of such things, shall we?" Mr. Weatherbee smiled warmly and patted Wendell's father on the shoulder reassuringly as they started down the trail to the village.

It took a little over ten minutes to reach the Glasswright's cottage during which Mr. Weatherbee engaged Mr. Glasswright in small talk that seemed to put the worried father at ease as probably nothing else could. They found Mrs. Glasswright in the kitchen area of the small cottage kneading dough like a mad women. Her cheeks were caked with flower which had turned gooey from her tears and she was muttering all manner of superstitious wards against evil as she mindlessly worked the over kneaded dough.

"There, there, Mrs. Glasswright, I'm here now and will do my best to put everything right as rain," the Wizard produced a fine pink handkerchief from his sleeve and offered it to the distraught women. She chewed her bottom lip for a moment before accepting the handkerchief looking at it and the Wizard as if they were the cause of all her woes. "If you haven't any plans for all that dough, Mrs. Glasswright, I'm very fond of fresh baked bread, but you must stop crying soon or it will be the saltiest loaf I've ever had the misfortune to stomach."

"Wendell's this way," Mr. Glasswright opened the door to Wendell's room and immediately had to jump back out of the way as hundreds of white rabbits spilled out.

Mrs. Glasswright gave a terrified scream and jumped from a stand still to the top of a nearby stool instantly. She started tracing every ward in her superstitious arsenal towards the rabbits that were quickly overrunning her home with one hand while holding her floor caked rolling pin in the other ready to club whichever of the fuzzy white monsters dared to try and eat her.

"Perhaps you should try and shoo away our furry little visitors and see to your wife while I have a look at your son in private," Mr. Weatherbee suggested and trying hard to keep a straight face as he carefully weaved his way through the rabbits towards the boy's bedroom.

"As you will, Mr. Weatherbee," Mr. Glasswright nodded, then to his wife he stated, "for the love of all Maggie, they're just rabbits. Start boiling some stew water and I'll start dressing them."

Mr. Weatherbee nodded approvingly towards Wendell's father thinking him a very sensible man as he stepped into the room and looked Wendell up and down. After this very cursory examination, the Wizard paused long enough to shoo the last of the lingering white Rabbits from the room then shut the door behind them. He then took a seat at the foot of Wendell's bed and patiently waited for the sick boy to awaken.

3

When Wendell awoke he didn't recognize the old man sitting at the foot of his bed at first though he did seem vaguely familiar. For a moment or two, they simply scrutinized one another in a kind of mutual examination which required no words. The old man had a short but very bushy grey beard that surrounded a smile that was very reassuring and contagious despite how rotten Wendell felt. His eyes were crystal blue behind the round lenses of his spectacles, which seemed far younger than his appearance would suggest. His nose was very large and rounded save for the perch his spectacles had worn into its bridge long ago. Long thick locks of unkempt grey hair hung down from the sides of his baggy leather hat which resembled an acorn with a bright white feather protruding from its side. He was dressed in weather worn and dirty tan robes lined with runes which glowed with soft iridescent white light. It was these runes of power that finally sparked Wendell's memory and all at once he blurted out the old Wizard's name.

"Bergstrom?" Wendell asked in wonder, forgetting his manners for a moment. "I'm sorry, Mr. Weatherbee."

"That's alright, Wendell, I'm Bergstrom to my friends and I'd very much would like to be your friend. Your father had the good sense to call upon me when it became clear that your condition was magical in nature. It's a good thing, too, for I know just the thing to help you if you're willing to trust me and do as I say?" the Wizard explained kindly as he stroked his bushy grey whiskers thoughtfully.

"Will it hurt?" Wendell asked reluctantly, remembering the Leech's frightening tools.

"No, Wendell, in fact I'm certain that it will make you feel immediately much better. Shall we proceed?" Bergstrom assured him, and after a moment Wendell nodded his acceptance. "Good. Now I want you to first close your eyes and visualize a brilliant white light."

Wendell thought this a bit strange, but everything about Mr. Weatherbee suggested that he was someone that he could trust so he followed the Wizard's directions. Closing his eyes, Wendell did his best to imagine a bright light in the darkness behind his eyelids. After a few seconds, Mr. Weatherbee spoke again in a soft hypnotic voice that seemed to make Wendell just a bit drowsy.

"Now when you've got this bright light clearly visualized in your mind I want you to open your eyes while simultaneously snapping your fingers," Mr. Weatherbee instructed.

Wendell hesitated a moment longer then opened his eyes and snapped his fingers. Instantly the room was filled with a brilliant white light and he felt as if something had been drained out of his body leaving him very fatigued.

"That was marvelous, Wendell; I couldn't have done better myself," Mr. Weatherbee admitted as he removed his spectacles and rubbed his eyes with the tips of his fingers. "Now, how do you feel, son?"

Despite the draining he experienced, Wendell did feel a lot better. The turning in his stomach had receded to merely an uncomfortable ache. His eyes didn't feel quite as itchy and the scratchiness in his throat subsided. He felt so much better in fact that he immediately glanced down at his hands thinking the Wizard must have magically cured him while he'd been distracted but then he saw that his skin was still covered in the ugly green bumps.

"Better Sir, but what did you do?" Wendell finally asked when he was unable to grasp how a flash of light could make a sick person become well.

"Not me Wendell, you. You have a bad case of Wizard Pox. It's a magical sickness caused when a person with magic in their blood like you goes for a long time without releasing some of that magic. See it builds up in your body when you don't use it and after a while makes you physically sick as it forces its way out. That's why rabbits have been appearing whenever you sneeze. What I've just showed you is a simple spell to create a flash of light. I want you to practice at it whenever you're in pain until this sickness goes away and it will drain the magical build up in a harmless way. When you get really good at it you won't have to even close your eyes before you do it, just snap your fingers and pop," Mr. Weatherbee smiled warmly though at the same time he seemed rather thoughtful.

"Does it cause you to see things?" Wendell asked after taking in the Wizard's explanation and digesting it for a few moments.

"What sort of things?" Mr. Weatherbee asked as he placed a warm hand on Wendell's forehead to check his temperature.

"Earlier a tiny man-like creature came out from under my dresser and stole one of my stockings. My father couldn't see it so I assumed I was feverish," Wendell explained as the Wizard withdrew his hand.

"Did it go back under the dresser?" Mr. Weatherbee asked as he rose to his feet eyeing the peace of furniture suspiciously as if it might bite at any moment.

"Yes Sir, along with my stocking," Wendell nodded before releasing a large yawn.

"Well let's see, shall we?" Mr. Weatherbee stated before flopping down on his belly so he could look under the dresser, "Ah, it seems a Brownie is building a nest down here. There now, don't be afraid. That's a good fellow."

After a moment or two of rummaging under the dresser, the Wizard withdrew his arm to reveal the tiny humanoid creature that Wendell had seen earlier held carefully in the palm of his hand. The Brownie was shaking with fear huddled in the center of Bergstrom's cupped palm. The Wizard fished in his pocket for a moment until he found a piece of hard candy wrapped in wax paper, unwrapped it with the tips of his fingers with one hand and then presented it to diminutive creature as he sat back down at the foot of the bed. The Brownie sniffed the candy for a moment with its oversized nose then took it greedily from the Wizard's seemingly giant fingers.

"You see him clearly? No transparency what so ever?" Bergstrom asked as the Brownie pushed the red piece of candy through the long hair under its nose and made crunching sounds as if chewing it up though Wendell saw no trace of its mouth.

"Yes, Sir," Wendell answered, captivated by the strange fairy creature.

"My my, you are a gifted boy aren't you?" Mr. Weatherbee stated to himself thoughtfully.

"What do you mean, Sir?" Wendell asked, meeting the old Wizard's eyes.

"Well you see, Son, most people can't see most magical creatures, like your father this morning. Even most Wizards can't see them until they've grown powerful and must rely on special potions or magical items to view the magical world. It seems that this illness has awakened something powerful within you and from now on you'll have to be careful. For as you begin to perceive the magical world, so too will the magical world begin to perceive you," the Wizard explained as he gently began to rub the back of the

Brownie's head with the tip of his finger. The Brownie appeared to like it for it leaned back into the Wizard's petting and made a squeaky noise that resembled a cat's purr.

"Then is it dangerous?" Wendell asked reluctantly, for he was just beginning to like the strange little creature.

"This? No, it's very harmless. Though they do have a habit of stealing only one stocking from a pair that often drives one to distraction. Most people that can perceive Brownies think them nothing more than simple pests but they've never taken the time to study the true benefits of these benevolent little friends. If you treat them kindly and give them little treats like candy or saucers of milk they make loyal little guardians who will warn you of danger and protect your belongings. They also will bestow little gifts upon people they like, but on the down side you'll have to get use to mismatched stockings. If you don't want to care for it I can take it outside and sprinkle salt around your door that will keep it from returning," the Wizard then paused expectantly--Wendell shook his head while releasing another large yawn, "Good, I think it's a marvelous first encounter for you to the world of magic. The warning I gave was directed more towards the darker creatures of magic. Some are bad or simply so different that they don't understand what can be harmful to mortal creatures like you or I. Normally they pay no heed to humans, however, because we can't see or hear them and they find it boring to torment someone who will only blame their antics on the wind or their own clumsiness. Now that you can perceive them however they'll notice you as well and that can be dangerous if you don't know how to deal with them."

"I'm going to put this little fellow back under your dresser then let you get some rest while I have a chat with your parents. Remember to practice the flash spell if you start to feel any pain and I'll come and check on you tomorrow," Mr. Weatherbee told Wendell as he knelt before the dresser and let the Brownie run underneath. He paused before opening the door and turn back as Wendell's eyelids were just beginning to slide shut again of their own accord, "I think it's best you don't mention the Brownie to your mother though, she seems a bit high strung as it is and it would probably send her over the edge. Farewell until tomorrow, Wendell, and sweet dreams."

"Good bye Mr. Weatherbee," Wendell whispered as his eyes shut all the way and he dozed off into a dream of swarms of Brownies trying to raid his sock drawer. It was more humorous than unpleasant as far as dreams go.

4

Wendell slept nearly all day waking only once when his father came in with his supper of warm rabbit stew. He then went back to sleep and didn't awaken again until the next morning. Wendell didn't feel much better when he awoke but thanks to Mr. Weatherbee's flash spell his symptoms were at least bearable. He was still practicing it when his mother arrived with his breakfast with disastrous results.

Wendell hadn't been able to do the spell without first closing his eyes despite the fact that it was getting easier, so he didn't see his mother open the door with a large bowl of porridge and cream. He open his eyes and snapped his fingers to produce the brilliant white flash of light only to be startled by the sounds of his mother's terrified shriek and the breaking of glass. His mother had dropped the bowl in her mad flight from his room leaving a large mess of shattered glass and milky oats across Wendell's bedroom floor. It wasn't the mess that disturbed Wendell, but the horrified look his mother had fixed him with before fleeing the cottage.

Wendell waited a long time hoping she would return, not just for his hunger but because he wished to apologize for frightening her. He spent this time watching the Brownie drink the milk off the floor. It avoided the porridge's oats after the first tentative sample but seemed to enjoy the creamy milk. On its hands and knees the Brownie pressed its head down into the spilt milk until its large nose seemed to lay flat and made a squeaky little gulping sound as it drank. Wendell couldn't help but laugh when the Brownie finally rose from its meal and revealed its face hair covered in cream and milk dripping from the end of its nose. The Brownie retreated under the dresser just seconds before Wendell's father entered the room.

"What happened, Son? Your mother is in a frantic state and refuses to come back into the house. She keeps babbling on about evil spirits and she thinks you're possessed," Mr. Glasswright asked as he removed a dirty rag from the back pocket of his trousers and began picking up the glass shards of the broken bowl that he placed within it.

"I was practicing the spell that Mr. Weatherbee taught me to help make me feel better and didn't see her come in. I didn't mean to scare her Father, honest," Wendell explained as tears welled in his eyes.

"Show me the spell, Son," Mr. Glasswright paused and looked at him thoughtfully.

"I don't want to frighten you away, too," Wendell told him as his tears weaved down his cheeks though the green bumps that had still not gone away.

"You won't, show me the spell," Mr. Glasswright assured Wendell gently.

Wendell didn't want to but was an obedient lad, so he cast the flash spell as his father commanded. His father winced as the light flashed but did nothing more but rub his eyes for a few moments thereafter.

"And that's it?" Mr. Glasswright asked after his normal vision had returned with something of an amused smirk on his weather worn features.

"Yes, Father," Wendell acknowledged as he wiped away his tears on his nightshirt's sleeve.

"And does it really make you feel better son?" Mr. Glasswright asked thoughtfully as he returned to picking up the broken glass.

"Yes, though it makes me tired as well," as if on cue, Wendell released a large yawn.

"Good. I think you should keep practicing it then, but not in view of your mother. I'll make sure she knocks from now on to make certain she doesn't accidentally catch you, okay?" Mr. Glasswright suggested as he finished with the glass.

"Okay," Wendell accepted his father's proposal though he was still very worried about his mother.

"Now, are you very hungry, or can you wait until I finish cleaning up this mess before I get you some more porridge?" Mr. Glasswright asked as he stood up and carefully wrapped the broken glass up within the rag. Wendell knew that he would reuse the glass once his father returned to his shop next to their small barn and provided that he wasn't back logged with orders his mother would have a new bowl by the end of the day.

"I can wait," Wendell answered before releasing another yawn. He was quite hungry but he thought that he could wait.

"Alright then, I'll fetch a mop and bucket and be back in a minute. Try to rest and don't worry about your mother. I'll have a long heart-to-heart talk with her," Mr. Glasswright told Wendell as he leaned over and mussed his hair lovingly.

Nearly as soon as his father left, Wendell went fast to sleep for he was both physically and emotionally drained. When he awoke, Mr. Weatherbee was once again sitting at the foot of his bed reading an old worn leather bound book with yellowing pages. Mr. Weatherbee was so intent upon the book's contents that he didn't notice that Wendell had awakened until the boy sat up in bed.

"Ah, you're awake. Your father had to return to his work but I promised him I'd look after you until his return. He left you some porridge there on the nightstand and if you'll but wait a moment longer I'll warm it up for you," Mr. Weatherbee explained as he marked his place with a scarlet lace then set the book aside.

"Did my mother come back?" Wendell asked hesitantly as the Wizard picked up the bowl of cold porridge. A shadow of sorrow crept across the old Wizard's features and he seemed to contemplate the bowl's contents for several seconds before he answered.

"Now listen carefully, Wendell." Mr. Weatherbee began while fixing Wendell with a serious look, "Your father wishes to protect you from the truth but I think your old enough to deal with it. He was going to tell you that your Aunt Margery has become ill and your mother has gone to take care of her until she's well but this is only part of the truth. The whole truth is that your mother is terrified of magic and the supernatural. Your father was unable to calm her down after she saw you cast the flash spell this morning so she went to your Aunt's house to recover from her fright. Now, Wendell, I want to make it perfectly clear to you that this isn't your fault and your mother still loves you. Do you believe me?"

"Yes Sir, but why is she afraid of magic?" Wendell asked to try to clarify his confusion. Thus far, he'd seen nothing that was scary about magic, in fact just the opposite. Even the white rabbits were very wondrous though they'd left many pellets about his room that his mother had to clean up late last evening.

"Magic by its very nature is mysterious and defies conventional understanding, and many people fear what they don't understand. I think it likely that your mother was told many scary stories about creatures of magic in her youth that frightened her greatly. As she grew up, she became more and more paranoid of the forces unseen that led her to all those superstitious wards against evil she so adamantly relies upon for protection. Seeing you cast that spell brought her face to face with her worst fears and she wasn't in any way prepared for such a confrontation. It happens from time to time, Wendell, you'll find people that are terrified of magic but it's a real tragedy that the first should be your own mother. It must have hurt profoundly to see her fear you," Mr. Weatherbee sighed deeply as he stirred up the porridge with the wooden spoon, "Now lets see if I can't warm this up, shall we?"

Wendell watched as Mr. Weatherbee held up the bowl before him and fixed the porridge with an angry glare. Within seconds the porridge began to bubble and steam as if it were still cooking over the fire.

"Oops, gave it a little too much there," Mr. Weatherbee admitted with a smirk as he placed the hot bowl in Wendell's lap. "Well you'll have to stir it until it cools. Best that you don't try that until you've had a lot more practice. It is far too easy to let the heat get away from you."

"What were you reading about?" Wendell asked after a few moments of stirring the porridge in silence. He was more than a little eager to change the subject away from his mother and her fears.

"Ah yes, I'd nearly forgotten," Mr. Weatherbee picked up the book and caressed the cover lovingly for a moment as if it were a valued treasure despite its worn and well used appearance, "My master wrote this book about all the creatures of magic he'd encountered in his youth. I brought it for you to read for it's full of ways on dealing with them without getting yourself into trouble as well as how to get out of trouble should it be unavoidable."

Wendell looked at the book disappointedly as Mr. Weatherbee offered it to him, but made no attempt to take it.

"Its okay, Son, as long as you take good care of it it's alright if you borrow it," Mr. Weatherbee encouraged him still holding the book out for him to take.

"It's not that Sir, it's just, I don't know how to read," Wendell admitted reluctantly as he met Mr. Weatherbee's gaze.

"Ah yes, I forget sometimes that education in these parts is expensive. No matter, today I'll read to you then perhaps tomorrow we'll see about starting to teach you to read, okay?" Mr. Weatherbee smiled and opened the book in his lap.

"Really? I don't think my parents can afford that and I'm not sure they'd pay for it if they could. There isn't much use for reading when you're making glass," Wendell told him before taking his first bite of porridge. It was to hot still and scalded his tongue.

"Well, you never know what the future will bring young Wendell and it's unwise to try. Teaching you to read would be my pleasure if you wish to learn and I can think of no better way to pass the time until you're well," Mr. Weatherbee smiled as if he found the situation amusing on a level that Wendell didn't quite understand, "Shall we begin?"

Wendell nearly forgot about his porridge and it was only slightly warm when he remembered, so engrossed was he in the story that Mr. Weatherbee read. They spent the morning and much of the afternoon learning about Fairies, Earth Spirits, and even Dragons. It seemed that Mr. Weatherbee's Master had been an adventurous soul who had sought out and studied these creatures despite the perils it often led him to. Still, he seemed to have faired fairly well through use of his quick wits and a few well-placed spells. What surprised Wendell most of all was how often Mr.

Weatherbee's Master had used the flash spell to distract creatures long enough for him to escape their clutches.

That afternoon when Mr. Weatherbee finally admitted that his eyes had grown too sore to continue, Wendell ventured a question that had been nagging at him for a while since the story began.

"Mr. Weatherbee, what happened to your master? Did he die doing his research?" Wendell asked thinking that it must be why the Wizard treasured the book so much.

"No, in fact at the very end of the book you'll here about how he encountered a ferocious Troll that broke his leg before he managed to escape. After that he just couldn't get around as well anymore so he settled down and wrote this book as well as a few others," Mr. Weatherbee explained with a heavy sigh. It was clear to Wendell that he missed his Master very much. "Anyway your father is about to come home and you should try and get some rest before supper. I'll see you tomorrow, Wendell, and we'll begin practicing your letters."

"Thank you, Mr. Weatherbee, I enjoyed those stories very much," Wendell scooted back down in his bed so he could lay flat.

"It was my pleasure, Wendell, but please, call me Bergstrom. Mr. Weatherbee always seems like your addressing my father," the Wizard chuckled as he departed the room with his book.

Wendell practiced the flash spell a few more times, now more than ever determined to get it right after hearing how useful it could be. Then he heard his father come home and he and Mr. Weatherbee talking in low voices. He strained to hear their conversation thinking they'd be talking about his mother but all to no avail. Soon he nodded off and didn't awaken again until his father came in with bowls of rabbit stew for their supper.

Wendell listened to the excuse his father made for his mother's absence but did nothing to let on that Mr. Weatherbee had told him the truth. His father tried hard not to show it but it was clear that her absence weighed heavily upon his heart as they ate. They chatted for a while telling each other about their day. Wendell's father had spent most of the day making windows for a family that had just moved to the northern outskirts of the village intending to start a dairy farm. He was excited for they had arranged to pay for there new windows in cheese and butter for the next three years and Wendell's father loved cheese above all other foods. The Glasswrights had but one milking cow that had been barter for a past commission and didn't produce enough milk to make cheese.

Wendell listened as his father talked on about the new family, named the Miller's, and how he'd be at their windows for the next two weeks. Then as his eyes began to blink more and more, and his yawns could no longer be stifled, Wendell's father mussed his hair and wished him goodnight taking their supper's dishes as he left. Wendell produced one more flash before he went to sleep to drain the last vestiges of his energy and put him down for the night. It worked wonderfully putting him under in seconds.

5

Over the next two weeks Wendell spent most of his waking hours with Mr. Weatherbee, learning how to read and write for neither of his parents were around. His mother was still at his Aunt's house on the southern outskirts of the village, while his father was busy making the Miller's new windows. Wendell struggled with the lessons that didn't come easy for him, but Mr. Weatherbee was an infinitely patient instructor who never once showed any frustration at Wendell's slow progress. At the times when Wendell got to frustrated to continue with his studies, they would take a break and either read from Mr. Weatherbee's Master's journal or simply talk about the world in general. The one subject they did not speak of that continued to weigh heavily upon Wendell's mind was the absence of his mother.

The continued absence of Wendell's mother was always at the back of his thoughts. Despite the Wizard's assurances that it wasn't his fault Wendell continued to blame himself for the disruption of his home and his mother's fears. He couldn't wait to get well for as soon as he did Wendell planned to go to his Aunt's house to apologize for scaring her and beg her to come home. Recovering from the Wizard Pox proved to be a slow process that not even Mr.

Weatherbee's magic could hurry along. It was in this second week of Wendell's sickness that the boy awoke to a strange sensation in the pit of his stomach.

It was either very late at night or very early in the morning when a tugging sensation awoke Wendell from his dreams. He could hear his father snoring at the other side of the cottage like a dull saw grinding away a log. At first he thought he was going to be ill but then he realized this sensation felt nothing like nausea. It felt more as if someone had tied a string to Wendell's naval and was gently tugging him with it. After a few moments Wendell sat up in bed and peered around the room. Nothing seemed out of place but just as he was about to lay back down Wendell spied the Brownie standing in the window seal above his bed.

Wendell tried hard to ignore the tugging sensation in his stomach as he climbed out of the covers and knelt up to see what the Brownie was looking at through the smoky glass. The Brownie's nose was cocked upwards towards Mr. Garroph's tower silhouetted inky black against the large full moon. Strange green lights flashed within the uppermost line of the tower's windows and after a few moments Wendell realized that the tugging sensation within his stomach was keeping time with these flashes. He swallowed hard, suddenly feeling afraid as he watched the eerie lights. He felt as if something was building up in the air like static electricity before a storm. All the hairs on Wendell's body began to stand on end and terror began to grow within him for he knew something unnatural was coming in the depths of his soul even if he didn't know exactly what. Movement caught Wendell's eye and he looked down to see the Brownie was also shivering.

Suddenly the tugging in Wendell's stomach became painful and he let out a strangled cry as he shifted his gaze back towards the tower. The lights had stopped flashing but instead had become steady brilliant rays bleeding out from not just the windows of the tower but from under the shingles of its pyramid shaped roof as well. Wendell felt something being draw out of him forcefully and painfully as his eyes grew wide with terror. It was growing stronger by the second as it siphoned away Wendell's strength. He was dimly aware of the Brownie's terrified squeak as the tiny creature jumped off the window seal and fled back to its nest below the dresser.

"No!" Wendell cried out against the unseen force draining him and instantly the sensation stopped and the lights in the tower flickered and died as if the boy's command had severed the string connecting him to magic above. Wendell sagged against the window seal taking in the air in great gasps. His body was drenched in sweat as his father burst into the room behind him.

"What is it? What's wrong?" Wendell's father asked holding up his flickering candle.

"I… I don't …know," Wendell stuttered in between breaths still very shaken from the experience.

"Looks like you had a bad dream, Son. Come on and lay back down, I'll tuck you back in."

Wendell gazed back out the window once more before complying with his father's wishes, but Mr. Garroph's tower stood cold and dark against the moon's cratered white surface. Wendell's fear began to fade away as his father tucked him back into bed then went to fetch him a glass of milk. As he drank down the milk his thoughts became sluggish and sleepy once more as exhaustion overwhelmed him. The last thing Wendell knew was his father's worried voice drifting in from somewhere far away asking if he'd knocked himself against the window seal when he awoke because he had a bloody nose.

6

The next morning Wendell awoke feeling much better than he had since he'd become ill. When he got up and checked the mirror on top of his dresser, he was excited to see the ugly green bumps were completely gone and his skin was once again clear and healthy looking. Quickly he dressed and left his room for the first time in weeks. Wendell found his father cooking his breakfast of porridge in the medium sized cauldron that hung above the hearth.

"Look father, I'm better!" Wendell called out excitedly as he rushed towards him. His father smiled wearily at him as he continued to stir the boiling oats.

"I'm glad, Son," his father told him with a heavy sigh. His father looked very tired with sunken cheeks and heavy drooping eyelids. His posture was that of an old man as he hunched over the cauldron.

"What's wrong?" Wendell asked not liking the listless way his father was staring into the cauldron's depths.

"Oh, I just didn't sleep well last night either. Don't worry; I'll be fine once I'm up and about. Why don't you bring me a couple bowls and I'll serve us up some breakfast," his father answered as he unhooked the cauldron from its hanger and drew it away from the fire.

Wendell ended up having to wash two bowls for there was not but dirty dishes piled high upon the kitchen counter. In fact it looked as if the whole cottage had been ransacked by Goblins in his mother's absence for everything was in disarray. Muddy footprints were tracked across the floor. Dirty laundry hung off the furniture. Half-eaten bread sat on the arm of his father's chair and the seat was full of crumbs. All Wendell's hopes of going to see his mother crumbled as he beheld his father's neglectful mess. He was going to have to spend the day cleaning before he could try to convince his mother to come home.

Wendell and his father ate breakfast together in silence; for his father was too tired to hold any type of conversation. When their meal was done his father told him to take it easy today so that he wouldn't have a relapse, then he mussed up Wendell's hair lovingly and left for his workshop.

Wendell sighed heavily as he looked around the filthy cottage not quite certain where to begin. Then he pulled a wash bucket from underneath kitchen counter and went outside to fill it at the hand pump. The bucket was nearly three-quarters full when Wendell noticed Mr. Weatherbee coming down the road just beyond their wooden fence. The Wizard was whistling a happy tune as he carried his Master's journal and the small blackboard under his arm that he'd been using to teach Wendell his letters.

"Hello Wendell, I'm glad to see your feeling better," Mr. Weatherbee greeted him warmly as he approached.

"Hello, Bergstrom. I'm sorry but I don't think I'll have time to practice my letters today, I've got to clean the cottage or mother will never come home," Wendell apologized regretfully.

"Oh, well perhaps I can help you. Two sets of hands should get the job done faster than one, right?" Mr. Weatherbee smiled as he handed Wendell the book and blackboard, hiked up the sleeves of his robes, and picked up the bucket which the boy had overfilled.

"That's all right Sir, I can do it myself," Wendell made a feeble protest as he followed the Wizard back inside.

"Nonsense, it's always good to do something with one's hands and a little hard work never hurt anyone. Unless of course they hit their fingers with the hammer instead of the nail," Mr. Weatherbee smirked with a wink.

Inside the cottage Mr. Weatherbee poured the water into the wash tub and then dropped in a thick bar of soap that hadn't seen action sense Wendell's mother had left. Once again he pulled up his sleeves, raised his arms above the tub, and then paused to give Wendell another wink before he invoked words of power. The spell hung in the air for several seconds after Mr. Weatherbee was finished reverberating through the air like the sounds of a distant storm. Wendell felt the air tingle and his hair prickle as the water within the wash tub began to bubble and churn. After a few seconds, the soapy water stilled within the washtub save for a few popping bubbles. Mr. Weatherbee glared at the water while placing his hands on his hips and tapping his foot with impatience.

"Hey! Wake up in there!" Mr. Weatherbee commanded after a moment then kicked the side of the heavy wooden washtub.

Wendell watched with fascination as the water within the tub started to rise and formed into a small vaguely man-shaped creature from the waist up. It formed two arms from its watery torso which it stretched as if a person just rising from a nap and a hollow formed on its shapeless head like a mouth opening in a large yawn. A gurgling sound emerged from the thing's mouth along with a few soapy bubbles before it closed and disappeared into a once more featureless face. Two bubbles formed just below the water's surface like eyes which looked around for a moment before coming to rest on Mr. Weatherbee.

"That's better now. Do you see those dishes?" Mr. Weatherbee asked in a commanding voice as he pointed at the heaping pile of dirty dishes. The water creature's bubble eyes turned slowly towards the dishes then back to the Wizard and it gave a nod along with a hissing gurgle. "I want you to clean each one without breaking them," Mr. Weatherbee commanded while shaking his finger over the creature.

The Water creature released another hiss then reached for the dishes with its featureless arms. Its arms seemed to grow thinner as they lengthened towards the dishes then flowed into the cracks underneath the pile. The dishes rattled against one another for a moment then began to hop one at a time onto the water creature's arms propelled by tiny geysers from underneath. As soon as a dish hit the creature's arms it would flow down its length into the creature's body as if propelled by a river's currant then sink slowly to the bottom of the wash tub.

"Be a good boy and fetch him another bucket of water or two, there are a lot of dishes here," Mr. Weatherbee broke Wendell out of the water creature's trance as he handed him the bucket once more.

"What is it?" Wendell asked completely oblivious to the bucket or Mr. Weatherbee's request.

"Just a small Elemental Spirit. They inhabit the elements around us but usually aren't that active unless some magic infuses them with energy like my spell. Now hurry up before the wash tub gets too dirty," the Wizard explained before gently propelling Wendell towards the door.

When Wendell returned with the sloshing bucket, he found Mr. Weatherbee directing a small Dust Devil in the center of the room. The small twister was picking up the dirt off the floor wherever the Wizard guided it and forming into a dusty core at the center of the funnel. Mr. Weatherbee looked up to peer at Wendell in the doorway and in his moment of distraction the Dust Devil touched upon the faded green wool rug resting in the center of the floor. The rug was instantly whipped back into the Wizard's face as the small twister began to drift away. After freeing himself of the rug, Mr. Weatherbee spent the next few moments coughing up the dust the rug had covered him with then he growled with annoyance as he shook his fist at the rug.

"Just dump that into the tub then go fetch another," the Wizard told Wendell once he'd stopped hacking and regained control of the Dust Devil.

Wendell obeyed, dumping the water into the tub where the Elemental was busy sloshing the water around the dirty dishes. The Elemental immediately made a happy gurgling sound as it swelled in size within the tub. The mouth hollow appeared once more beneath its bubble eyes and formed into a crude smile at Wendell for a second or two before disappearing once more. Wendell hurried out again to the hand pump and started to fill the bucket as fast as he could so that he wouldn't miss any of the excitement.

"What's going on?" Wendell's father startled him from behind. His father was coming back from the river with two full buckets of sand.

"Mr. Weatherbee's using magic to clean the house! Come on, you have to see this!" Wendell encouraged his father excitedly as he finished filling his bucket and then staggered under its weight.

"Alright," Mr. Glasswright set down his buckets and followed Wendell with an excited grin.

When they entered the cottage, Wendell's father released a long whistle of astonishment. On top of the Dust Devil 'sweeping' and the Elemental washing dishes, Mr. Weatherbee now had all of the dirty cloths standing in an orderly line before the wash tub waiting their turn to 'bathe.' On one side of the tub the Elemental was still at his work while on the other, one of Mr. Glasswright's tunics was scrubbing itself against the washboard with a soapy brush not unlike a man taking a bath.

"Start filling the other tub now, Wendell, so they may start to rinse," Mr. Weatherbee directed, "Good morning Mr. Glasswright. I hope you don't mind that I'm helping Wendell with his chores."

"Not at all, Mr. Weatherbee," Wendell's father laughed and clapped his hands in excitement.

As Wendell rushed over to the empty wash tub as fast as the sloshing bucket of water he was carrying would allow, Mr. Weatherbee pointed at a scrub brush sitting on the counter and chanted off another spell. The scrub brush immediately came to life scrubbing the now empty kitchen counter. Below, the tunic jumped into the wash tub Wendell was filling and submerged itself three times in the water. After that it hopped out onto the tub's rim and began shaking itself dry like a sopping wet dog.

"Hey! Cut it out!" Wendell exclaimed as he caught most of the water the tunic was casting off. His father doubled over with laughter as Wendell tried to shield himself from the splashing water with his hands.

Grinning from ear to ear, Mr. Weatherbee pointed at the kitchen window which then opened on its own. The tunic hopped up onto the opened window's seal and proceeded to hang itself on the close line just outside. When it was properly secured, the tunic reached down with its sleeves and pulled the lines in opposite directions so it was wheeled outward into the morning light to dry. Below the window a pair of stockings were next in line for the tub.

Wendell was just about to run for another bucket of water when the cottage was filled with an earsplitting scream. All eyes turned to the cottages entrance where Wendell's mother stood wide eyed with terror and as white as a ghost.

"Maggie?" Wendell's father whispered hoarsely still winded from his laughter. Mrs. Glasswright paused only a moment longer before she fled out of sight. "Maggie!" Mr. Glasswright called after her as he gave chase.

"Oh bugger," Mr. Weatherbee sighed as his shoulders slumped in defeat. All his spells ended in that instant as he shook his head in disgust.

7

By the time Wendell's father returned home, it was growing late and the house was clean. He said nothing as he walked into the kitchen and began to chop up vegetables for soup. Mr. Weatherbee tried to apologize and then take his leave but Mr. Glasswright stopped him asking that he please stay for dinner so they may talk. He then sent Wendell out to fetch more water as he returned to preparing dinner. Wendell had never seen his father look so haggard and it frightened him.

Dinner was a quiet affair for no one was willing to break the somber silence. When it was done Wendell started to pick up the dishes intent on cleaning up, but his father stopped him saying he would take care of it and that he wished Wendell to go to bed. Both he and Mr. Weatherbee wished him goodnight as Wendell went to his room frightened and annoyed that he was not going to be included in their discussion. He sorely wanted to know what was going on with his mother as he changed into his warm nightshirt and cap.

Wendell lay in his bed straining to hear the adult's conversation in the next room, but both his father and Mr. Weatherbee were very careful to keep their voices low. No matter how hard he tried, Wendell could only catch the occasional word or two, but nothing that shed light on what they were discussing. Then after awhile Mr. Weatherbee went home and Wendell could hear his father quietly doing the dishes. When Wendell could stand the silence no more he climbed back out of bed and went out to speak to his father.

"When is mother coming home?" Wendell asked. Mr. Glasswright paused for a moment without turning to face his son.

"I don't know, Son," Mr. Glasswright answered as he started scrubbing the cauldron he'd been scouring once more.

"Is she mad at me?" Wendell asked on the edge of tears.

"No, but she's having a very hard time coming to terms with the events of the last few weeks. She's very terrified of magic and her fear seems to be beyond all reason," Mr. Glasswright explained slowly as he continued to focus on the cauldron before him.

"What if I promised to never do magic again? Then would she come back?" Tears began to roll down his cheeks as Wendell said the words and his stomach knotted.

"It isn't that simple. Mr. Weatherbee says that the magic has awakened in your blood now. If you try to repress it not only will it make you sick again, but in all likelihood it would come out in wild surges that would hurt you or others around you. It isn't something you can ignore, Wendell, it's a part of you now," Mr. Glasswright explained quietly. Wendell digested the news bitterly as he wiped away his tears on his linen nightshirt's sleeve, "Mr. Weatherbee says he's willing to take you on as his apprentice. He likes you a lot and thinks you'll make a fine Wizard. He'll teach you to control your power so you'll remain safe. It would mean you'd have to go live with him, however."

Wendell didn't know what to say, he'd never even considered leaving home within his meager dozen years of life. It was a frightening suggestion even though he truly enjoyed Mr. Weatherbee's company. He lowered his eyes to the floor and watched a teardrop splash on the top of his bare foot. When he looked up his father was staring down at him grimly. It was clear to Wendell that this decision was taking a harsh toll on his father as well.

"Why don't you try and get some sleep and I'll do the same. Tomorrow Mr. Weatherbee will be coming by and we'll all sit down and talk it over," His father suggested with a long gloomy sigh.

"Alright, Father," Wendell acknowledged as he wiped away his tears once more.

"And, Son," his father stopped him before he could open his bedroom door, "No matter what happens know that I love you."

"I love you, too, Father," Wendell told him before slipping back into his room.

Wendell didn't fall asleep right away for too many thoughts were rolling around in his head. When he did finally get to sleep his dreams were tainted with a dark sense of impending doom. Something malevolent was drawing near; Wendell could feel it watching him. Closer and closer it crept towards him until the fear of it drove Wendell from his dreams.

Wendell awoke with a start. His sense of panic started to melt away as he realized he was safe in his bed until he noticed he could still feel the malevolent presence drawing nearer. Once again Wendell saw that the Brownie was standing in the window sill, but this time it was looking down instead of up at Mr. Garroph's tower. Despite his growing fear, Wendell had to know what was stocking the night outside the cottage. He apprehensively sat up peeked out the smoky glass window without raising his head more than a few inches above the sill.

The Brownie released a low squeak as it placed a finger to where its lips might have been and pointed toward the corner of the barn. A small shadow detached itself from the deeper shadows of the barn. Like a thief, the shadow crept towards the house cautiously.

As the shadow drew nearer Wendell was able to make out a few details. First of all it was a small creature barely three feet tall and wrapped within a hooded cloak that was dark as pitch. As it slinked forward, Wendell could see its eyes glowing with a dull red light within the shadowy depths of its cowl and a long pointed nose jutted forward like a dark carrot. It's thin legs tapered down to small hooves beneath its layers of dark clothing that seemed to be in constant motion even when the creature paused to cautiously spy on its surroundings. It was nearly under Wendell's window when the boy began to hear its low hateful voice releasing a long seemingly endless string of blasphemous curses. Wendell jumped below the window sill with a slight gasp as the creature raised its gaze towards the window.

The curses stopped in the same instant and all grew so quiet Wendell feared to breath. After a few moments of which felt like a lifetime to the boy the silence was broken by the creature sniffing loudly on the other side of the window that was quickly followed by a low grunt of approval. Wendell didn't know what to do. He was afraid to call out to his father for the creature seemed dangerous despite its diminutive size. The Brownie caught his attention by placing its hands around where its mouth should be as if it was about to call out, but instead of its normal squeak it released the frightening bark of a large Dog.

A harsh cry of alarm flowed up from under the window followed by more terrible curses as the creature fled. Wendell saw it just disappearing around the corner of the barn once more when he poked his head above the window sill. The Brownie stopped its loud bark and released a squeaky whistle that sounded like a long sigh of relief.

"That was great, thank you," Wendell acknowledged in a cautious whisper to the Brownie. The Brownie released another short squeak then gave a bow that almost touched its oversized nose to its oversized toes. Then it sat down on the window sill cross-legged peering out into the night. "Do you think it'll come back?" Wendell asked after a few moments of scanning the yard outside.

The Brownie answered with a shrug and a squeak then pointed at Wendell and signaled for him to go to sleep with his hands clasped beside its tilted head before it turned back to its vigil. Wendell felt better knowing the Brownie was intent on guarding him and crawled back under the covers. As he closed his eyes, the Brownie started to sing a soft squeaky lullaby from the window sill above. It was a comforting song even if Wendell had no clue what words if any the Brownie was putting to the music. His fears gradually melted away and sleep embraced him once more, but this time it was good sleep untainted by evil dreams.

8

When Wendell awoke he was reluctant to get out of bed for he had the impression that his future was going to be shaped by this day's events. After a few minutes of procrastination, he decided that hiding from it would do no good and mark him as a coward so he got up and dressed. He noted that the Brownie had vacated the window sill and was nowhere to be seen. Wendell promised himself that he'd bring his tiny rescuer some type of treat for last night's heroic rescue as he left the bedroom.

Wendell's father was coming in from the barn as the boy exited his room. He carried a steaming half-full bucket of creamy milk in one hand and a bucket full of eggs in the other. Mr. Glasswright looked as if he'd had little to no sleep throughout the night as he set his bounty upon the counter with a large yawn.

"Good morning. Would you like me to cook this morning?" Wendell offered.

"Can you cook up these eggs? Since your mother hasn't been baking we're starting to get a stockpile and I don't want to take them to market when there's work to be done here," his father asked as he crumpled into his chair at the head of their small table.

"Of course, I've watched mother do it many times," Wendell smiled as he pulled the heavy cast iron skillet off its wall hanger. He tossed another log on the hearth's soft glowing embers then set the skillet on the iron bracket above. Next he retrieved a wooden spoon and scooped a generous helping of lard from its jar into the pan where it slowly began to melt. His father watched him through half-lidded eyes as he quickly chopped up the last green onion that had been hanging in the pantry and tossed it into the now sizzling lard. Wendell then began to carefully crack eggs into the pan one by one. He only lost one piece of shell in the process but was able to scoop it out of the runny mixture with the other half of the shell.

"You've learned well from your mother," Wendell's father commented quietly as the boy began to scramble the eggs with the wooden spoon. His father's praise brought to many conflicting emotions to the surface so Wendell chose to remain silent and concentrate on the cooking food. Soon the eggs were done and he served them up on two of their thick glass plates.

Unwilling to breach the barrier of silence that had fallen between them as they ate, Wendell concentrated instead upon the tiny bubbles suspended within the glass of his plate as he idly poked at the eggs without appetite. He fancied those bubbles imagining what it would be like to be within one looking out at the world through the aqua colored glass. He liked his father's work and felt a dull ache in the depths of his heart as he realized for the first time he wouldn't be able to follow in his father's footsteps.

"Don't play with it, eat it," his father commanded before shoveling another bite into his mouth.

"Yes, Sir," Wendell sighed and dutifully took his first bite of the fluffy scrambled eggs.

"Excellent work," his father grunted after he finished the last bite and pushed the plate away. He sat back and rubbed his eyes for a moment, then gazed across the table at Wendell as if there was something more he wanted to say. After a moment his shoulders sagged as he let out a long sigh and then pushed himself up out of the chair, "I've got to ground down some lime for the windows. After you finish your breakfast I want you to clean the dishes. When your done you can play but stick around the yard and when Mr. Weatherbee gets here come fetch me."

"Yes, Sir," Wendell acknowledged as his father poured himself a glass of milk and drank it down in a few noisy gulps. Then he paused to muss Wendell's hair before he left for his shop.

Wendell finished his breakfast but before he started on the dishes he filled a saucer full of milk and took it carefully into his room. He set the saucer upon the floor before the dresser then lay down so he could peek underneath. In the farthest corner pressed up against the walls was the Brownie's nest of stockings. It looked for all the world like a small bird's nest with the stockings twisted around one another in ways Wendell doubted any Human could replicate if they tried. The Brownie poked its nose over the edge of its nest and sniffed with an inquisitive squeak.

"Here you go, little guy," Wendell whispered as he slid the saucer up next to the nest. "Drink it quickly so I can clean the saucer when I'm done with the rest of the breakfast dishes, okay?"

The Brownie whistled and nodded its head before it climbed out of its comfortable looking home to inspect the saucer's contents. Wendell smiled as he got back up. Discovering the Brownie had been the best part of this whole experience he thought as he returned to the kitchen.

By the time Wendell's chores were done the sun had come up with the promise of a warm day ahead and he couldn't stand the thought of spending any more time indoors. He headed out enjoying the crispness of the air which only lasts for the first hour or so after dawn. Already the village was stirring as his neighbors went about their daily routines.

Wendell first headed for the ground outside his window wishing to confirm that last night's prowler wasn't just an unpleasant dream. Sure enough he found small goat like tracks leading from the barn to his window and back again pressed lightly into the dirt. A cold shiver ran down Wendell's spine and he decided he would have to speak to Mr. Weatherbee about it when time allowed. He followed the tracks around the barn but they were soon lost in the field of wild grass where his neighbor's cows stood grazing.

Frustrated, Wendell returned to the cottage but then continued past it to the river that ran behind their cottage. He spent the next hour or so engaged in the simple activities that make a boy's childhood worthwhile: sSkipping stones, catching frogs, and flipping rocks to watch the crayfish zoom away quickly put most of his unpleasant thoughts right out of mind for awhile. He then saw something that brought home the fact that things for him had changed and would never be the same.

Wendell had just managed to catch a large crayfish nearly eight inches long. As the fresh water lobster bared its claws daring the boy to place a finger within its reach the river water before him began to swirl against the current causing a small whirlpool to form. Wendell watched the water funnel in wonder momentarily forgetting about his captive crustacean. The crayfish latched onto this momentary lapse in Wendell's concentration quite literally by sinking one of its jagged pincers into the boy's thumb.

"Ah!" Wendell cried as he instantly tried to shake the crayfish loose with a panic-fueled wave of his arm. The crayfish held on just long enough to make certain it had taught Wendell a lesson then let go to drop back into the river shallows with a plop. Wendell sucked his hurt thumb as he watched the Crayfish jet away backwards into deeper water and out of sight before a giggle of amusement brought him back to the water that had distracted him in the first place.

The river water at the center of the whirlpool began to geyser upward then formed into the shape of a beautiful girl with Elvin features. When she was completely formed the water around her stilled and her flesh lost its watery transparency becoming a solid white with slight aqua undertones. Her hair hung sopping wet behind her and appeared to be a dark green that was almost black. Her eyes were large and slanted, colored a deep crystal clear aqua green full of mischievous playfulness as she gazed upon him. Her face was almost a perfect heart-shape accented by the crow's peak of her hair. High well-rounded cheekbones surrounded her playful chubby lipped smile before turning into long pointed ears behind. She giggled again as Wendell tried to advert his eyes from her nakedness seemingly amused by his sudden change in color.

She was a Naiad. Wendell remembered a story from Mr. Weatherbee's Master's journal of his contact with the mischievous fresh water fairies. The journal had warned that while the Naiads weren't evil they were dangerous for they often forgot that mortal creatures couldn't breath underwater. It also had told of their love of music and dance and how the old wizard had convinced one to retrieve an amulet from the bottom of a lake by singing it a song. Wendell wasn't much of a singer, nor did he think it likely there were any treasures worth retrieving at the bottom of the muddy river except for perhaps the crayfish that had just escaped him.

"Come play with me," the Naiad beckoned, exposing far more of herself than Wendell was comfortable with. Her voice was sweet and full of mirth.

"Sorry, I can't. I have to go," Wendell lied, slowly backing up the sandy shore away from her.

"Please?" She pouted, protruding her lower lip with an expertise only young girls can truly master. Then she smiled again as a new thought entered her beautiful head, "I can show you some magic."

Wendell hesitated with interest anew. He was reasonably certain he was far enough up the shore to be safe from her for the journal had also said Naiads couldn't leave the water. The Naiad dipped her index finger into the water and began to twirl it in small circles. After a moment she drew it upwards causing a small globe of water to follow her finger into the air. She placed her other hand beneath the sphere-- although it didn't touch her skin--and held it up before her. She gave him a mischievous wink then pursed her lips and blew upon the globe. The water sphere instantly changed from clear to a soft glowing blue and the Naiad smiled.

"Look, I can use it to tell your future," she told Wendell with a delighted giggle.

"Really?" Wendell took an unconscious step forward despite his apprehension.

"Ah huh. Let me see," she looked deep into the glowing sphere, her fine high-arched eyebrows nearly met as her forehead wrinkled with concentration, "I see. I see you're in great danger."

"What kind of danger?" Wendell asked as his mind quickly jumped back to the creature that had been prowling under his window last night. There was a note of panic in his voice.

"You're in great danger of...getting wet!" the Naiad exclaimed a second before she blew on the globe again. The water sphere instantly shot straight into Wendell's face, splashing him with cold water as the Naiad giggled with mirth. Wendell wiped his face indignantly with the sleeves of his tunic as the Naiad continued to point and giggle. He started to walk away but she called to him again, "Come play with me."

"I have to go now," Wendell lied again over his shoulder. The Naiad splashed the water before her in a frustrated tantrum then stuck out her tongue towards him before disappearing back into the water. His new vision was going to take some getting use to Wendell pondered as he marched back toward the cottage.

9

When Wendell came back around the cottage, he found his father and Mr. Weatherbee standing before his father's shop talking. They broke off their conversation as he approached with the uncomfortable looks people get when they've been caught talking about someone behind their back. Wendell slowed as he closed the last few feet between them knowing that this was the moment he'd been dreading and that it couldn't be ignored a moment longer.

"Good morning, Wendell. Were you having trouble waking up? A little cold water works every time," Mr. Weatherbee greeted him warmly as he noticed Wendell's wet head.

"Not exactly, Sir. I got splashed by something in the river," Wendell explained cryptically lowering his gaze, "How are you this morning?"

"Very fine indeed, I've been out walking and the morning air seems to have invigorated these old bones like nothing else could," Mr. Weatherbee smiled and stretched his arms before him with his fingers interlocked. Most of the old Wizard's knuckles cracked as he did so with audible pops.

"Shall we step inside and have a sit down while we discuss Wendell's future?" Wendell's father suggested raising his arm to guide them into the cottage.

"Forgive the rudeness of my interruption but Wendell's future is exactly why I've come, Mr. Glasswright," A strong self-assured male voice put in from behind them before any of the three had taken a single step towards the small domicile.

They all turned as one towards the voice and found yet another Wizard standing at the gate that Wendell presumed was the reclusive Mr. Garroph. He stood a head taller than both Wendell's father and Mr. Weatherbee draped in robes of purplish blue. Over his shoulder was draped a dark purple cloak with a wide open cowl pulled back far enough to reveal his features but drawn forward enough to shield him from the sun. He had a pale face with sunken flesh around thick strong bones that seemed to suggest he avoided sunlight regularly. His face might have been handsome once upon a time but the years and a seemingly neglectful lifestyle hand conspired to make him haggard and unattractive. Short white hair clung to his scalp like moss and what few unruly tangled strands did hang were held back by a rawhide headband with runes burnt across its surface.

The Wizard's most prominent features were his eyes sunk deep under his strong brow above an average looking nose. His eyes were so dark brown that it was nearly impossible to tell where his irises ended and the pupils began. Those eyes were both penetrating and uncomfortable as they added force behind his gaze and Wendell got the impression that if he put his mind to it the Wizard could peer right through him as easily as looking through a window. Those eyes were locked upon Wendell's father as if only he existed in the world and after a pause just long enough to give him a chance to come to terms with his appearance the Wizard continued on as if he'd been expected all along.

"We haven't been formerly introduced, Mr. Glasswright, but I am your neighbor, Mr. Garroph. It has come to my attention that your son has developed some meager magical power and I'd like the opportunity to train him in its use. Therefore I've come to offer you 50 crowns to take him on as my apprentice which I feel is a more than generous sum," Mr. Garroph smiled as he removed the heavy purse of gold coins from under his cloak and offered them to Wendell's father in the palm of his hand.

50 crowns was an unbelievable sum that made Wendell hold his breath as his father stared at the purse in open disbelief: with 50 crowns one could buy most if not all of the village; with 50 crowns Wendell's family for the next two generations wouldn't have to work another day in their lives. Wendell couldn't believe his apprenticeship would be worth so much. Normally it would be his family who would have to pay for his training, not the other way around. He looked to his father and saw that all these thoughts and more were going through his mind.

"We had planned on having Mr. Weatherbee train Wendell, but I'll leave it up to you, Son. Who would you prefer to train under?" Wendell's father asked after contemplating the purse for a few moments.

Mr. Garroph's gaze shifted for the first time to Wendell like the eyes of a hawk which have just spotted a rabbit in an open field below. It was almost like receiving a physical blow to Wendell as he felt the full impact of the Wizard's gaze. He started to open his mouth to answer but his words died upon his tongue as he heard Mr. Garroph's voice within his head.

'Think boy, I can show you the path to power! Your family will be taken care of for life and all I ask for in return is your unquestioning loyalty. It's a fair exchange is it not?' Mr. Garroph thoughts invaded Wendell's mind with cold hard reason, but before

he could come to any conclusion another voice, that of Mr. Weatherbee entered into the mental conversation.

'Come, come Scott, loyalty isn't the only price you've paid for your power nor would it be all that you'd take from the boy. What about your soul? Wasn't that the first sacrifice you made along your path to power? That and your humanity were lost long ago and tell the truth, have you gained any comfort from the power you've acquired or has its acquisition become the soul purpose of your existence?' Mr. Weatherbee asked in a mental voice filled with pity.

'Stay out of this, old man. Your meddlesome interference is never welcome. Go back and tend to your bees and leave me and the boy alone. Your parlor tricks are nothing compared to what I can teach him. Let him decide for himself what he would learn,' Mr. Garroph's voice returned in anger. Wendell broke his gaze away from the tall Wizard and looked at Mr. Weatherbee. The older Wizard looked back at him and smiled knowingly.

'Yes, free will. That is another price you would pay along the path Mr. Garroph would teach you. The choice is yours, Wendell, and don't think that there shall be any love loss between us should you choose to apprentice under Mr. Garroph. Follow your heart and I'm certain you'll make the right choice,' Mr. Weatherbee winked at him.

Wendell was suddenly left alone within his own thoughts and he released a long sigh of relief. Carefully avoiding Mr. Garroph's gaze, he looked to his father who was watching him closely.

"I think I'd prefer to train under Mr. Weatherbee, Father," Wendell surprised himself with the sense of relief he felt as he spoke the words.

"Are you certain, Son? It seems like a big decision to make so quickly," his father asked, placing a reassuring hand upon Wendell's shoulder.

"Yes, I'm certain," Wendell answered shifting his gaze to Mr. Garroph. For a moment he thought the tall Wizard would be angry and possibly try to lash out at him. He felt that Mr. Garroph was dangerous and greatly feared his anger. He surprised Wendell however by tilting his head with the semblance of a pleasant smile.

"As you will young Sir, it seems I've come too late to sway your mind," Mr. Garroph withdrew the purse back under his cloak then nodded to his father, "Good day to you then Mr. Glasswright, Mr. Weatherbee."

They all watched Mr. Garroph exit the yard closing the gate behind him, but only Wendell seemed to notice something disturbing about the Wizard as he turned left at the road that would take him back up to his tower. Despite that he walked under the bright morning sun, Mr. Garroph cast no shadow whatsoever. It was a small detail that seemed harmless enough to Wendell's mind, but it still filled him with an uncertain dread as he watched the Wizard go. His father was the first to break the silence after Mr. Garroph was lost from view behind their neighbor's old red barn.

"Well, that was different. Don't think I've ever seen that much money in my whole life. Best that we never mention this to your mother or else I'll end up getting slapped for passing up the opportunity," Wendell's father sighed thoughtfully before turning his gaze first to Mr. Weatherbee and then to Wendell, "Still, I think you made the right choice, Son. That fellow is more than a little creepy and I doubt that all that money would be any comfort while I was kept up at night worrying about you."

"You are a very wise man, Mr. Glasswright, perhaps this will ease the wrath of your Mrs.," Mr. Weatherbee held out a small purse to Wendell's father as he patted him on the shoulder. Mr. Glasswright accepted the purse with no small amount of surprise, "I'm afraid its hardly more than 20 talons but I've never been one who puts much value in monetary wealth. Use it wisely."

"Thank you, Mr. Weatherbee, but by all rights it should be we who are paying you for Wendell's education," Mr. Glasswright protested, trying to hand the purse back.

"Nonsense, we Wizard's put far greater value upon the bond between Master and Apprentice than any other profession for it is a bond that often lasts throughout this life and beyond. A Smith will train an Apprentice to shape metal so he can provide wealth and security for his family but a Wizard will train an Apprentice to shape the universe to his will. Therefore paying for the right to teach someone like Wendell is only proper. Please keep the money, I insist," Mr. Weatherbee explained. After a moment, Wendell's father shook his head in disbelief and pocketed the purse in his trousers.

"Well, I guess you should go and pack. I can't see as there's any more reason to delay Mr. Weatherbee and I have work to do as well," Wendell's father sighed as if the full impact of Wendell's imminent departure had just settled on his shoulders.

"Yes, Father," Wendell acknowledged, and then he went ahead as the two adults continued to talk.

"Will we be able to visit him?" Wendell's father asked before the boy had made it to the door of their cottage.

"How about on Sundays? That way there will be no chance of you interrupting any of his training," Mr. Weatherbee answered as Wendell went inside.

Wendell retrieved one of the many potato sacks his mother had neatly folded and placed on the bottom shelf of the pantry then headed for his room. It wouldn't take him long to pack for he owned little beyond his clothes. He spent the next minute or so filling the course burlap sack with his clothes, not bothering to fold anything as he packed them away. He was about to leave when a small squeak drew his attention to the Brownie at his feet.

"I've got to go live with Mr. Weatherbee now," Wendell stated as he knelt before his diminutive friend. The Brownie released a sorrowful little squeak and hung its head. Wendell chewed his lower lip for a moment as his thoughts raced, "Would you like to come with me? I could take your nest as well and I'm certain Mr. Weatherbee wouldn't mind."

The Brownie looked up and thought for a moment before it nodded its head and gave a happy little squeak followed by a whistle.

"Great! Hold on a moment while I get your nest," Wendell smiled and then laid down on his belly. The nest of stockings was surprisingly firm and held its shape perfectly as Wendell drew it out. The Brownie gave a frightened little squeak as he lifted it into the air and placed it gently in the top of the sack. "Relax, I won't ruin it," Wendell tried to reassure it with a smirk. "Now, would you rather ride on my shoulder or in my pocket?"

The Brownie pointed up towards his shoulder and gave another squeak. Wendell placed his cupped hand before it so the Brownie could jump in, and then raised it to his shoulder where it disembarked. Wendell picked up the burlap sack and started to leave but paused in the doorway to look back at his empty little room a moment longer. I'm leaving home he thought as he gazed at the small confines of his former life. Somehow it hadn't felt real until that very moment as he stood looking back from the threshold. The Brownie gave him a soft squeak of encouragement from his shoulder.

"Your right, I mustn't dwell upon past," Wendell sighed as he turned away and left his room behind.

10

After saying his goodbyes to his father, Mr. Weatherbee led Wendell towards his tower whistling a pleasant tune, but soon after they broke away from the village the old Wizard stopped at the base of the hill. Wendell watched in silence while Mr. Weatherbee pulled a live Dove and several pieces of wax paper wrapped candy from his pocket. The Dove he let fly away with a bit of annoyance then he unwrapped one of the sweets idly lost in thought.

"There you are, my little friend, and one for you as well, Wendell," Mr. Weatherbee stated as he handed the unwrapped candy to the Brownie who was still perched on Wendell's shoulder and another to Wendell, "Tell me, have you ever met Mr. Garroph before Wendell?"

"No, Sir," Wendell answered as he unwrapped his piece of candy. It was a green gum drop.

"I find it curious he took such an interest in you. That was no small sum he offered your father," Mr. Weatherbee told him as he unwrapped a piece of candy for himself.

"Well, there has been some strange things going on lately that I've been meaning to tell you about, but I guess I kind of got distracted with what's been going on with my mother," Wendell admitted as he half-chewed half-sucked on the Gum Drop. It tasted like sugary limes.

"Go ahead then, I'm all ears," Mr. Weatherbee prompted him as he began to walk again, but much slower than when they had started and he clasped his hands behind his back.

So Wendell told him about the lights in Mr. Garroph's tower and how they had made him feel, then he went on to tell him about last nights prowler and how the Brownie had scared it away. Mr. Weatherbee listen intently until Wendell was done then asked a few questions about minor details that had been left out. He seemed especially interested in how Wendell had cried out to break whatever spell had been draining him. That point beyond all others intrigued the Wizard. By the time Wendell finished they had climbed to the top of the hill and he got his first close look at the old Wizard's tower.

The yard around Mr. Weatherbee's tower was surrounded by a tall fence constructed of interwoven pieces of iron that snaked in no discernable pattern but looked intimidating as a whole. A small neat looking vegetable garden sat directly before the tower on either side of a brick paved walkway. On either side of the garden set upon stout wooden benches were two large oval beehives of red clay that stood taller than Wendell and were half again as wide. The tower itself was approximately 30 feet wide at the base and narrowed slightly towards the top 70 feet above. It was--for the most part--a featureless round tower of dark gray granite bricks until near the top where a few narrow windows could be seen below its overhanging wood shingled cone roof. A set of stairs wound up from the ground nearly 10 feet before they came to the tower's single heavy reinforced door of iron-studded oak. A fat, ugly Gargoyle perched on the high-arched eave above the door appeared to be the structure's single artistic embellishment and it wasn't very artistic.

"Everyone listen up! This is Wendell. He's going to be my new Apprentice so try to make him feel at home. Wendell, this is everyone," Mr. Weatherbee waved his had around the yard as he made the introduction but the only living creatures Wendell saw were the bees, and they were too busy at their own business to pay much attention to the old Wizard or Wendell. Unperturbed by this lack of response, Mr. Weatherbee marched up the path towards the tower.

When Mr. Weatherbee reached the door he had to spend several moments fishing in his pocket for the key, mainly due to the seemingly endless line of brightly colored handkerchiefs tied end to end which he had to pull out first. By the time he was done he had a 2-foot pile of handkerchief rope at his feet and Wendell released an involuntary giggle at the old Wizard's frustration. After giving Wendell a stern look of mock disapproval, Mr. Weatherbee bid him to hold the large brass key while he busied himself with pushing the handkerchiefs into his closed fist one by one with his index finger. When they were all neatly tucked within his fist, he blew on it and opened his hand and another white dove flew out of it with no trace of the handkerchiefs. Smug in his success, Mr. Weatherbee took back the key with a wink and opened the tower's door.

Wendell blinked with startled amazement as he looked within the tower for the dimensions of the interior far exceeded those of the tower's exterior. Before him a 20-foot corridor led to a wide open chamber beyond that seemed at least twice again its length. Along the corridor large columns of dark gray marble supported the vaulted ceiling high above, each embellished with a life-like sculpted dragon head with wide open jaws. Within these Dragon's mouths burned blue flames that lit the way before them. The floor of the corridor was a checkerboard pattern of grey and white marble tiles. Despite the grandeur of the architecture everything was quite dusty save for a well trodden path down the center of the hall and many cobwebs that hung defiantly throughout the upper reaches. Mr. Weatherbee waved Wendell in then closed and locked the door behind them before handing the key back to the boy.

"You keep that, I'm certain I have another somewhere around here," Mr. Weatherbee patted his pockets thoughtfully but did not delve into them again, "Now let's see, the door to the right is a broom closet and the one to the left is a cloak room."

"How is this possible?" Wendell interrupted the Wizard's tour still taking in the unnatural dimensions of the place in dumbfounded awe.

"How is what possible?" Mr. Weatherbee looked around seemingly oblivious to what was bothering the boy.

"It's bigger on the inside than the outside," Wendell stated placing a hand tentatively on the wall to make certain it was real.

"Ah well, extra-dimensional space is a bit of an advanced subject but I suppose I can teach you the basics," Mr. Weatherbee placed a hand on Wendell's shoulder and guided him slowly down the corridor while he explained, "See in the beginning the Creator; don't ask me who or what he, she, or it was. I leave those types of questions up to religious people to sort out. Anyway, the Creator made the universe but by all accounts it was a bit of a rushed job and there was quite a bit of unused space left over. Now it's important to understand that all magic leaves traces after it is cast, kind of like if you walk across the carpet with muddy feet. When these traces build up in places like a Wizard's home, for instance, the magic tends to attract the unused bits of space like a magnet. Now when this space enters the physical universe it must either become a part of the world around it or else it creates a void space which implodes within itself and winks out of the Universe again. The magic that has built up within my home makes it rather easy for the space to simply add on to existing rooms slowly over time. So you see, when I first built this tower it did in fact conform to the dimensions it was designed to but as the magic has built up while I lived here, so too did the rooms begin to grow. If I were to leave and the magic was given enough time to fade away the tower's growth would halt and it would be set as it is. Why, I know an Enchantress who lives in a cottage smaller than your parent's home but because it's been in her family for over five generations and she comes from a long line of magically talented ancestors it seems like a huge castle within."

"That's not even the strangest side effect to the magical build up though," Mr. Weatherbee went on as they exited the corridor and entered the central heart of the tower. It was a round chamber nearly 40 feet across with a winding stairwell corkscrewing up the walls and out of sight high above. An antique suit of platemail armor and a small endtable of dusty mahogany were the only furnishings at the foot of the stairwell. Light filtered down from several tall narrow windows up the tower's length even though only a few had been visible from outside and all of those at the very top.

"The strange part is what the magic tends to add as time goes by. Take that corridor for instance. When I had this place built I was severely limited on funds for I hadn't been expecting to move in the first place. Those two doors I pointed out were all that lay between the entrance and this chamber along with a small non-decorative stone sconce. Then after a few years of living here it lengthened into the corridor you saw complete with those dragon heads and there perpetual flames to light the way. If you live here long enough I'm certain you'll find far more interesting puzzles than the size of the rooms," chuckled Mr. Weatherbee.

Mr. Weatherbee stopped at the foot of the stairs and gazed up the central shaft with a small barely audible grunt.

"I think I'll meet you at the top. I don't think my old knees could take the strain of walking up these," Mr. Weatherbee smiled as he stepped back away from Wendell. He put his hands down at his sides and made small flapping motions with his long dexterous fingers. Instantly he began to rise away from the marble floor, gaining speed as he went. Just before he'd risen out of sight, Mr. Weatherbee called back down to Wendell, "Take your time coming up the stairs. I wouldn't want you to strain anything."

Wendell let out a deep sigh which the Brownie seconded with a squeak as he started up the stairs. It was a long and painful climb to the top.

SECTION 2

11

Wendell was in a sorry state 322 steps later when he reached the top of the tower's stairwell. Sweaty and sore he sat down on a leather upholstered bench that was the only piece of furniture at the top. Before the bench was a small balcony that overlooked the stairwell below, while a corridor leading off this small viewpoint started through an archway right next to it. The Brownie squeaked its reassurances and patted him on the ear.

"Thirsty?" Mr. Weatherbee asked from his side holding out a wooden goblet to him. Wendell was too thankful to wonder if the old Wizard had appeared by magic as he took the goblet and gulped down the cool water within. Mr. Weatherbee walked over and leaned over the balconies' rail for a look while the boy drank, "Quite a hike, aye?"

"Thank you, Sir," Wendell gasped when he finished then sagged in his seat for a moment before rising. After 322 steps, Wendell had to know what it looked like from the top. He leaned over the rail and looked down. The Brownie leaned a bit further using a lock of

Wendell's hair to anchor itself in place. Below they could see every circular row of the stairs spiraling downward and in a moment of vertigo Wendell actually imagined that they were slowly spinning in an almost hypnotic pattern.

"Perhaps we shouldn't take in the view until you've gotten a little more use to the heavier magical fields within the tower, shall we?" Mr. Weatherbee pulled him away as he began to stagger against the rail. He led Wendell down the corridor decorated with moth eaten tapestries and to the first of four doors on the right, "This will be your room. I know it's not much, but feel free to make whatever personal touches you feel necessary to make yourself feel more at home."

Mr. Weatherbee opened the door to a bedchamber that may have easily contained his parent's cottage and had a bit of room to spare. The chamber itself was rounded as a pie wedge centered from the door. Two tall narrow windows lined the outer wall with their wooden shutters latched open to let the sunshine in. Under one was a plain wooden desk with a comfortable looking red leather upholstered chair while resting under the other was a large bed piled high with thick blankets and draped with transparent cloth mosquito netting. The only other furniture in the room was a large wardrobe of hand-carved mahogany that had scenes of fey creatures dancing in the woods carved into its doors with stunning detail. Mr. Weatherbee entered and proceeded to show Wendell around.

"I've taken the liberty of putting some appropriate clothing here in the wardrobe for you and before I hear any complaints robes are a sign of our illustrious profession and yes you must wear them," the old Wizard opened the wardrobes doors to reveal the interior. The upper portion of the wardrobe was packed with robes of many different colors hanging upon wooden coat hangers. Below were two narrow drawers with decorative brass handles beside two shelves to place his shoes. On the inside of one door was set a large mirror while a variety of wizardly hats hung off pegs on the other.

"The hats are optional, but you'll find many spells are easier if you have one. Under the bed is a chamber pot that will dump whatever waste you put in it into an extra-dimensional void so be careful with it. Oh, and its best if you sleep with the netting pulled down, some of the spiders here get quite large. Now put your things down on the bed so we can finish the tour, you may unpack later."

Wendell followed Mr. Weatherbee's instructions putting his bag on the bed and then followed him out of the bedchamber into the corridor where the tour of the tower continued. Directly across the hall was the kitchen and washroom though Mr. Weatherbee didn't show it to him saying that it was unwise to disturb the cook without need. Instead, he led Wendell to the next set of doors telling him that the one on the right was his bedchamber while he turned to the left hand door.

"And this is the dining hall," Mr. Weatherbee stated as he opened the door to a huge hall lit brightly by a great iron chandelier with perhaps 200 candles. As they entered, a door was just shutting on the left hand side of the great hall which Wendell assumed led back to the kitchen, but he wasn't able to catch a glimpse of the cook he only saw the fruits of their labor. Two large bowls of steaming vegetable soup and flat bread had been set out at opposite sides of the long oak table designed to seat twelve comfortably and probably twice that in a pinch. "Ah, I guess its lunch time," Mr. Weatherbee commented as he headed for one end of the table happily.

The soup was by far the best Wendell had ever had, seasoned with exotic spices he'd never tasted before. The flat bread tasted rich even without the honey that had been put out for it in small earthware jars for it had generous sprinklings of several whole grains baked throughout its savory crust. Never before had Wendell imagined that something as simple as bread and soup could be a dish of Kings but whoever Mr. Weatherbee's cook was had done just that. The only failing the meal had lay in the enormous size of the great table which made normal conversation next to impossible. Still the old Wizard tried shouting down the great table's length throughout the meal attempting to make Wendell feel at home. Wendell got the distinct impression that Mr. Weatherbee had been very lonely for a long time and was overjoyed at the prospect of having someone around to talk to.

After their lunch was consumed, Mr. Weatherbee guided Wendell to the door at the end of the corridor which opened to another spiraling stairwell though far narrower than the first that surrounding a central support pillar decorated with carvings of grim faces upon each side of its surface. As Wendell climbed the stairs behind the old Wizard, he was given a terrible fright when one of the grim visages gave him a wink as he passed by. Wendell cried out in surprise and nearly tumbled back down the stairs before Mr. Weatherbee snatched him back by his flailing arm.

"What is it, a spider?" Mr. Weatherbee asked fearfully as he glared about the ceiling distrustfully.

"It, it winked at me," Wendell answered excitedly as he pointed at the stone visage accusingly.

"Did it now?" Mr. Weatherbee leaned over and examined the sculpture closely. The face stayed very still and stone like under his scrutiny. The Wizard wrapped his fist on the carving's forehead a few times but it didn't move again. "Probably just your mind playing tricks on you. I know this tower probably seems very spooky compared to your parent's cottage but soon it will grow to feel like home," he told Wendell as he turned away but no sooner had his gaze shifted than the carved face stuck out its long stone tongue towards the Wizard.

Wendell let out a little giggle at the sculpture's antics and Mr. Weatherbee shot him a questioning look with one of his bushy grey eyebrows raised. The carving immediately resumed its grim motionless demeanor as the old Wizard's gaze shifted from the boy back to it.

"What's so funny?" Mr. Weatherbee asked Wendell when he found nothing out of the ordinary to explain the boy's sudden outburst of humor.

"Oh nothing, I was just amused by my own silliness is all," Wendell lied. This seemed to be an acceptable excuse to the Wizard for he started back up the stairs shaking his head and muttering something about the strangeness of youth into his bushy whiskers with something of a cross between disapproval and longing. As Wendell followed him, he looked back over his shoulder and the carving gave him another wink before it was lost from sight.

The narrow stairwell exited into the huge round chamber above through a large trapdoor in the wooden floor that was already open. It was the top of the tower for above their heads was the huge cone of roof rafters tapering into the darkness. When they first entered only a single candle burned upon an ornate brass stand at the center of the room beside the largest book that Wendell had ever seen resting on it's own stand, but then Mr. Weatherbee clapped his hands and all around the room candles on brass candelabrums spontaneously ignited to push back the gloom.

The huge chamber appeared to be part workshop, part laboratory, and part study as Wendell gazed around it in wonder. Along the wall next to a stone hearth was a large table stacked with all manner of bottles, beakers, and jars along with other strange apparatuses of twisting tubes, wires, and crystals for which Wendell had no name. Continuing around the chamber there was set another table and workbench cluttered with carpentry and metal working tools to more exotic jeweler's files and lenses. Next was some very tall and wide bookshelves that had a small selection of aged volumes but was far more devoted to strange jars and bottles with neat little labels pasted onto their fronts. Some of these containers seemed to contain rather mundane powders, herbs, and liquids while others had what looked to be the internal organs of creatures either dried or suspended in liquids. Then there was the space for the stairs where Wendell and the Wizard stood before coming to two large high-backed leather upholstered chairs on the other side of the hearth. A small endtable sat between these chairs with a decorative wood-framed marble chessboard. Its pieces were carved of what looked to be obsidian and rose quartz that must have cost a small fortune. However, all this seemed but meaningless window dressing in comparison to the great central tome.

As Wendell tried to take in all that lay within the chamber his eyes constantly drifted back to this worn and weathered old tome as if its very presence defied interest beyond its thick rough yellow pages. It contained power that Wendell could feel radiating outward and drawing him to it like a moth to flame. The book was bound in leather but had a sleeve of tarnished silver around it that created a hinged bracket and lock. This sleeve was made up of intertwining swirls and knots that formed seemingly hypnotic patterns overlaying the leather. As it drew him into its silvery surface, Wendell could almost make out words hidden in the patterns but the combination of his poor literacy and the weaving of the silver made him unable to grasp what it may have written there. The silver bracket's lock was a puzzle of some kind for there was no sign of a keyhole that Wendell could detect. Only a large knotted pattern protruded from the spot where a keyhole should be. It appeared as a silvery rose in full-bloom that weaved like the rest of the bracket with its cord-like silver strands. It was Mr. Weatherbee's voice that finally broke the spell and returned Wendell's consciousness back to the here and now.

"Something, isn't it?" the old Wizard smiled gently as he gazed at Wendell and the boy suddenly wondered how long he'd been lost within the great tome's patterns, "I first saw it some 350 years ago and it captured me just as it did you. It is the Arcanus Silverratuss Librus, or the magic silver library if you want the literal translation from Elvin. It has been passed from Master to Apprentice for at least 22 generations each adding his or her personal spells to it during their ownership. The earliest spells are little more than undecipherable symbols inked in blood mixed with charcoal. There are very few legacy tomes such as this and once you've taken your oath of apprenticeship its fate will be bound to yours as it has been to mine and all my Masters before me. I'm telling you this because this is point of no return my boy. If you step within that circle and take the oath there is no turning back, you will be bonded to me and this book in a way both unnatural and unbreakable. I could try to explain it further but some spells by their very nature defy explanation or definition so they remain mutable within themselves and may adapt to our ever changing world. What I can tell you is your perspective of me will change, as will mine of you to that of loyal Apprentice to Master and vise versa. You will sometimes be able to sense my desires when they pertain to you and will be unable to share my secrets. There may be other side effects as well, the most common of which is we'll feel each other's pain when the other is hurt, but again the spell is very mutable so nothing is ever certain. You must now make your choice Wendell; I've given you what warning I may."

As Mr. Weatherbee crossed the circle of symbols burnt into the floor surrounding the tome that had escaped Wendell's previous notice there was a slight distortion in the air as if he'd passed through some kind of invisible barrier. The Wizard took a position beside the tome and simply watched the boy expectantly, his face betraying neither his desires nor fears. A small part of Wendell wanted to flee the tower for he knew that his world would never be the same after he crossed that line, but only a small part. Mostly Wendell was already captured by the thought of learning things most would never know. The thought of unlocking the secrets of the Universe drove him forward with but a moment's hesitation.

Crossing the circle was far harder than it appeared for the very air resisted Wendell's intrusion. Again, he felt the tugging sensation within the pit of his naval as he struggled through the unseen barrier that tried to block his way. Then all of a sudden, he was through and would have fallen flat upon his face if not for Mr. Weatherbee's quick reflexes as the old Wizard caught him. Wendell sagged in the Wizard's grasp totally wiped out from the experience that had been far more exhausting then climbing the stairwell up the tower for it not only drained his body but seemingly his mind as well. Mr. Weatherbee seemed not at all concerned as he continued to hold the boy until his strength returned; in fact, he seemed rather pleased that Wendell had made it.

When Wendell was able to feebly stand once more on his own, Mr. Weatherbee bid him to take a position next to the tome while he went about opening it. The Wizard accomplished this by tracing the edges of the silver rose pattern three times clockwise then three times counter clockwise. As the last circle was completed, the silvery cords unwound themselves and withdrew until they were only on the leather covers so the book could open. Then, instead of opening the tome, Mr. Weatherbee leaned forward and spoke to it in a commanding tone.

"Show me the Oath of Apprenticeship," the Wizard commanded and the tome instantly responded. The book opened on its own and flipped a third of the way through its pages before coming to rest on the desired spell. At the center of both pages was a handprint in dark blue ink, the one on the left with fingers pointed upwards while the one on the right with its fingers pointed sideways towards the spine. Every inch of the pages surrounding these handprints was filled with spidery text in the same blue ink of which only a few letters Wendell could pick out that he recognized. Mr. Weatherbee scanned the text with his lips moving slightly as he read for several minutes before he spoke again. "This is a very complicated spell written in ancient Elvin so you will not be able to understand it nor can I begin to translate it to you when you have not been educated in the subtleties of this dead language's grammar. Therefore, you must trust in what I've told you about the oath and do as I say. First, you must place your right hand on the handprint on the right page while I do the same upon the left. Then we must clasp our free hands with palms together and fingers intertwined. I will then start reciting the spell and at each of the two breaks before its completion I'll look to you and you must state clearly 'So swear I Wendell Glasswright.' The first part of the oath is swearing your allegiance to me and the second is swearing your oath to keep this book and its secrets safe from anyone who would try to steal them. The last part of the oath binds the spell unbreakably in place. It is important that you don't break contact with me or the book until the casting is completed. Do you understand?"

"Yes, Sir," Wendell nodded, getting a bit anxious.

"Then let us begin," Mr. Weatherbee smiled as he placed one of his old bony hands upon the page and the other before Wendell.

As soon as Wendell placed his hand upon the page and grasped the Wizard's, Mr. Weatherbee began to chant off the spell and as he chanted, his words began to echo and reverberate with power. This was not like the simple spells Wendell had previously witnessed or felt, and by the end of the first line, he grew afraid of the terrible power that was building around him. The air became saturated with it causing all the hair on his body to stand on end and goose flesh to rise. The letters on the tome's pages flared with a fiery blue radiance and an unnatural breeze chilled the air. Outside the circle, ghostly shapes began to manifest and take the form of phantom Wizards. As these apparitions manifested they added their own unearthly voices to Mr. Weatherbee's chant causing it to echo louder than before. So distracting was it that Wendell almost missed his cue and let his oath burst forth with surprise when he noticed that they all were looking to him expectantly.

Mr. Weatherbee then chanted on and if anything, the spell grew worse. It started with a tingling in Wendell's stomach that steadily grew outward until it felt as if his skin was going to crawl off his flesh at any moment. His heartbeat was racing with terror until the boy feared it might thunder out of his chest. All the candles were suddenly extinguished causing the only light to be that of the books pages and the soft glow of the spectral Wizards of the past. Then the book's fire changed from blue to an even brighter green and Mr. Weatherbee's face was cast with harsh shadows that gave him an unholy aspect as the second portion of the spell drew to a close.

Once again, Wendell swore but this time his voice was filled with terror as he yelled it out above the echoing spell's roar. He wanted to break away and flee but his brain kept telling him it would soon be over and to trust in Mr. Weatherbee's word. As the old Wizard started chanting the final portion of the spell Wendell felt real power wash through him for the first time. It was terrible, wonderful, and intoxicating all at the same time. He felt as if he could destroy mountains with by his will alone or create a mighty tempest with the fancies of his heart. Green fire sparked from between his and Mr. Weatherbee's hands where they made contact with each other and the book. Then came the pain.

It was not physical pain that suddenly assaulted Wendell but the pain of having magic alter the nature of his soul. Terrible pain that held him rigid and unthinking as he begged aloud to make it stop through teeth clenched so tightly if he could have formed thought he'd have feared they would shatter. It lasted an eternity or a moment then it was gone and Wendell felt himself falling but had no will or the energy to attempt to catch himself.

Through blurry eyes, Wendell watched as each of the Ghostly Wizards bowed to his Master one by one before fading back into the ether realms from which they came until only one lingered though dimming slowly. Wendell's Master tried to touch the Specter's hand with tears running like rivers down into his beard. For a second it seemed they would clasp hands just as he and Wendell had during the spell then the Apparition's hand passed through his Master's without the slightest hesitation. Wendell's Master recoiled from the touch with a shiver and Wendell felt his deep despair. Then the ghost spoke with the hollow echo of the past intruding upon the present.

"Rejoice, my Son, for today you've added another link to our most sacred of chains. Train him well for he is your link to the future just as you are mine. Complete the circle," the Apparition stated as he continued to fade away. When he was no more than a tiny distorted haze in the darkness, his final words echoed back from the great beyond, "Know always that I am proud of you, my Son."

As the Apparition disappeared so too was the chamber cast in utter darkness and Wendell felt himself sinking into it no longer able to remain conscious. He was spent in both body and soul. No dreams or nightmares troubled his sleep for even in his unconsciousness his soul knew that his Master was watching over him.

12

When Wendell awoke he was seated in one of the red leather chairs before the hearth. His Master sat across the gulf divided by a chessboard looking sorely worn out and haggard. A warm fire now blazed within the hearth and was consuming not just a small pile of logs but fragrant incense as well. The incense made Wendell feel exceptionally relaxed and clear headed despite the fatigue he still felt throughout his whole body.

"How do you feel?" His Master asked gently, his voice was a bit raspier than usual.

"Worn out, but better than before," Wendell answered and the old Wizard smiled knowingly. After a few minutes of doing nothing but watching the flames within the hearth dance, Wendell ventured the first of many questions on his mind, "Master, were those all really the spirits of the Wizards who've come before us to serve the book?"

"Yes. It is one of a very few occasions in which they may move freely between the worlds of the living and the dead. They must add their power to keep our legacy intact for with each casting of the Apprenticeship Oath it demands more energy to continue the cycle. Somehow the spell pulls them through the divide to accomplish this then sends them back when it is complete. There are more powerful spells in the book but that is one of the more unique ones," His Master told him while still lost in the depths of the flames.

"It was terrifying," Wendell admitted with a shiver. What he left unspoken was how good it felt as well. So much power had been surging through his body that Wendell thought he now knew how Gods must feel. He longed to feel it again, but perhaps not right now he decided as he felt the dull ache from it to the very marrow of his bones. His Master made no reply.

"You miss him very much, don't you?" Wendell ventured after sitting quietly as long as a twelve year old boy can.

"He was taken from me before his time. It was painful to be reminded of that fact is all. We were very close," the old Wizard whispered more to the fire than to Wendell, "One day we will be reunited but it will be a bittersweet reunion. Such is the cycle of life and death."

"How was he taken?" Wendell asked before he thought better of it. His curiosity somehow overcame his new longing to please his Master for a horrible moment. His Master turned his gaze upon him but the harsh shadows of the firelight hid whether or not the question had upset him, "I, I'm sorry. I shouldn't pry."

"An evil Wizard named Melbourne Veld ambushed him while he was shopping in the city. He waited until my Master's attention was fixed on a gem he'd enchanted with a fascination glamour then unleashed enough Hell fire to overcome his defenses and level three of the surrounding city's blocks. I doubt my Master noticed the attack at all," the old Wizard told him after a few moments. His tone held no sadness or anger, but just stated the facts with dry candor. He paused for a moment then went on and as he spoke it seemed as though he was confessing some terrible deed to Wendell that pained him but needed to be told nonetheless, "When I learned what Melbourne had done I swore an oath of vengeance upon him. I went to his tower intent on challenging him to a Wizard's duel, but he'd already fled before the law could catch up to him. I spent many years tracking him across this and other lands before I finally caught up to him and his Apprentice, Scott Garroph. I challenged him and he laughed at me for he was old and powerful. He underestimated the depth of my fury and it cost him more than his life. In the madness of my anger, I cursed him to a place far worse than hell. I trapped him within the dreams of the God of Madness to be lost forever beyond the constraints of time in an ever changing landscape of insanity. It is the darkest magic I've ever done and I often fear what the cost of it will be upon my soul.

"With his Master dispatched I then turned my wrath filled gaze towards Scott intent on finishing it once and for all, but he was young and begged me for mercy. He swore to all the powers that he had nothing to do with my Master's death nor did he feel any compulsion to avenge his fallen Master who'd been a cruel and bitter man. Something in his voice broke me from my rage and I told him I'd allow him to live as long as he gave no hint of following his Master's evil ways.

"After that, Scott and I found ourselves lost in a foreign and dangerous land far from home so we decided to travel back together out of necessity. In that time I can't say that we ever became friends for his Master's abuse had left its mark upon him, but we did grow to respect one another. Scott has a brilliant mind, full of uncanny cunning that saved both our lives more than once. After we returned, we parted company and he took up residence in his Master's tower and me in mine. I made no secret of the fact that I kept an eye on him for I knew that he was ever in danger of falling down the same dark path as his Master and I felt responsible for I had given him his life."

"Years went by and I'll admit I grew lax in my vigilance. Scott had become a recluse within his tower and no word of any wickedness by his hand reached my ear. Then one day he just vanished, thwarting every attempt I made to locate him by magic. I knew he was up to something so I started a very long search to find him. It took me twenty two years to find him living here in your quiet little valley for he is very good at covering his tracks, and even then it was only by chance. A traveling merchant I had dealings with had sold some books to Scott as he was passing through and recognized his name when I mentioned him in passing. I immediately moved here certain that I'd find him knee deep in the dark arts terrorizing the surrounding area but that was not the case.

"While the Villagers often blame him whenever their milk goes sour or a five legged calf is born I've not had any solid evidence that he's up to no good. Like before he's become a recluse, ignoring the world beyond his tower walls. The experiences you've told me of this morning are the first real hints of misbehavior I've heard of in the ten years I've lived here, and they are hardly conclusive. The drain of power you felt was likely an unknown side effect of whatever magic he was performing, for Scott's ego would never allow him to rely on others for his magic, but it does hint that he's playing with some very powerful forces. Even the Infernal that was prowling your yard wasn't actively causing harm. In all likelihood he merely sent it out to track down who had disrupted his spell for he would have instantly recognized it if it had been me. Again he attempted no harm, but instead tried to purchase you as his Apprentice," here Wendell's Master paused and turned back towards the flames, lost it thought. Wendell digested all that he'd been told for a minute or two then another thought burst into his head.

"His shadow!" Wendell blurted out excitedly, "He didn't cast a shadow even though the sun was shining brightly this morning. I didn't think it was all that important before and had nearly forgotten about it."

"Noticed that did you, well it is another clue but hardly conclusive of anything. Shadows can be manipulated in many different ways by magic and not all are baneful. In fact shadow plays are some of the very first magic parents teach their children in Wizard families because of its harmless nature. His shadow's absence is not in itself an ill omen, but does raze the question of where is it? Now the absence of his reflection would be far more significant for it would be indeed prove that his soul is lost or in the possession of another. Only ill ever comes from such a loss," Wendell's Master got up and put another log on the fire, "I think that's quite enough of dark subjects for one night, I've probably said far to much as it is. You should go to bed now. Tomorrow we'll begin your training in earnest and you'll need to be well rested."

Just the mention of sleep made Wendell yawn and he rose from the chair stiffly, fully conscious of his body's aches and pains.

"Good night, Master," Wendell sighed, reluctant to leave the old man's presence as he headed for the stairs.

"Good night, Wendell," Bergstrom smiled behind him, amused by the fact that the boy was now completely unable to address him by his name. It was the reversal of rolls that had taken him back into the past along with seeing his Master's spirit, "I'm the Master now, so what should I teach him first?" he asked the fire as he sat back down. The fire refused to answer but chose to continue its hungry dance upon the logs. It didn't matter though, for soon the answer came to him without aid and the old Wizard chuckled behind his bushy grey beard.

13

"Wake up, Wendell," Mr. Weatherbee called in from the doorway very early the next morning. Wendell yawned as he rose and rubbed the sleep from his eyes. It was not yet light out and the air within the tower was cold as the grave. His Master smiled at him then began to withdraw. "When you've finished dressing, come to the dining hall so we may eat and plan your day. Try not to take to long."

"Alright, I won't," Wendell told him as he headed towards the wardrobe wishing he'd worn his stockings to bed. The cold flagstones sapped the heat from his toes in seconds.

Wendell opened the wardrobe's doors and quickly delved into the drawer into which he'd dumped his clothing. He found two mismatched stockings and quickly pulled them on. As he rose he glanced up and caught his reflection, stifling a yawn before it quickly moved to mimic Wendell's movements.

"Hey!" Wendell exclaimed in a mixture of surprise and annoyance at his reflection's misbehavior. Though it initially startled him he seemed to be accepting the towers magical nature much better this morning, or else Wendell's mind was simply too tired to rebel against the abnormality of the situation. Wendell's reflection shrugged as if to say he was sorry but what was he going to do about it before it fell into line.

Picking out a robe took longer than Wendell had planned for it seemed like most of the ones that his Master had assembled were either far too flamboyant for Wendell to comfortably wear in public or were far too big. In the end, he settled for a midnight blue robe that was only about a half foot to long for its course heavy linen promised to keep him warm. He also chose a stocking cap that matched its color remembering what his master had said about hats making it easer to cast some spells. When he was done changing, he looked himself over once more in the mirror. He made such a pathetic showing that his reflection shook its head and slumped its shoulders in humiliation.

"No one asked you anyway," Wendell growled as he hiked up his over-long sleeves so he could shut the wardrobe doors on his annoying counterpart. Perhaps he could get his sister Wendy to hem them up the next time he went down to the village: Wendy had always been quite cunning with a needle and thread, making all her own dresses. Thinking of his older sister inevitably led to thoughts of Wendell's mother of whom she greatly resembled, so he tried to put them out of his mind as he headed towards the dining hall.

Wendell found his Master already halfway through the steaming hot breakfast pudding that filled the great chamber with an aroma of apples and cinnamon. Mr. Weatherbee wasn't paying much attention when he came in and sat down at his end of the long table for the old Wizard was busy scratching a quill over a piece of parchment while idly shoveling pudding into his mouth between words. Wendell's mouth exploded with saliva as he sat down and inhaled the pudding's delectable vapors. He was just bringing the first spoon full of the desert towards his mouth when his Master called out to him.

"Ah, there you are. Come down here a moment, won't you?" Mr. Weatherbee waved him over. Wendell took the bite of the delicious pudding as he rose. The burst of flavor was rich and even better than he'd anticipated. So good in fact that he didn't notice that his robe had gotten caught under the chair and he pulled it over with a loud crack as he started to walk away. Mr. Weatherbee looked amused as he watched the boy untangle the garment and right the chair, "You'll get used to wearing robes soon enough, just be careful going up and down stairs until then. Now I have a list of ingredients I want you to gather in the valley today while I'm away. Do so as quickly as you can then come back and practice your letters. I've put a black board and some chalk in your desk among other things and the rest of what you'll need you can find in the entrance hall closet."

"Where are you going Master?" Wendell asked with displeasure as he took the parchment from Mr. Weatherbee. He'd hoped they'd be spending the day together and the idea of the old Wizard's absence was strangely upsetting.

"I've some business to see to in the city and I may also stop to visit an old friend. Just concentrate on gathering what's on the list to keep your mind off my absence," Wendell's Master smiled before taking another bite of his pudding.

As Wendell started back toward his end of the table slowly, he struggled to read what was on the list. The parchment contained only three items: a lock from a fair-haired Maiden, Widow's tears, and a lucky horseshoe. Wendell turned to ask how he was supposed to go about getting these items but he found his Master's seat vacant. The Wizard was gone and Wendell was alone in the great feast hall. With a heavy sigh, Wendell returned to his seat and ate his breakfast.

When the pudding was devoured, Wendell decided to help the cook by returning the dirty dishes to the kitchen as well as compliment his culinary skill. He gathered the dirty bowls and spoons and made his way through the servant's entrance to the kitchen. Through the door he found a kitchen of massive proportions as most rooms he'd seen within the tower.

The kitchen smelled of baking bread and dried herbs that seem very homey and welcoming to the Apprentice. A great brickwork oven dominated the center of the room with its stout metal door thrown open to warm the chamber. To one side of this oven, the chamber was devoted to cleaning: several large wooden tubs lined the walls with linen sheets and Wizard garments hanging above upon cloths lines to dry. Wendell quickly located the tub devoted to dishes and dumped his load into the soapy water. Immediately a large Elemental swelled up as if to swallow the discarded dishes that sank down into its watery depths. Though it startled Wendell he was not surprised to find it there since he'd already witnessed his Master's use of such creatures for cleaning.

The other half of the chamber was devoted to the kitchen and Wendell poked around for a moment wondering about the absent cook. Three cauldrons of varying sizes hung within the massive hearth--the smallest of which was still stained with the apple cinnamon pudding. Upon the hearth's wide mantle rested more herbs and spices than Wendell had known existed within the world: he saw common ones such as salt, pepper, and mustard seed as well as exotic ones like cloves, basil, and linseed oil that he knew his mother would have killed to own, and then there were those that he had never even heard of like Float Root and Amber Vine amongst the impressive and very expensive collection.

Two large tables were set parallel before the hearth cluttered with knives, whole grain flower, rolling pins, pots, and pans. Above these bundles of vegetables had been hung from chains lined with hooks, as well as salted meats and strings of fresh garlic. The kitchen looked as if it had been in use just moments before Wendell entered but now was just as empty and lonely as the abandoned feast hall. Frustrated, Wendell continued on through the door that led towards his own quarters knowing he probably didn't have time to linger if he wanted to collect everything upon the list. As he started down the corridor towards the Tower's central stair, Wendell could have sworn he heard someone humming from the kitchen behind.

14

After carefully descending the stairs, Wendell sat down upon the bottom step to catch his breath for a minute before continuing on to the closet. He was uncertain what exactly he would need but assumed he'd know it when he saw it. He opened the door of the closet and was able to form a perfect O with his mouth just before the wall of junk collapsed over him like an avalanche. Shaken but unscathed Wendell spent the next twenty minutes cleaning up the mess of snow shoes, croquet mallets, butterfly nets, fishing poles, Yule decorations, an old brass oil lamp, wicker baskets, tangled rope, bird cages, a bear trap, rusty tools, a hunting horn, a very dull axe, a cracked flower vase, stuffed animals with loose stitching, beeswax candles, worn winter galoshes, bowling balls, lawn darts, glass bottles, birthday decorations, paint brushes, camping gear, bird whistles, wooden buckets, brass spittoons, a harpsichord, chamber pots, a ship's anchor, cloth mosquito netting, a plate mail gauntlet, a magnifying glass, wooden panpipes, a chain leash and collar, canoe paddles, potato sacks, linen handkerchiefs, a spyglass, a locked box that rattled, manacles, a can of horse glue, brooms, a weaver's loom, moth-eaten blankets, feather dusters, blacksmith's tongs, a leaky oil can, Solstice decorations, mops, a book on subtropical fish, a stringless lyre, a sack of goose feathers, worn scrub brushes, a picnic basket, tangled red ribbon, a sack of marbles, hopelessly tangled fishing tackle, an ear horn of brass, balls of tangled yarn, a foot stool with a broken leg, a thirty pound mace, and one stuffed beaver. Of the cluttered assortment of miscellaneous junk, Wendell took only a pair of old shears and a small glass vial with a cork stopper. The rest he fought valiantly back into the seemingly infinite and somehow just a tad too small depths of the closet before he threw his weight against the door and prayed to any God that would listen it wouldn't burst open again when he moved. The Gods were merciful and Wendell fled before they had a chance to change their minds.

Once outside the Tower, Wendell started down the hill towards the village wondering where to begin. He knew only one Widow in the village who was Granny Rosa, but knew of no fair-haired Maidens since all the women and men in these parts had brown or black hair. He knew the place to find horseshoes was the Black Smithy or on a Horse, but doubted any of them would be considered lucky. This list was going to be harder to gather than it first appeared Wendell thought as he scanned the parchment again thoughtfully.

Wendell entered the village intent on going to see Granny Rosa since hers seemed the most obtainable component on the list, but as he made his way down the lane of small cottages he saw something that distracted him from his bazaar little scavenger hunt. Trevor Smith had a girl Wendell's age pinned against the back side of a cottage between his large meaty arms. Wendell didn't know who the girl was but he was more than familiar with the bully who had plagued him and the other children of the village since he was old enough to walk and talk. Trevor was the son of Thornton, the village blacksmith, and like his father had grown head and shoulders taller than anyone else their age. The meaty thirteen year old took sadistic delight in tormenting every child smaller than himself, which is to say everyone who wasn't old enough to be working in the fields or learning their trade. The bully was as husky as he was large with short dark brown hair and an unpleasant face. His eyes were dark and beady as well, not exactly intelligent but sharp and full of predatory cunning. The girl he had pinned between his gorilla-like mitts was a very fair creature indeed.

She was a milkmaid Wendell deduced from the wooden carrier that had one bottle of milk amongst several empties clutched before her protectively. Her freckly face would be very pretty if not for the fact that she was very afraid at the moment as she stared up into Trevor's looming mug. She was dressed in a simple blue and white work gown and had a white bonnet tied around her head to ward away the morning's chill. Wendell was able to hear some of what was going on before either the bully or milkmaid noted his presence.

"Let me go, I have a delivery to make!" The Milkmaid pleaded as she tried to squirm out from under Trevor's arms.

"Not until you pay the toll. Give me a kiss," Trevor grinned wickedly as he leaned to the side to block her escape.

"My father would whip the hide off my backside if he heard I was kissing boys. Just let me go!" The milkmaid cringed, looking even more horrified.

"That's the price. Take your time in deciding, I've nothing better to do today," Trevor chuckled with an evil leer.

"Leave her alone Trevor!" A voice that Wendell had a horrified feeling was his own told the bully before he had a chance to stop it.

Trevor blinked with disbelief as he turned towards Wendell like a confused giant. The milkmaid took advantage of his moment of distraction and quickly slipped out from under his arms, causing her milk bottles to clink together as she did so. Instead of fleeing as would have been prudent, the milkmaid raced behind Wendell and stopped as if he had some chance of protecting her from the bully's wrath. Wendell gulped audibly as recognition sparked in Trevor's eyes and his unpleasant features twisted into the sadistic grin of a cat that has just found a small helpless animal to toy with.

"Nice dress, Wimpell. So what, now you're a mighty Wizard who's going to teach me a lesson?" Trevor chuckled as he advanced menacingly.

Wendell tried to back away but was blocked by the milkmaid behind him.

"Go on. Turn him into a frog or something. Anything is bound to be an improvement on that ugly mug," The milkmaid goaded Wendell on with a push to the back loud enough to be heard by the bully.

"Yeah, Wimpell, show me some magic," Trevor laughed as he snatched the front of Wendell's robes and jerked him upward until he was barely touching the ground with the tips of his toes.

As Trevor pulled back his meaty fist that was certain to destroy Wendell's nose, the Apprentice closed his eyes and tried to visualize the brilliant white light. It was much harder to do under the threat of an immediate pummeling but luckily Trevor hesitated to savior Wendell's apparent fear giving him the time he needed to focus on the spell.

"Closing your eyes isn't going to make this hurt any less," Trevor chuckled as Wendell visualized the light before his eyes and snapped his fingers.

Trevor cried out in surprise as the flash exploded right in front of his meaty face and he automatically dropped Wendell as he tried to protect his eyes. Wendell hit the ground running and didn't even pause as he snatched the dumbfounded milkmaid's hand and dragged her away. Within a few steps Trevor's roar of anger spurred her into a more energetic flight and the two ran as fast as their baggy clothing would allow. They didn't stop until they had put more than half the village behind them and then they slumped behind a barn completely out of breath. Wendell didn't even want to think about the pummeling he was going to receive the next time he encountered Trevor.

"I really think you should have turned him into a frog but that was pretty good, too," The milkmaid stated critically once she'd regained her breath, "Thank you, Wimpell."

"It's Wendell, and you're welcome. Trevor's going to pound me good for that next time though," Wendell stated gloomily as he took off his stocking cap and scratched his head.

"Oh. Well, you were wonderful all the same, Wendell. My name's Mary Miller," she beamed a beautiful smile at him that made Wendell feel more than a little warm and uncomfortable, "I don't know how I would have gotten out of that if you hadn't come along."

Mary took a step towards him expectantly and Wendell backed into the barn's wall somewhat frightened as he fidgeted with his cap in front of him. He noticed all of a sudden that he felt something within the blue cloth hat and he looked down at it in surprise. Wendell opened the headwear and peered within to find a bundle of green straw like things tied together with a red lace. Curious he grasped the bundle and pulled it out to reveal them to be the stems of a small bouquet of pink roses.

"Pink roses are my favorite! How did you know?" Mary exclaimed with delighted surprise as she took the bouquet from Wendell's numb grasp. She leaned in and kissed him on the cheek before he could gather his wits to protest and sent a strange electrical sensation through his body from where her lips met his flesh.

Wendell babbled something completely incoherent as he held his cheek that made Mary giggle with mirth as she stuck her cute freckly nose into the flowers. Suddenly Wendell was finding it impossible to focus on anything but her, but looking at her made him feel queasy at the same time. The twelve year old fidgeted with his collar as he looked down at the ground uncomfortably and that's when he noticed a piece of metal sticking out of the loose soil at his feet. Wendell leaned down and brushed the object off to reveal it to be a worn old horseshoe with the rusted remnants of one last nail. Wendell picked it up and examined it curiously wondering if it might be lucky.

"What are you going to do with that?" Mary asked curiously.

"I was just wondering if it was a lucky horseshoe. I'm supposed to find one along with a couple other things for my Master," Wendell explained as he focused on the horseshoe to avoid Mary's gaze.

"I would think that not being nailed to a Horse's hoof would be considered good luck and you did find it by a lucky coincidence," Mary reasoned as she continued to smell her little bouquet with smug satisfaction.

"I suppose," Wendell acknowledged her rational as he removed and discarded the rusty nail before tucking the horseshoe into his belt pouch.

He chewed his lip for a moment then looked at her sheepishly. "Well I guess I better be going. It was very nice meeting you Mary."

"Wait. I only have one more bottle of milk to deliver to Granny Rosa, after that I could help you?" Mary offered hopefully.

"That's who I was headed to meet before I ran into you," Wendell blurted in surprise, "I need some Widow's tears."

"I think that horseshoe is far luckier than you imagined, Wendell," Mary stated knowingly as she stepped away from him. She took a few steps down the road then turned and looked at him expectantly. "Are you coming?"

"Yeah," Wendell stated as he straitened his cap upon his head and followed her while trying to avoid tripping on the hem of his robes.

"You better start coming up with a plan on how you're going to make Granny Rosa cry," Mary stated after they had walked down the dirt road for a minute in silence, "I won't help you hurt such a sweet old lady."

"I wouldn't dream of it," Wendell assured her truthfully. Mary smiled at him again as if he'd passed her test satisfactorily.

"So how are you going to get them?" she asked curiously.

"I haven't the foggiest idea," Wendell shook his head as he wracked his brain for the answer.

15

Granny Rosa was not really Wendell's grandmother or any of the other village children for that matter. She had no children of her own so she compensated by adopting all the village children as her own to spoil rotten whenever possible. Granny Rosa lived in a small cottage at the base of the hill upon which Mr. Garroph's Tower perched on the eastern side of the valley. She was as venerable as the surrounding hills but hadn't lost a bit of her energy despite the years she'd accumulated. Granny Rosa supported herself by weaving but her true passion in life was baking sweets for any child who would happen by. Wendell had never passed the cottage without smelling some form of pastry, cookies, or candy in her oven wafting out the open windows and door like an irresistible lure and this morning was no exception.

"Lemon Tarts," Mary stated after sniffing the air with her freckly little nose as they approached the door of the cottage that was cracked open to let the place breath. Wendell grinned as he extended his fist to knock on the open portal for the smell was quite enticing.

"Come in, the door's open," Granny Rosa called out stating the obvious. She shot them a toothless grin of pure joy as Mary and Wendell entered.

Granny Rosa as normal was perched upon a tall stool before her loom with her back before the oven. She was bent like a bow as she manipulated the color threads of her latest blanket with withered claws that seemed to possess uncanny skill despite their liver spotted appearance. Her cheeks sagged around her smile having far to much excess skin to take an active roll in the expression and her blue gray eyes were magnified behind her thick lenses as she squinted at both of the children in turn.

"Sorry I'm late, Granny Rosa, but I had a bit of trouble getting here," Mary apologized as she removed the full milk bottle from her carrier and offered it to the old woman.

"Busy collecting flowers from bashful little gentlemen?" Granny Rosa grinned as she spied Mary's bouquet of pink roses then looked towards Wendell's blushing face.

"That and dealing with a bully," Mary giggled as she saw Wendell's discomfort.

"Was it that horrible little Smith boy again? Despite how many parents complain they never seem to rein him in," Granny Rosa shook her head in disgust causing her silvery bun to wobble on the back of her skeletal head, "Why just last week Jeremiah Tanner nearly knocked me down as he dashed in here with that cruel little Goblin child right on his heels. Had to almost ruin my broom giving him a good thrashing for disturbing my peace. Not that I think it did the least bit of good mind you."

"That's the one. He wanted me to give him a kiss to leave me alone until Wendell came to my rescue," Mary shivered at the thought.

"You know your father's going to be awfully cross if you've been fighting, Wendell. Not that I don't think Trevor couldn't do with a good punch to the nose mind you. Seems like that's the only way to get through to his type," Granny Rosa stated with disapproval as she starred down her nose at the boy.

"He wasn't fighting. Wendell used magic to distract that Troll faced oaf then we ran. He was wonderful!" Mary boasted with pride making Wendell all the more uncomfortable.

"So you really have become Bergstrom's Apprentice then, aye? Wonderful gentleman, always knows just how to make an old gal blush," Granny Rosa smiled as she tied off her thread then moved to the oven.

"Yes, Granny," Wendell acknowledge awkwardly as he wondered if the whole village was gossiping about him, "That's actually why I came."

"Oh, has Bergstrom need of a tapestry or something for that drafty old Tower?" Granny asked as she fished out a tray of steaming hot lemon tarts with a thick rag and set them on the counter to cool.

"Not exactly, no," Wendell scratched his head suddenly uncertain as to how to breach the subject, "You see this morning he gave me a list of things I had to gather before he returns tonight, and one of those things is Widow's tears. Since you're the only Widow I know I was hoping I might get some from you."

Granny Rosa stopped fanning the tarts with her rag and stared at Wendell for a moment before she broke into a mirthful cackle.

"That sounds like the kind of mad errand old Bergstrom would send you on," Granny Rosa shook her head as she chuckled, "I'd like to help you, Wendell, but I haven't wept in years. How could I be sad when I've got such wonderful company like you about?"

"Did Mr. Weatherbee say they had to be tears of sadness?" Mary asked thoughtfully.

"No, the list just says Widow's tears," Wendell unfolded the piece of yellowed parchment to be certain.

"Maybe we could make her laugh until she cries?" Mary suggested as she placed the empty milk bottle the old woman gave her into her carrier and set it on the counter.

"I don't know if my old heart could take that much humor these days," Granny Rosa shook her head doubtfully as she began breaking the tarts of the cookie sheet with a wooden spatula, "One good joke could be all it takes to do me in."

"Onions!" Wendell blurted out snapping his fingers. A bright flash of light went off before his eyes as he did so. It took moment of rubbing his eyes to recover then he finished his thought, "If you were to chop up some onions that might make you cry with little to no danger to your health, Granny."

"I suppose I could chop up some onions early for tonight's soup for a good cause such as helping our village's newest Wizard," Granny Rosa stated thoughtfully as she handed both children one of the lemon tarts that were still hot but cool enough to touch, "You'll have to go out in the garden and pick them though."

"Thank you. That seems more than reasonable, Granny," Mary nodded before she took a tentative bite of her tart, "These are excellent."

"Thank you, Granny, I really appreciate this!" Wendell grinned before he munched down two thirds of his tart in one bite and scalded his tongue. Mary laughed and rolled her eyes at his impatience.

"Yes, well as I said Bergstrom is a gentleman and we could use a lot more men around following in his footsteps," Granny Rosa nodded to herself as she climbed back up onto her stool, "The onions are growing in the back two rows of my garden. Bring me the two largest ones you can find, Wendell, while Mary and I chat."

"Yes, Granny," Wendell acknowledged as he headed to the door. He got the suspicious feeling they were going to be talking about him as he exited the cottage.

It took Wendell only a minute or two to locate the two largest purple onions the small garden had to offer, then he picked and wash them at Granny's hand pump. When he returned both Mary and Granny Rosa wore smug smirks as they looked at him, but neither made any comment about what they'd been discussing. Wendell had thought that girls got more understandable with age but Granny Rosa seemed to be an exception to the common rule. He waited patiently for the old woman to finish the currant line of the blanket she was working on while he munched down another tart. Then Granny once more tied off her threads and set about chopping the onions.

At first Wendell's hopes were crushed for Granny Rosa seemed all but immune to the onions vapors as she quickly diced them. Then she placed the tiny cubes into her cauldron with her hands, looked at him with a heavy sigh, and proceeded to rub her eyes with her onion sticky fingers. Within a minute, tears were streaming down her saggy cheeks and Wendell handed her the corked vial.

"You owe me one, kid. Now go fetch me a bucket of water so I can rinse this stuff out," Granny Rosa sniffled as she put the vial up to her eye to fill it.

By the time Wendell returned Mary held the vial that was half full of Granny's tears and the old woman busied herself with rinsing out her eyes.

"First time I've ever purposefully done that," Granny chuckled as she dried her eyes on her cooking rag, "Stings twice as much when you know what's coming."

"Thank you very much, Granny. I don't know how I would have gotten these without you," Wendell acknowledged as he eyed the tears within the vial speculatively.

"Well at least you didn't run up and kick me in the shin or pull my hair. Good Wizards are much more preferable to bad ones. Take another tart with you and be sure to tell Bergstrom I'm looking forward to his next visit," Granny Rosa chuckled as she climbed back up onto her stool.

Wendell and Mary said their farewells to Granny Rosa as they picked out another lemon tart each, then they left the cottage munching the pastries happily. It was just starting to get hot as they walked up the dirt lane waving greetings to the villagers who were about their daily chores. Everyone's mood seemed to be as pleasant as the weather and Wendell felt content until Mary asked the question that reminded him about the task at hand.

"So what else do you have to collect?" Mary asked after finishing the last of her tart.

"The hardest thing of all," Wendell sighed as he opened the parchment and read the last item again while shaking his head gloomily. "A lock from a fair-haired Maiden. I don't know anyone with fair hair around here."

"Is that all?" Mary giggled at him with amusement sparkling in her blue eyes.

"Do you know somebody?" Wendell asked hopefully.

"Hold these," Mary smiled as she handed him her milk bottle carrier and bouquet of roses. After he'd taken the items, she untied her bonnet and shook loose her long straw blond hair that fell down her back in a thick tangled mass, "I washed my hair this morning after I got up but it was to cold to wear down. Do you have something to cut off a lock?"

"Oh, um yeah. I have some shears in my pouch," Wendell stammered as he gazed at her completely flustered. He'd never been very interested in girls before but with her hair loose Mary was absolutely beautiful even if it was mussed from being bundled up wet beneath her bonnet. Mary seemed very pleased with his reaction and giggled at him again as he fished out the shears for her.

"A token of my affection for my dashing hero," Mary smiled as she snipped off a small lock and presented it to him, "Just don't tell my mother. She dotes on my hair as if it was magic spun gold."

"I can understand why. It's very beautiful!" Wendell stated before he even thought about what he was saying. Mary positively beamed with delight as she loosed a happy little sigh.

"So what's next on your list?" Mary asked as she returned the shears and took back her belongings with a bit of a blush.

"That was it. I'm suppose to return to the tower now and practice my letters, but I think I'm going to stop at my sister's and see if she can hem up these robes first," Wendell admitted reluctantly.

"Well I suppose I should be getting home as well," Mary sighed gloomily this time, "I had a lot of fun with you though. Perhaps we can do it again soon, if you aren't to busy learning Wizardry that is."

"I'd like that, Mary. Be careful going home, Trevor's going to be looking for both of us for the next few days at least," Wendell warned as he scratched his head disheveling his stocking cap.

"I will," she stated, shifting her eyes from him to the ground then back again. She seemed to be waiting for something but Wendell was at a loss as to what. After a moment she sighed again, "Well, goodbye then."

"Goodbye, Mary," Wendell stated as he watched her turn away. She took a few steps then turned around and shot him a frustrated look.

"You're not very good at this, Wendell. Your suppose to kiss your damsel farewell," Mary stated crossly tapping her foot impatiently with her fist full of flowers resting on her hip.

"Oh. Sorry!" Wendell apologized awkwardly looking very embarrassed.

"Well?" she asked after they looked at each other for a moment uncertainly.

"Right!" Wendell jumped as if she'd just lashed him with a whip. He approached her more than a little frightened, leaned in and kissed her on the cheek.

"That's more like it," she sighed happily before she planted her own kiss on his cheek, "See you soon."

Wendell watched her walk away as he rubbed his tingling cheek where she'd kissed him. He tried and failed to understand why girls who liked him you were so much scarier than those that don't. It was a confusing conundrum that he thought maybe he should ask his Master about once he returned. That thought mixed up Wendell's feelings even more. At least with Mary he'd been able to ignore the fact that his Master wasn't around. Now that she was gone the weight of his absence felt even more profound and Wendell sighed heavily as he turned towards the village center where he'd find his sister at her husband's tailor shop.

16

"Hello, Wendell. How are you feeling?" Fredric greeted Wendell coolly as he entered the tailor's shop.

Fredric had always been polite but somewhat aloof with Wendell since the time he'd betrothed his sister six years ago. Wendy had always assured him that Fredric did in fact like him but everyone in his family had the same reserved demeanor that made it hard to tell. She had confessed once that it had taken her nearly six months to realize he fancied her because his manner was such that it had been impossible to tell and she had been taken completely by surprise when he'd tried to kiss her for the first time.

Fredric was currently kneeling before a wooden mannequin sewing a pocket onto its fine leather surcoat. He was a young man who's black hair was just starting to thin. His features were average looking if somewhat long, save for his ears that protruded noticeably. He had a face that seems to be searching for perfection in all it beholds that was often lined with frustration because it failed to find it. He was a quite talented tailor who'd been offered several jobs in the city for his skills. Wendy told their mother once while Wendell had been listening that Fredric turned down these offers for her so she could remain close to the family and that she loved him all the more for it.

"Very well, Sir, is my sister around?" Wendell asked uncomfortably. He didn't like disturbing people at work even if Fredric didn't seem the least bit distracted.

"She's at the market grocery shopping. Is there something I can help you with?" Fredric asked as he pulled out one of the pins holding the pocket in place and stuck it into the corner of his thin lipped mouth.

"I was hoping she could hem up these robes, but perhaps I can come back tomorrow," Wendell sighed as he started back towards the door.

"No need, just give me a moment and I'll take care of it," Fredric told him as he continued his long even stitches.

"I don't want to disturb your work, Sir," Wendell paused at the door.

"It's no trouble. The Knight who commissioned this coat won't be back for two more weeks and I'll be done with it by the day after tomorrow at the latest," Fredric explained as he tied off the thread and cut off the excess with his shears, "Why don't you come over here and I'll see what I can do?"

Wendell obeyed, walking over to his brother-in-law and stood still as the tailor folded up the sleeves to respectable levels then pinned them in place. He then repeated the process on the lower portion of the robe after brushing off the dust it had been accumulating as it dragged behind the boy.

"I'm only going to stitch this just enough to keep it out of your way. I think by the end of summer you'll have grown another two inches at least and it will need adjusting again. This is good linen and should last you several years with care," Fredric explained as Wendell stood hoping he wouldn't get poked by a misplaced needle.

"My Master gave me a whole wardrobe to choose from and I thought this one looked the best despite it being oversized," Wendell admitted as he began to look around the shop. There wasn't much to it, just enough space for a few dress mannequins, a cutting table, and several bolts of cloth. Fredric and Wendy lived in the rooms behind this which were small but cozy.

"Well you made a fine choice. Take good care of it," Fredric stated as he continued to quickly sew the left sleeve.

As Wendell gazed towards the back hall he spied a Brownie creeping down the small corridor. It seemed much older than his with shaggy gray fur covering most of its body. Only its arms, boots, and over-large nose were visible protruding from its excessive body hair. It was carrying a small spool of thread upon its shoulder as it strolled down the hall.

"You've had a lot of stockings go missing, haven't you?" Wendell smiled as he watched the Brownie place the spool of thread under one of the mannequins as if it had fallen then return back the way it had come.

"How did you know?" Fredric asked as the door opened and closed behind them, "Be with you in a moment," Fredric stated after glancing up for only an instant.

"You have a Brownie living here. I just saw it put a spool of thread under the mannequin over there then head back towards your apartment. They steal stockings to build their nests, but only one from a pair for some reason. They're really quite friendly and helpful if you give them treats like candy and milk," Wendell told him before he glanced over his shoulder to see who had entered.

Wendell was very surprised to find his mother standing behind them white as a ghost as she stared down the hall. Wendell immediately became choked up with emotions and didn't know what to say. She stiffened visibly after a moment and Wendell turned to see that the Brownie had returned this time with a large wood button in its arms.

"You can see it!" Wendell blurted out in surprise as he saw how his mother's eyes followed the Brownie across the room. She turned her wild fearful gaze upon him for a moment as if Wendell was a complete stranger.

"There's nothing there!" she declared defiantly after a moment then she fled the shop slamming the door behind her.

Fredric had stopped sewing and was now staring up at Wendell in confusion. Wendell sniffled but was determined not to break down into tears in front of the tailor no matter how hurtful his mother's reaction was. There was a long moment of uncomfortable silence then Fredric squeezed Wendell's shoulder with sympathy in his eyes before he continued his work.

"What did you say to my mother? She nearly trampled me in the street," Wendy asked as she pushed her way into the shop with an arm load of groceries in cloth sacks. Then she saw Wendell and her expression changed to one of gloomy understanding. "Oh. Hello, Wendell. Father told me she was reacting poorly but I had no idea it was so bad. I'm so sorry, little brother."

Wendy set down her groceries upon the trimming table and came up and enveloped Wendell in her plump arms from behind. She resembled their mother so closely that Wendell broke into the tears he'd promised himself he wouldn't shed. She just squeezed him all the more tightly as he let it all out. When Wendell started to dry out, Fredric paused in his stitching and removed a handkerchief from his back pocket to give to the distraught Apprentice.

"What happened?" Wendy asked quietly as she straightened his cap and then came around so she could face him.

"I was telling Fredric about the Brownie you have living here in the shop when she came in behind me. I didn't have any idea it was her until I turned around. Then I noticed she could see it, too. My Master thinks that she's afraid of magic because someone told her frightening stories as a child, but if she's able to see creatures of magic like we can then it means they've noticed her as well. The bad ones have probably been tormenting her all her life and she's just been trying to pretend they don't exist. No wonder she's afraid of me. I would be to if I'd had to live with that all my life with no one to explain to me how to deal with what I saw," Wendell shook his head and slumped his shoulders in defeat.

"Okay, so what's a Brownie?" Wendy asked as she looked from Wendell to Fredric trying hard to understand.

Wendell sighed heavily then told them everything he knew about Brownies including how his had scared away the Infernal that had been prowling around his window. When he was done they asked a few more questions while Fredric finished his work. When Wendell's robes were complete, he told them he'd look for the Brownie's nest and they followed him as he went from room to room searching under the furniture.

Wendell finally found the nest of tightly rolled stockings well hidden under the corner of their bed. The industrious Brownie had suspended its nest that was easily twice the size of Wendell's from the bedposts using web like nets it had woven out of thread. It took a bit of shimming, but Wendell was able to catch the little old Brownie and carefully pulled him out from under the bed.

Fredric was completely unable to see the old Brownie but Wendy discovered that she could see it faintly if she squinted her eyes. It appeared some what transparent to her but she could definitely tell where it was and after several minutes of inspection decided it was fairly cute. At Wendell's suggestion they brought the Brownie a saucer full of milk and Fredric got excited when he saw the milk being drunk by a creature he couldn't see. Wendell offered to take it to the tower with him but Wendy thought it would be cruel to transplant a creature so old from its home after discovering it was there when it had caused them no harm before then save for some missing stockings. Fredric agreed and when Wendell left was still filling the saucer full of milk repeatedly just so he could watch it disappear again. Wendell sincerely hoped that the Brownie knew its own limitations otherwise he feared that Fredric may feed it to death.

17

The rest of Wendell's day was fairly uneventful. After returning to the tower he spent the rest of the afternoon practicing his letters upon the blackboard in his room, taking a few short breaks to play with his Brownie. He named it Squeaker after realizing that he hadn't given it a name. The Brownie seemed to like the title and gave him a squeaky whistle of approval.

It was growing dark before the Master of the tower reappeared and Wendell was in the dinning hall eating. Bergstrom greeted him warmly despite looking worn out from his travels before he sank into his chair behind a covered silver platter that concealed all but his hat from view. Their dinner consisted of roast chicken covered in a warm red gravy that was very sweet, corn on the cob covered in melted butter and shredded cheese, and warm dinner rolls with butter and honey that gushed out of their centers when one bit into them. Wendell's Master was very preoccupied with the delicious meal so the Apprentice spent most of the time trying to figure out how the mysterious cook had managed to get the honey-buttered filling into the round rolls without cutting their surface. When both Wizard and Apprentice had eaten their fill and then some, Bergstrom told Wendell to get the items he'd been able to gather and meet him in the attic.

Wendell was more than a little excited as he raced from his room anticipating learning something mysterious and grand that the strange items would be used for, but when he reached the attic he found his Master sitting in his leather chair before the fire simply watching the flames of the warm little blaze. Wendell was directed to have a seat in the opposite chair as his Master examined each of the items in turn with little interest. He then set each item down beside the chest board and fixed Wendell with a curious expression before he spoke.

"Tell me about your day and how you obtained these items," Bergstrom instructed him as he sat back in his chair and rested his hands atop his full belly.

Wendell proceeded to tell the Wizard all about his day leaving out no details no matter how small. Bergstrom listened without interrupting though he did chuckle from time to time especially when he heard about how Wendell had pulled a bouquet of pink roses from his hat for Mary after escaping Trevor. He also seemed to find Granny Rosa's assistance very amusing as Wendell's story continued. When Wendell spoke of the encounter with his mother at the Tailor's shop the Wizard's expression changed to sympathetic sorrow but the boy controlled his emotions and continued on. When Wendell was finished the Wizard was silent for a moment before he spoke, digesting the events that had transpired thoroughly.

"Well that does explain why Mary Miller was so insistent that I be added to her daily route when I met her upon the road this evening. I think your going to have to be very careful of that one, she very tenacious," Bergstrom chuckled as he turned back to the fire.

"How was I able to pull the roses from my hat, Master?" Wendell ventured after waiting as patiently as a twelve year old boy can for his Master to continue.

"Some magic is reclusive and shy. It likes to hide in places that feel comfortable to it, where it can feel secure. Wizard's hats and pockets often seem like good hiding spots to this kind of magic. After a time the magic will build up, especially when you've been sleeping in a place of power like this. When such magic is exposed or in imminent threat of exposure it will try to take the form of something that will conceal its true nature. This is very useful to Wizards for the magic doesn't actually think about what its changing into, it just takes a form that it senses will be welcomed or useful to whoever is about to discover it. Today as you were fidgeting with your hat in your hands the magic within was scared that you were about to discover it so it changed into a form sfor it would be welcomed. You weren't really thinking about anything other than your own discomfort, I imagine, so it latched onto the form of something that would be pleasing to Mary to help you break the ice. Magic such as this can be very intuitive and insightful to a Wizard's needs," Bergstrom explained with an amused grin.

"So magic is alive?" Wendell asked after a moment.

"Yes and no. Magic is the force that is a byproduct of life. It has many characteristics that mimic those of life but it isn't actually alive unless it changes into a living form. It grows with imagination and dreams of things that would be impossible without it. It's fueled by our desires but has no real will of its own. If we believe in it we can use magic to alter reality but it can't so much as conjure a bubble without some will to shape it. Even wild magic, which is chaos incarnate, is fueled by will. It either is feeding off an unintelligent subconsciousness or was set in motion long ago by someone who was incompetent or to short-sighted to understand the ramifications of what they were setting into motion," Bergstrom paused lost in thought for a moment before he continued, "When I speak about the emotions of magic I'm not suggesting that the magic is actually feeling these things for it is a force without feeling of its own. It does however get imprinted with the emotions of those who fuel it. That's why you felt scared and unwell when Mr. Garroph's magic was drawing strength from you. His dark emotions had been imprinted upon the magic causing it to feel unwholesome and evil. When you've become more in tune with your senses you'll be able to tell good magic from bad instantly when you are within its proximity.

"By this same type of impression, magic can also develop life like behaviors. For example, the magic fueled by the will and desires of a shy person reacts as if it were shy and reclusive. Magic fueled by an angry person tends to react violently, and so on. Some times these impressions can be very useful such as with the shy magic that will accumulate in your hat and pockets. Others can be baneful. An example of this is when angry magic accumulates it often causes foul weather or violent wars to break out before its energy is spent. As Wizards we must be especially careful of what spells we cast when under the influence of strong emotions for the magic we generate is far stronger than that that occurs naturally and the emotions we imprint upon it can alter its effects in unforeseen ways," Bergstrom warned as he shifted into a more comfortable position within his chair.

"So I can pull anything out my hat that I will?" Wendell asked hopefully.

"Perhaps. Such magic is unpredictable at the best of times and it takes practice to conjure specific items at will. The shy magic often latches onto subconscious desires that are stronger and far less predictable than what we actively want to appear at the moment. I've been trying to figure out for years why the shy magic often forms into live doves every time I reach into my pockets. It will also be limited by your personal strength as a Wizard. The stronger you are the more magic you'll accumulate within your hat, pockets, and sometimes even your sleeves. The more complex the object the more magic it requires to conjure. A bouquet of flowers is a relatively simple object in comparison with say a pocket watch. What a Wizard can conjure from his or her pockets is often a good indication of the level of their power. You'll have to explore your own limitations to find what you can and can't conjure, but seeing as you've managed to conjure something without any formal training already I'm willing to bet that your limitations will only be set by your own imagination. A word of warning, however, don't ever try to use conjured items as spell components. The magic reacts badly when you try to fuel magic with magic creating a paradox that will have disastrous consequences. No matter how good at conjuring you become there are no short cuts when a spell calls for material fuel."

"So what are we going to use these components for?" Wendell asked excitedly as he looked at the items he'd colleted resting upon the table.

"I was wondering how long it would take you to get around to those," Bergstrom smirked as he lifted the lock of Mary's hair and examined its straw colored strands, "We aren't going to do anything with them. You are, though perhaps not at this moment. I sent you for these items for a few different reasons. First of al,l each of these items are not inherently magical but when looked at from a certain point of view may be perceived as embodying an essence that may be drawn upon to fuel magic. A lock of a fair-haired Maiden could be perceived as the essence of beauty or perhaps feminine youth. Tears of a Widow could be perceived as the essence of sadness or loss even if Granny Rosa felt neither of these things when she shed them. Wonderful old gal, always makes the best pastries.

"It is these essences that some spells require to create their magic for the magic itself has no concept of what that essence is without something tangible for it to draw upon. As an example, say I wished to cast a glamour to appear as a young Maiden to trick a Knight into doing something he wouldn't normally do for an old Wizard like me. Now my spell can create an illusion simply enough but the magic really has no concept of what a beautiful maiden is so it requires an essence of that beauty to draw upon to create an image that will be pleasant to the eye of said Knight. Now I have the lock of a fair-haired Maiden that I perceive as containing the essence of beauty. This component will satisfy the magic's need for that essence because I believe that the lock contains it and my will and desires fuel the spell's power and give it shape. Do you understand, Wendell?" Bergstrom asked as he set down the lock in the center of the chest board before him.

"I think so, Master, but why can't the spell just draw upon your memory of what a beautiful Maiden looks like?" Wendell asked in confusion.

"That's a very good question that I'm glad you asked. Remember how I told you magic is shaped by our desires and will? Well my memory of what a beautiful Maiden looks like has little to nothing to do with my desire to trick the Knight. Magic doesn't read your mind, it reads your desires. I don't actually desire to appear as the Maiden but to trick the Knight. While I can perceive the way of going about making my desires become reality by appearing as the beautiful Maiden the magic can't and will require the essence of that which is beyond the scope of my desire if I wish it to achieve that goal. Do you understand?" Bergstrom asked after explaining it carefully as he leaned forward in his chair.

"I think so. It sounds complicated at first but I think I get it," Wendell scratched his head, disheveling his cap.

"Alright then, now the more complex the spell the more essences it will require. Going back to the previous example, let's say that I wish for my glamour to not just appear as a beautiful Maiden but a sad beautiful Maiden that will inspire the Knight to wish to aid her. The spell will now require the essence of sadness in addition to the essence of beauty to achieve the desired effect. Therefore, I add the Widow's tears for to me they embody the essence of sadness," Bergstrom picked up both the vial of tears and the worn old horseshoe in his hands. He set the vial down beside the lock of Mary's hair and contemplated the horseshoe a moment before continuing, "Now with the Maiden's hair and the Widow's tears I have the means to complete my glamour but I have no assurance that the Knight will be sympathetic to this maiden regardless of how sad or beautiful she is. Human emotions are tricky things at best and because I want to be assured of success I decide to add a bit of the essence of luck to my spell to tip the odds in my favor. This old horseshoe I perceive as symbolizing the essence of luck and therefore will make the final component in my spell.

"This is a simple example of the kind of objects complex spells require and why. I had you gather these to give you a taste of the kind of items you'll often have to track down and inspire you to think of creative ways of obtaining them. I am very proud of how successful you were for I had thought the Lock of a fair-haired Maiden would create quite a poser for you in these parts. I was unaware that the Miller's had a fair haired daughter," Bergstrom grinned within his bushy beard as he gathered the objects up once more, "From now on I will often be giving you lists of such components to track down. Sometimes I will name a specific object and you will have to determine what essences it may embody. Other times I will name the essence and you will have to find something you believe embodies it and be prepared to explain why. As you gather these items, I want you to try and come up with theoretical spells that may call for them. When you come up with a promising one, we will begin researching the words of power that may bring about your desired effect. I've put a blank notebook in your desk to write down your ideas. Make certain you write them down legibly so that I can check upon your progress from time to time. These items you may keep in your room as well until you find a use for them, though I'd be reluctant to part with a favor from your first love interest if I were you. Such a keep sake is one of a kind and will have a powerful essence all its own that you'll not likely be able to replicate."

"Yes, Master," Wendell blushed as he took his objects back and put them in his belt pouch. He was silent for a moment as he thought about what he'd been told then he ventured another question as the Wizard waited patiently, "Why can I see magical creatures so clearly and my sister can only see them partially when she squints? If my mother has the sight shouldn't all her children have it equally?"

"Nothing is assured with magical bloodlines, though your sister may find it gets easier to see the more often she uses her sight. Why you should have such a strong gift while your other siblings don't is just another aspect of magic's mysterious nature. Do you regret having your gift?" Bergstrom asked quietly.

"No. I regret that its estranged me to my mother but the more that I experience of the magical world the more I feel I was meant to be a part of it. If that makes any sense?" Wendell answered after contemplating the question.

"It does. Knowing ones place in the world is a gift in itself. Be careful though, not everything in this world is pleasant and without the proper care much of it can be very dangerous," Bergstrom smiled grimly before turning his gaze towards the fire, "I think that's enough for tonight. Go get some sleep, Wendell, there's no telling what trials tomorrow will bring and its best to prepare with a good nights rest."

"Yes, Master, sleep well," Wendell sighed as he walked away, not really wishing to be parted but compelled to obey.

18

"Wake up, Wendell, its time to get up," Bergstrom broke into Wendell's sleep seemingly moments after he'd closed his eyes. Wendell opened one eye to see only the faintest glow of dawn out the window. Despite the early hour his Master seemed to be in good spirits, "Oh come now, lazy bones, it promises to be another warm sunny day."

Wendell got up mechanically with a great yawn for someone his size as his Master withdrew back into the corridor. He was halfway to the wardrobe when it dawned on his sleepy mind that his feet weren't touching the flagstone floor or going numb with chill. Wendell looked down to find that a large Bear fur rug now rested under his feet between his bed and the wardrobe. It was a great Cave Bear hide that completely stretched across the opening with thick bushy fur that felt wonderful between the boy's toes even if its head was a bit frightening.

Wendell looked around and found that the rug wasn't the only change to his bedchamber. Beside the window above his desk now stood a tall Mahogany bookshelf decorated with a Snakelike Dragon doing battle with a Knight upon its side. The objects he'd gathered yesterday were sitting on one of the shelves at eye level though Wendell had set them upon the desk before going to bed. Well at least his room was getting more comfortable Wendell thought as he made fists with his toes and liking the way the Bear fur felt between them.

"Good morning," Wendell greeted his yawning reflection as he opened the Wardrobe door. His reflection smiled as it scratched his head uncertainly.

Wendell put on his mismatched stockings then pulled on his blue robes, but before he put the cap upon his head he thought he'd try to conjure something useful. Wendell held it before him as he had the day before, closed his eyes and tried to visualize a hair brush. After a moment he reached into the hat and grip what he thought was a hair brush's handle, but as he opened his eyes and withdrew it he found instead a fancy wood and cloth umbrella with strange plants painted over its surface. His reflection found his failure most amusing and it laughed at Wendell silently while opening and closing the umbrella's reflection as if it were a great new toy. Wendell hung the umbrella from one of the wardrobe's hat pegs and stuck out his tongue at his reflection before closing the door.

Wendell's breakfast was waiting on the table within a covered silver platter but his Master seat was vacant with only dirty dishes before it to testify that he'd already finished eating. Wendell removed the platter's cover to reveal a warm cheesy omelet filled with diced bell peppers, mushrooms, and onions with two pieces of flat bread and a small jar of honey. Wendell devoured the breakfast ravenously until only the tiniest of crumbs remained. He then set off to find his Master, curious as to what today's lesson would be.

Wendell first searched the attic but Bergstrom wasn't there. He then went to his room and knocked upon the door but still the Wizard didn't answer. Wendell was about to head down the winding stair to the ground floor of the tower but as he was passing the door to the kitchen he heard the clatter of pots and pans in water. Wendell listen to the sounds of someone washing dishes within the kitchen for almost a minute before he threw open the door determined to catch the reclusive cook before he could hide once more.

Wendell did catch sight of the cook this time but he instantly wished he hadn't. Floating before the wash tub from the waist up was the ghost of an overweight cook with a large billowing hat washing dishes that

Wendell could see through his semi-transparent torso. The cook half-turned and gazed at Wendell sucking all the warmth from his body as their eyes met. The spectral cook's features lay transparently over a ghostly white skull and pinpricks of fiery green light burned within the inner most depths of its sockets. Its misty transparent lips formed into a terrifying smile over its pearly white fangs a split second before Wendell fled as fast as his legs could carry him.

Wendell raced down the corridor and onto the spiraling stairwell with break neck speed. He flew down the stairs with speed only true terror can muster and was still running at full steam when he reached the bottom though he had been winded enough to stop screaming. Out of the tower he shot as if from a cannon and barely was able to stop before running headlong into Bergstrom and Mary upon the walkway before collapsing in a blubbering incoherent and completely exhausted heap.

"What is it, Wendell? You look like you've seen a ghost!" Mary exclaimed as she knelt beside, him causing the empty bottles in her carrier to clink together.

"You went into the kitchen, didn't you?" Bergstrom asked with a stern look of disapproval, "I told you it wasn't wise to disturb the cook. Don't worry, I'm sure the grey in your hair is only temporary."

"What's wrong with disturbing the cook?" Mary asked in complete confusion as she examined some of Wendell's gray frosted hair between her fingers with alarm.

"He, he's dead!" Wendell managed to spit out between his chattering teeth.

"What happen, was there some kind of accident?" Mary covered her mouth in alarm.

"No, he's been dead for many years now. What Wendell is trying to say is he's a ghost who haunts our kitchen. You should have known it takes a life time or two to perfect that kind of culinary talent. Our ghost was the royal chef of King Theo Rosevart III until he stepped upon a rolling pin dropped by his Apprentice and cracked his skull against the oven. My Master's Master was called upon to remove his spirit which was haunting the royal kitchens. When he discovered that all the ghost really wanted was to continue perfecting his art, he devised a spell to transport and anchor him to our kitchen. When I moved here I used the same spell to transport him to this tower's kitchen. He is really a pleasant fellow once you get use to his appearance and the unearthly chill that surrounds him. Just never insult his cooking if you value your life," Bergstrom explained as he helped Wendell back to his feet and brushed the dust from his robes, "I'm sorry, I guess I should have given you a better warning. I've all but forgotten the curiosity that plagues twelve year old boys."

"He's horrible!" Wendell stated still shivering with the unnatural chill, "I thought my blood was going to freeze in my veins when I looked into his, his eyes!"

"Yes, well most spirits stuck upon the mortal plane tend to be a bit unpleasant. Just don't ask him to show you what's under his hat. That's even more unpleasant," Bergstrom shivered as he straightened Wendell's hat.

"What did he look like?" Mary asked curiously.

"Better wait until he's had a proper chance to warm up before he tells you. He's probably going to have nightmares as it is," Bergstrom suggested, giving Wendell a reassuring pat on the back, "How about instead I send you on an errand to get your blood pumping again. If you're out in the sun for awhile things won't seem half as bad. Miss Miller can accompany you if she likes, that is assuming you're done with your deliveries?"

"I altered my route so this would be my last stop," Mary grinned smugly.

"I had a feeling you might," Bergstrom smiled knowingly as he dug in his pocket. Mary laughed and clapped her hands when he produced a live dove that fluttered away with a surprised cue. His next fishing expedition into the unpredictable pocket produced another piece of neatly folded parchment, "Ah, here we are. You should be able to find all of these things in the north woods. Should be just the place to forget about unnatural spirits on a summer day like this, but don't stress your selves to find everything at once. I understand if you want to take time off to play. I myself need to tend to this garden. Going to visit sick children every day for the last couple of weeks has really made me fall behind on my weeding."

Mary looked at Wendell who was still as white as a sheet on the clothesline before she decided to take matters into her own capable hands. She took the parchment from Bergstrom then grasped Wendell's hand and dragged him down the walkway. Bergstrom smiled after them as he withdrew a pair of worn leather gloves from his pocket and proceeded to go to work on the garden that had far more weeds than vegetables at this point. Within minutes he was lost in conversation with the bees and the Gargoyle that perched above the Tower's door. If their lack of response to the old Wizard's banter disturbed him he never gave pause as he plucked the weeds one by one.

19

"What does it say?" Mary asked eagerly as they walked down the north road toward the village outskirts. She'd been so eager to know what was on Bergstrom's list that she'd forgotten that she didn't know how to read. With a frustrated sigh she'd begrudgingly handed the parchment list over and was now leaning over as if her proximity to Wendell might overcome her illiteracy, "Come on, don't keep me in suspense!"

"Essence of birth, Essence of Growth, and Essence of the wild," Wendell read off slowly furrowing his brow in thought.

"What's with all the Essences? I thought he was going to send us after more objects?" Mary scowled with disappointment.

"These are objects, just not specific ones. We have to find something that personifies birth, growth, and the wild," Wendell explained while still looking at the list thoughtfully.

"Oh, so if we found a bird's egg that would be considered the essence of birth?" Mary asked, growing excited once more.

"Hey, yeah, that's a good one!" Wendell acknowledged, making Mary beam with delight, "We'll have to keep our eyes open for bird's nests when we get to the woods, but we'll probably have to settle for egg shells this late in the season. All the eggs will have hatched by now. What do you think would personify growth?"

"That's even easier, silly," Mary giggled at him, "Flowers, trees, bushes, you name it. They all grow."

"Yes but do they personify growth?" Wendell asked to cover his embarrassment at not realizing how simple the answer was.

"I'm not sure. I guess you'd have to find something that grows really fast to be the essence of growth. A weed maybe, or better yet blackberry bushes. They grow really fast and never really stop," Mary nodded knowingly, "They may be considered the essence of the wild even because once they get going they pretty much overrun everything else around them unless you constantly trim them back."

"You're really good at this. I'm glad you came along," Wendell smiled as he put the list back in his belt pouch.

Wendell regretted saying it a moment later when Mary let out a long sigh and took his hand. It wasn't so much that holding her hand bothered Wendell as it was that he was painfully aware of how uncomfortably sweaty his palm was in her firm little grip. Mary seemed oblivious to this short coming as she gazed at him smugly while they continued to walk along the dusty wagon-eaten road. His discomfort did free Wendell of any lingering feelings of dread from having seen the ghost of the cook. Mary's affections distracted Wendell to the point that they could have easily been walking through the land of the dead and he wouldn't have noticed.

Within just over a quarter of an hour, Wendell and Mary passed the last of the northern farms and crossed the old worn stone bridge that marked the end of the village and the beginning of the wild. Beyond the bridge lay the sparse wood of Maples, Ash, Walnut, and Oaks as the road climbed up the gentle sloping hill out of the valley towards the distant city of Lavittia beyond. It was a peaceful and warm wood that imparted a carefree sense of idleness to all who spent time within its old proud trees. Here one could sit in the shade or play in the sun surrounded by the earth's natural beauty and forget the toils and troubles of the world beyond. The wood was most popular amongst the Village's children and the men who aspired to fish the upper reaches of the snaking little river, but woman also dared the serene wilds for wild mushrooms, berries, and nuts from time to time. As soon as the children reached the far side of the bridge, they laughed and began to run toward the trees hand in hand caught up in the playful magic of the wood as only children can.

Wendell and Mary couldn't have explained why they were overcome with energetic mirth, nor would they have cared to as they plunged deeper into the trees leaving the road far behind. Once comfortably lost from view of any that may disturb their private free time, they slowed to a more comfortable pace content as they continued to hold one another's hand. Wendell was a bit apprehensive since he'd not been here since acquiring his gift of sight, but nothing unnatural immediately leaped out at him and he gradually began to relax. That is until Mary yelled excitedly and nearly pulled his arm out of his socket as she dragged him towards a nearby Oak tree.

"Look at that!" She pulled him physically towards the ground where she picked up a large green Acorn triumphantly, "The essence of birth, or growth"

"Birth I think," Wendell smiled at her as she placed the Acorn in his free hand.

"Alright, how many should we gather?" Mary asked as she collected a few more off the ground.

"Not more than a handful I should think. I can't see devising that many spells that require the essence of birth and they are pretty common if I need more," Wendell decided as he gathered a few as well.

"You're going to make your own spells?" Mary asked as she handed him the rest of the acorns.

"I'm supposed to be coming up with ideas on how to use these ingredients to write down in my notebook. When I come up with one that looks promising, Master is going to help me research words of power to create the spell," Wendell explained as he secured the handful of Acorns in his belt pouch.

"Wow, that sounds exciting. I wish I could learn magic. Its way more fun than being a milkmaid," Mary admitted longingly.

"Master says it isn't all good, some of its very frightening and dangerous," Wendell stated in an attempt to make her feel better. Then he thought of his mother, "And my Apprenticeship didn't come without a heavy price," He stated gloomily.

"How much did your father have to pay? My father has already started saving my dowry in an oak chest he keeps on the mantle. It might be enough to cover an Apprenticeship, that is if Mr. Weatherbee is willing to train girls?" Mary queried as they stood up and brushed the dirt and twigs from their clothing.

"That isn't the kind of cost I was talking about. As far as money goes, my Master paid my father. That's apparently the way of it with Wizards because even Mr. Garroph tried to pay my father to train me. I think you have to show you have some magical talent before they're interested," Wendell said as he looked around the surrounding trees to avoid letting Mary see the sadness thoughts of his mother had invoked within him.

"Oh. So what was the cost you were talking about?" Mary shot directly towards his heart like an arrow.

Wendell remained silent for a long time before he turned toward her. Mary looked him directly in the eyes but made no attempt to press him further seeing that whatever it was on his mind was obviously painful. Finally Wendell decided that he might as well tell her before she heard some exaggerated rumor from the village's grapevine. Secrets didn't ever remain secrets for long in a village as small as theirs.

"My mother is afraid of magic and the supernatural. And now since the magic has awoken in my blood she's afraid of me, too. I became my Master's Apprentice because she wouldn't come home while I was there," Wendell told her quietly, wiping away the tears that rolled down his cheeks with his sleeve as the truth crossed his lips.

Mary almost knocked him down as she embraced him in a fierce little hug. After a few moments, Wendell melted into her embrace and squeezed her back. He could smell her hair that protruded from beneath her bonnet that had the faint aroma of roses as he leaned beside her head. They held each other quietly for a few minutes then when Mary spoke he was surprised to find she was crying, too,

"Don't worry, Wendell, I won't abandon you like she has," Mary sniffled as she pulled away just enough to look at him, "Even, even if we're not meant to be together. I'll always be your friend."

"That means a lot to me, Mary," Wendell admitted as he brushed away one of her tears and she smiled at him.

"We should probably get back to gathering those items," Mary sighed as she rested her head against his chest listening to his heart beat.

"I suppose," Wendell agreed, but squeezed her tightly instead of making any attempt to proceed.

It was a moment that the two children would never forget. In that moment, concealed within the sleepy sunny little glade beneath an elder Oak, something happened that neither one had sought out or expected. In that moment, their love ceased to be a childish game of frivolous fancy and became a bond stronger than either would have ever imagined possible before then. In that moment Wendell and Mary truly fell in love.

True love of course means something very different when you're twelve than at any age thereafter. For Wendell and Mary it meant that from that time on they spent every moment they could with one another, whether it be scouring the valley for objects from one of Bergstrom's yellowed parchment lists or simply playing games of imagination to pass the time. They were inseparable friends with an intimate closeness that rarely needed words or actions to define. It was simply a bond that they both felt more acutely apart than when they were together and neither could rest easy without the other because of it. This was the way of things over the next three and a half years, during which Wendell and Mary grew together and slowly approached the people they would eventually become.

At fifteen and a half Wendell was no longer the small thin boy he'd been, but had grown tall and husky as his father had before him. His brown hair had grown long and wild without his mother's constant gardening and now rested near the small of his back. Despite Bergstrom's hopes, Wendell had not lost the gray frosting that had grown from his temples since his first encounter with the tower's ghost cook, but he had accepted this mark and even come to secretly like it feeling it somehow gave his features a dignified quality no other youths possessed. His face had lost all traces of childhood and had developed a strong jaw and hawkish nose. He was not the most handsome lad in the village but they all envied him none the less for the Apprentice Wizard had something that they all longed for and that was the eye of Mary.

At fifteen and a half Mary had shed her pretty youthful appearance to become the most beautiful young woman in the village. She'd grown tall and fair in a way that caused other women to envy her and men to run headlong into things as she passed due to her distraction. She was aware that she could have her pick of any man but she had long ago chosen Wendell and hadn't regretted her choice since. Her father had once suggested that she think before she settled upon the Wizard's Apprentice, but Mary had simply smiled and told him that he'd grow to love Wendell as much as she if he'd but give him the chance and if not then they'd be forced to elope without her dowry after they came of age. Her father and mother had made the effort after that to get to know Wendell and he was already accepted as an imminent addition to their family.

Physical growth wasn't the only changes that had occurred in the three and a half years after that fateful summer. Wendell was making so much progress with his magical studies that Bergstrom was often heard boasting that he would one day even surpass his skills with almost fatherly pride. In truth Bergstrom rarely taught Wendell any longer, but was more of a wellspring of experience the young man consulted before experimenting with whatever challenge had tickled his fancy. They were more like partners now, often collaborating on arcane projects that neither would have dared without the other's aid.

It was not all good changes for Wendell, however. The rift between him and his mother had done nothing but grown over the years. In the beginning Wendell had continued to reach out to her, but after being spurned again and again he'd finally given up. Now whenever they encountered one another around the village they simply ignored one another. Despite this mutual agreement of avoidance his mother's loss never ceased to weigh heavily upon Wendell or his father's hearts.

Mr. Glasswright visited Wendell every Sunday rain or shine. He was not the happy spirited man he once had been for the family rift had taken its toll upon the senior Glasswright and his health suffered because of it. He often fell into gloomy states of depression during which he couldn't bring himself to eat or drink. He'd lost so much weight that he appeared nearly twenty years older than he actually was. Wendell often wondered what his father's life was like at home but Mr. Glasswright was always cryptic about the state of things between him and his mother. Their time together on Sundays was so short that Wendell didn't have the heart to press his father about the problem and tried to simply enjoy his company in the time they had.

Despite these trials, Wendell was happy. Life in the valley went on as it always had and he enjoyed it. Time marched by lazily in his secluded corner of the world but he did not long for a life of excitement. He only longed to share his life with Mary and the others he'd grown to love.

20

"Be careful, Wendell!" Mary commanded from the base of their old Oak as she watched him climb higher.

Wendell just grinned to himself wondering if she'd fall to pieces if he fell or beat his broken body in a fury because he hadn't heeded her command. In a few moments the Apprentice Wizard thought he'd climbed high enough and started to carefully work his way outward on a the thick knotted branch upon his belly. Clenched within his teeth was a strange mobile of his own design constructed of silver wire, crystals, and rune stones tied up in a neat little bundle. When he reached the point that to go farther would mean to risk breaking the limb he sat up and proceeded to unwrap his latest experiment.

"This had better be worth the risk or you're going to get it!" Mary threatened, but Wendell knew this was more fueled by frustration than fear. He'd refused to tell her what the mobile was supposed to do and the suspense was eating Mary alive, "If that thing just turns sunlight into bubbles I'm going to be very disappointed."

"Don't worry, it'll be worth it. I promise!" Wendell grinned mischievously down at her while he secured the mobile in place.

Once the mobile was secured, Wendell spoke a few words of power as he dripped a few drops of honey upon the central rune stone of the device. The rune stones immediately began to glow faintly and the crystals began to vibrate to produce a soft tinkling. Satisfied that the device was working as it should Wendell set the honey jar on the limb above it then started to scoot away backwards. After a few feet, Wendell got frustrated as his robes got tangled on the limb so he slid off and hung from it by his hands. Mary immediately let out a worried little gasp but said nothing as he hung above for a moment longer before letting go.

Wendell had yet to master true flight but by flapping his hands at his sides could easily slow his fall. Soft as a feather he landed beside Mary with a smirk and a wink, but the fiery little milkmaid wasn't about to let him get away with making her worry.

"Owe!" Wendell exclaimed as she punched him hard in the shoulder with a little fist of steel.

"Warn me if you're going to do something like that next time!" Mary narrowed her eyes crossly, uncertain if he'd been taught a proper lesson as Wendell rubbed his shoulder.

"Sorry! I forgot I hadn't shown you that trick yet," Wendell apologized, trying hard not to smile.

"So what is it suppose to do?" Mary asked after dismissing his misbehavior and casting her gaze towards the mobile for a moment.

"Just wait. Oh, I nearly forgot. You'll need to take a sip of this," Wendell stated as he pulled his latest vial of Third Sight Potion from his belt pouch and handed it to her.

Potions of Third Sight had been Wendell's first endeavor in the art of Alchemy, mostly because Mary would get very frustrated when he saw something magical that she could not. Now he was in the habit of making a fresh batch every week just so Mary could keep up her relationship with Squeaker. The milkmaid doted upon the Brownie and lavished it constantly with little treats. It had gotten to the point that Squeaker would let out a sad little whistle whenever he entered his room without her due to her spoiling it rotten at every opportunity.

Mary took a small sip of the potion and as normal made a horrible face at its bitter taste. Her blue eyes immediately dilated until little of her irises remained and again she cast her gaze upwards towards the mobile. She chewed her lower lip for a moment then looked to Wendell impatiently.

"Just wait; I don't know how far they'll have to travel," Wendell whispered as he looked towards the device eagerly.

It took a few minutes before the magical lure's first victim made its appearance and Wendell was more than pleased when Mary gasped in awe of the beautiful little Fairy. It fluttered about chaotically upon brilliant wings like a butterfly that held every color of the rainbow. Its tiny naked form resembled that of a petite prepubescent girl child save for the antennae that wriggled from her brow. Her skin was the palest hue of blue that was possible before the color was lost to white completely. Her eyes sparkled a brilliant green like two tiny emeralds upon her heart-shaped face. Long pointed ears jutted out from her wild bushy blue-white hair that bristled upward in blatant defiance of gravity. The Fairy was unnaturally beautiful despite the aura of weirdness that surrounded its tiny form and Wendell was beside himself with pleasure when Mary threw her arms around his neck and kissed his cheek with a happy little giggle.

"Shhh. I don't want her to notice us," Wendell whispered in Mary's ear as he enveloped her in his arms from behind.

Two more Fairies arrived and began to flutter around the magical mobile just as the first began to examine the contents of the honey jar still resting atop the limb. They appeared much as the first except for slight differences in the hues of their hair and skin. One of the newcomers was male and he twittered at the first inquiringly as her head and shoulders disappeared beneath the honey jar's rim. Their language seemed to be reminiscent of small bird calls and Wendell thought it would be impossible to distinguish them once they were concealed within the tree's leafy canopies. The first fairy emerged from the jar with a face plastered with golden honey and twittered to the others excitedly before plunging in once again.

"Are they dangerous?" Mary whispered, trying hard to contain her giggles.

"No, not normally. Unless something threatens their woods, but they do like to play pranks on the big folk who can see them. They are mischievous spirits who have a strange sense of humor," Wendell explained as he breathed in the scent of roses that always perfumed Mary's hair, "If they should notice us just pretend that you can't see them and they should quickly lose interest."

"Where do they live?" Mary asked as she watched all three of the fairies tiny naked butts wag in the air below their wings as they crowded around the jar's rim to feast on honey.

"Here now, probably. My lure should continue to fascinate them whenever the sun strikes the crystals. I made it just strong enough that it should call to them within a few miles, but weak enough that they'll be able to ignore it when they're hungry or tired. If we continue to bring a jar of honey each time we come I don't think they'll bother us when we sit and watch them," Wendell told her thoughtfully.

"Oh!" Mary exclaimed as all three Fairies suddenly flew away quickly to northwest knocking over the honey jar in their haste. The jar shattered on the Oak's gnarled old roots with a gooey splash of ceramic shards and honey. "Oh no, what do you think scared them away?"

Wendell didn't answer because he wasn't really listening. At about the same time the Fairies had taken flight he'd felt a cold dread grow in the pit of his stomach as an evil presence approached. It took Wendell only a moment to sense that whatever the presence was it was coming from the southeast as if it was just leaving the village. Mary stiffened as she noticed something was distracting him and she remained silent for a few moments before she queried as to what was the matter.

"What is it Wendell? What's wrong?" Mary asked quietly as she scanned the wood in the direction of his gaze clutching his arm for reassurance.

"I'm not certain, but I think we should hide," Wendell suggested after scanning the wood a moment longer distrustfully. The feeling of the evil presence was getting stronger by the second.

"Okay, but where?" Mary asked as she scanned the open glade without seeing any likely hiding spots that would conceal them both.

"There, against that tree," Wendell pointed to a towering Maple whose trunk had a partial hollow of rotted dead wood at its base. He took Mary's hand and pulled her into the hollow quickly as he continued to cast his gaze behind, "Stand with your back to the trunk. Be very still and very quiet," Wendell directed as the evil presence began to make him feel nauseous.

When Mary had obeyed, Wendell squeezed into the Maple's hollow beside her. He then tore a small piece of the Maple's bark off and held it in his open palm while putting out his other hand like a shield before him. Quickly he recited an incantation that resonated with power as the air before them began to distort and shimmer. Within a few seconds the bark within Wendell's palm was consumed as if by fire until nothing but white ashes remained. The air before them stopped shimmering but took on a shaded appearance as if the sunlight was passing through a smoky glassed window. Wendell sagged a little from the spell's drain then brushed the ashes from his palm before taking Mary's hand.

"What just happened?" Mary whispered unable to contain her curiosity.

"I concealed the hollow with an illusion. Now be quiet, it's almost here!" Wendell answered in a hoarse whisper, giving her hand a gentle squeeze.

His warning came not a second to soon for as soon as Wendell had spoken they heard a foul voice muttering curses approaching the glade. Within a few more seconds, the almost forgotten form of the Infernal was spied shuffling through the trees toward them. Mary released a choked little cry when she spotted the evil little creature's repulsive features and Wendell quickly clapped his hand over her mouth to keep her from making any further noise. The Infernal stopped dead save for its small hooves that continued to prance and grasped the rapier that hung sheathed from its belt.

Wendell had not thought of the Infernal in years but now seeing it in the light of day brought home the terrible memory of it prowling around his window long ago. Its aspect was no less frightening compounded by the aura of cold unnatural evil that seemed to precede it. Now Wendell could make out the pointed stubs of small ivory horns that protruded from its greasy black hair just below its cowl. The Infernal's skin was like dusty coal save for where it faded to a dull reddish tone upon its lips and around its eyes. Those eyes had glowed with a hateful red fire in the darkness but were nothing more than glossy solid black orbs in the light of day. Now Wendell could see that it was dressed in a short kilt, tunic, and vest beneath its cloak all of which were colored the same dull black of its skin. If ever there was a being to walk the earth with villainous intent none had achieved the appearance quite as well as the malevolent Infernal.

"The Boy!" the Infernal hissed like a curse after sniffing the air with his long pointed nose. He drew his rapier fluidly from its sheath then sniffed the air some more.

Wendell felt a cold dread as the Infernal scanned the woods carefully but was relieved when its hateful gaze passed directly over their hiding spot without pause. After a moment the broken honey jar drew the Infernal's attention and it pranced quickly over to investigate. It poked at the jar's fragments with the tip of his gleaming slender blade and sniffed the air some more.

"Fairies.!" the Infernal hiss with a new level of venom behind the word before he spit upon the ground as if to seal his contempt. "Bah, no time to pluck their wings today. Must seek the filthy Goblins and see if it's ready. The Master will be cross if I tarry and inflict more pain. The boy is of no consequence any longer, the plan has changed."

And with that comment, the Infernal sheathed his sword after a final look around to be certain he was alone and pranced out of view. Wendell waited nearly five minutes before he released Mary's mouth and put a finger to his lips. Slowly he crept out of the Maple's hollow and looked towards the direction the Infernal had gone. The villainous creature was nowhere to be seen and Wendell waved for Mary to come out.

"Come on, it's gone now," Wendell stated with assurance for the Infernal's proceeding feeling of dread had faded away to nothing.

"What was that thing?" Mary asked as she gazed back towards the Maple. No sign of the hollow could be seen upon its seemingly flawless trunk and she tried to touch the illusion's surface to be certain it was still there. Her hand passed through it without hindrance of any kind for the image had no substance and was nothing more than visual trickery.

"Trouble. Come on, let's go back to the village in case it comes back," Wendell extended his hand to her.

"It knew who you were, Wendell. Don't try to protect me from the truth," Mary shot him a look that would have caused the Infernal to cringe as she took his hand.

"It's an Infernal. A creature summoned from a much darker dimension to do the evil bidding of the one who brought it here. Specifically Mr. Garroph, or at least so me and Master believe. It came looking for me once just before I started my Apprenticeship to see who had disrupted its Master's spell. I haven't seen it since that night and had nearly forgotten of its existence until now," Wendell explained as he quickly guided her back towards the road.

"It would have killed us if it had found us, wouldn't it?" Mary asked with a shiver as she gazed back over her shoulder.

"I wouldn't allow anything to hurt you, Mary," Wendell stated without a doubt as they reached the road, "I'm not certain, though. It's evil and dangerous but it obeys its Master's will and I don't have any idea how Mr. Garroph feels about me. I haven't seen him since the day he tried to purchase me from my father."

"I think it would have tried to kill us," Mary stated quietly as they slowed their pace as they approached the bridge. She didn't stop looking over her shoulder distrustfully until they had crossed the river and were once more surrounded by the familiar and comforting fields of vegetables, "Do you know where the Goblins it spoke of are?"

"No, they could be anywhere. Goblins live underground and move about nomadically to wherever they find precious minerals and ores. They are very cunning metal smiths and jewelers. That's probably what Mr. Garroph has commissioned them for," Wendell stated thoughtfully then smirked as a new thought occurred to him, "Perhaps I should go ask him. The Goblins could craft you a marvelous wedding ring."

"Be serious, Wendell!" She smacked him playfully on the shoulder, "We still have months before we come of age and I don't want you going anywhere near Mr. Garroph if that's the kind of creatures he employs."

"Alright, I was only joking," Wendell cowered away from her in mock fear, "Besides, I was thinking about asking Suzy Ingrum anyway. You're just too violent for me."

This time Mary hit Wendell in earnest as her cheeks flared with her fiery temper. Wendell laughed as he ran away and she quickly gave chase. By the time they reached her family's dairy farm they were both laughing and out of breath. The fear of the Infernal was all but forgotten as they stopped before the gate of the large farm.

"Did you like the Fairies?" Wendell asked as they embraced.

"Yes. You really are quite clever when you're not making a complete fool of yourself," Mary stated, arching a fine blond eyebrow daring him to disagree.

"I wouldn't pester you half as much if you weren't so beautiful when you're angry," Wendell smirked as he brushed a few fine hairs out of her eyes.

"And I wouldn't be half as violent if you didn't seem to enjoy the pain," she smirked back at him. They both sighed happily knowing that they loved one another completely and were probably getting to old to change.

"I'll see you tomorrow," Wendell stated.

"Don't do anything to provoke Mr. Garroph," she directed.

"Why would I? He's never done anything to me," Wendell stated as if the thought had never crossed his mind, "Don't worry so much. I want nothing to do with Mr. Garroph and I'm sure he feels the same way about me."

"I hope so," Mary sighed as she gazed up at the menacing square tower that loomed over the east side of the village. "I truly hope so."

SECTION 3

21

As soon as Wendell left Mary at her family's dairy, he dropped his guise of carefree happiness and adopted the aspect of deep worry that had been gnawing upon his heart since encountering the Infernal. Because of his love for her he would happily play the fool to shield her from this evil, but as Wendell headed back to his Master's tower he knew in his heart that Mr. Garroph was far from apathetic towards him. He'd disrupted the Wizard's plans three and a half years ago when he'd refused his offer of Apprenticeship and Wendell doubted he'd forgotten or forgiven that small slight. Though his experience with Mr.Garroph was extremely limited Wendell had noted the quiet rage that burned beneath the surface of his polite façade. Now it was apparent Mr. Garroph had a new plan and Wendell was certain that he, his Master, and perhaps the whole valley were in terrible danger.

Wendell found Bergstrom in his garden talking to his bees. Immediately upon seeing his face the elder Wizard knew something was wrong and inquired to what ailed him. Wendell paused before he spoke unable to shake the sense of danger that gnawed at him. After a moment he decided prudence was preferable no matter how unlikely it was they may be overheard.

"Not here. Let's talk within the circle," Wendell stated as he looked around the tower's yard distrustfully.

"All right, Wendell," Bergstrom stood up and brushed himself off. He then gazed towards the beehives with a stern look before he issued a command, "Guard the tower. Repel anything that approaches."

Wendell was not surprised when two large swarms flooded out of the hives and started circling the fence's perimeter in opposite directions. He'd suspected for a long time that his Master had kept the bees for more than their honey production. Bergstrom doted upon them and talked to them constantly, that they were guardians was no small stretch of the imagination.

Wendell started to walk towards the tower but before he'd taken more than a single step Bergstrom grasped his arm and jerked him about. There was a sudden uncomfortable tug within the teen's gut as he was spun about and when he completed the turn he found himself no longer within the garden but standing before the Legacy Tome within the tower's attic.

"Now what's this about, Wendell?" Bergstrom asked as he clapped his hands to ignite the candles throughout the chamber.

"You never told me you could teleport us both like that," Wendell stated as he tried to steady his nerves from the disturbing after effects of the translocation spell.

"Well if I taught you all my tricks you'd never get any exercise going up and down the stairs, now would you?" the old Wizard chuckled, "Now out with it. What's happened that we should need this kind of privacy?"

"Mary and I encountered the Infernal in the woods this afternoon," Wendell stated grimly before taking a few deep breaths. The teleport was something very knew and he wondered how many times his Master had done it before he'd gotten use to it.

"I assume that since the woods aren't ablaze with Hell fire that she's okay. Put your head between your knees and breathe in through your nose and out through your mouth," Bergstrom instructed as he pointed towards their chairs before the fire and beckoned them. The chairs immediately walked over and entered the circle causing waves of distortion to ripple through the air as they breached the invisible barrier. The chairs came to rest facing one another before the Legacy Tome and Wendell was more than happy to get off his feet until the vertigo passed.

"She's fine. I used an illusion to conceal us within a tree hollow but I think it would have likely sniffed us out if it hadn't been on errand for its Master. The foul little thing defiantly knew my scent and could even smell that there had been Fairies present in the trees moments before it arrived," Wendell explained before he followed his Master's advice, sticking his head between his knees to breath.

"Ah, so your lure worked? I bet Mary enjoyed that," Bergstrom chuckled lightly as if the Infernal was of no consequence what so ever.

"She did until the Infernal scared them away and ruined the mood," Wendell sighed heavily shaking his head as he sat up. The breathing had helped to calm his stomach within seconds. "The nasty little bugger talks to itself and let an interesting tidbit slip out before it left. He said he had to go see the Goblins to see if it was finished and that I was of no consequence any longer for his Master's plans had changed."

"No hint as to what the Goblins are crafting for him?" Bergstrom asked hopefully to which Wendell shook his head with disappointment, "Anything else? Think carefully, no matter how insignificant it might have seemed at the time."

"Only that the Infernal seemed disappointed that it didn't have the time to stay and pluck the wings off the Fairies. Oh and a passing comment that his Master uses pain to keep him in line," Wendell shrugged, "Neither seemed very surprising or consequential."

"I would have to agree," Bergstrom stated quietly before sitting back in his chair. The old Wizard was silent for a long time then he looked at Wendell curiously, "Do you think you got a good enough look at it to visualize it accurately within your mind?"

"Right down to his knobby ivory horns, why?" Wendell nodded, positive that he could do as his Master asked. Good visualization skills were fundamental in spell casting or one would have unpredictable results.

"It's a long shot at best but we may be able to scry him. Mr. Garroph has many wards upon his home and person to thwart such magical detection but its possible he overlooked his minion. The Infernal is rarely visibly active and then usually only at night concealed by darkness. Its possible Scott wouldn't see the need to waist energy warding him," Bergstrom explained as he walked over to one of his shelves of spell components. He searched the shelf for a moment before he found a fist sized crystal ball, a small bundle of white sage, and a brass censer. These he brought back to his chair. "Now before we begin I must warn you not to ever attempt this magic upon powerful Wizards such as myself or Mr. Garroph. We tend to like our privacy and our wards can be quite devastating to those who attempt to invade it. Even many mid-level Wizards may be able to detect you watching them even if they can't prevent it so you must be very careful whom you target your vision upon."

"Can non-Wizards sense it?" Wendell asked curiously as his Master lit the sage on fire with the nearby candles.

"Sometimes, but unless they've had some instruction in magical defense they'll likely only get a vague feeling their being watched. Even if they do recognize the scrying for what it is without spell casting there isn't a whole lot they can do about it beyond attempting to feed the watcher false information," Bergstrom informed him as he watched the sage burn for a few moments then blew out the flames allowing the bundle to smolder and produce a great amount of fragrant smoke. He then placed the smoldering sage within the censer and set it between their feet.

"The sage isn't necessary for this magic but since it's your first time I thought it would help you clear your thoughts and relax. Scrying is more of an art form than proper magic and occasionally you'll find those who can do it that don't have an ounce of magic in their blood. What is most important is that you clear your mind of everything save for the visualization of your target. Then when you are ready you look upon a reflective surface and concentrate upon the person, place, or thing that you wish to scry. There are no words of power that can aid you just your will and desire to see your target. When you get better at it as I have done you'll no longer need a reflective surface and may simply see your target in the air before you. Truly gifted Seers can listen to their targets as well but its best to get down the basics before you attempt that. Now close your eyes and cup your hands before you," Bergstrom instructed as he placed the heavy crystal ball within Wendell's hands, "Now clear your mind of everything but the Infernal's face and when you believe you have his features locked into your mind's eye look into the crystal and will yourself to see him."

Wendell did as he was instructed, clearing his mind of all thoughts but the ugly face of the Infernal. It wasn't that difficult for most magic he'd learned called for focused concentration. When he thought he was ready he opened his eyes and gazed at the crystal ball within his hands. For a moment the image of the Infernal he'd etched into his mind was super imposed upon the crystal then the image changed and solidified into a life like image of the Infernal squatting amongst several other ugly little humanoids playing some kind of game with handfuls of bone dice. The image was completely silent but seemed completely life like as if the

Infernal and what Wendell assumed were Goblins were actually within the crystal sphere. Within a few moments Wendell found it was the easiest thing in the world to hold the image in place and he decided to be daring and attempt to hear them as well.

"I say you're a liar and a cheat, Quick," One of the Goblins croaked in a voice that sounded like it should have belonged to a bullfrog.

"Say that again and I'll make certain that your last meal is your own steaming guts, Marrowlicker. These are your bones so if there's any cheating going on you're to blame," the Infernal hissed coldly giving the dice a good shake before he cast them against the wall. All the Goblins howled with laughter as the Infernal cursed apparently very displeased with the way the dice had landed.

"That's another silver you owe me, Quick. Pay up so we can play again," a short pudgy goblin with sickly green skin and a completely bald head beckoned with his clawed fingers.

"Bah, your loaded bones are no fun. Where is your cousin so I can be on my way?" the Infernal grumbled irritably as he placed a talon in the Goblin's greedy palm.

"He'll be along shortly. That was no simple trinket your Master commissioned, but Droolsnarl's the best at what he does. Your Master will be pleased despite the wait," the Goblin boasted before he bit into the silver coin with a sharp fang then examined the dent before depositing it in his leather vest's pocket apparently satisfied with its authenticity, "Come on Quick, I know you have a few more coins to spare. I can smell them."

"Bah, one more round. But if you roll Dead Man's Sevens one more time expect to taste my steel for your greed, Toadfart," Quick grinned menacingly towards the pudgy Goblin who suddenly looked very uncomfortable as he fondled the dice within his claws, "What's wrong Toadfart? Did you think I hadn't noticed?"

"I think your right, Quick. I think Marrowlicker loaded these bones. They just don't feel right in my hand now that you mention it," Toadfart agreed quickly and made a show of setting down the dice. He yelped with surprise when Quick's blade was suddenly resting upon his pudgy throat.

"How about we let fate decide? You throw those bones and if you roll anything but Dead Man's Sevens I'll kill Marrowlicker and take his money, but if you roll the Sevens I'll slit your throat ear to ear and take yours. Now roll!" Quick commanded with the cruelest of grins.

Toadfart gulped audibly as he raised and shook the dice with the rapier pressed against his throat just hard enough to keep his chin up. Wendell watched in fascination as the Goblin named Marrowlicker licked his wide blubbery lips and tried to discreetly draw his short sword behind his back. The dice flew against the wall but before they could come to a rest both the Goblins were gurgling with slit throats while Quick wiped his rapier clean with a dull black handkerchief. The other Goblins were frozen with disbelief as Toadfart and Marrowlicker toppled over thrashing upon the stone floor.

"What a surprise, Dead Man's Sevens. Guess you win, Toadfart," Quick chuckled as he peered down at the dice. As one the other Goblins began to howl with laughter, Quick began to rifle through the still twitching Goblin's pockets for coins.

"Mary isn't going to believe..." Wendell began to say but immediately the image before him changed to the Miller's dining table where Mary was passing a bowl of rolls to her father.

Mary suddenly stiffened for a moment then looked around in confusion nearly dropping the rolls in her father's lap. After a moment she looked directly at Wendell with a strange expression across her beautiful features.

"Wendell?" She asked with disbelief. It surprised Wendell so much that he lost his concentration and the Crystal Ball's image faded in an instant until all he could see was a magnified view of his palms beneath.

"Well that was interesting. Not very illuminating, but interesting," Bergstrom chuckled as Wendell sagged in his chair suddenly feeling the magic's drain, "I thought you would be good at scrying since your sight is so strong, but to be able to hear your target as well on your first attempt. That's no small feat. Bet your feeling it now though?"

"I feel like I haven't slept in a week. How was Mary able to sense me?" Wendell asked curiously as he stifled a yawn.

"Your bond is strong enough that she probably just recognized your presence. You had her drink some of the Third Sight Potion to view the Fairies today, she may have seen a distortion as well or she's just growing more perceptive from prolonged contact with our world. I wouldn't worry too much about it unless she catches the Wizard Pox. If that happens your in for some real trouble. That girl's tenuous enough without magic. With magic she could probably enslave the world," Bergstrom chuckled as he scratched his bushy beard thoughtfully.

"We didn't learn what Quick was after though," Wendell sighed gloomily.

"No, but we did accomplish something. First of all we now know that Quick isn't warded against scrying and that means we can spy on him often as long as we're careful. Secondly I now know what he looks like and despite your obvious talent for scrying I have far more endurance when in comes to maintaining such spells. And finally you've successfully learned a new and very useful form of magic that with practice will become easier and far less draining. I'd say that this has been a very profitable exercise even if we didn't accomplish the goal we set out to, wouldn't you?" Bergstrom smiled as he leaned down and snuffed out the sage completely in the censer's sandy bottom.

"I suppose, but I still would like to know what they're up to," Wendell grumbled as he tried to hand back the Crystal Ball.

"No, you keep it. Like I told you before I no longer need it," Bergstrom put up his hand.

"Master, may I ask a sensitive question?" Wendell asked after looking at the crystal ball in his hand for a moment thoughtfully.

"Of course Wendell, anything," Bergstrom looked at him curiously.

"I don't want you to feel as if I'm in any way dissatisfied with my training, but I've noticed that you haven't been instructing me the way you use to and well today you've shown me two forms of magical knowledge you possess that you've never even hinted at before now. Are you in some way dissatisfied with me or my progress?" Wendell asked reluctantly fearing how the old Wizard may respond.

"I am very pleased with your progress, Wendell, and I have never once been dissatisfied with you, quite the opposite in fact. You have an intuitive grasp of the arcane like no other Wizard I've met. I have slowed down your education for two very important reasons. The first is you've already learned twice as much as any other apprentice your age. While this is by no means a bad thing you are still very young and I'm reluctant to place the responsibilities of more advanced powers on your shoulders until you've matured a bit more and passed a few of life's harder tests. Magic is very wonderful when used properly but can be the bane of all life if used recklessly or in the heat of passion. You're quickly coming upon a profound change in your life as you're about to enter your manhood. I assume you and Mary have already made plans to be wed after your birthdays?" Bergstrom paused and waited for Wendell's nod, "Well that is going to test you in ways you've not foreseen. Even the happiest of couples sometimes argue and fight. As Wizards we must be always vigilant of our emotions because it is far too easy to accidentally summon storms when we're angry, slay those who frighten us with a word, and even cause unforeseen havoc when we are joyous. Have you ever stopped to think what may happen when Mary is in labor with your first child?"

Wendell remained silent under the elder Wizard's scrutiny for such thoughts had never occurred to him. It was frightening to think that a simple lover's spat could end in serious harm to the one he loved and the thought of Mary in labor was just sobering. Bergstrom let it sink in for a few moments then he continued with a gentle smile,

"Now that is the possible negative ramifications of teaching you more powerful magic, but now I'm going to tell you the positive reasons I've slowed down your training. The simple fact of the matter is you don't need it. The more I've given you free reign to delve into your own interests and ideas the more I've been truly astonished with what you've come up with on your own. Take your latest experiment, for example. You created a lure to charm Fairies with no other intent than to impress Mary, but did you ever stop to consider how valuable an item your little mobile would be in an area plagued by Fairies? With a couple of your devices the Fairies could be lured away from the populous harmlessly or drawn to an area where they're required. You haven't explored the potential of such creatures beyond their ability to make Mary smile, but I know a Wizard in the east who creates enchanted apples with a combination of keeping Fairies in his orchard and a few simple spells. I think he'd pay handsomely for one or two of your little devices. With what knowledge you already possess you're more than ready to make your mark upon the world and by simply giving you little nudges here and there instead of teaching you a spell I've encouraged your creativity and imagination which are far more useful tools than say calling down meteors to smite your enemies or teleporting from the bottom of this tower to the top. Wouldn't you agree?"

"I guess so, but I really do get tire of going up those stairs, Master," Wendell ginned wearily.

"Then don't. I have complete faith in your ability to overcome such a simple problem," Bergstrom laughed as he picked up the censer and returned it to its place on the shelf, "Now that I've explained my reasoning do you trust me to continue guiding your training?"

"Of course, Master, and I'm very relieved to know that I've not displeased you," Wendell acknowledged adamantly.

"Good, then I suggest that we go down and eat dinner before we offend the cook with our absence!" Bergstrom smiled as he directed his chair back to its place before the fire. Wendell nodded his agreement and directed his own chair back before stuffing the Crystal Ball into his pouch then following the elder Wizard to the stairs, "So how many Fairies did your mobile attract and what type?"

"Three Moon Sprites. You're honey was very popular with them," Wendell grinned at his Master's interest.

"It's a shame we live so close to the village or I'd have you set them up around the tower. I'd like to experiment with adding a touch of their magic to my bee's honey," Bergstrom sighed longingly.

"We could try setting up a few hives in the wild?" Wendell thoughtfully suggested.

"They make to tempting a snack for the bears."

"Well luring Fairies wasn't too hard, I can't see repelling bears as being any more difficult," Wendell chuckled.

"What type of essence did you use for the lure?"

"Honey!" Wendell chuckled.

22

"You were watching me last night, weren't you?" Mary more accused Wendell than asked.

"It was accidental. Master showed me how to scry and during the attempt I thought of you and there you where. I'm sorry. I didn't intend to invade your privacy like that." Wendell apologized honestly.

Mary was sitting on Wendell's bed stroking the back of Squeaker's head as he watched the rain pour down outside his window. This downpour was very out of season for summer and it had made Wendell introspective. Squeaker released a long string of happy squeaky purrs as Mary continued to stroke its thick head fur.

"I didn't mind really, it just startled me. I'm glad I wasn't drinking or you may have caused milk to come out of my nose and father would have never let me hear the end of it," Mary smirked as she changed the pattern of her stokes to gentle scratches along side Squeaker's head where the ears of a Human would be. The Brownie shuddered with pleasure as it leaned into her fingers.

"What did you see when you notice me?" Wendell asked curiously.

"Nothing, I just knew you where there. It was as if you had walked into the room but I couldn't see you," Mary shrugged.

"Master and I had a serious discussion about my magic last night." Wendell stated quietly as he watched the rain splatter against the lead linings of the multi facetted window and accumulate upon the edges before poring over to the masonry below, "He warned me that my powers could be very dangerous when we argue or when you're in labor with our children. It's very easy to generate magical effects when lost in the heat of strong emotions."

"Yes, I could see how that could be a problem. I guess you'll just have to let me win all of our arguments," Mary stated with an amused smirk.

"I'm being serious Mary. It could be very dangerous," Wendell turned towards her, hugging his shoulders for warmth. While comfortable, the tower was very drafty and his mood didn't help to ward off the chill.

"So was I. I would of course win them all anyway but we really can't have you destroying the furniture with lightning bolts and such. I mean really, what would the neighbors say?" Mary asked raising one eyebrow and trying hard not to smile.

"You're being very difficult about this," Wendell sighed, shaking his head in frustration as he came over and sat down beside her.

"I love you, too, Wendell," She leaned over and kissed his cheek, "I'm just not all that concerned is all. I know you'll never hurt me."

"Not intentionally, no. But even the happiest of couples fight. What happens if in the heat of an argument I loose control? I couldn't live with myself if I caused you harm," Wendell sighed again as he conjured a piece of candy from his pocket and handed it to the still purring Brownie she had in the cup of her hand. Squeaker unwrapped the lemon drop greedily and handed back the wax paper before crunching into it.

"I think you're worrying far too much about it. You're the gentlest person I know and I've never once seen any hint that you weren't in complete control of your powers," Mary tried to reassure him as he quickly folded the wax paper into the form of a bird, "If loosing control frightens you, then don't."

"You make it sound so simple," Wendell stated doubtfully as he placed the tiny bird in his hand then blew on it to give it the appearance of life. The wax paper bird instantly began to flap its wings and in a moment took off from his hand and began to soar around the room. Squeaker gave a happy squeak and clapped its hands before continuing to crunch on what was left of the candy within its concealed mouth.

"It is simple until you start agonizing over it," Mary smiled as she watched the wax paper bird fly about.

"How is it you always seem to be able to untangle difficult problems and make me feel better?" Wendell asked as he watched her. She turned towards him and lit up the room with her beautiful smile before releasing a giggle of amusement.

"That's simple, too. I'm more powerful than you, silly!" Mary smirked at him smugly before kissing him on the lips.

Squeaker let out a long squeaky laugh at the befuddled look that crossed Wendell's face as he gazed into Mary's completely self-assured eyes. It was far too easy to believe she was anything but absolutely correct as Wendell lost himself in her gaze.

23

Two days later Wendell was headed into town to visit his sister Wendy, who had become pregnant with her first child. This was an exciting event for the whole family for Wendy and Fredric had been trying to conceive since the beginning of their marriage and their repeated failure had weighed heavily upon the couple. Wendell was to meet Mary at the Tailor's shop but as usual had lost track of the time and was running late. As he entered the first row of cottages at the bottom of the hill he was preoccupied with what would be a suitable gift to conjure for his sister when Mary's voice drew his attention towards a small barn belonging to the Ingrum family.

"Leave me alone, Trevor, or you'll be sorry!" Mary threatened coldly from the other side of the structure just loud enough to catch Wendell's ear.

"What, a pasty faced wizard is good enough for you but a real man isn't? Give us a kiss. I won't tell Wimpell," Trevor's rumbling chuckle caused Wendell's blood to burn.

"Get off me!" Mary exclaimed before letting out a shriek of surprise that Wendell took for pain.

When Wendell came around the corner he found Mary on the ground with Trevor leaning over her. She had tripped over the Goat's feeding trough but in Wendell's anger it appeared that Trevor had pushed her. The ugly mountainous Smith's son looked up at him in surprise as he was offering Mary a hand up. Wendell didn't notice the sky above darken with angry black clouds forming out of the clear morning air but Trevor and Mary certainly did.

"Get away from her, Trevor!" Wendell growled and thunder rumbled above to emphasize the command.

"I'm alright, Wendell! Trevor was just leaving!" Mary stated as she struggled to rise, but her gown snagged upon the head of one of the trough's protruding nails and tore as she rose.

"No I wasn't!" Trevor stood up squaring his muscular shoulders before Wendell, "You don't scare me with a bit of foul weather, Wimpell. Everyone thinks you Wizards are so special because you can do a few tricks but I know the truth. You're just a bunch of lazy tricksters who've never had to do an honest days work in their lives!"

Another thunderclap rolled overhead as Trevor sneered down at Wendell defiantly. Mary tore her gown even further as she hastened to get between the two as they glared at each other with mutual hatred.

"Stop it right now before someone gets hurt!" Mary commanded as she stepped in between them while trying to keep her modesty by holding the torn cloth of her gown together.

"Stay out of this, Mary!" Trevor ordered as he forcefully pushed her out of the way causing her to fall once again.

Wendell had only felt the kind of power that surged within him once before when he took his oath of Apprenticeship. He balled his fist and his eyes glowed frightfully as the lightning bolt arced down from the storm clouds above. Trevor's eyes grew wide and a moment to late he discovered that not all Wizardry was simple trickery and that some was indeed to be feared. He felt the burn of the fiery electricity and cowered before it with a scream of utter terror but the bolt did not but scorch the hair off his arms, Bergstrom intercepted it with a mystical shield. The arc of lightning impacted the hemispherical barrier of energy with a thunderous crack, sending lesser arcs flying off in several directions. One of these arcs cut through the Ingrum's fence and half-dozen terrified Goats beyond. Another flew straight into the barn, igniting a mound of hay instantly upon impact.

"Control yourself, boy!" Bergstrom commanded in a voice like thunder and for the first time ever Wendell saw anger and the true power in his Master. Gone was all hint of the kindly old man who amused all by pulling live Doves from his pockets and talked to things that weren't alive. In his place was a terrifying Wizard whose very presence radiated magic so powerful it would have been humbling to the bravest of souls.

A gust of icy wind that distorted the air and chilled all present to the bone blew into the barn and instantly froze the burning hay and put out the flames. Everyone turned and found Mr. Garroph walking towards them with a hand that was still covered in frost. The Wizard wore a stern mask but Wendell thought he detected a sparkle of amusement in his eyes as looked upon the Apprentice. Bergstrom nodded towards the other Wizard regaining a bit of his composure and Mr. Garroph returned the gesture with a bit more elegance.

"Would you be kind enough to escort young Mr. Smith here to his father while I sort out this mess, Scott?" Bergstrom asked as the other Wizard approached.

"Of course, Bergstrom," Mr. Garroph tilted his head before he leaned over and picked up the shaking bully by the arm.

"Please inform Mr. Smith that I will be along shortly to speak with him," Bergstrom stated as he removed his cloak and wrapped it around Mary to conceal the ruins of her gown. They watched Mr.Garroph lead Trevor away until he turned the corner then Bergstrom turned a very unpleasant glare of disapproval upon Wendell.

"Master I..." Wendell began but Bergstrom cut him off instantly.

"Go cool down!" The elder Wizard commanded as he pushed Wendell in the chest with an open palm with a strength and quickness that was surprising for a man of his age. Wendell fell backwards and landed softly in the snow.

The Apprentice blinked and looked around to find he was now sitting atop a snow covered mountain amidst a vast range of icy peaks that stretched as far as the eye could see. The cold of the mountains hit him like a physical blow despite the sunny clear skies above and his head swam with a shortness of breath in the thin air. Wendell stood up and immediately hugged himself as he stamped his feet for warmth. He thought about trying to make his way off the mountain but after looking around once more he realized there was nowhere to go.

After dancing in place for almost a minute, it occurred to Wendell he might be able to improve his lot and with shaky hands he took off his cloth hat and attempted to conjure a warm winter coat. The Apprentice was less than amused when he pulled a pair of swimming shorts from the worn midnight blue hat. He released a curse he knew would have caused Mary to smack him for blasphemy before he attempted to clear his mind and try again. This time he pulled a sun umbrella out of the hat and swore the Gods were mocking him.

It was nearly an hour before Bergstrom came to fetch Wendell and by then the Apprentice was in a very sorry state. The elder Wizard found the boy huddled within a beach towel that did little beyond covering his shoulders. Bergstrom looked remorseful as he offered the boy his hand. Wendell took it and was drawn upward into the tower's attic before the fire. Shuddering with frostbite, Wendell almost toppled into the flames in his enthusiasm to get warm. Bergstrom patted him on the shoulder gently then sat down in his chair without a word.

"I'm sorry, Master," Wendell sniffled once he'd warmed up enough to think clearly again.

"I'm sorry, too, Wendell. You aren't the only one who lost their temper. I shouldn't have sent you to the north like that," Bergstrom shook his head remorsefully.

"I deserved it, I almost killed Trevor," Wendell sighed deeply before releasing a large sneeze.

"You were sorely provoked. Or so Mary told me," Bergstrom stated quietly.

"I didn't mean to. The power just surged up before I could stop it," Wendell explained as he rubbed his hands above the flames.

"It happens to the best of us from time to time. Next time try to avert your gaze to something nearby. Property is far easier to replace than a human life," The elder Wizard suggested quietly, "I've paid the Ingrums for their fence and the dead Goats though they'll probably still be a bit skittish around you for years to come. I don't think Trevor will ever bother you or Mary again. By the time I got to the Smithy to speak with his father the boy's hair had lost all color from his fright. I really don't think he believed magic was real until he saw that bolt of lightning coming down towards him."

"How did you know what was going on?" Wendell asked as he turned towards his Master.

"You weren't exactly subtle, now were you? What with the sky becoming overcast in a matter of seconds accompanied with thunder and lightning. It would have been hard to ignore you even if I hadn't felt your anger. You caused such a ruckus you even coaxed Mr. Garroph out of his tower to see what was going on," Bergstrom chuckled with grim amusement.

"I guess I didn't really notice until the lightning," Wendell admitted turning back towards the fire, "He seemed amused by it though."

"Well, Scott always has had a compulsion to flaunt his power over the powerless. He's matured a bit over the years but it probably appealed to him greatly to have the villagers reminded that even the weakest of us can call upon forces well beyond them. That and the fact that he could appear to be coming to Trevor's rescue instead of being blamed for the milk going sour," Bergstrom explained thoughtfully.

"Was Mary upset with me?" Wendell asked quietly, afraid of the answer even as he asked the question.

"Scared for you would be more my analysis of her mood. I think she'll save being upset until she's certain you're alright and then you'll be in for an earful at the very least," Bergstrom chuckled with amusement, "I took her to your brother-in-law's shop to have her gown repaired. I figured they'd take care of her while I came to fetch you. I wouldn't be surprised to find she's marching up the hill as we speak to be certain I haven't turned you into a Frog or something."

"That's what she wanted me to do to Trevor the day we met," Wendell laughed, causing himself to sneeze several times in a row before he regained control of his nose.

"That would probably be an improvement on the boy's looks," Bergstrom chucked with a mischievous sparkle in his eyes.

"Can you?" Wendell asked curiously.

"Not really, no," Bergstrom shook his head and scratched his beard looking a bit uncomfortable, "I could implant the suggestion that he was a frog in his mind and give him the compulsion to eat bugs like a frog, but it would only last a few hours at best then he'd return to his normal unpleasant self. I'd rather you didn't experiment with such magic, however. It's far too easy to cause permanent harm to your subject without proper training and you're not ready for it yet."

"Yes, Master," Wendell acknowledged as he wiped his runny nose on his sleeve.

They were silent for a long time save for Wendell's sniffles and the occasional sneeze. Then the door bell's ethereal chimes echoed through the attic and Bergstrom grinned.

"That I believe would be your fair Miss Miller. You rest there and I'll go fetch her," Bergstrom smiled as he rose from his chair, but he paused before leaving, "You might consider playing up the severity of you're cold, Wendell. It might just save you from her temper."

The old Wizard winked before he disappeared causing Wendell to grin. Wendell was amused by the notion until he heard Mary chiding Bergstrom mercilessly for his callousness as they were coming up the stairs. Then a strong sense of self preservation caused Wendell to throw himself into the chair. He'd just conjured a blanket to throw over himself and began to feign sleep when Bergstrom led Mary into the chamber.

"Oh, Wendell!" Mary rushed to his side, all her anger forgotten in an instant as she gazed upon his sickly looking face.

"Mary?" Wendell wheezed pathetically as he cracked open his eyes, "I'm sorry, Mary. I, I didn't mean to scare you," Wendell apologized with just the right amount of sniffling to seem truly on the edge of death's door.

"Shh, be quiet, Wendell. It's alright now. You need to rest," she stated as she kissed him on the forehead.

"Um, err, if you'll look after Wendell, Mary, I'll just go down and get the cook to prepare him some chicken noodle soup," Bergstrom withdrew with eyes that were watering as he struggled to contain his laughter.

"I should think that's the least you can do," Mary glared after the Wizard as he walked away with a look that could have frozen a Fire Giant's blood. Wendell bit his lip in alarm hoping that Bergstrom wouldn't be offended but the old Wizard just walked on until he disappeared down the stairs. Wendell barely returned to the proper visage of death incarnate before Mary turned back to him and once again instantly melted from anger into the embodiment of loving concern, "Is there anything I can do to make you more comfortable?"

"Just sit down and hold me, Mary?" Wendell scooted to one side of the large chair and opened the blanket for her to join him.

"Of course, my dearest," Mary smiled as she sat down beside him and embraced him warmly.

As they snuggled together under the blanket, Wendell wondered how long he could continue to be sick before Mary got wise to his ruse. She felt so good embracing him that Wendell found himself musing over simple glamour's that would give him the appearance of contracting a fever, mumps, and even more severe ailments of the flesh just so she would comfort him more. Her tender affections did much to alleviate the tension and guilt of that morning's events.

24

The weeks that followed Wendell's loss of control were hard on the Apprentice, for people who had always before been friendly towards the boy now treated him with a cautious respect or outright fear that he had trouble getting use to. Trevor's bleached white hair seem to constantly remind them that Wizards weren't exactly safe to have around regardless of how pleasant they may appear and the untimely death of livestock was even more abhorrent to the little farming community. Of course those who actually knew Wendell were inclined to believe that Trevor had provoked him, but they were in the minority regardless of how adamantly they spoke on his behalf.

Wendell found himself shunning the villagers more and more often for he was ill at ease with their sideways glances and hushed toned remarks. Most hurtful to him by far were mothers who would gather their children indoors as he approached as if he'd consider doing them harm if given half the chance. Bergstrom sympathized with his plight, but counseled to just act as he always had for some new scandal would erupt soon enough to give them something to gossip about and Wendell's act would be all but forgotten. Wendell wasn't so certain however as days turned into weeks and the villagers continued to treat him as something dangerous within their midst.

On a Monday morning, Wendell set out once again to see his sister for he had little else to do. Mary had more responsibilities these days and he didn't expect her for a few more hours so he headed into the village eager to be certain Wendy was well. He made his way into the village, ignoring the looks of disapproval and fear he received and was cutting across the small market square. He ran into Trevor who was carrying a barrel full of coal towards the Smithy. Both boys stopped when they realized who approached and a hushed silence fell across the square.

Wendell had not encountered Trevor since the day of lighting and though he'd heard about the bully's change in hair color he was ill-prepared for the reality of it. Not a single black hair remained on Trevor's round head and the white gave him an elder look despite the youthfulness of his ugly features. Wendell felt horrid enough as he gazed at his childhood nemesis but it was even more awkward because he could feel half the village staring at them. Wendell drew upon his inner strength and decided that he must at least attempt to make things right.

"I'm very sorry, Trevor. I never meant to loose control like that, please forgive me," Wendell apologized, causing the larger boy to blink with surprise. There was a long moment of awkward silence then another thought occurred to Wendell, "If I can come up with a way to restore your hair, do you think you could forgive me?"

"I don't want anything to do with magic," Trevor grumbled as he touched his hair self-consciously with his free hand.

"None of us do!" Wendell's mother yelled from one of the nearby vegetable wagons, causing both boys to jump. A few of the other villagers growled their agreement and still more nodded their heads, "Why don't you just leave and never come back?" his mother suggested with a cold air of authority that was down right frightening to the boy.

"Are you really going to side with a woman that abandoned her own flesh and blood?" Mary asked as she walked up beside Wendell carrying a basket full of vegetables. She glared at Wendell's mother with nothing but contempt as she addressed the others, "Is that the kind of person you want to follow?"

"He's evil!" Wendell's mother pointed at him red faced with a seething rage that everyone present found repulsive even if they'd agreed with her only moments before. When next she spoke spittle flew from her mouth and her words were hissed like a curse, "I never should have born him!"

Many people gasped aloud and more than a few backed away from Maggie Glasswright as if she was a serpent in their midst.

"Mother..." Wendell choked and took a step towards her but stopped when she immediately stepped back and traced one of her superstitious wards against evil in the air towards him. Tears ran like rivers down Wendell's cheeks and he was stunned by her reaction.

"Why you evil old hag! How dare you!" Mary started towards her with her tiny fists balled red faced with fury. This sparked Wendell into motion and he grabbed his love around the waist before she could take more than a pace towards his mother.

"Yes, hold your harlot back unclean spawn. I should have thrown your putrid little body into the river the day you were born!" Maggie hissed before spitting upon the ground towards him and stomping off.

Many of the villagers turned white in the horror of Mrs. Glasswright's curse but Wendell couldn't see them. He was to busy fighting to keep a hold of Mary who was determined to spill his mother's blood. After a few moments within which Wendell appeared to be fighting a down hill battle, Trevor set down his barrel of coal and picked her up as if she weighed nothing at all.

"Where should we take her?" Trevor asked wincing both from Mary's blows and the long winded string of venomous curses towards Wendell's retreating mother.

"The Tailor's shop," Wendell stated thinking it was the closest and Wendy had the best chance of calming Mary down since she was pregnant. Trevor nodded and began to march in that direction, ignoring the gruesome fates Mary threatened to bestow upon him if he didn't put her down. Wendell wiped his eyes on his sleeve and paused only long enough to retrieve Mary's discarded vegetables and basket before he gave chase.

Fredric and Wendy started with surprise as Trevor fought Mary through the door of their shop. After Wendell came in he dropped her in a heap in the center of the floor then backed up against the door folding his meaty arms so she couldn't get pass. Mary sat where she'd been dropped, scarlet purple with rage breathing so heavily that Wendell feared she'd pass out. She glared at Trevor with venomous daggers but made no move to launch at the ugly giant who watched her without flinching.

"What's happened?" Wendy asked as she approached Mary cautiously holding her swollen belly. She squatted down before her so she could look Mary in the eyes.

"Mother...Mother cursed my birth in the village square and called Mary a harlot," Wendell choked out as fresh tears tumbled down his cheeks, "I think she was trying to get the villagers to drive me out."

"It backfired though. No one wanted to side with someone who speaks of drowning infants," Trevor shook his head in disgust. His statement caused both Fredric and Wendy to grow very pale.

Wendell knelt down beside Mary and put his arms around her. After a few moments Mary's breathing settled down a little and her color subsided to an angry flush rather than that of an angry plum. When it was clear that she was no longer going to try and rush the door Trevor nodded with a grunt towards Wendell and started out the door.

"Thank you, Trevor. That was very decent of you," Wendell told him before he could exit. Trevor got an uncomfortable look upon his ugly features before he just shrugged and left.

"Are you alright, little brother?" Wendy placed a hand on his cheek. Fredric came up beside her and offered her a stepping stool so she could sit down.

"I think so. I knew she was scared of me but I never dreamed she wished me to die or that she'd try and attack me publicly. And what she called Mary was just unforgivable. I would never try to dishonor her before we're married," Wendell shook his head in disbelief.

"I know, Wendell. You're a decent young man and Mary is a pure young woman," Wendy sighed as she leaned forward on the stool and hugged them both.

"She seemed down right deranged," Mary grunted as Wendy broke away, "And I think most of the village saw it to."

"Well I'm going to go have a chat with father and maybe our brothers as well," Wendy stated as she hoisted herself off the stool using Fredric's arm, "This has been going on far too long and bringing it out in public is just inexcusable. You and Mary don't deserve to be treated this way and it's high time someone put a stop to it."

"I don't know if that's such a good idea, Wendy. You didn't see the hatred in her eyes. I don't want this rift between us to endanger you or the baby," Wendell tried to dissuade her as Wendy headed towards the shop door.

"Your concern is heartwarming, little brother, but my mind is made up," Wendy smiled at him determinedly before she exited the shop.

Wendell hugged Mary tightly for a few moments then helped her to her feet. Fredric watched them sternly for a moment or two then gave them one of his very rare thin lipped grins.

"I know something that will cheer you up," The Tailor stated as he walked back towards one of the tall cupboards that lined the back wall.

From the cupboard the Tailor drew out the beginnings of a fine white gown hanging from a wooden hanger. Most of the gown's pieces were only held together with pins but already it looked like a fine garment that any noblewoman would be proud to wear upon their wedding day. Mary instantly stepped forward and hesitantly touched the gowns sleeve as if it were a sacred object that she both loved and feared at the same time.

"It's beautiful," Mary whispered reverently. "Who's it for?"

"You, my dear. Wendy and I thought it would make a fine wedding present and save quite a bit of your dowry. I started on it a few months ago and have been adding a little more to it between commissions ever since," Fredric grinned at Mary's state of shocked disbelief.

He was completely unprepared for it when Mary threw her arms around his neck and kissed him upon the cheek with a girlish giggle of pure pleasure. Whether it was the fact that he was unaccustomed to such blatant displays of emotion or that he was uncomfortable with being touched by anyone but his wife was uncertain, but Fredric stiffened under Mary's assault as if she'd nearly given him heart failure. Mary of course was completely oblivious to the Tailor's discomfort for she couldn't stop looking at the gown.

"I think that means she likes it," Wendell clapped Fredric on the shoulder to restart his heart.

"Like it? I love it!" Mary snatched the gown from Fredric's hand greedily and took it to the mirror so she could get an idea what it would look like upon her, "It's the most beautiful gown I've ever seen."

"Careful, Fredric, I think you're in danger of becoming her favorite in-law," Wendell teased as he watched Mary display the gown upon her breast with childish mirth she hadn't displayed in years. She sounded as if she was twelve again with her happy little giggles.

"I don't know if I could survive that!" Fredric blushed as he rubbed his cheek where she had kissed him with a mock look of horror that took Wendell off guard. Until that moment, Wendell hadn't been aware that his brother-in-law was capable of humor.

25

For the next two days Wendell retreated to the tower's attic and worked upon a new project. He paused in his work only to visit with Mary when she came by to inquire about his absence. Once Mary determined that Wendell was not locking himself away in depression and was merely obsessing upon his work, she kissed him on the cheek and left him to it. Mary was a practical girl who didn't mind him ignoring her occasionally, mostly because his efforts usually produced something wonderful for her. This wasn't one of those times though he hadn't bothered to tell her that.

Wendell finished his project near supper time on the third day and paused only long enough to scratch down the formula before he headed to the village. When he reached the Smith household it took no small amount of courage to knock on the door and even more when the Bear like form of Mr. Smith answered.

"What do you want?" Mr. Smith growled with displeasure after glaring at Wendell for a moment. The Blacksmith was a giant among men who loomed over Wendell.

"May I please speak to Trevor, Sir?" Wendell asked meekly as politely as he could manage.

"Who is it, Pa?" Trevor's voice asked from within.

The Blacksmith glared at Wendell distrustfully a moment longer then stepped to the side so Trevor and Wendell could see one another. Trevor got the curious expression of one who is both intrigued but senses the possibility of a trap.

"Says he wants to speak to you," His father grunted to Trevor but made no attempt to leave them alone.

"Well?" Trevor asked after a moment.

"I made this for you, or more specifically you're hair," Wendell held up the large bottle of dark liquid dye, "I know you said you didn't want anything more to do with magic so I made it without using any. I'm pretty sure I got the color of your hair right. All you'll have to do is sprinkle some on, rub it in, and then rinse it out with water and the color should last a week or two. If you like it I'll make more when you run out."

Trevor took the bottle and looked at it thoughtfully for a moment.

"What's in it?" He asked distrustfully.

"Mostly walnut oil, boiled down tree sap, and liquid charcoal. It took me almost two days to figure out how to blend it so that it would stain your hair without leaving a gritty residue," Wendell explained awkwardly, very aware of Mr. Smith's distrustful glare.

"And this isn't some type of trick?" Trevor asked suspiciously.

"No, Trevor, it's not a trick. It's an apology and a thank you," Wendell smiled awkwardly before he started to turn away.

"I'm sorry, too. I shouldn't have pushed Mary," Trevor told him quietly before Wendell had fully turned, "Thank you."

"You're welcome, Trevor," Wendell nodded before he left them.

Despite recent events Wendell felt much better as he started back towards the tower. Somehow making peace with Trevor made Wendell feel as if he had a chance to resolve all the issues in his life. It was a small thing but it was a wrong that had been righted and that felt good to him.

By the time Wendell reached the dining hall Bergstrom was nearly done with his meal, but the Apprentice was in such high spirits he didn't care. When his Master inquired as to what had made Wendell so merry he was proud to learn that he'd made peace with the Blacksmith's son. As Wendell dug into his dinner, Bergstrom talked to him about his latest theory about the fluidic nature of time and a special clock he had thought of while weeding this morning. His bees had given him the idea for the magical timepiece because bees have a far better grasp of time the elder Wizard informed him. Wendell listened with interest until they were interrupted by the ethereal doorbell's chimes.

"I wonder who that could be at this hour?" Bergstrom stated as he rose from his chair, "Finish you're dinner and think on what I've told you. It seems like I'm forgetting something but I can't for the life of me think of what that may be and you don't want to make any mistakes what so ever when you meddle with time."

"All right, Master," Wendell acknowledged with his mouth half full of roast beef just before the old Wizard disappeared.

Wendell took two more bites which he washed down with some wine and was about to take a third when he was suddenly overcome by his Master's fear and pain as if he was experiencing them first hand. *'The book! Protect the book!"* his Master's voice stabbed into his brain like a red hot iron. Wendell jump to his feet knocking over his chair and ran as fast as he could towards the attic. Within a minute he was entering the circle and could swear he sensed something like a sigh of relief as he approached the Legacy Tome.

Wendell looked down at the formidable tome and wondered what he should do now. Then it occurred to him that the Legacy Tome probably had several defensive spells to thwart any attempts to capture it. Quickly he traced the rose patterned lock to open it then when the silver sheath had receded he commanded it,

"Show me a spell to repel intruders within the tower!" Wendell exclaimed and was more than a little relieved when the thick tome's rough pages began to turn.

The spell the tome opened to was entitled 'Security Labyrinth' and looked to be a complex bit of magic. Wendell started to read the spell's description but before he'd made it through the first sentence he felt the familiar sense of evil that always preceded the Infernal drawing near. Certain that he was almost out of time Wendell began to recite the spell's incantation as carefully as he could and hoping that the Legacy Tome had not led him astray.

As soon as the spell was complete, Wendell almost fell to the floor as a wave of energy surged out from within him omni-directionally. The only noticeable change to Wendell as he pitched forward on top of the book to keep from collapsing to the floor was as the wave passed over the stairs the hatch closed and locked itself with a snap of its heavy iron bar. The presence of the Infernal's evil was still there but it no longer seemed to be advancing. A little more relieved Wendell took the time to read the spell's description since he was in no condition to move anyway.

By means of the Security Labyrinth spell, a Wizard may alter the dimensions of each room within his dwelling to create a maze to disorient and lose would-be invaders. Intruders will be unable to navigate the altered chambers correctly and will often find themselves returned to the dwelling's entrance where they may start over again or leave. Wendell read upon the page that had beside it a plate that illustrated a Wizard walking down a corridor that was warped and twisted upon itself holding his head as if confused.

"What should I do now?" Wendell asked the tome with a heavy sigh. The Legacy Tome didn't answer but Mr. Garroph's cold voice did within his head.

'You should give up and give me the book, Boy. You are not my enemy. There is no reason to fear as long as you don't choose to stand in my way," Mr. Garroph's voice reasoned with oily smoothness.

"What have you done to my Master?" Wendell asked reluctantly.

'He is secure in my possession, and there he will remain. It took me many years but I finally came up with a suitable punishment for the death of my Master. Fear not, Bergstrom is going to live for an exceptionally long time,' Mr. Garroph chuckled wickedly. His amusement was short lived however as he released an angry growl of frustration, *'Whatever this spell is you must cancel it at once or suffer my wrath, Boy.'*

"What spell?" Wendell asked innocently as he tried to think of what to do next.

'Don't test my patience! You have more to lose than you know, or did you think I hadn't noticed you're fair little Mary? She's a bit young and hot tempered for my tastes but perhaps I can make an exception,' Mr. Garroph threatened viciously.

"Touch her and you'll come to a much worse end that you're Master!" Wendell threatened feeling the power of his anger beginning to boil within his blood.

'Give me the book and both of you will never need have fear of me again,' Mr. Garroph stated in a voice that said he was nearly at the end of his patience.

"Show me a spell to shield my mind from another's thoughts," Wendell commanded the tome and it instantly flipped a half dozen pages to a spell entitled 'Intellectual Fortress.'

'Don't you dare, Worm!' Mr. Garroph hissed, but Wendell was already reciting the three word incantation.

Within seconds there were no thoughts in Wendell's head but his own and he was pleased to find the spell drained him not at all. He needed to make certain Mary was safe and find a way to free his Master from whatever Mr. Garroph's prison. Mary would have to come first, since he had no clue as to how to confront Mr. Garroph and live. Wendell quickly pulled the crystal ball from his belt pouch and proceeded to attempt to scry her.

It wasn't easy for Wendell had a lot on his mind, but after a few attempts he was able to see her sitting on her bed brushing her beautiful hair while humming a soft tune. Once more she sensed his presence and after a moment looked directly at him.

"I know you're watching me," Mary narrowed her eyes with a playful smirk.

"Can you hear me Mary?" Wendell asked hopefully.

"I bet you were hoping I'd be bathing before bed!" she grinned at him as if the idea was tempting.

Any other time Wendell would have been very intrigued by Mary's scandalous mood but right now it just frustrated him. He needed to warn her, but how? Then he thought about Mr. Garroph's mental contact. He'd seen both Mr. Garroph and his Master do it with no form of incantation what so ever. He had a feeling that it was just a matter of will but was it dangerous as well? After a moment Wendell decided the danger of Mr. Garroph out weighed the risk and concentrated on projecting his thoughts towards Mary.

At first nothing happened and Wendell felt like he was pushing up against a barrier of some kind. He tried harder but again he couldn't seem to project anything beyond the barrier. Wendell took a deep breath, focused his thoughts, and then slammed them into the barrier with all his mental might. There was excruciating pain but the barrier shattered like a glass window and he suddenly felt the surface of Mary's mind.

"Oh my, Wendell you've hurt yourself!" Mary dropped her brush in surprise as he made contact.

'It's nothing! You're in danger! Mr. Garroph's imprisoned Master somehow and he threatened you if I don't give him the Legacy Tome. You and you're family have to get out of there and hide. He may already be coming for you!' Wendell projected towards her quickly.

"It's not nothing Wendell! I, I can feel your pain. You've got to stop this at once!" Mary screamed as tears began to roll down her cheeks. Wendell was getting light headed with the pain and figured she was probably right, but refused to let go of the contact until he knew she was going to follow his instructions.

'Not until you promise to run. You and your family have to get out of there right now!' Wendell gritted his teeth as the pain intensified.

"Alright, I promise! Now please stop!" Mary was weeping as both her parents rushed into her room.

'I love you,' Wendell projected before he released the painful power. He watched her start to physically drag her parents from the room before his concentration was broken by a large drop of blood splattering over the crystal ball's surface.

Wendell put his fingers to his nose and found it to be bleeding in a steady trickle. Quickly he pinched it off and leaned his head back wondering what he'd just done to himself. He needed a plan he thought quickly and it had better be a good one.

"Show me a spell to locate a person anywhere," Wendell commanded the tome and it quickly flipped two thirds though its pages to a spell entitled 'Seeking the Lost'.

Quickly Wendell read through the spell and found that it wasn't that difficult as long as you had the proper components. Wendell memorized the list then started searching his Master's shelves. Soon he had everything except for the most vital component of all, something personal belonging to the target individual. Wendell looked around quickly but saw nothing he would consider personal to his Master. Almost everything within the attic was a tool not something intimate like the spell was asking for. Then a thought occurred to Wendell and he went to his Master's chair. He searched it top to bottom in hopes of finding a hair or a nail clipping but there was nothing. Frustrated, Wendell let out a heavy sigh and then another thought occurred to him. The chair itself was one of his Master's most intimate possessions. It was a long shot but the alternative was going down and searching his bedchamber that Wendell wasn't certain he'd be able to find with the Security Labyrinth spell in effect. Wendell returned to the shelves and retrieved a silver handled knife they used for chopping up herbs. He cut a small square out of the leather upholstery and returned to the book.

Wendell placed all the components upon the square of parchment he'd prepared the recited the incantation. As soon as the final word of power was uttered all the components were consumed by fire that danced across the parchment's surface for several seconds thereafter. When the fames went out Wendell saw charred lines had been scorched into the parchment's surface to form a map of the tower. A tiny arrow sat where he was standing pointed at the stairs. Wendell took a few steps towards the stairs and was pleased to see the arrow moved upon the map with him. Satisfied that the seeking spell was working Wendell returned to the Legacy Tome.

"Show me a way to transport you," Wendell commanded hopefully.

The Tome responded to flipping all the way to the inside of the front cover where four words of power had been inscribed with silver point. Wendell recited the words and the tome instantly closed and began to shrink until it was small enough to fit within his palm. Wendell laughed aloud as he picked up the now tiny tome and placed it within his belt pouch. He was probably going to need a magnifying lens to return the Tome to its original size but at least he wouldn't break his back carrying it in the meantime. Satisfied that he was prepared Wendell went to the stairs, threw back the bolt and opened the hatch. With the Seeker map in hand, Wendell set out to find his Master.

26

The stairwell coming down from the attic didn't seem any different to Wendell, but when he opened the door at the bottom he found himself peering into his own bedchamber instead of the corridor it normally connected to. While disorienting, Wendell was not surprised and proceeded into his room as he gazed down at the Seeker's Map within his hands. The arrow that represented him has now pointing back towards the door that had closed behind him. Wendell was about to turn and exit the room when the door knob began to rattle before him.

In a panic Wendell looked around quickly for a place to hide but the Wardrobe and under the bed just seemed too obvious. Then the Apprentice looked down at the bearskin rug at his feet and a brilliant flash of inspiration struck him like a kick to the head. Wendell had experimented with extra-dimensional space before but he wasn't certain if enough would have accumulated under the rug to hide him. He knew it was there for he often deposited the dust he swept up under it, but he was uncertain if the same principle could be applied to a human being. As it was Wendell hadn't the time for doubts for he heard the door's catch release behind him.

Wendell lifted the bearskin rug and dived beneath as the door to his bedchamber creaked open and suddenly found himself in a strange and very dusty void. Wendell had to cover his nose and mouth to keep from sneezing as he peered around curiously. The void was very dark and had no gravity. The only features within the void that he could perceive were the bottom of the rug above him and large clumps of dust that drifted around him chaotically.

"Dam that boy!" Mr. Garroph's voice hissed from above the rug as Wendell heard footsteps cross the flagstone floor. "I was just going to kill him, Bergstrom, but this spell is so irritating I'm going to have to come up with a special torture for him as well. There's no point in shouting, I can't hear a word you're saying."

Wendell decided to risk peeking outside the rug for it sounded as if Mr. Garroph had his Master close at hand. Cautiously he lifted the heavy Bear head no more than an inch or two. Standing before it in the center of the room no more than an arm's length away was Mr. Garroph. He was focused upon a small bottle resting in the palm of his hand that appeared to be made from a large hollowed-out diamond. The bottle had another smaller diamond stopper and within it was the tiny animated form of Bergstrom, gesturing towards Mr. Garroph rapidly.

"Come now, Bergstrom, just because I've won doesn't mean you have to be rude," Mr. Garroph chuckled wickedly after watching his captive's silent gestures for a moment. "You've been looking over my shoulder like a hawk for so very long. Now tell me honestly, how does it feel?"

Wendell wracked his brain for how to get the bottle away from Mr. Garroph but he couldn't think of anything that wouldn't end in him being discovered and killed. Then the sound of a loud barking dog made the Wizard jump nearly half a foot and he dropped the bottle clumsily. Wendell didn't have time to think about it, he just reacted instinctively as the diamond bottle tumbled towards the ground.

With one hand Wendell beckoned the diamond bottle to his grasp while with the other he directed the bearskin rug to attack the startled Wizard. The bottle flew to him like an arrow as his cover leapt off and enveloped Mr. Garroph, biting and clawing like a very flat bear. Mr. Garroph let out a cry of alarm as Wendell jumped to his feet and ran. He didn't even slow down as he scooped up Squeaker from atop of the nightstand on his way to the door. Wendell plunged through the door just as Mr. Garroph began a dreadful sounding incantation that made the hairs on the back of his neck immediately stand on end. Squeaker let out a high pitched whistle of alarm as Wendell toppled through the portal and the door slammed shut behind him.

"Are you alright?" Wendell asked the Brownie as he picked himself up. Squeaker nodded but was trembling all over. "You were wonderful! Remind me to give you a special treat as soon as we get out of here."

The Brownie shook its hairy head and held up two fingers.

"Two treats?" Wendell asked with a smirk and the Brownie bobbed its nose in affirmation, "You got it."

Wendell set the Brownie on his shoulder then peered down at his Master within the diamond bottle. The old Wizard smiled up at him despite the beads of sweat on his brow and his heaviness of breath.

"Hold on a moment and I'll have you out of there," Wendell stated but his Master just shook his head as Wendell grasped the diamond stopper.

Wendell tried pulling and twisting the stopper but the diamond wouldn't budge in the slightest. Bergstrom waited patiently for Wendell to exhaust his efforts with a knowing smile then pointed out from the bottle once he had the boy's attention once more. Wendell looked where the old Wizard pointed and found that he was in his Master's bedchamber that he'd only ever glimpsed before.

Bergstrom's sleeping quarters were a simple affair much like Wendell's own. He had the same style wardrobe, desk, and bed but lacked the shelves upon which Wendell kept his spell components or the bearskin rug. There were a pair of fuzzy pink slippers resting beside the bed and a large old chest at its foot. Bergstrom was presently pointing at the desk.

Wendell walked over to the desk feeling a bit uncomfortable intruding within his Master's private sanctuary, even though he knew it was a silly notion as his Master was directing him to do so. Once there, his Master made a motion as if pulling open a drawer then pointed to the front of the desk where three drawers were set in a line.

"This one?" Wendell pointed at the top drawer but Bergstrom shook his head and held up two fingers.

Wendell opened the middle drawer and looked within. There was a tiny decorative brass chest, several crow quill pens, a stack of parchment, and a thick bundle of letters tied together with a scarlet lace. Wendell pointed to the chest hopefully but his Master shook his head. Wendell then pointed to the bundle of letters and Bergstrom nodded vigorously. Wendell picked the letters up and started to untie the lace but Bergstrom stopped him by raising his hand then made a gesture indicating he should put them in his pocket.

"You want me to take these, anything else?" Wendell asked as he put the letters into his belt pouch.

Bergstrom looked around the room for a moment scratching his grey beard then snapped his fingers and pointed towards the chest. Wendell went to the chest with the bottle resting in his palm and opened the heavy iron-studded wood lid and feeling thankful that it wasn't locked. Within the chest sat a pair of old boots with a hole worn in one toe, a large leather pouch with runes scorched across its surface, and a twisted oak wand. Wendell immediately reached for the wand but Bergstrom shook his head with a look of such utter dread that Wendell recoiled from it as if it were a snake. He then pointed at the pouch and Bergstrom nodded with a grin. Wendell picked up the pouch which felt empty then pointed at the boots. Bergstrom laughed and shook his head as if the notion was very amusing then motioned Wendell towards the door.

"We should we go now?" Wendell asked as he placed the pouch's strap over his shoulder so it hung at his waist. Bergstrom nodded and then made as if jogging in place, "I should run?"

Bergstrom nodded and gave him a wink.

"I'm going to put your bottle into my belt-pouch until we're out of the tower in case I have to run or cast spells," Wendell explained apologetically. Bergstrom sighed heavily then nodded in agreement, "You, too, Squeaker, I wouldn't want you to fall."

Squeaker made a whistle of acceptance and leaped into Wendell's palm so he could be tucked safely away. Once the Brownie and his Master were secure, Wendell went back to the door and hesitated before opening it. He took a deep breath then grasped and turned the knob. The door opened to his room again and a very angry looking Mr. Garroph amidst the scorched and shredded pieces of his rug.

"You!" The Wizard hissed like a curse just before Wendell slammed the door closed again.

Wendell took another deep breath and opened the door a second time. This time the door opened to the dining hall where the remains of Wendell's dinner still rested upon the table. He walked in and the door slammed shut behind him just as the door to the kitchen was opening. The Infernal Quick entered the huge chamber and shot him a wicked grin of sadistic pleasure as he brought his rapier forward with an audible swish. Wendell tried to go back to the door, but as he grasped the door knob a small dagger flew by his arm with only an inch to spare and wedged itself between the wood and stone locking it in place.

"Going somewhere, Boy?" Quick asked him as Wendell turned back around, "I think my Master wishes to have a word with you."

"Get out of my way or you'll be sorry!" Wendell threatened as he took a step forward menacingly. The Infernal laughed and cut the air before him with swift slashes of his blade.

"Think you got the guts to tangle with me do you? Why don't we see? I can spill them on the floor easy enough and you'll be alive long enough to answer all my Master's questions as pretty as you please," Quick chuckled confidently as he pranced forward with the clicking of his small hooves upon the flagstones.

Wendell didn't waste any more words on the evil little creature but gestured towards the nearest chair at the table and directed it to attack. Quick glace towards the piece of furniture and just barely managed to jump to the side before it trampled him under its carved bird-like taloned legs. The chair immediately reared up on its hind legs and began to kick at the Infernal as if it were a horse and Quick was forced to parry the blows with his rapier with a venomous curse. Wendell sent two more chairs after him then started towards the kitchen door.

"Oh no you don't!" Quick growled as he leapt on top of one of the chairs then sprang off to intercept him. The Infernal did a mid-air summersault before landing in front of Wendell with his cloak billowing behind. He laughed aloud as he slashed playfully at the boy's gut, forcing Wendell to withdraw.

As the chairs galloped toward the Infernal to defend their Master, Wendell swept off his hat and reached inside. Quick laughed with sadistic pleasure when Wendell drew a gleaming long sword from his hat, obviously delighted with the prospect of clashing steel. His black eyes boggled in his head when--instead of attacking with the blade--Wendell tossed it into the air with his own wicked little smirk. The long sword tumbled once in the air then stopped as if some invisible swordsman had grasped it. The blade cut a couple of slashes through the air as Quick had done moments before then darted towards the Infernal with deadly speed. Quick yelped with surprise as the long sword started thrusting at him with a deadly barrage and it was all the Infernal could do to parry the deadly assault.

Wendell watched as the sword and chairs forced Quick back into the corner then started towards the kitchen door once more. The Infernal yelped with pain as Wendell grasped the door knob and he saw the long sword had finally struck home and impaled the foul creature through the heart. Wendell felt the mildest sense of remorse as he watched the villain fall, but it was more regret that it had been necessary than anything approaching sorrow. As the Infernal crumpled to the floor it burst into a cloud of foul black smoke that rolled outward for a moment before dissipating and the long sword clattered lifelessly upon the floor.

Wendell opened the door and was relieved to find himself looking out the entrance of the tower. He ran down the steps and had started down the walkway when he heard Mr. Garroph's voice uttering an incantation behind him. Wendell was nearly burned as a wall of flames erupted in front of him and was forced to skid to a halt. He turned to see Mr. Garroph on the steps grinning down at him wickedly secure in the knowledge that he had won.

"Give me the book and I'll reward you with a quick death," the Wizard beckoned with his claw-like hand.

Wendell looked around desperately but the wall of flames had encircled him so that the only way out was through the Wizard. Knowing he was out of options, Wendell straightened and looked Mr. Garroph in the eye defiantly. Wendell knew that it would mean his death but his oath was still as strong and unyielding as the day he'd sworn it. Mr. Garroph raised his eyebrow in disbelief as Wendell defied him.

"No!" Wendell cried out and started to gather his power for one final desperate spell that would probably do nothing but annoy the Wizard further.

It wasn't necessary, however, for as Mr. Garroph opened his mouth to respond the ugly Gargoyle upon the eve above his head stepped off its perch and flattened the Wizard with a gruesome wet crash of breaking stone. Wendell winced with repulsion as the flames around him flickered down to nothing and went out. Hesitantly he walked towards the messy remains, he wanted to be certain Mr. Garroph was in fact dead. As he approached the upper half of the shattered Gargoyle turned its head towards him and grinned while extending a claw to give the bewildered boy a thumbs up. Seconds later the Gargoyle cracked and fell to pieces amongst the gory remains.

"Messy business, that," Bergstrom stated as he walked up beside Wendell and peered down at the remains, shaking his head in disgust, "Poor Churchill, always have missed his singing voice since today."

"How did you..?" Wendell started to ask as he looked at his Master in shock.

"Get out of the bottle? I haven't yet," Bergstrom smiled as he led the Apprentice away from the remains and down the walkway, "Don't bring me out though. There's no telling what would happen if I were to see my future self. The Universe doesn't react well to blatant paradox, but it can ignore a discrete one from time to time. Time to time, that's a good one," Bergstrom chuckled mirthfully tickled with his play on words.

"Then I guess you successfully made your clock?" Wendell asked, fighting the urge to look into his belt-pouch to see the present version of his Master.

"Yes and no. The clock was a complete failure but don't tell me that or I'll never learn from my mistakes. The pocket watch however works quite well, at least most of the time," Bergstrom chuckled as he held up a golden pocket watch suspended from a fine platinum chain. The timepiece's silver hands where ticking away in reverse over ruby inlays and its casing was covered with runes, "Took me nearly a decade and I still have a few bugs to sort out."

"So why have you come back? I mean, I'm glad to see you in all but isn't this a bit dangerous?" Wendell asked awkwardly as they started down the hill towards the village.

"Well I need to seal both towers, but I thought it wouldn't hurt to visit you for a moment or two. It's hard to keep up one's friendships when one is constantly moving back and forth through time. I must say it's good to see you so young again, Wendell. It's been an age since you were the boy you are now. It's always bothered me you were forced to grow up so fast on account of me," The old Wizard admitted remorsefully.

"Why would you need to seal your tower? Aren't we going to continue living there?" Wendell asked wishing that his Master wouldn't keep referring to his future in the past tense, it was giving him a head-ache.

"I will, but not for awhile. We can't have curious villagers poking about things that are better left undisturbed by the ignorant. Now I'm not certain how much of this I should tell you, but as I remember it was very bothersome and frustrating trying to explain things to you from inside that horrible bottle. I'm going to set you on the course and you can just play along and seem very clever when its my present self's turn, alright?" Bergstrom winked at him with a mischievous smirk, "You don't possess the power yet to open that bottle so I directed you to those letters to lead you to certain old friends of mine who may. You're going to have to leave your peaceful little village behind for awhile and venture out into the harsh world beyond to seek them out. It isn't going to be easy but obviously you're eventually successful. Any questions?"

"If I'm not going to return to the tower then where am I going to live?" Wendell asked worriedly as he started to rub his temple.

"Well you and Mary don't need some old man about all the time after your married so you move over there," Bergstrom pointed towards Mr. Garroph's tower, "After you've cleaned it out a bit your family finds it quite comfortable."

"When I had to warn Mary Mr. Garroph had threatened her I hurt myself contacting her with my mind. Is it serious?" Wendell asked still feeling the lingering pain.

"Unfortunately you have done permanent damage but it isn't very serious. You weren't ready to use telepathy for one thing and to compound the problem you forced your thoughts through the Intellectual Fortress barrier you cast to block out Mr. Garroph. As a result you're often going to get migraines and the use of that power will always be less than pleasant," Bergstrom patted his shoulder reassuringly as they entered the village, "Anything else before I go?"

"Just one more thing. What's this pouch for?" Wendell held up the pouch that was covered in runes.

"It's a Pouch of Needful Things. It uses the same basic principles you use when you conjure something from you're hat only the pouch will always give you something useful to the problem at hand. It was one of my very first creations and proved very useful when I was traveling abroad. Conjuring has the draw back of being unpredictable whereas the pouch may not always give you what you expect, it will always give you something you need. Use it sparingly though, for to be effective it requires more magic to function and you wouldn't want it to be drained when your need is great," Bergstrom smiled and stopped as they reached the deserted village square. He looked Wendell up and down as if trying to memorize his features as he was, then embraced the boy warmly, "Now I have to go if I'm going to accomplish what I came here to do before my time is up. Take care, Wendell, and give my best to Mary. She was rather cross with me the last time we spoke because I meddled with one of her potions."

"Wait a minute, Mary can't do magic!" Wendell blinked, startled in disbelief.

"Not yet she can't," Bergstrom winked mischievously as he was disappearing from view.

27

"Oh, Wendell, are you alright?" Mary pounced upon Wendell as soon as he opened the Tailor shop's door.

"Yes, I'm fine," Wendell lied as he hugged her tightly.

Wendell was surprised to find how many people were squeezed into the crowded shop all looking towards him expectantly: Fredric, Wendy, Mr. and Mrs. Miller, Wendell's father, his elder brothers George and Mathew, and their wives Peggy and Donna. The only people missing of his immediate family were Wendell's eldest brother Vernon and his mother. His father was the next to embrace Wendell almost before Mary had released him.

"Where's Bergstrom? Did he teach Mr. Garroph a lesson?" the Senior Glasswright asked, squeezing Wendell's shoulders. Even though it had only been a few days since Wendell had seen the man he couldn't help but notice how much grayer his father looked since Sunday.

"Not exactly, no," Wendell sighed wishing that his headache would go away. "Can I sit down for a moment? I'm very tired and sore."

"Of course, Son. Do you have another stool around here, Fredric?" Mr. Glasswright inquired to his son-in-law.

"I'm afraid Wendy is using the only one. Sorry." Fredric apologized uncomfortably.

"The floor will be just fine," Wendell stated as he moved into the room and promptly collapsed in the first open spot on the floor that he came to.

"So what's going on Wendell? Don't keep us in suspense!" Mr. Miller inquired as he squatted down beside them, "Mary told us that Mr.Garroph threatened her life and we had to flee because of it."

"Mr. Garroph is dead," Wendell stated evenly as he opened his belt pouch, "He won't threaten anyone ever again."

"Wendell, you didn't?" Mary gasped putting a hand to her mouth.

"No I didn't. Not that I wouldn't have if I could. The Tower's Gargoyle dropped upon his head just as he was about to kill me," Wendell carefully fished out Squeaker and handed him to Mary.

"What is that?" George asked curiously as he gazed at the Brownie.

"You can see it?" Wendell asked with mild amusement, "How about you, Mathew?"

"Sort of, it's pretty hazy though," Mathew squinted at the Brownie as if he were trying to bore a hole through it with his gaze.

"This is Squeaker, my Brownie," Wendell introduced the little creature. Squeaker immediately gave him an indignant whistle and shook its head, "I'm sorry. This is Squeaker, and I'm its Human."

Those that could see the Brownie laughed as it nodded in agreement. Wendell conjured a piece of candy from his pocket for Squeaker, but it shook its head again and gave him another whistle as it held up two fingers.

"Sorry, I forgot!" Wendell admitted as he conjured another piece for his greedy little friend. Then he sighed heavily as he withdrew the diamond bottle containing Bergstrom.

"Oh no, what happened?" Mary asked as she snatched the bottle away and held it up to eye level so she could gawk at the Wizard properly. When she was done jarring him from one side of the bottle to the other Bergstrom waved at her with a weary smile.

"Please be careful Mary," Wendell winced as she tilted the bottle for a better view, "Mr. Garroph trapped him in there somehow and I don't have the power to release him."

"That's horrible. What are you going to do?" Wendy asked as everyone gathered around to gawk at the tiny imprisoned Wizard.

"I think he directed me to fetch these letters so they could lead me to someone who can free him," Wendell told them as he drew the bundle of letters from his pouch while carefully avoiding Bergstrom's suspicious gaze. Wendell released a heavy sigh, "I think I'm going to have to leave the village for awhile."

"How long do you think you'll be gone, Son?" Mr. Glasswright asked after a few moments of awkward silence.

"I don't know. It may take awhile," Wendell paused thumbing through the letters and look at Mary. Surprisingly Mary seemed not concerned in the least as she continued to scrutinize Bergstrom as if he was a fascinating new pet. Wendell licked his lips for a moment then pressed on with his thoughts fearful of the temper tantrum he expected from his lover, "Unfortunately, it means we may have to postpone the wedding indefinitely."

"That's alright. We can get married as soon as we get back!" Mary told him as she got a little cat-like smirk and gleefully gave the bottle a little bit of a shake.

"Give me that!" Wendell snatched the bottle back with a reproachful glare, "You can't come; it would be far too dangerous."

Mary raised an eyebrow at him with a look that said she loved him but he was about to loose yet another argument.

"He's right Mary. You're better off staying here where it's safe," Mr. Miller jumped to Wendell's aid.

"Why is it you men always think us women-folk need to be sheltered from the world? On any given day I have twice as much common sense as Wendell and could easily take him in a fight yet for some strange reason you seem to think its me whom needs protecting. Now I could waste the rest of the evening arguing with you at the end of which I'll win, or you can accept it now and we can start making useful plans that may be a bit more productive. Which is it going to be?" Mary asked confidently and after a moment Squeaker released a squeaky chuckle from where it rested on her lap.

"You're too young to leave home. Tell her, Margaret," Mr. Miller looked to his wife for support. Mrs. Miller's face was as stern as stone as she turned from her husband to Mary.

"Would you like me to pack you some winter clothing as well dear? Its summer now but I wouldn't want you to get caught unprepared," Mrs. Miller asked, ignoring her husband's look of shock completely.

"Margaret?" Mr. Miller almost whined in disbelief.

"I think our summer clothing will be fine. Wendell can conjure warmer clothing should it be needed, but we probably should have a couple thick blankets for at night," Mary answered her thoughtfully.

"Well when your father is done losing this argument, come back to the house and I'll have everything ready for your trip," Mrs. Miller squeezed her daughter's hand before she stood up and made her way to the door.

"Margaret, you shouldn't be walking alone at night," Mr. Miller called after her, causing the middle aged woman to pause.

"Oh don't worry, if you're afraid I'm certain Mary will hold your hand on the way home," Mrs. Miller smiled sweetly at her husband before disappearing out the door. Mr. Miller looked down at his daughter who gave him exactly the same sweet smile his wife had a moment ago. The dairy farmer's shoulders slumped in defeat after a moment then he rushed out after his wife without another word.

"One down, who's next?" Mary turned her smile on Wendell and raised her eyebrow, daring him to open his mouth.

"You really are a terror, you know?" Wendell sighed as he looked down at the letters in his hand.

"I love you, too!" she threw her arms around his neck and gave him a warm kiss on the cheek.

Wendell had the horrible suspicion that his life was going to be a long series of such defeats until the day he died and it was only going to get worse when Mary learned magic. He tried to ignore her smug little smile as he began separating the letters in front of him. Despite the number of the correspondences, there appeared to be only three people responsible for the letters: a Mr. Giles of Lavittia, a Mr. Blackwood of Slumberdale, and a Miss Hartford of Mucklemire Swamp. Of these places Wendell had only ever heard of Lavittia, but then he'd be the first to admit that his knowledge of the world beyond the valley was severely limited. Lavittia was nearly 120 miles to the north or so the Merchants who occasionally stopped in the valley claimed.

"Master, I don't know these places. Which is the closest?" Wendell asked as he set the bottle before the letters on the floor. Bergstrom pointed to the stack from Miss Hartford of Mucklemire Swamp, "Is she powerful enough to free you?"

Bergstrom shrugged his shoulders after scratching his beard thoughtfully for a moment.

"Of these people who is the most likely to be able to free you?" Mary asked after Wendell scowled with frustration. Again Bergstrom scratched his beard thoughtfully then pointed to the pile from Mr. Giles of Lavittia. Mary chewed her lip for a moment then asked another question, "Lavittia is in the north, are these other places as well?"

Bergstrom grinned up at Mary then pointed at the letters from Miss Hartford and nodded. Then he pointed to the letters from Mr. Blackwood and shook his head. He looked around for a moment then pointed to the east towards Fredric and Wendy's back rooms.

"I guess we're headed north," Mary stated thoughtfully.

"If you wait a few weeks the mid-summer caravans will arrive. I'm sure you could barter passage on one of their wagons," George put in as he leaned over Bergstrom's bottle thoughtfully, "Why do you think he can hear us but we can't hear him?"

"If his voice could carry through the diamond then so could his spells. As to why he can hear us I'd say that Mr. Garroph likely enchanted it that way just so he could gloat over my Master," Wendell explained as he looked down at the elder Wizard, "Better questions would be how does he get air and will he need food and water?"

Bergstrom shook his head and then pulled a roasted chicken wing from his pocket. He took a bite of it then waved his other hand over it to transform it into a tankard of ale. The old Wizard raised the tankard to their health then took a long pull, causing golden ale to leak into his beard. When he had finished he wiped his mouth on his sleeve then waved his hand over the tankard again to cause it to vanish. Wendy and Peggy both clapped at his little display and Bergstrom gave them both a theatrical bow which caused his acorn shaped hat to fall off his head. As the Wizard's hat hit the floor of his diamond prison a live dove took flight from its depths and everyone laughed as Bergstrom tried to run around and catch it using his hat like a net.

"Something tells me he's not going to starve," Mr.Glasswright chuckled as he shook his head.

"I don't think we can wait for the caravan. Master shouldn't have to stay in there any longer than he has to. We'll set out tomorrow and if the caravan catches up to us so be it," Wendell decided as he watched his Master's antics with concern. No matter how cheerful the old Wizard seemed Wendell knew captivity was taking its toll upon his soul.

After a moment of silence, Squeaker released a strange chirp and leapt down from Mary's lap. The Brownie's call was answered a moment latter by the extremely fury Brownie that lived in the Tailor's shop who was standing at the far side of the hallway. Wendell and the others that could watched as the Brownies met in the center of the hall. They immediately clasped each others hands palm to palm and rubbed their oversized noses together. After a few moments of this strange greeting they began to chirp, whistle, and squeak to one another rapidly as the furry Brownie led Squeaker into the back rooms and out of sight. Wendell was pleased that Squeaker had found a friend and wondered why he hadn't thought to introduce the two sooner.

"Strange little buggers," George shook his head with amusement.

"So why are you all here?" Wendell asked as he looked at his father and brothers curiously. Rarely did this many of the family gather without reason. George looked at their father then Wendy before dropping his eyes to the floor. Mathew got an equally uncomfortable look and couldn't meet Wendell's gaze. After a moment Peggy came up behind him and clasped his hand with a gentle squeeze of reassurance. Wendell had a sinking feeling when Mary reached over and took his hand. "What's happened?"

"You're mother declared that you were officially dead to her and forbid us to speak your name or associate with you," Mr. Glasswright stated quietly as he gazed evenly at Wendell, "So I told her to pack her bags and get out of my house. She's gone to live with Vernon and his wife, and from the way he talks I'd say it's a safe bet that you can't expect to ever be welcome in his home. After they left we were discussing how best to explain this all to you when Mary showed up dragging her parents behind her saying Mr. Garroph was up to no good and you had hurt yourself to warn her. Me, your brothers, and Fredric were about to head up the hill when you walked in looking a bit worse for wear but alive and kicking as it were."

"I'm so sorry, Father. You must believe I never wanted any of this to happen!" Wendell sniffled as tears trickled down from his eyes.

"You don't have anything to be sorry for, Son. Maggie isn't the same woman I married and I've had all I can take of the new one. Its been tearing me up for some time as I tried to love what she's become but now that she's gone I'm starting to feel better already. You're a good boy and that's all I've ever wanted you to be. It's a shame that she can't see that but its about time we all put that out of our minds and start looking to a brighter future," Mr. Glasswright stated as he looked around the room at his children and their spouses until at last his gaze fell upon Mary, "Fredric showed me the gown he's making and I think you're going to make the prettiest bride this old valley has ever seen. I'm looking forward to it and the grandchildren that will come after."

Mary--for once--was at a complete loss under the elder Glasswright's gaze and she finally had to lower her eyes bashfully as her cheeks flushed bright red. Mr. Glasswright seemed amused by this response and released a mirthful chuckle before he started talking to them seriously once more.

"Now you two have to be careful as you're traveling abroad. Most folks in communities like this are honest enough but the more people there are the more scoundrels get thrown into the mix who love to take advantage of young folk like you. Be wary and vigilant. Whenever possible let people talk and you listen carefully. Most bad folk will let slip their bad intentions long before they get around to them. If you're paying attention chances are they'll not catch you unawares. Be especially wary of those who offer to buy you drinks for their usually trying to cloud your judgment so they can get their way," Mr. Glasswright warned them wisely, "You free Mr. Weatherbee and head strait back home. Don't get bewitched by foreign wonders along the road. True happiness comes from a simple life surrounded by family that loves you. The rest is just illusion no different than one of your wizardly tricks to amuse and distract the simple minded. Now come here both of you and give me a hug so I can go home and go to bed."

"You sound as if you once did a fair bit of traveling yourself, Father," George commented as Wendell and Mary gave the old Glasswright love.

"Well you don't see any Glassblowers around here to learn my trade from do you?" Mr. Glasswright asked as he stood up with a smile and headed for the door, "It took me a half-dozen and one years to realize that there wasn't any place better than the quiet little valley I started from. Once I did I came home built my house and never had the desire to leave again."

They all thought about what the senior Glasswright had said for a few minutes after his departure then they began saying their farewells one couple at a time, until Wendell and Mary were the last to leave. Fredric and Wendy agreed to take care of Squeaker while they were gone as they departed into the bright summer night. Wendell and Mary walked slowly, enjoying one another's company as they gazed up at the stars holding hands. No words were spoken and none were needed. Both knew they had to enjoy this short time they had left for tomorrow everything would change.

28

As if an ill omen of things to come, it was raining when Wendell and Mary set out the next morning. It was the steady rain that usually comes only in spring and has the endurance to last for hours. Wet and weary they trudge up the muddy north road that led out of the valley under the assault of this steady downpour and by the time the terrain began to level off that afternoon their clothing and packs were soaked to the bone and both were completely miserable.

"I've had enough of this!" Wendell declared stopping amongst a thicket of trees that surrounded the road, "I'm soaked, hungry, and am simply done for today."

"Alright, why don't you start a fire while I set up something to sleep under?" Mary suggested with the cool tone of one who's on the edge loosing control of their anger.

"Fine!" Wendell growled as he dropped the heavy pack he was carrying and marched into the trees to gather wood.

Neither Wendell nor Mary was angry at the other. Their foul moods were simply the byproduct of being cold, wet, and having to trudge away from the home that neither wanted to leave. They both realized this of course and the time apart did help a little, but what helped more was that the rain stopped a few minutes later.

When Wendell returned with an arm load of branches and twice as many marching dutifully behind in a long single file line, Mary had constructed a crude lean-to and had her clothes hung up to dry. Whatever lingering resentments the day had seeded within Wendell were quickly forgotten as he looked upon what lily white skin Mary had allowed to protrude out from under the blanket she was wrapped in. He was painfully conscious of the fact of how beautiful she was and how far they were from the village and its laws.

"Wendell, you're staring," Mary smirked as he piled wood in the shallow pit he'd dug.

"I'm sorry," Wendell stated unconvincingly--even to himself--as he cast his gaze downward and realized that he'd put far too much wood on the pile.

"Liar!" Mary accused with a mischievous giggle.

They were both quiet until Wendell had made the wood pile a more manageable size then ignited it with an angry glare. Then Mary broke the silence with a suggestion that both excited and terrified Wendell at the same time, "You should hang up your clothes and come sit beside me," Mary told him without a trace of humor as she brushed her hair.

Wendell's heart skipped a beat within his chest and for a long moment he just stood frozen staring at her. Mary stared back as if the suggestion was the most perfectly normal thing in the world as she continued to detangle her long blond mop with long even strokes. When it became clear that Wendell wasn't going to comply without further encouragement, Mary paused her brushing and raised an eyebrow at him.

"Well?" She asked expectantly.

"I, I'm not certain we should," Wendell found himself rather reluctantly saying.

"It's alright, Wendell. There's no one around for miles, the only one who will see you is me," Mary sighed as if he was being rather silly.

"Anyone but you I wouldn't mind as much," Wendell admitted with a bashful blush that made Mary giggle.

"We're going to be married soon. I'm pretty sure that means we're going to see one another's naked bodies at some point. Why not now?" Mary reasoned as she began to brush her hair again.

"I don't think it would be proper," Wendell admitted even though a part of him really wanted to comply.

"Would it be more proper for you to get sick during the night because you slept in soaked robes?" Mary raised her eyebrow again daring him to try and argue her logic.

"Probably!" Wendell answered stubbornly.

"Wendell, come here," Mary commanded as she set her brush down upon her pack, secured her blanket about her, and stood up.

Despite the many magical powers Wendell had mastered, the power to defy Mary's will had always eluded him. Occasionally he tried and sometimes he could resist, but in the end he'd always submitted to her commands. This time he didn't struggle very hard, for the truth of the matter was he was very cold for his robes were sopping wet. Wendell came to her reluctantly and stood before her shivering.

"Put up you're arms," she commanded as she tucked the edge of her blanket tightly beside her breast. Wendell sighed and started to complain, but her eyes narrowed into a frightening glare so he bit his tongue and raised his arms. Mary pulled his robes over his head laying bare all that he was. She glanced at him with a smirk of approval then began to ring out his robes of the excess water, "Now take off your boots and stockings, wrap yourself in the other blanket, and then set Bergstrom beside the fire. I'm sure he's tired of seeing nothing but the inside of your pouch all day."

Wendell complied with a minimal amount of grumbling for he really did feel much better once he was wrapped up in the only slightly damp blanket rather than the soaked robes. After he'd put the grateful elder Wizard's bottle on a rock so he and his dove companion could enjoy the fire, Wendell returned to the lean-to and sat down beside his love. Mary immediately leaned against him for warmth with a smug little smile.

"Now do you see? If I hadn't come along you would have caught your death of cold the very first night out," Mary rubbed it in with a tired little yawn.

Wendell thought about telling her that if she hadn't been there he wouldn't have been the least bit shy about stripping off his wet clothes, but he was too weary to start another argument and Mary did feel wonderful pressed up against him. They soon fell asleep within each others arms and were lost in pleasant dreams of being together.

29

The next two days passed slowly as Wendell and Mary continued north upon the wagon-worn road. The weather returned to the summer norm, making their walk more pleasant save for blisters as they passed through rolling wood covered hills. They were in the wilds that separated the old northern communities from the younger southern ones. They saw no other travelers as they walked until mid-afternoon upon the third day of their trek, when they met a Tinker headed south.

This Tinker turned out to be a friendly old soul who was more than happy to chat about the lands ahead. From him Wendell and Mary learned that two more days ahead they would reach the village of Willowdale, which was the first of the northern settlements. Just beyond this community, the road would fork to the northeast and to the northwest. Both roads eventually led to Lavittia, but the Tinker swore that the northwestern was the safer of the two. The northeastern road skirted Mucklemire Swamp about two miles beyond the fork. The Tinker confessed to never hearing of a Miss Hartford dwelling in the swamp, but many of the Willowdale locals often spoke of the Mucklemire Witch with cautious respect or outright dread.

When the Tinker had continued on his way, Wendell removed Bergstrom from his pouch and asked if Miss Hartford was in fact the Mucklemire Witch. Bergstrom nodded his head to indicate that she was but it was clear from his glare that he did not care for that title in the least. They had lunch beside the road under the shade of a tall pine, then packed up their gear and continued on.

The next day the woods gradually thickened into a dark and dense forest which cast the road into perpetual gloom. As the two walked through this shadowy wilderness, they heard many strange creatures the likes of which they had never encountered before. One terrible growl frightened Mary so badly that she clutched Wendell's arm and wouldn't let go until he stated that she was cutting off his blood flow with her tight little grip. After that she eased up, but would not release him as she continually scanned the trees distrustfully.

That night was terrible and neither Wendell nor Mary got much sleep as they listed to the beasts of this untamed forest huddled beside the fire. It was a horrible feeling of exposed nakedness that crept into their hearts and filled them with dread. In the darkness beyond the fires light, a thousand phantoms of their imaginations watched and waited for the two of them to fall asleep or the fire to burn out. Needless to say, they did not allow either of these things to happen and they paid a heavy price for it the next day.

Like listless zombies, they trudged through the forest the next day making slow progress but determined to continue on to happier places. They didn't reach the end of the forest by nightfall, but by then were far too tired to care whether they were eaten in the night. They slept within one another's arms oblivious to the sounds that had so frightened them the night before and woke up stiff but well rested. By mid-morning the forest thinned again until ending altogether and Wendell and Mary saw a thriving village clustered around a small river in the fields beyond.

Willowdale was not unlike their own little village though it was nearly twice its size. The buildings tended to be designed more like log cabins with high stone foundations, but Wendell and Mary found this to be a small cosmetic difference of little note. The people of Willowdale were friendly as they shopped in the market square to replenish their supplies and they were able to hear news of ill tidings from the north.

The market was a buzz with rumors of two noble Lords whose petty feud had broken out into outright war. Many warned Wendell and Mary to be very wary if they were headed through the lands just south of Lavittia for although the Lord's forces were unlikely to bother them, many highwaymen were taking advantage of their distraction as the two forces clashed. As they left the village they discussed what they had heard and both Wendell and Mary hoped that Miss Hartford could free Bergstrom so the north could be avoided. They had been so preoccupied with the gossip that it wasn't until they reached the fork in the road that the two realized they'd forgotten to ask for directions to where the swamp Witch dwelt.

True to the Tinker's word, the land soon began to descend into a wetland marsh as Wendell and Mary walked the northeastern road. After another mile, a thick damp mist obscured the land ahead turning it into a haunting place of shadowy trees amidst the stagnant vapors. The smell of mildew and moss was the first indication that they were nearing the swamp then suddenly the land beyond the east side of the road was gone replaced by still and inky black water.

Wendell and Mary slowed their pace as they scanned the swamp for some hint of the Witch's dwelling, but all they spied was the occasional swirl of something moving beneath the water and some very large frogs. The two began to get increasingly frustrated as they continued and then they came to an old wooden mailbox that was pitted and slowly being overtaken by stringy yellow peat moss sticking out of the swamp water just beside the road.

"This must be the place," Wendell stated as he tried unsuccessfully to penetrate the fog with his gaze.

"I'm not going into the water," Mary stated with finality as she watched a large snake with black, white, and orange stripes swim by.

Wendell didn't blame her apprehension as he spotted the snake she was watching. He once again wished he'd been able to master flying so he could cross the water, but he'd not practiced the art since the day he'd hung his fairy lure in their old oak tree. What they needed now was a boat he thought and then he remembered the Pouch of Needful Things. Wendell didn't know quite what to expect when he reach into the pouch and felt something hard, but he was completely unprepared to draw out the front end of a Canoe. Mary's eyes boggled in her beautiful head as Wendell struggled to pull the Canoe out of the pouch a half foot at a time. The mouth of the pouch only seemed to widen minutely, but the eight foot boat bulged through seamlessly anyway without resistance. Wendell heaved the wooden watercraft into the swamp then reached into the pouch again and was delighted to find the handle of a paddle. He delved into the pouch a third time hoping for a second but apparently the pouch's magic was drained for all he found was the leathery bottom.

"That was very bazaar," Mary told him as Wendell steadied the Canoe so she could climb in.

"It surprised me a bit, too," Wendell admitted as he climbed in behind her and pushed them off with the paddle, "I was told the pouch would produce needful things but not what the limitations of those things may be. I always figured the things I conjured would be limited to what could fit through the openings of my hat or pockets. It may be worthwhile to test the limits of such conjuring further."

They were silent as Wendell paddled them deeper into the churning mists, until no land was visible around them only trees that looked like the knotted skeletons of Giants as they loomed up out the swamp. Soon the two heard a series of splashes that seemed to be drawing nearer and Wendell halted his paddling so they could listen. After a few moments, they saw this splashing was caused by figure walking quickly across the water at an angle that would bring them close to the two in the canoe.

It was hard to tell any details about the person as he or she continued their hurried pace across the water's surface, for they were completely covered in a cloak that continually seeped mist from its pale grey fabric all around them. In the person's hand before them was held a small square wooden cage that contained something shadowy and obviously alive. The figure turned its shadow-cloaked hood towards them for a moment, then quickened their pace to a hurried sprint. The figure was almost out of sight completely before Wendell thought to call to them.

"Miss Hartford?" Wendell called out hopefully.

"Bugger off! I don't want any!" the figure called back in a decidedly feminine voice that rasped with age and then she was gone.

"Well that went well," Mary stated sarcastically after a moment.

"Maybe we should just head on to Lavittia," Wendell stated thoughtfully.

"Don't be silly, Wendell. We're here now and she obviously lives close by. Let's keep going," Mary told him as she clutched her brown linen cloak around her to ward off the fog's chill.

"Alright, but if she turns us into frogs for disturbing her remember that it was your idea," Wendell grinned at her wearily.

"She probably just thought we were trying to sell her something," Mary decided aloud as Wendell paddled in the direction the woman had previously fled.

"Because traveling salesmen often venture into the middle of eerie mist-filled swamps with their own Canoes to make a few extra coins, right?" Wendell asked mockingly with a chuckle.

Mary didn't answer him as Wendell continued to paddle on. Within a few more minutes, they came to a small island of thick wild grass whose sole features were a large dead-looking oak that had many herbs hanging from its limbs to dry by leather twine and a small round thatch hut. They disembarked from the canoe and Wendell pulled it ashore, then they stood looking at the Witch's dwelling with apprehension.

"I guess you better knock on the door," Mary stated as she pushed him forward.

"Right," Wendell shot her a look that seemed to say 'Why me?' but didn't move to actually do so.

"Well go on," Mary pushed him forward more insistently.

"Fine," Wendell stated with something far less than enthusiasm as he stepped up to the door and started to knock. Before his fist touched the poorly nailed wood, the door opened abruptly to reveal the scowling Mucklemire Swamp Witch.

The Witch wasn't a bent warty old hag whose hideous visage could crack mirrors and wither plants. She was in fact an attractive old woman despite her obvious displeasure at seeing Wendell and Mary at her doorstep. She was dressed in a plain tan gown that was still damp at the bottom with swamp water. She'd taken off the cloak that bled fog but had replaced it with a thick brown shawl bundled around her shoulders. Her features hinted that she had once been a great beauty as her sharp blue eyes quickly scanned them from behind thin rectangular lenses that perched on the top of her small nose. She had fine long black hair that hung limply around her head with only the slightest hint of a wave.

"Miss Hart..." Wendell began with his fist still poised in the air to knock but the Witch cut him off completely.

"Oh, its you again. Well I'm very busy at the moment so come in and be quiet. I'll be with you as soon as I can," then she disappeared into the gloom of the hut leaving the door wide open behind her.

Wendell looked back at Mary but his lover simply shrugged. He then cautiously entered the hut with her clinging behind him as if Wendell might disappear if she didn't hold on tight.

Not surprising to Wendell, the Witch's hut was far larger on the inside than the out. The door opened to a great domed chamber nearly 50 feet wide that appeared surprisingly neat in contradiction to the muddy swamp outside. One side of the hut had a small bed with a chest at its foot that looked rather lonely against the barren wall. The other side of the hut had shelves covering most of the walls containing all manner of jars, bottles, tins, baskets, cages, vials, and many other containers with strange and often grotesque ingredients for witchcraft. Two fire pits blazed before the shelves over which hung large iron cauldrons suspended by chains. One of these cauldrons was producing a steady stream of vile green smoke that fell heavily around it to accumulate on the floor. The other cauldron was covered with a lid that rattled and seeped small wisps of steam. The Witch danced between the two stirring the covered one quickly before replacing the lid with a snap before anything but steam could be revealed and tossing more foul ingredients into the other seemingly on whim.

Wendell approached then stopped and waited patiently just far enough to be certain he was out of the way. Mary, however, soon grew bored and began examining the foul things that had been accumulated upon the Witch's shelves. The Witch paid them no mind whatsoever and seemed oblivious to their presence as she continued her strange dance between the cauldrons. That is until she stopped and started mumbling to herself as if deep in some complex thought.

"Essence of night, that may do it," The Witch muttered after mumbling for a few moments.

"Would this do?" Mary asked as she held up a jar full of dried bat wings toward the Witch.

The Witch immediately shot her a curious look as if suddenly seeing Mary for the first time. After a moment she beckoned the girl forward, removed a bat wing, and tossed it into the cauldron curiously. The cauldron immediately belched forth a large puff of red smoke before returning to its former green appearance. This reaction seemed to please the Witch and she smiled at Mary sweetly.

"Thank you, Dear. Now fetch me the essence of earth and wisdom," the Witch directed as she closed the lid on the jar of bat wings.

The Witch watched Mary like a hawk as the girl put the jar back where she'd found it then began to search the shelves carefully. The first ingredient Mary found almost immediately in the form of a rather large jar of worms amidst some loose soil. The second ingredient took her far longer but after several minutes of searching she found a small vial containing several gray hairs.

"Very good!" The Witch chuckled as she threw a few of each into the cauldron. This time the smoke turned a golden yellow and stayed that way. The Witch then took the jar and vial from Mary and thrust her large wooden spoon into her hands, "Keep stirring that until it's done."

"How will I know when it's done?" Mary asked as she began to stir the bubbling mixture. The Witch just released a wild cackle of amusement and shrugged before she returned the worms and gray hairs to the shelves. She then marched over to Wendell and looked him up and down again with a scowl of distaste.

"Who are you and what do you want?" the Witch blurted out after she was finished with her examination.

"My name is Wendell Glasswright and that's Mary Miller, Miss Hartford, and we have a problem," Wendell introduced himself as he began to dig his Master out of his pouch. He stopped however as the Witch burst out into a cackle that made him wince with dread.

"You don't say. Imagine the very idea someone would come to see the Mucklemire Swamp Witch without having a problem. The seas would boil and the moon would turn as blood," the Witch cackled on until tears were coming out of her eyes. This continued for several moments before the Witch regained control of her mad humor then she dried her eyes and looked at him with a smirk, "Alright then, hit me with you're best shot, ok?"

Wendell didn't bother trying to explain, he just drew forth the diamond bottle and presented his Master to the Witch. The Witch froze loosing all trace of her chaotic mirth. She carefully took the bottle from Wendell's hand and readjusted her lenses so she could better see the Wizard.

"Bergstrom?" the Witch asked uncertainly. The old Wizard waved then blew her a kiss, "Scott did this, didn't he? I told you to just kill him, but no, you have to give everyone the benefit of the doubt. Bet you wished you'd listened to me now, don't you? Wait until I get a hold of him. I'll have his gizzard to use as my bootlaces. By the time I'm through he'll long for what you did to his Master as a reprieve from my wrath!"

"Mr. Garroph is dead," Wendell put in meekly, hesitant to interrupt the Witch's rant. She narrowed her eyes and glared at him.

"How long? There may be still time to get some justice," The Witch growled frighteningly.

Before Wendell could answer, Bergstrom caught her attention again by banging on the inside of his prison. The old Wizard shook his head and fixed her with a reproachful glare. The Witch's shoulders sagged and she sniffed noisily as a tear rolled down her cheek.

"I'm sorry, Bergstrom. I know I promised not to dabble with any more Necromancy but seeing you like this just makes me so angry. I hope Scott's death was extremely unpleasant to say the very least," she apologized and Bergstrom's eyes softened on her.

"The tower's Gargoyle jumped on his head and crushed him," Wendell explained quietly.

"Good for Churchill. I always liked that hunk of stone. He has such a beautiful singing voice," the Witch sighed and wiped her eyes with the corner of her shawl. She then gazed at Wendell again thoughtfully, "So this is the Apprentice I keep hearing so much about. You could have said something earlier," she shook a finger at Wendell as if he'd just been caught with a hand in the cookie jar.

"I did try!" Wendell tried to defend himself.

"No matter, what's done is done," the Witch dismissed his attempt with a shake of her head. She then extended her hand to him, "I'm Miss Aggie Hartford, but you may call me Aggie. Thank you for bringing Bergstrom to me. It's going to take some thought, but I'm sure I can break this spell."

"Thank you Miss Hartford, I mean Aggie. It means a lot to me," Wendell took her hand.

"Miss Hartford! I think it's done!" Mary interrupted them. Wendell gasped when he looked over to see Mary bathed in harsh orange light that was radiating from the caldron causing her hair to stand straight up behind her. Aggie just cackled and told her to keep on stirring.

30

"Come here, Mary," Aggie beckoned Mary to the cauldron she'd just emptied with a vanishing spell.

It was Wendell and Mary's third day at the Witch's hut and she'd just sent him to Willowdale to buy some groceries. At least that had been the old Witch's excuse. The truth of the matter was she wanted some time alone with the fair-haired girl who she'd known for a very short time, but already felt a special kinship toward. As Mary drew close to the cauldron, Aggie pointed into it and raised an eyebrow.

"What do you see there Mary?" Aggie asked. Mary leaned over the cauldron chewing her lip nervously.

"Nothing, just blackness," Mary answered quietly, feeling as if she'd fail some important test but didn't wish to lie to the old woman.

"Look closer. Do you wish to know what I see?" Aggie asked gently with a smile.

"Yes," Mary answered in a barely audible whisper as she stared into the cauldron harder.

"I see infinite possibilities," the Witch leaned over and whispered in her ear. She then went over to her shelves, but instead of picking out some ingredient she merely swept her hand across the top shelf to gather dust then returned. Aggie blew gently at an angle as she dropped the dust in. Instead of falling to the bottom of the empty cauldron as it should have the dust swirled in a spiraling pattern just below the rim as if it had been caught upon the surface of invisible water. "There's a whole Universe of possibilities in the space you see before you. Far more than any one person could explore even if they live a hundred normal lifetimes."

Aggie glared at the wood below the cauldron and it instantly ignited. She noticed Bergstrom was giving her a curious look from within the diamond bottle that rested on a nearby stool and the Witch gave him a mischievous wink before she moved behind the enthralled girl. The swirl of dust within the cauldron began to change as the cauldron quickly heated up taking on brilliant hews of color that danced across the girl's enthralled face.

"You love Wendell very much, that's plain to see. Soon you will marry, settle down, have children, and what then? Will you live happily giving all you are to your family as you slowly wither year after year? Will you be content to watch your husband's powers grow while you become ever weaker? Will Wendell be satisfied to watch you wither away while the magic slows his ageing down to a barely perceptible crawl? Look upon Bergstrom and guess how old he is. Then multiply that number by ten and you may come closer to the mark. Wendell will feel your loss for centuries after you pass, unless…" Aggie left Mary hanging as the beautiful clouds of colored dust began to condense into minute stars that sparked in the girl's eyes.

"Unless what?" Mary whispered as a single tear trickled down her cheek and hung precariously over the tiny developing Universe on the tip of her chin.

"Unless you want something more," Aggie whispered in her ear as she stroked the back of her hair.

"Wendell is all I've ever wanted. I could never leave him!" Mary looked at the Witch in horror, causing the tear drop to plummet through the Universe which caused untold chaos as it disrupted the space that suspended it.

"I wasn't suggesting you should," the Witch cackled as she placed a warm wrinkly hand on Mary's cheek and used the other to brush away her tears, "I think he'll make a fine husband that will love you as no other in this world could. But that doesn't mean you're not allowed to want more. Do you think he only yearns to make you happy? If so, why does he work so hard to perfect his magic? Why not just spend all his time with you? What I was asking is would you like to learn something of his art?"

"But I can't learn magic; I don't even know how to read," Mary gasped in disbelief.

"Neither do I," The Witch chuckled.

"But your letters..." Mary rationalized.

"Are a product of my will, not my knowledge. Wizards are a stodgy lot that can't seem to take magic seriously unless they've thoroughly dissected it and write their findings down in dusty old tomes," Aggie smirked as she shot Bergstrom a mischievous glare. The old Wizard seemed to be pointedly ignoring her as he fed his dove birdseed from the palm of his hand, "You have the will to make magic happen and the talent to interpret what you need from the physical world to fuel that magic. The only question that remains is do you have the desire to learn? It's okay if you don't. The vast majority of people in the world don't and live simple lives with little ups and little downs. But I think you'll be unsatisfied with that kind of life because you'll want to be close to Wendell. You'll see the things that most are completely ignorant of. You see what others take for trickery is real and obtainable for some but not others. So I'll ask again, do you want more?"

"Yes," Mary whispered after searching Aggie's eyes deeply for several more seconds.

"Then start by mending that which you have broken," Aggie instructed gently as she gestured to the cauldron's contents.

Nothing remained of the Universe's neat little swirl. Stars half-formed bounced around the cauldron's interior, leaving trails of burning energy in their wake. The brilliant-hued clouds of dust were dissipating in every direction at once. In short it was all coming apart and all because of one small carelessly shed tear that still rested at the very center of the cauldron's round bottom. All this Mary looked upon and despaired for it seemed as if it was all lost spiraling out of control.

"How can I fix it?" Mary asked the Witch hopefully.

"Sometimes the best way to fix things is to start over from the beginning," Aggie smiled as she waved her hand over the cauldron to make its contents vanish. Then she nodded to Mary.

Mary smiled and went to the shelves to collect more dust excitedly. Aggie watched as she mimicked what the elder Witch had done to get the Universe started and wasn't surprised in the least when she got it right on her very first attempt. She waited until it had properly developed then retrieved an empty vial with a cork, a sheet of parchment, and a wooden ladle from her shelves. Aggie bid Mary to open the vial and hold it steady as she folded the parchment into a neat funnel to place on top. Then Aggie carefully scooped the universe out the cauldron with the ladle and poured it through the funnel into the vial. When it was all inside the vial Aggie bid Mary to cork it up tight. The tiny Universe continued to swirl within the glass brilliantly.

"What is it for?" Mary asked as she admired her handiwork. She absolutely loved the swirling colorful gasses and tiny but brilliant stars.

"It is simply to remind you of the most important rule of magic. That which you create, for good or for ill, you are responsible for. Cherish it, Mary. It's your first step into a much larger Universe than you ever dreamed was possible," Aggie smiled as she vanished what was left within the cauldron.

"Look, Mr. Weatherbee! Look what I've made!" Mary exclaimed excitedly as she set the Universe in front of his bottle prison. Bergstrom smiled at her and winked but as soon as her back was turned shot Aggie a questioning look.

"Why should you men have all the fun?" Aggie asked him quietly once Mary was distracted once again. Bergstrom just sighed and shook his head before he returned to stroking his dove.

SECTION 4

31

"Ahhh! It's no good!" Aggie cried out with despair after watching her latest potion fail. She threw the nearly empty bottle away from her in disgust, ignoring it as it shattered against the wall by her bed and began to eat a hole through the wood and thatch with an angry hiss. Aggie's shoulders slumped and she began to weep as she looked down at the diamond bottle before her, "I'm sorry, Bergstrom. I, I don't know what else to try."

Mary came over and put her arms around the old woman to comfort her as Bergstrom gave her a weary smile. Wendell quickly ran over to the dissolving wall and vanished the acidic potion and the broken glass below. It was their third week at the Witch's hut and this was the last of a long line of failed attempts to free the bottled Wizard.

"I guess that settles it. We have to go on to Lavittia," Wendell sighed as he returned to the others.

"Dam Scott, why did he have to be so cruel? If he'd only killed you I'd be able to do something, but this. This is beyond me!" Aggie growled as she waved towards the bottle. Bergstrom got a very uncomfortable look and loosened the color of his robes.

"Well, let's just hope this Giles has more luck," Wendell commented rather thoughtfully.

"Giles? You're not going to put you're life in Reginald's hands are you?" Aggie looked at Bergstrom in horror. The old Wizard rolled his eyes at her as if she was about to start a very old argument...which she was, "He's evil and power hungry. Why he'd step on a baby if he thought it would advance his career. There's got to be someone other than Reginald. What about Odis of Berkwood? He seemed like a trustworthy fellow."

Bergstrom shook his head and made a motion as if he was being hung by the neck.

"Dead, huh? The locals found out about the grave robbing didn't they?" Aggie sighed. Bergstrom nodded his head as if it were expected, "What about Sir Charles of Northrock? He seemed pretty capable."

Bergstrom again shook his head then made as if stomping with a drunken stagger. He then pantomimed looking up in terror followed by clapping his hands together horizontally.

"Flattened by a Giant, aye?" Aggie muttered and Bergstrom nodded with a sympathetic look as if he still felt the loss, "What about Mad Anne?"

Bergstrom sighed heavily and twirled his finger beside his ear while crossing his eyes above a large grin.

"Finally went completely mad, huh?" Aggie sighed. Bergstrom nodded, "Vellick the Vile? I know he's evil but anyone has to be more trustworthy than a politician."

This time Bergstrom just glared at the Witch.

"Is Reginald Giles really that bad?" Wendell asked.

"Yes!" Aggie answered as Bergstrom shook his head no. Both of them glared at the other with annoyance. Then Aggie grumbled a bit of an explanation, "Reginald Giles is the Duke of Lavittia's Court Magician and Chief Adviser. In actuality, he rules Lavittia just don't tell the current Duke. Whenever the Lord of the city dies another takes his place and Reginald retains his position. It's been going on like this for at least four centuries. Anyone who speaks up against Reginald either mysteriously becomes his friend overnight or has a tragic 'accident' the next day."

"That's horrible!" Mary put in as she stood behind the Witch with her hand on Aggie's shoulder.

"That's politics. It's a very bloody business," Aggie shook her head with disapproval, "Well, I guess I'll just have to come along. There's no way these kid's are ready to deal with Reginald by themselves."

Wendell didn't know if he should thank Aggie or run away screaming in terror. Mary looked very pleased, but then the Witch had been teaching her magic whenever Wendell wasn't around. Over the last three weeks, the old Witch would inevitably find some errand to send Wendell on so she could continue Mary's training. Wendell hadn't minded much because it made Mary happy and he knew they be parting company with the Witch soon, but now it seemed as though that parting was getting pushed further away. He looked at Bergstrom but the old Wizard just shrugged.

"I suppose I should get packed," Aggie looked around her hut thoughtfully, "Take Bergstrom and your packs outside. I won't be long. I like to travel light."

Wendell and Mary obeyed, gathering Bergstrom and their things before heading out to wait in the canoe. About a minute went by during which they could hear Aggie humming a happy little tune within the hut. Then there was a loud cracking sound just before the hut was torn apart by what appeared to be a tornado centered within the middle of the destroyed dwelling. For a few moments the children watched aghast as all of Aggie's belongings from her various grotesque witchery ingredients to her bed swirled around the small twister then everything was sucked down into one of the Witch's black iron cauldrons. Aggie then stepped up to the cauldron and waved her hands over it until it shrunk down to the size of an apple. She then picked up the cauldron and placed it in a satchel she'd dawned around her shoulder and then tied up the drawstrings of her cloak.

"All ready!" the Witch smiled as she climbed into the canoe carefully.

Wendell had the feeling this was going to be a very interesting trip as he paddled them away from the grassy little isle.

32

Despite Wendell's initial reservations, Aggie turned out to be a very pleasant traveling companion. She filled their long trek northward with pleasant conversation that was very informative. She taught Wendell and Mary the names of all the plants, animals, and minerals they passed along the road as well as their uses both in the arcane and mundane. Wendell found her grasp of the natural world to be simply staggering. She knew a half dozen uses for virtually every herb and could specifically identify animals by their sound, tracks, or excrement at a glance.

Impressive as Aggie's knowledge was it was not perfect, Wendell soon discovered. Aggie had little grasp on social customs for she'd spent the majority of her life in isolation. This became apparent when the subject of Mary's dowry came up in conversation and Aggie just looked at her blankly. Mary had to explain the concept, which the Witch found just a bit sexist and offensive. Aggie also had little grasp of most of the mechanics and theories behind magic that seemed very simple to Wendell, who'd learned them at the beginning of his Apprenticeship. To Aggie, such concepts were completely inconsequential to the making of magic. She simply willed magic into happening or it didn't. If a spell or potion failed she would simply try to get the same results in a different way, why it had failed didn't matter to her in the least and she admitted freely she often failed when she experimented with new ideas. When he told her that her way sounded a bit dangerous and impractical, Aggie just cackled with mirth and told him that's exactly what most Wizards say.

The three walked for two days before they left the swamp behind and ventured into another dense forest. Unlike the last one, the children had entered this one held no fear whatsoever for Aggie explained what every sound was and often why the creature was making it. Their progress did slow, however, for the Witch often stopped to gather herbs and other less pleasant ingredients she said could only be found in forests like this. Whenever the Witch gathered as much as she could comfortably carry, they would have to stop so she could 'unpack' her hut and put her newly acquired treasures away. It soon became clear to both Wendell and Mary that they might well have come of age and then some before they were able to make it home.

In the early morning of the third day, the three met a very skittish Merchant traveling south. The Merchant nearly jumped out of his skin when Wendell waved hello and it took a few minutes to convince the poor fellow they meant him no harm. Apparently the Merchant had traveled from Lavittia hoping to flee the strife that was tearing apart the north for safer opportunities in the south. Unfortunately he'd run into not one but three groups of Highwaymen along the road and had to bribe away most of his wares to get away with his life. Now the Merchant was traveling south with not but the clothes on his back and his ornery mule that had a bad habit of biting him whenever he turned his back. Wendell sympathized with the Merchant's plight so much that he conjured him a large gold nugget to help him in the days ahead. Flabbergasted, the Merchant spent the next few minutes thanking him and blessing his children's children for at least seven generations to come before he finally continued on his way. As soon as the Merchant was out of sight, Aggie turned on Wendell with anger over what he'd done.

"Of all the foolish things to do that was perhaps the most block headed!" Aggie began pausing only to draw more wind, "I suppose you thought you were doing that man a favor, but let me explain just how wrong you are! The way people handle the bad things that happen to them is what defines their character! When you give him gold for nothing but the price of a sad tale you take away that challenge and reinforce the idea that it may be more profitable to continue spinning such yarns. And that may only be the tip of the iceberg your ship's about to crash into! What do you think the first thing that fellow's going to start talking about when he gets to Willowdale? I'll give you a hint and say it won't be his ornery mule! He's going to tell everyone who'll listen about the generous young Wizard who's handing out gold like it was candy! You're fame is going to spread across the land faster than we can walk! Every pathetic soul for miles is going to seek you out to see if they can get a shiny nugget of their very own! Every Highwayman will be on the lookout for the boy Wizard with gold in his pockets and don't get me started on the nobility! At best they'll want to stick you in a nice little cell where they can force you to conjure and endless supply of those nuggets to fill their coffers! At worst they'll want to kill you so you won't ruin the economy or threaten their status! Nothing will displease the rich faster than the thought of the poor having the chance of being on equal footing! I mean really, what's the point of having gold if everyone has it? Next time you want to help someone conjure a loaf of bread or maybe a single coin! Hopefully that fellow will just think you're the son of a prospector and not that you actually produced it by magic! Why if you had told him your name, I'd leave you right here and now because you certainly be marked for death and a danger to anyone around you!"

Wendell had lost all color about halfway through Aggie's tirade. He'd never even stopped to consider what ramifications giving the Merchant gold might have. It got even worse for as soon as Aggie was done yelling at him, she brought out the diamond bottle and told Bergstrom exactly what had happened. More painful than ringing ears was the look of deep disappointment his Master wore as he shook his head at Wendell. The only one that wasn't upset at him was Mary. As soon as the Witch stormed down the road muttering about the foolishness of Wizards, Mary took his hand and gave him a sympathetic squeeze as they continued on.

That night Aggie didn't talk to Wendell save for to growl 'Good night!' before she entered her hut and slammed the door behind her. Wendell and Mary laid under the stars together talking about inconsequential things until she fell asleep clinging to him. Wendell stayed up far longer going over his mistake repeatedly and what he may have done instead to help the poor Merchant.

33

Aggie was in a bit better mood come morning and even graced Wendell with a 'Good morning' after she'd finished packing up her hut. The three started down the road again and by mid-morning the Witch was chatting away as if the encounter with the Merchant the day before had never happened.

After a few hours, the trio broke free of the forest and spied a large town in the distance across the rolling grassy plain. Even though they were still a few miles away, they could tell that the sprawling town could have easily housed two villages the size of Willowdale and still have a bit of room to spare. This community of large two and three story buildings was clustered around the southern shore of a good-sized lake sprinkled with small fishing boats. Despite the warnings about larger communities Wendell's father had given him and Mary, the two couldn't help but get a bit excited at the prospect of seeing this sprawling mecca of civilization. Aggie was far less enthusiastic about the town and began to grumble about thieves, conmen, and other riff-raff as they started across the plain.

About halfway across the plain, a fearsome roar erupted from somewhere above in the bright sunny sky that gave the children pause. Both looked up curiously but all that could be seen above was a small dark speck against the sun. Wendell and Mary proceeded then to look toward Aggie inquiringly, but found the Witch was standing very still with a look of utter terror upon her face as she stared up at the speck in apparently paralyzed shock.

"What is it Aggie?" Mary inquired as she tried to get a better view of the growing speck by shading her eyes with her hand.

"R-r-r-run!" the Witch stuttered out after a moment as she grasped both children by the wrists and yanked them into motion.

"What are we running from?" Wendell cried as he ran while trying to keep the dark blotch against the sun in view. Another terrible roar drowned out the Witch's answer as she tried to propel them even faster.

"Dragon!" Aggie screamed after the roar had ceased just as both children had guessed the answer.

Dragons are rare: not because they are particularly slow to breed or that they are hunted, but because they have a unique lifecycle amongst creatures of magic. Dragons tend to grow very large. There are small varieties but these are more popularly referred to as Drakes. True dragons eventually grow to about the size of a large two-story barn not including the long snakey tail and great bat-like wings. It is a slow process that takes hundreds of years. During this slow growth process, the dragons sleep in caves deep within the earth. Unfortunately from time to time, they do wake up with a ravenous hunger. Even more unfortunate is that dragons tend to look at humans in about the same light as a hungry wolf looks at rabbits in the fields.

"Were not going to make it!" Aggie cried as she looked over her shoulder at the dragon who was swooping down upon them, "Keep running!" the Witch commanded, as she pulled the hood of her cloak over her head and broke away hard to the right.

The Witch's cloak instantly began to produce a thick rolling blanket of fog behind her as she ran into the open field. Wendell was dimly aware of horns beginning to sound throughout the town ahead but he was to busy watching the dragon, the Witch, and dragging Mary by the hand to pay them much mind. The dragon didn't seem all that interested in Aggie as it continued to focus on the two fleeing children until the Witch stopped and gave it a reason to pay attention to her.

"Over here, Lizard Lips!" Aggie taunted, as she pulled a small vial from her purse and threw it at the passing dragon with all her might.

The vial hit the dragon in the haunch and exploded in a brilliant green flash, causing the reptilian to roar with pain. The dragon stalled in the air with a powerful flap of its great wings and immediately focused its angry bird-like visage on the mist-shrouded Witch.

"That's right, Bird Brain, over here!" Aggie cackled wickedly as she threw another vial at the scaly monster.

The second vial hit the dragon right in its beak-like snout and exploded in a brilliant purple flash. The dragon roared as it shook its scaly head in pain and anger. When it had shaken off the blast, it tucked one of its leathery wings in and wheeled about toward the Witch with a menacing snarl that released puffs of fire from the sides of its mouth. Aggie got a particular look that said 'Oh bugger!' a split second before she ducked low and ran into her thick blanket of fog as the dragon flapped towards her with blinding speed.

"Wendell, stop! She'll be killed!" Mary screamed as she stopped dead in her tracks and pulled him to a halt like an anchor, "We've got to do something!"

"Like what?" Wendell asked as he watched the dragon breathe a stream of fire into the fog bank that was still rapidly growing.

"I don't know! What about your pouch?" Mary cried as tears streamed down her cheeks.

Wendell didn't see a canoe helping the dire situation much and could think of no object that might. But Mary's tears were enough to make him try regardless of his doubts so he thrust his hand into the Pouch of Needful Things. Wendell's hand grasped something that felt for all the world like the feathery head of a feather duster and he yanked it out with haste. What sprang from the pouch was not an instrument for dusting thankfully but a knight in shining armor upon a snow white war stallion. Wendell drew the knight out by the white feathered plume atop of his helmet and the momentum of it carried him and his horse forward with excited neigh. The knight brought the horse to a halt before the children then looked around with confusion written all over his handsome square-jawed face. This confusion only lasted until he spotted the dragon, then it changed into a look of grim determination.

The knight pulled down his cross-slit visor, lowered his lance, and kicked his horse towards the dragon all in the same motion. The war horse reared and kicked its front hooves in the air for a moment before it leapt forward in a break-neck charge. Wendell and Mary watched the knight race towards his prey with the tiniest glimmer of hope penetrating their dumbfounded states of shock.

We've all heard poetic fables of knights on white horses fighting horrific dragons to save a lady fair but the battle that erupted as soon as the newly conjured knight closed the distance with the dragon was not one of these. It was a very bloody engagement between a man and a very angry fire-breathing reptile.

The knight caught the dragon completely by surprise as it had once again stalled in the air and was using its powerful wings to blow away Aggie's fog while spraying its fire in a wide arc. The dragon let out a horrible roar of pain as the knight's lance tore through the leathery membrane of its great left wing and instinctively whipped around its scaley bird-like head and bit off half of the offending weapon with a frightening snap. The knight didn't pause as the dragon fell heavily to earth, throwing the remains of his ruined weapon at its head as he veered his horse to the right and attempted to race behind the scaley beast. The lance's ruined shaft bounced off the monster's forehead with a dull thud doing little but to agitate it further. The dragon countered by chopping down its long snakey tail right in front of the horse. The horse reared at the last moment to save both of their lives. Unfortunately the night was unprepared for his stallion's quick maneuver and the weight of his heavy plate armor caused him to topple backwards off his mount's back and land with a heavy clatter of steel upon the ground.

This may very well have been the end of the knight but for the fact that the dragon was momentarily distracted by his horse. The white stallion, finding itself suddenly without a rider and confronted by a very frightening large angry reptile, quickly decided that the time for heroics on his part had passed and the time to flee as fast as his hooves could carry him had arrived. This decision made the stallion quickly leap right over the dragon's tail and ran like the gates of hell had been opened behind him. The dragon tracked the horse uncertainly for a moment, which gave the knight needed time to roll to his feet and draw his sword. The gleaming steel blade sliding from its sheath solidified within the dragon's mind which meal it should deal with first and with a hungry growl that vibrated through the knight's chest, circled to face him.

What was going through the knight's mind as the angry dragon began to stalk towards him is uncertain, but he raised his shield defiantly and waited for the dragon to attack. Like a snake the dragon struck at him, but the knight somehow managed to be quicker. He jumped to the side and struck the dragon across its snout as if a Master disciplining an unruly mutt. The dragon hissed flames as it recoiled just as fast as it had struck and shook its long head with frustration, causing great gobs of blackish blood to fly from the deep cut across its snout that smoldered when they fell into the wild grass beneath. The dragon narrowed its angry yellow red eyes at the knight just before it opened its mouth wide and breathed fire toward him.

Now it is a little known fact about dragons that very few knights have uncovered that when they breathe fire they have a large blind spot directly below their heads. Few learn of this blind spot and fewer still successfully exploit it, but that's exactly what this knight did. As the scorching stream of fire shot towards him, the knight did not cringe behind his shield but instead dove foreword beneath it. After several seconds of maintaining its flames, the dragon closed its mouth and gave a smoky-satisfied snort. Then the scaley monster growled with annoyance as it searched the scorched ground before it for the expected extra crispy treat that was the normal reward for such acts. The dragon looked from side to side suspiciously after a moment wondering why this meal was being so difficult before the knight's sword was jammed up through its throat into its primitive predatory brain.

Having a sharp pointy piece of steel stabbed through one's brain is a surprising experience for all creatures great and small. The dragon, who was still working under the assumption that it was still alive, reacted to this surprising new sensation by tossing its head from side to side in an attempt to dislodge the pointy piece of steel. This reaction did not dislodge the steel but did throw the now very bloody armored knight who was gripping it about two dozen yards away. The knight landed in a painful crumpled heap and immediately began to thrash about in a wild attempt to remove his smoldering armor. It was at about this time that Wendell and Mary awoke from their stunned states of gawking in disbelief and ran to aid the knight as the dragon's body finally realized that it was in fact dead and gave up attempts to remove the steel and crumpled to the earth.

"That was Amazing!" Wendell exclaimed as he pulled away the last peace of the knight's red hot armor with his cloak.

"Thank you," the knight winced as he poked at one of many rising blisters where the dragon's blood had burn through his tunic and into his shoulders.

With his steel plated shell removed, the knight appeared to be a handsome fellow with short thick curly black hair. His features were strong and proud in a way that normal people are almost never born with. He was well muscled and despite the dragon's blood scorching dressed in noble attire. After a moment of probing his burns curiously, the knight looked up at Wendell then Mary with another look of confusion.

"Oh no, Aggie!" Mary suddenly started and looked around fearfully.

"I'm fine. Just need some rest is all," Aggie stated as if trying to convince herself of it as she stumbled from the dissipating mists.

"You better sit down," Mary suggested after running over and stomping out the Witch's smoldering cloak.

Aggie's clothing and face were scorched black save for two tiny clean rectangles behind her lenses. One side of her hair was now shorter than the other and her Mist cloak was all but ruined. Despite this scorched and ill-used appearance, Aggie appeared to have come through the near death experience without physical harm though her mental state was still somewhat in question. The old Witch was very listless and uncharacteristically quiet as Mary helped her down into the grass beside the knight.

"That was a very foolish thing to do, Aggie," Mary scolded the old Witch like a child before she embraced her tightly.

"Yes, it was," Aggie nodded her agreement quietly above Mary's arms, "I must be losing my wits in my old age," she stated soberly as Mary withdrew.

"What's your name?" Wendell asked the knight as he squatted down beside him.

"Sir Gawain," The knight told him uncertainly. He still seemed very confused and Wendell couldn't blame him. "I can't seem to recall what my first name is though."

"What can you recall?" Wendell asked as he watched a group of riders break away from the town and head down the road towards them.

"Not much. I know that I'm a knight of noble birth but I can't seem to remember who my parents were or even if I have parents," Sir Gawain scratched his head in confusion, "I can't seem to remember being knighted either, but I know how to fight dragons and ride a horse like it was second nature."

"Where did you come from?" Aggie narrowed her eyes and asked him suspiciously.

"I don't recall," the knight shook his head in confusion.

"Wendell?" Mary looked at him expectantly.

"What have you done now, Boy?" Aggie locked an angry glare at the Apprentice, full of accusation.

"Don't be mad at him, Aggie. I told him to do it," Mary admitted rather sheepishly.

"Told him to do what?" Aggie growled shifting her eyes between the two.

"I pulled him out of the Pouch of Needful Things," Wendell sighed as he looked into Sir Gawain's deep brown eyes sorrowfully, "I was just trying to get something to save your life and he's what came out."

"Oh my!" Aggie exclaimed in utter loss. This one was beyond even the Witch's vast experience.

34

"To the Dragon Slayer!" a townsman toasted across the Inn's common room and the crowd roared in answer for almost the twelfth time that evening.

Wendell raised his own tankard in response, but only mocked drinking to Sir Gawain's health. He'd promised Mary he wouldn't indulge in the seemingly endless stream of ale before she'd escorted Aggie to bed. The only reason he was still up at all was the fact he felt responsible for the knight. He watched quietly as men clapped the knight on the back and congratulated him over and over again. None of them questioned the act itself but Wendell sure was.

Wendell knew that a lone knight slaying a dragon was the stuff of children's fairy tales. A dozen maybe, but not one. This of course brought up the question of what had Wendell actually conjured from the Pouch of Needful Things? He had watched Sir Gawain throughout the evening and after seeing how the knight treated everyone with courtesy and kindness in a very humble way, he had come up with an interesting answer. Wendell suspected that he had not in fact pulled a knight from the pouch but had instead pulled out a hero.

Although Wendell had little to no experience with nobility, he was fairly certain that they didn't treat the common man as equals regardless of how many drinks they bought him. He was also certain that they didn't react uncomfortably to being the center of attention or donate the money they'd been given for a dragon's skull to the local orphanage. There were other little things as well, like despite how many drinks Sir Gawain had thrown back he still seemed completely sober. If that wasn't enough, Wendell had noticed that despite some rather blatant and very unlady-like efforts, Sir Gawain was seemingly completely oblivious to female advances. He thought that would change in an instant should one of the barroom beauties suddenly become a damsel in distress. Sir Gawain was just too good and larger than life to be a kKnight. He was a hero, Wendell was certain. So what did that mean?

Wendell wasn't sure. He really wished he could talk to his Master about it but Aggie had taken the diamond bottle with her. The old Witch was at a loss as well. She'd just cautioned Sir Gawain to imply that he was from a distant land until they could get things straightened out. Sir Gawain was seemingly incapable of lying, but the implication that he wasn't from these parts was true enough.

"Please friends, thank you all but I've had enough," Sir Gawain announced to the disappointed crowd gathered around him. He shot Wendell a look of expectancy as he carefully navigated his way towards the stairs. Wendell followed a moment later leaving his untouched ale upon the table.

"I was beginning to think I would never get away," Sir Gawain admitted as they entered the room they'd rented.

"How do you feel?" Wendell asked more to confirm what he believed he already knew.

"Tired and a bit sore," the knight admitted with frustration as he poked at one of his burns.

"I mean how's your head? You drank an awful lot this evening," Wendell asked as he sat down upon one of the two single beds.

"I'm nowhere near my limits if that's what you're asking," Sir Gawain scratched his head as if that thought was a bit confusing.

"No, of course not," Wendell smiled, knowing any normal man who'd drunk as much as the knight would have passed out an hour ago.

"I should be drunk, shouldn't I?" Sir Gawain asked uncertainly.

"Don't worry about it. It's inconsequential at the moment," Wendell sighed, hoping it was true.

"I need a name. It feels wrong not to have one," Sir Gawain sighed.

"How about Justin?" Wendell threw out the first name to pop into his head.

"Sir Justin Gawain?" the knight tried it out. It didn't really roll off the tongue but he didn't seem to mind, "Thank you Wendell."

"You're welcome, Justin. Is anything else bothering you?" Wendell asked, hoping half of what was bothering him hadn't occurred to the knight.

"What should I do now? I can't see as there's much call for dragon slaying," Justin stated gloomily.

"I think you should come with us, at least until you feel you've got a better grip on what you want to do with you're life," Wendell suggested, hoping neither Aggie nor Marry would mind.

"Where are you going?" Justin asked curiously.

Wendell had a thought as he opened his mouth to respond. If his theory was correct then not only would Justin be incapable of refusing but he'd probably feel good about the prospect.

"We're on a quest to free my Master from an evil Wizard's curse," Wendell threw it out there watching the knight closely.

The change was instantaneous. Justin sat up straighter and puffed up his chest. All sense of confusion and uncertainty were gone from his features and his eyes gleamed with eagerness. Wendell thought it was likely that Justin was near unstoppable as long as he was set on a heroic quest. That was exactly what the magic had conjured him for.

"I'd be honored to aid in such a noble and worthy task," it wasn't so much an answer as a declaration to the world, "The evil fiend will suffer for his wickedness."

"Actually the evil Wizard is already dead," Wendell couldn't help but grin.

"Oh. Well, what kind of curse is it?" Justin seemed a bit crest-fallen not to have an evil Wizard to vanquish, but was no less determined.

"My Master has been trapped in a magic bottle none of us can open. We're on our way to see a Wizard we hope is powerful enough to help," Wendell's explanation seemed to take a bit of the wind out the knight's sails, "But the way is likely to be fraught with all kinds of danger. I mean just look what happen to us today," Wendell added hopefully.

"Well, it still seems like a worthy task, I suppose," Justin sighed, "The lack of an evil Wizard is disappointing though."

"Well you never know when one will pop up," Wendell smirked as he lay down on top of the bed and pulled his hat down over his eyes, "Heck, there might even be a damsel in distress by the end of this. You just never can tell."

Wendell knew that Justin was grinning at that prospect.

35

"Well I'll be a Baboon's twin. I think you're right, Wendell," Aggie stated as she watched Sir Gawain ride his war stallion ahead of them with a proud canter, "It does explain why his horse showed up just seconds after he whistled."

"And why his armor retained that mirror-like finish with only a single wipe of a cloth," Mary put in, "Do you think it's safe to be around him?"

"I suspect there's no safer place in the entire world," Wendell admitted thoughtfully.

"Unless he attracts danger," Aggie muttered skeptically.

"I don't think so," Wendell shook his head, "But I doubt he'll be able to ignore anyone in trouble regardless of the danger. We'll have to keep a close watch on him either way."

Despite Justin's hopes, no evil Wizards or damsels in distress confronted the party as they headed away from the town of Lakeview. They traveled north for a little over two hours before coming to a small village called Windydale. They were surprised to find that news of Justin's exploits had already proceeded them and they were met by a crowd of locals who wanted to see the humble Dragon Slayer. The small party was bogged down for almost an hour and couldn't escape until Justin agreed to give a first hand accounting of the battle. On the bright side, the villagers did provide them all with a free lunch.

Over the next three days this would become the norm, as they passed through nearly a dozen small communities that were usually no more than an hour apart. Word of mouth seemed to have traveled like wildfire across the land and the four never lacked food or a place to stay. At the end of the third day, three Highwaymen with crossbows leapt from concealment to waylay them between villages. But after taking one look at Justin, the Brigands threw down their arms and ran back into the forest screaming 'The Dragon Slayer' in fear. Justin decided these lost souls seemed sufficiently remorseful for their evil ways and decided not to give chase after them.

On the fourth day, they came to the castle of Trent Guard perched atop a large man made mound. There a Lord by the name of Baron Trenton road out to greet them along with a retinue of ten knights and their squires all eager to meet the mighty Dragon Slayer. Again the four expected to have to relate the tale before being allowed to go upon their way, but Baron Trenton wouldn't hear of it and insisted they stay the night as his guests. Reluctant to anger the first nobleman they'd encountered, they agreed and were escorted up to the castle.

Baron Trenton was not what Wendell had expected a nobleman to be as they spent the evening feasting in drunken revelry. The Baron was a loud obnoxious man fond of crude humor and booze. He was very friendly despite these shortcomings though his constant boorishness and back slapping wore thin as the night progressed. More interesting by far was his Baroness, who was by contrast a quiet and insightful young woman only a couple years Wendell's senior.

From the Baroness Trenton, the four were able to learn far more about the lands and happenings further north. About a half-day ride ahead, they would come to Castle Brinswick which was owned by the Baroness's brother Baron Brinswick IV. After that they would enter the forest of Widow Wood and there is where their real danger would begin, for just beyond the forest lay Widow Guard Castle which belonged to Count Kelvin Helmsbrent, one of the feuding lords at war.

Count Helmsbrent had always been of cool disposition towards his eastern neighbor Count Ulbright due to an ancient family dispute that's been all but forgotten. Last month the Count's only son was hunting in the forest and mistakenly crossed over into Ulbright's lands. Some of Ulbright's men chanced upon the lad and his retinue and mistook it for some sort of invasion. They sent word to their Lord as they spied upon the band, but before Ulbright got there a fight broke out and Helmsbrent's son was killed. Apparently Count Ulbright punished the men responsible and tried to make amends for the bloody deed. But Count Helmsbrent went mad with grief upon seeing his son's body and attacked Ulbright and his men. War was declared soon after and now both refuse to listen to reason as they continue to launch skirmishes upon one another. None of the surrounding noble houses wish to become involved with the blood feud and it is all they can do to simply see to it that it doesn't spill over into their lands. Trade is already being disrupted and crime is on the rise, the Baroness informed them as her husband led several knights in a very off key song about Goblins stealing a young couple's clothes while they were bathing in a river.

The next morning the four thanked the Baroness for her hospitality and said their farewells. They would have liked to have thanked the Baron, too, but he had overindulged in drink and had yet to rise. The Baroness walked them to the castle gates and before they left handed Sir Gawain a letter to deliver to her brother as they passed Castle Brinswick.

The four passed through two more small villages before they reached the small castle of Brinswick that evening. Baron Brinswick IV was a slight man who resembled his sister so closely that the four would have sworn they were twins. The Baron received them graciously and was very delighted to find they carried news from his sister. He to insisted they stay the night as his guest for the road through Widow Wood was not safe in these troubled times.

As they sat down at the Baron's table to what looked to be a very subdued affair in contrast to his brother-in-law's, Wendell got a curious tingling sensation up the back of his spine just before the world around him froze. Wendell blinked with a shiver as he gazed around the large table in wonder. The Baron was frozen leaning to speak with Sir Gawain with a goblet poised as if ready to drink. Mary was frozen with a bite of roast pork upon her fork before her open moth as her eyes were focused on a Minstrel standing at the other end of the table playing his Lyre. Aggie was frozen making a humorous face at a small giggling girl sitting at the servants table across the hall. Wendell could even see particles of dust frozen in the air around him. Everything from the candle flames to the pouring wine seemed to be suspended from the flow of time except for him.

The snapping of fingers drew Wendell's attention to a disembodied hand in the air behind the Baron's chair. The hand beckoned to him with its finger and Wendell got up and walked to it. He stopped about a foot away from the hand and looked at it curiously a moment before it extended forward quick as a viper, snatched his robes, and drew him to another place and time.

"Hello, Wendell," a very familiar voice greeted him as he reeled with disorientation in the hand's supportive grip.

Wendell blinked a few times to bring the man holding him into focus and was amazed to find he was looking at a much older version of himself. This future Wendell was a few inches taller with more definition to his lean muscles. His face had deeper lines and a long narrow strip of a black beard hung from his chin. He was dressed in robes of midnight blue with black trimming but his hat seemed to be the same cloth cap that he'd always worn.

"You shouldn't be doing this, the paradox!" Wendell gasped at his future self.

"Normally that would be a worry but look around Wendell. We're out of phase with reality," Future Wendell smiled as he gestured behind his younger self.

Wendell turned and looked with wonder upon the giant chamber they were standing in. The chamber appeared to be part dining room, part kitchen, part laboratory, and all chaos. A long table with eight chairs sat in the center of the chamber. A female toddler with wispy straw colored hair sat at one end of the table silently clapping with a beautiful chubby faced grin that showed off the two front teeth she had. At the other end of the table a large frog was being silently scolded by a furious looking older version of Mary, who was waving a wooden spoon over it menacingly. All around the room about them potions, cauldrons, cooking utensils, brooms, plates, silverware, and a very frighten looking cat were flying about chaotically as if caught up in Mary's rage. Behind her a large hearth was erupting with billowing green flames and a half dozen Brownies were running for cover under a low stepping stool.

"If we were to step into reality there'd be a problem, but if we're out phase even if only slightly reality assumes we're some other Universe's problem and simply ignores the paradox," the Elder Wendell informed him with a mischievous grin. Then he nudged Younger Wendell with his elbow and pointed at the frog, "She thinks that's us."

"She looks really upset," Younger Wendell stated as he watched Mary turn an ugly scarlet purple.

"Well she kind of caught us kissing an Enchantress this morning," Elder Wendell smirked, "Its not as bad as it seems, she's just blowing off steam. She knows we were ensorcelled at the time. You think this is bad you should see what happened to the Enchantress. It's not pretty! Mary bewitched her so that she explodes then reforms again about every five seconds. The poor girl only gets about a second to scream in between the cycle. If she's lucky, Mary will let her out of it when she feels the girls learned her lesson in a decade or two."

"So why did you bring me here?" Younger Wendell inquired as he looked at the mirthful toddler in wonder.

"To give you a warning, Baron Brinswick's wine is poisoned," Elder Wendell stated bluntly.

"Who's trying to kill him?" Younger Wendell turned immediately and asked.

"I suspect Reginald Giles or his Apprentice Donavan but I haven't found any proof. The important thing is that you save the Baron. Oh, wave to Wendy."

"Wendy?" Younger Wendell turned back to find the toddler pointing and giggling at him.

"In honor of our sister's memory," Elder Wendell sighed as the younger Wendell waved stiffly to the toddler.

"Wendy's dead?" Younger Wendell asked in a voice choked with conflicting emotions.

"Yes, but that was near two hundred years ago. She and Fredric had long and happy lives," Elder Wendell informed himself.

"She has Mary's hair," Younger Wendell smiled even as a lonely tear trickled down his cheek.

"And our eyes. Got to watch that one, she doesn't miss anything," Elder Wendell paused to make a silly cross-eyed face at the girl.

"We're going to see them all pass away, aren't we?" Younger Wendell asked soberly.

"We learn to show them how much we love them at every opportunity and we honor their memories by watching out for those who follow. Our family is far larger than you can imagine now and it's still growing. It's never easy to watch those we love pass, but it always balances out in the end...not that there really is an end." Elder Wendell explained thoughtfully.

Two straw-haired boys raced through the chamber silently laughing before disappearing through another set of doors. They didn't seem to pay any mind to the chaos as they passed, they just ducked under a flying plate on their way through. Wendell had to laugh as he saw one of them looked like a much younger version of his brother Mathew.

"How many children do we have?" Young Wendell asked in mirthful disbelief.

"I don't want to ruin the surprise but let's just say more than a few," Elder Wendell winked at him, "Uh-oh, Mary knows something's up. We've got to hurry."

Younger Wendell looked and saw Mary looking from Wendy towards them suspiciously. Mary immediately began to squint towards them as if she was searching for something.

"Remember to save the Baron when you get back and watch out for Reginald and his apprentice. No matter how helpful they may seem they're not our friends," Elder Wendell warned himself.

"But if that's true shouldn't we avoid them and Lavittia all together?" Young Wendell asked furrowing his brow with concern.

"If you do Bergstrom may never be set free. Oh, and that's another thing. We're too young to have learned this yet but Bergstrom has a weakness that may very well be his undoing. He trusts Reginald blindly and won't listen to a word against him. Not even when it comes from Aggie, Mary, or us. It rests upon our shoulders to watch out for him," Elder Wendell explained soberly.

"I bet you think you're really funny, don't you?" Mary growled with fury as she pushed out of reality and into the out of phased realm the Wendell's were occupying as if passing through a gelatinous shimmering in the air, "I bet you just loved watching me talk to that frog."

"Now honey, be careful," Elder Wendell stated as he moved away from his younger self cautiously. Mary glared at him furiously as she removed a small vial from her shoulder pouch and held it above her head ready to throw it at him.

"How long did you think you could get away with making a fool out of me?" Mary advanced shaking with fury.

"You just seemed so certain the spell was going to work that I didn't want to disappoint you is all," Elder Wendell laughed at her mischievously.

Mary growled as she threw the vial at the elder Wendell's feet. The vial shattered as he muttered some incantation and a vile yellow smoke enveloped him. As the smoke cleared, Younger Wendell gasped as he saw his elder self had been turned to stone and Mary snorted with a nod of approval. She turned too looked at him and her face instantly transformed from anger to reminiscent joy.

"Oh don't worry. I'll change you back tonight when its time to vanish the trash," Mary sighed as she approached him almost hesitantly. She reached out tentatively and touched his cheek gently enough to feel like a feather brushing up against his skin. "Were we ever so young and beautiful?"

The young Wendell looked upon the older Mary carefully noting the lines time had etched into her flesh. He was surprised to find this mature version of his love was no less attractive than the Mary he'd left a few minutes ago in Baron Brinswick's hall. Her hair may have lost a bit of its luster and her eyes may have lost a bit of their youthful innocence but she was his love none the less.

"You're still the most beautiful woman I've ever looked upon, Mary," Wendell smiled as he brushed away her tears. Behind Mary the statue of elder Wendell winked at him.

"I love you to, but you need to go back now," Elder Mary sighed happily before she gently pushed him away and back into the past.

Wendell blinked with disorientation as time within Baron Brenswick's dining hall began to sluggishly move forward once more. Wendell moved around the Baron's chair as time began to accelerate steadily towards its normal pace.

"I'll take that!" Wendell snatched the wine goblet from the Baron's hand just before the drink touched his lips and tossed it over the table into the center of the hall. The music stopped and everyone gasped as the spilt wine bubbled and hissed while eating into the stone. All eyes turned to Wendell as the Apprentice returned to his chair and started to quietly eat his dinner.

36

"Who is responsible for this?" Baron Brinswick demanded of Wendell with quiet rage, as he gestured towards the patch of pitted floor that had been stained scarlet by the poisoned wine.

"I don't know," Wendell told him honestly before he took a bite of roast pork and chewed it carefully before swallowing.

"How did you know, Wendell?" Mary asked him after a moment.

"I can't tell you," Wendell stated cryptically before taking another bite and washing it down with some wine while avoiding her gaze.

"So what can you tell us, Wizard?" The Baron asked with annoyance.

"This is very good pork," Wendell answered before taking another bite and smiling.

'Who warned you?' Aggie's voice intruded into Wendell's mind like acid behind his eyes causing him to wince.

'I did,' Wendell thought back at her reflexively even though the projection was excruciatingly painful.

'Well, I guess you can be trusted. Forgive me, Wendell; I didn't know you'd been scarred,' Aggie apologized as she withdrew her painful mental contact as gently as she could.

"What is it Wendell? What's wrong?" Mary looked at him worriedly as he closed his eyes and squeezed the bridge of his nose.

"Nothing, just a headache," Wendell sighed and patted her hand with a weary smile.

"Please, Wendell; I must know who wishes me harm," Baron Brinswick pleaded as he moved to lean on the table before Wendell.

"You'd know that better than I, Baron. Who would profit by your demise?" Wendell put down his fork and looked at the upset Baron.

"I don't know. Since I have no wife or sons, it would fall to the Duke to decide who inherits my lands," Baron Brinswick shook his head after a moment's thought. Aggie immediately made an unpleasant sound in the back of her throat as if she might be choking on something, "If you have a thought, spit it out, Woman."

"Nothing really, just thinking about who pulls the Duke's strings is all," Aggie gave the Duke a glare of annoyance for being referred to as 'woman' and not by name.

"Reginald? But I've never been rash enough to say any word against the Magician," the Baron shook his head as he grew pale with real worry.

"Just because you haven't given offense doesn't mean the vacuum of power created by your death wouldn't serve his interests. But that's only an old 'woman's' opinion, so take it with a grain of salt," the Witch stated before she returned to her meal.

"I, forgive me, Madame. I spoke ill but didn't wish to cause offense," the Baron apologized awkwardly but sincerely.

"You're forgiven; just don't let it happen again," Aggie gave him the disapproving glance of a mildly-cross Grandmother. After taking a bite of her food, she smiled and spoke with her mouth full, "This really is excellent pork."

"Yes, my cook is quite gifted when it comes to preparing meat," the Baron commented off-handedly, choosing to ignore the Witch's unrefined eating habits. He grew thoughtful for a moment then turned back to Wendell, "Thank you for saving my life. I owe you a great debt that shall never be forgotten and you must never hesitate to call upon me when you are in need. Now I must ask that you excuse me. I have much to think about. Please indulge of my hospitability and know you are welcome."

Baron Brinswick began to withdraw from the hall but before he left he stopped before his wine goblet where it still lay in the center of the hall. He contemplated the discarded vessel for a few moments, then withdrew a silken handkerchief from his pocket and carefully picked it up within the cloth so none of its silver surface would touch his skin. With the goblet held before him, the Baron then withdrew from the hall and the four travelers didn't see him again until the next morning at breakfast.

"I trust that you all rested well?" The Baron inquired as he entered the hall early the next morning. The Baron still wore the same clothes he'd worn the night before, but if his apparent lack of sleep bothered him he didn't let it show. Actually he seemed in a good mood despite the last night's events, as he selected a large ripe apple from the fruit bowl that had been provided for breakfast.

"Very well my Lord. Your hospitality was excellent," Justin tilted his head and the Baron smiled.

"I'm glad to hear it. Outside I've had horses prepared as a small token of my appreciation and wonder if you would allow me the honor of accompanying you on to Lavittia?" the Baron surprised them all as he began to peel his apple carefully with his dagger so that the skin was removed in one long spiraling strip.

Wendell, Mary, and Aggie all looked at one another with something between uncertainty and apprehension. But before any of the three could come to a conclusion as to how to respond, Justin took the matter out of their hands.

"You're company would be very welcome, My Lord," Sir Gawain smiled, genuinely pleased by the notion.

"Thank you. Dangerous roads are better traveled in the company of friends," the Baron smiled, tilting his head before discarding the apple's skin back into the fruit bowl and taking a bite.

When they exited Brinswick's Keep, they found not only the horses that had been prepared for them but the Baron's entire retinue of twenty knights, a half-dozen squires, and another half-dozen retainers all packed up and ready to depart. Their departure was slowed for both Wendell and Mary had to be taught the basics of riding. The Baron saw to the lessons personally. Aggie it turned out was an accomplished rider but had her horse's tack removed save for the saddle blanket before she would mount the beast. The lack of stirrups didn't hinder the Witch in the least for she simply whispered into the horse's ear while scratching its chin and the animal laid down before her so she could climb aboard. If the Witch gave the beast any more guidance as she sat side-saddle chatting away none of the others saw it.

Widow Wood Forest was a dark wood of giant old growth redwoods that averaged 3 to 5 times the length of a horse in thickness. The Baron informed them that the forest had been named for the giant spiders that could be occasionally found inhabiting the upper reaches of the redwood's canopy. Despite the ill fate the name implied the Baron also told them that these spiders rarely attacked travelers, they preferred to eat the giant moths that also claimed the forest as their home. The real danger of the forest, he informed them, were Highwaymen or running into one of the skirmishes between the warring Counts and being mistaken for enemies.

As they rode easily doubling their normal pace thanks to the horses, Baron Brinswick began to teach Wendell, Mary, and by proximity Aggie the manners and etiquette that would be expected within the Lavittian Court. Because of Sir Gawain's heroic act of slaying the dragon, they would be encouraged to interact with the nobility of the Court and any slip-up in the way they conducted themselves could have serious consequences, even if it was only ignorance and not inclination. Wendell and Mary took to most of these lessons easily for although they lacked the refinement of nobility, they had been raised to be well mannered and polite since they were old enough to walk. Aggie did not, and found the whole business to be rather bothersome and couldn't seem to see the point. Despite these setbacks, Baron Brinswick was very patient and did what he could to polish the old Witch's behavior. His success was very limited, but he said she'd made progress nonetheless.

Over the next two days the party encountered no one, but this surprised them little since they were accompanied by so many well armed knights. They did get the chance to see one of the giant brown Widows as it hung low from the trees wrapping a huge paralyzed moth in its webs. The arachnid was not unlike the ordinary Black Widows they occasionally found back home save for its dull brown color and the fact it was the size of a horse. The giant spider paid them no mind as they quietly passed and for that Wendell was truly thankful.

On the third day the party stumbled onto the remains of a battle along side the road, and Baron Brinswick called a halt so the bodies of three knights could be buried before they traveled on. He informed them that the three were Count Helmsbrent's men. The Baron's men quickly buried the three in shallow graves beside the road then propped their shields against their down turned swords as a simple marker. No words were spoken, for none needed be said.

That evening the party broke out of the forest and made camp in the sight of a very large castle. No more than ten minutes after their fires had been lit, a large host of knights led by Count Helmsbrent himself came to investigate. Baron Brinswick told them to remain calm for this had been expected and that he would speak to the Count. The Baron walked to the edge of the encampment and waited patiently for the host to arrive.

"Greetings, Milord!" Baron Brinswick called out, raising his open hand as the host drew near.

The Count called a halt by raising his mailed fist, and his knights formed a line at his sides that numbered at least sixty. The Count raised his visor revealing a grim haggard visage, as he scanned the Baron and the encampment carefully before he rode forward to speak to the Baron.

"Greetings, Baron," the Count put his gauntlet to his helm in a salute. His voice was cold, hollow of feeling despite his politeness, "To what reason do I owe the privilege of you're company?"

"We are merely traveling through to Lavittia on a personal errand," Baron Brinswick explained without detail.

"You are welcome to enjoy the hospitality of my table this evening, Baron," the Count invited as if it was a formality. No one but a fool would have mistaken his tone as welcoming.

"Forgive me, Milord, but due to your current conflict with our mutual neighbor I can not chance being mistaken to be supporting your cause and must regretfully decline your generous invitation," Baron Brinswick stated politely.

"As you will. For your protection, I must insist on posting a guard near you're camp while within my borders," The Count responded without seeming surprised in the least by the Baron's refusal.

"I would appreciate the extra security. I must inform you that we chanced upon a battle ground a few hours ago along the road. Three of your men lay unattended so I saw to their burial. Their shields mark the graves if you would care to see to other arrangements," Baron Brinswick informed him grimly.

"Thank you, Baron. You're act is appreciated," The Count responded coldly.

"I wish to offer my personal condolences to you're recent loss," Baron Brinswick placed his hand upon his heart with a slight bow.

"Fare journey to you," Count Helmsbrent repeated his salute and then road back to his men. Ten of his knights were commanded to keep watch over them, before the Count and his host returned to Widow Guard Castle. These men made their own large fire a hundred yards away, but rested not as they watched throughout the night.

In the morning the party rode on shadowed by their ten restless guards until near noon when Widow Guard Castle was lost from sight, then they departed without a word. The Baron explained that the guard was necessary not only to make certain their party was not enemies in disguise, but so that Ulbright's forces couldn't attack them and claim his death was Helmsbrent's doing to draw other houses into the blood feud against him. These things tumbled around Wendell's mind throughout the day and he wondered what he was truly getting himself into when he'd warned himself about the Baron's poisoned cup.

Just after noon the next day the party spotted the towering walls of Lavittia across the plains, and both Wendell and Mary were in awe that any community could be so huge. Baron Brinswick and Aggie were amused by the children's naivety as they rode on towards the great northern capital of their land.

37

The city of Lavittia was truly a marvel for Wendell and Mary to behold as they gawked from behind Baron Brinswick and Sir Gawain within the column. From the time they passed through the great southern gate, their eyes continually raced from one wonder to the next unable to find purchase for more than a few seconds before finding something new. Buildings of white stone towered sometimes four or five stories high around the narrow cobblestone streets often adorned with fairy creatures at play. Elegant marble statues adorned most intersections, depicting the elder pagan Gods that had been all but forgotten in the children's distant part of the world. Here Priests often sat at their feet pedaling their Patron's blessings and accepting their worshiper's offerings by proxy.

The city's architecture was grand, but the people who dwelt within it were more exotic still. Humans were by far the most common and they came in varieties of color Wendell and Mary had never seen. Amongst these humans were other peoples as well like hairy Dwarfs were sitting on wooden scaffolding to chisel designs in newly-erected pillars. Ugly green skinned Goblins were hawking fine jewelry in suspicious little packs. They saw nimble Gnomes whose movements were as quick and animated as birds while they rushed about the streets determinedly. Tiny Halflings whose voices squeaked as they greeted all they passed with friendly salutations as they drove wagons full of produce to the markets. Why Wendell even spotted a willowy Elf walk by who seemed to be looking for some shop and marveled at his unearthly beauty. Everywhere he looked, the wonders continued seemingly without end.

Merchants with wares the likes of which the children had never imagined called out to hawk their goods or simply haggled with one another in the streets. Two-headed monkeys, cloth enchanted to change color depending on the mood of its wearer, apple wine that allowed the imbiber to dream as vividly as life, Goblin crystals that hovered around what ever object was closest, clay statues that would work as thoughtless slaves, and a hundred other strange and exotic wonders were for sale. If that wasn't mind boggling enough, Baron Brinswick informed them that the true markets of Lavittia held wonders that made these street hucksters seem shoddy by comparison.

The city wasn't all fabulous as Wendell and Mary soon found. Some areas they passed reeked so badly of human excrement that they had to hold their noses to prevent becoming ill. Diseased and dismembered Beggars were common on street corners, pleading for talons to buy their bread. Many of the Gentry they passed were served by pathetic looking slaves which the Baron informed them were often the children of those who could not pay off their debts or those born of slaves who knew no other existence. At one point a group of dirty children in tattered rags approached with outreaching hands begging for coins, and to Wendell and Mary's horror the Baron's knights instantly drew arms to dissuade them from coming near. When the column had passed these pathetic creatures, the Baron informed them that such groups would strip you clean of anything they could grasp within seconds if you didn't react thusly, but even he seemed disgusted that such action was necessary towards the city's young.

These and countless other things the children saw as their column slowly snaked through the crowded narrow streets ever towards the gleaming white marble palace that towered at the city's heart upon a walled off hill. The Palace's was made up of six great spiraling towers spaced evenly around a grand central dome, which was enchanted to reflect rainbow hues as if made of a crystal prism. Three story wings jutted from beneath these towers not unlike the legs of an insect covered by neat rows of narrow arched multi-paned windows. The spaces between these wings were walled off into sectional courtyards and beyond them the Palace grounds were covered in vast beautiful gardens subdivided by pools and sculpted hedges. Peacocks, Geese, and Swans haunted these gardens amidst the Gentry and an army of diligently-silent grounds keepers and stony-faced guards. It was a world onto itself that Wendell, Mary, and the others were suddenly plunged.

38

"It's beautiful," Mary sighed longingly as she watched the gown of one of the Ladies across the hall shift from an iridescent white to a deep sparkling blue while the woman talked with her friends.

"If you like it that much I'm certain I could figure out the enchantment they used to make the cloth," Wendell smiled as he leaned foreward on the bench they'd been told to wait upon to examine the gown closer.

"You'd better not!" Aggie hissed loud enough to make everyone in the Palace hallway stop and stare at her. Aggie gulped audibly and continued in a hushed tone when her audience lost interest a few moments later, "Hasn't Bergstrom told you it's considered very rude to copy another Wizard's creations without permission? That's the kind of thing that starts Wizard duels or worse, lawsuits."

"Oh. He never mentioned that," Wendell stated a bit chest fallen.

"Daft bugger, what have you been teaching this boy?" Aggie glared into her shoulder pouch with disapproval where she was keeping the diamond bottle. She continued to stare into the pouch for a few moments in silence before she spoke into it again shaking her head with disgust, "Well I'd call that pretty fundamental!"

"You're the ones who wish an audience with Reginald Giles?" a servant with a very nasal voice asked as he approached the bench.

"That's right, where is his royal muckedy muck?" Aggie shot back as she closed the pouch hastily. The servant got a very annoyed look under his powdered wig.

"The Court Magician is a very important and busy person, who should I say is calling upon his precious time?" the servant asked as if Aggie was someone who the guards should be called upon.

"Tell him Aggie Hartford, Bergstrom Weatherbee, and their protégés would like a word or two if he's not to busy shuffling around the nation," Aggie growled irritably at the man of whom she was taking an instant dislike.

"Very well," the servant acknowledged as if he believed her request was a complete waste of his time. He gave her a crisp and very insincere bow before pivoting on his heels and disappearing down the corridor from which he'd come from.

"Insolent Cur, I should curse his nose to swell three times its size just so everyone can see what a snob he is," Aggie muttered as she narrowed her eyes at his retreating back.

"Calm down, Aggie. We need Reginald's help, remember? Assaulting his staff with curses probably isn't the way to go about getting it," Mary squeezed the elder Witch's shoulder in an effort to cool her temper.

"Like Reginald would notice. He's probably never looked at a servant's face in his life!" Aggie retorted crossly.

"His Excellency has agreed to grace you with and audience, Madame. Please follow me," the servant stated with a cross between disbelief and annoyance when he returned a few minutes later.

"Dam right he has! He knows I'll level the Palace if he doesn't," Aggie muttered with irritation as they got up to follow the nasal-voiced servant.

The servant led the three down the adjacent corridor past several sets of doors until coming to his destination. He lightly knocked upon the door before him with his snow white gloved fist, waited a moment, and then opened the doors to a large impressive study. The study was furnished with a huge desk of ornate mahogany polished to a mirror finish. In front of the desk sat three small oak chairs that seemed unworthy to even rest within the mahogany desk's shadow. Behind the desk resting comfortably within the plush spacious arms of a large leather upholstered chair sat a fat jolly looking Wizard in royal purple robes with black trim.

This Wizard's white hair had been painstakingly curled into thick locks around his head that fell to precisely a half an inch above his shoulders. He had a white whiskered goatee that seemed a bit too small for his chubby round cheeks under a large fleshy round nose. He sat with one hand resting upon the desk before him weighted down with glittering gemstone rings on each finger including his thumb.

Poised behind this obese Wizard like a starved waif was a lean albino boy near Wendell's age, dressed in plain robes of black with white trim. The boy's short hair was as white as snow and plastered against his scalp with some type of oil that made it glisten. His skin was the same colorless hue save for a generous speckling of creamy white freckles across his small pug nose. In fact the only real color he had lay within his slightly slanted eyes that seemed to pop out of his head with a light crystal blue. Wendell thought he'd be handsome if his appearance wasn't so unnatural looking.

"Ah Aggie, always a rare and special treat. I love what you're doing with your…hair these days," the fat Wizard began but stumbled when he realized Aggie's hair was very lop-sided.

"Do you really like it, Reginald? I just had a dragon style it for me the other day," Aggie smiled wickedly as she teased her hair playfully.

"And who are these fine young people?" Reginald pressed on fluidly casting his gaze upon Wendell then Mary.

"Wendell Glasswright and Mary Miller," Aggie presented them.

"You don't say. From what Bergstrom writes you're quite the rising star amongst our profession, Wendell. I'm Reginald Giles and this is my Apprentice Donavan Kellroot. I'm very pleased to make you're acquaintance," Reginald tilted his head towards Wendell but didn't seem acknowledge Mary at all. His jolly demeanor quickly changed to one of mock distress as he glanced towards the door, "You seem to be missing someone however. I could have sworn the servant announced Bergstrom as well. Was he delayed for some reason?"

"Nope! I've got him right here," Aggie continued to smile as she drew forth the diamond bottle and set it on the desk in front of him. Bergstrom waved to Reginald with a happy smile and his dove resting on his shoulder.

"Oh my!" Reginald chuckled for a moment as he leaned over the bottle for a better look. After a moment he leaned back again and beckoned to his Apprentice, who automatically leaned down so Reginald could whisper in his ear. Donavan gave a slight nod, then withdrew to disappear through a door concealed within the paneling behind his Master's chair. As soon as the boy was gone Reginald leaned forward once more to speak to Bergstrom, "Not having a very good day are we, old friend?"

Bergstrom just smiled and shrugged.

"Forgive my rudeness, please wont you sit down," Reginald smiled as he directed them to the three small chairs in front of the desk.

"Don't mind if I do," Aggie stated as she waved her hand over the chairs transforming them into one very large plush leather upholstered coach that dwarfed the Magicians chair. She made an elegant show of straightening her dress after she sat down in the center of the couch and shot him another smile. The slightest hint of annoyance twitched in the corner of Reginald's right eye for just a second.

"I take it the power to open this bottle is beyond you?" Reginald asked Aggie with a jolly grin.

"I don't know about beyond me, I just don't know how. But then I've always left playing with toys to you boys," Aggie countered, still smiling as Wendell and Mary sat down to either side of her.

"Ah Aggie, it's been far too long!" Reginald chuckled deeply making his blubbery flesh jiggle, "Well as it happens I do think I can help you out of there, Bergstrom, but my aid isn't going to be free. You know what I want. What do you say, do we have a deal?"

Bergstrom sighed heavily slumping his shoulders in defeat, then after a moment he reluctantly nodded.

"Good!" the Magician clapped his hands together excitedly as he sat back in his chair with a cat that just ate the canary-like grin, "It should only take my Apprentice a moment to fetch that which I need. So you really tangled with a dragon, aye, Aggie?"

"What did you just agree to Bergstrom?" Aggie growled irritably, ignoring the Magician's question completely.

Bergstrom just shook his head as he stroked his dove sorrowfully.

"Something very valuable," Reginald taunted with a childish giggle of delight.

Aggie shot him a glare that warned there could be bloodshed in his immediate future, but before the Magician could react Donavan returned as silently as he'd left. The albino Apprentice handed his Master something small that fit in the palm of his hand then returned to his stance of readiness behind the lefthand corner of the Magician's chair.

"I'm sorry, old friend, but this likely won't be pleasant. Are you ready?" the Magician waited until Bergstrom sighed and nodded once more ,then he grasped the diamond bottle in one hand.

With the other hand Reginald brought forth a silver bottle opener covered with runes and popped the diamond stopper off the bottle as easy as if it held no magic what so ever. There was a whistling sound not unlike a boiling tea kettle seconds before Bergstrom began to scream. Wendell felt his Master's excruciating pain as the old Wizard was sucked out of the diamond bottle eyeball first and as if his body had no bones whatsoever. With a loud , Bergstrom was deposited onto the floor in front of the desk very shaken but in perfect health. A moment later, a second pop followed and the dove was ejected with a very excited cue. The bird dropped a large splatter of white excrement and two tail feathers on top of the Magician's desk as it flew around the study once then landed on Bergstrom's hat with an indignant shake of its feathers.

"Donavan, please," The Magician nodded towards the mess the dove had left in front of him as he placed the diamond stopper back on top of the bottle. Donavan stepped forward and dutifully vanished the offensive mess with a wave of his hand then buffed the spot using his sleeve.

"Oh, Bergstrom!" Aggie embraced him warmly, planting several kisses upon his cheeks and lips. A moment later she backed off with embarrassment that she tried to cover up by snapping at him angrily, "That better of taught you a lesson about giving evil Wizards the benefit of the doubt, you insufferable fool!"

"As I remember you weren't being very good when we first met but I gave you the benefit of the doubt," Bergstrom grinned wolfishly as both Wendell and Mary embraced him at the same time.

"That's different. I'm not a Wizard, I'm a Witch," Aggie nodded as if the difference should have been obvious.

"And still the most beautiful one I know," Bergstrom stated with sincerity. Wendell and Mary couldn't believe it as they watched Aggie blush with embarrassment and release a girlish giggle as she toyed with the burnt side of her hair unconsciously. Reginald ruined the moment by clearing his throat expectantly.

"Of course, your payment," Bergstrom sighed as he conjured a peace of yellowed parchment, a quill, and an ink well from his pockets and turned back to the desk so he'd have a flat surface to write on, "This is really painful you know, Reg."

"You're just lucky I had a similar problem a couple years ago when a Genie tricked one of the Duke's friends into taking his place within his bottle," Reginald chuckled as he contemplated the enchanted bottle opener with amusement.

"What is that you're writing? Just what did you agree to give him?" Aggie asked narrowing her eyes distrustfully at the Magician.

"Something very dear to my heart," Bergstrom stated as he finished writing and slid the parchment over to Giles. "It's my great great great great Grandmother's recipe for enchanted saltwater Taffy."

Aggie blinked with surprise and looked at him expectantly.

"It cures any form of indigestion, heart burn, gas, and poison in your system when you chew it," Bergstrom shook his head with self-disgust, "It's been a family secret for generations."

"And now its mine!" Reginald chuckled greedily, as he scanned the recipe carefully with a sparkle in his beady eyes.

39

"I really do hate that man sometimes," Aggie growled crossly after they'd left Reginald's study. The Witch had decided she and the children should leave when the Magician had brought out a twenty year old bottle of Blackwood Apple Wine to toast Bergstrom's freedom.

"I know what you mean. Did you see the way he just dismissed me as unworthy of his notice?" Mary growled in a manner frighteningly similar to the Witch.

"What? No, I was talking about Bergstrom. Reginald I hate all the time," Aggie grunted with a bit of a smirk at her protégée.

"I disliked him as well. His friendliness is a mask to hide what is really going on in his head," Wendell admitted thoughtfully. He didn't want to tell them everything his future self had told him but he thought the general admission of the Magician's character would be safe.

"Where are we going?" Mary asked when she noticed they'd passed Baron Brinswick's apartments where they were staying.

"Well I have an errand to run in the city. I suggest you two go out enjoy the Palace Gardens. It's going to be at least three days before we can leave," Aggie growled with irritation.

"Why three days?" Wendell asked curiously.

"One day for those two idiots to get really drunk, one day for them to wasted in the enchanted slumber the wine causes, and finally a third day for them to get over the hangover," Aggie sneered as if the whole business offended every sensibility she had.

Aggie bid Wendell and Mary farewell after they exited the Palace and they watched her stride away determinedly towards the main gate still muttering curses about blockheaded Wizards. When the old Witch was lost from sight, Mary took Wendell's hand and led him into the Palace Gardens. The two found the entrance to a hedge maze and entered in the hopes of getting lost so they could enjoy some private time together. After wandering the maze for awhile, they chanced upon a pleasant little stone bench surrounded by neatly trimmed roses. Here they decided to waste away the afternoon together. Unfortunately this plan was not meant to be, when Donavan and his friends arrived.

"Sorry, are we interrupting something?" Donavan's somewhat mocking voice asked as Wendell and Mary were kissing.

Wendell and Mary broke their embrace to find the Magician's apprentice, a pretty young Lady, and another boy in gray Wizardry robes staring at them with amused smirks. The young Lady was dressed in a fine brown and red noble gown and had fiery red hair hanging down from under her transparent scarlet wimple. She had sparkling green eyes, large teeth, and so many freckles one could easily mistake them for the actual pigment of her pale white skin. The boy Wizard was at least two years younger than the rest of the children with short bowl-cut brown hair. He was an average looking youngster with ears that protruded just enough from his head to be amusing.

"Actually yes, you are," Wendell answered truthfully. The young Lady laughed showing off her toothy grin until Donavan looked at her with annoyance.

"We were just wondering if you'd be willing to give us a demonstration of your magic? the way your Master boasts about you we'd be honored for a lesson," Donavan asked with thinly disguised mockery.

"Alright," Wendell agreed with a smirk. He reached into his pocket and conjured three pieces of waxpaper-wrapped candy which he offered to them. Mary laughed as the young boy ran up and took one of the candies without seeing the look of disapproval on Donavan's face.

"Is that it? My little sister can conjure those," the freckly Lady stated, as she conjured a dove from her sleeve and began to pet its head as it cued softly.

"Yep, that's it," Wendell grinned at her.

"See, I told you Bergstrom's just an old fool. All those stories about him are probably just lies he circulated to improve his standing," Donavan goaded with a wicked smirk.

"Mr. Weatherbee doesn't lie," Mary growled dangerously at the Magician's Apprentice.

"Who asked you, Peasant?" the Lady asked as she vanished the dove with a twirl of her hand then placed it on her hip with a toothy sneer.

"Why you little..." Mary began before Wendell clapped his hand over her mouth.

"What exactly can we do for you, Milady?" Wendell asked quickly not liking how hot Mary was becoming under his tight grip.

"You can start by letting go of you pretty little girlfriend's mouth so she finish whatever it was she was about to say," the Lady narrowed her eyes at Mary and gritted her large white teeth.

"That would be very unwise, Milady, for we have not the freedom to speak as freely as you," Wendell stated politely as he glared into Mary's stormy eyes.

"Go ahead; I don't need my title to deal with some stupid little peasant trollop," the Lady grinned down at Mary mockingly.

At this point steam spouted from Mary's ears, scorching Wendell's arm into releasing her. The young boy Wizard upon seeing this reaction stopped sucking on his lemon drop, turned deathly pale, and ran as fast as his short legs could carry him. Both Donavan and the Lady turned a bit pale as well, looking confused and it occurred to Wendell they hadn't guessed that Mary could do magic as well until that moment. Despite this sudden revelation the two held their ground, watching Wendell's love turned a very ugly scarlet purple in dumbfounded fascination.

"What did you call me?" Mary asked in a quiet voice that terrified Wendell far more than any screaming fit she had ever unleashed.

"I called you a stupid little peasant trollop," the foolish young Lady repeated her insult, despite the warning signs of the apocalypse that was about to be unleashed.

"That's what I thought you said," Mary said quietly as her eyes began to glow with inner fire.

Marry smiled at the foolish young Lady with all the malice she could muster. It was a hideous smile that could fill one's entire life with the most terrifying of nightmares and probably did. The only thing that could have made such a smile worse is if it had been cast by a very angry Witch, as was the case. Upon gazing at this fearsome smile, the foolish young Lady produced the sound of a donkey.

"Hee-Hah!" the young Lady blurted forth with surprised confusion.

The young Lady instantly clapped her hands to her mouth, only to find she now had a lot more mouth. She became comically cross-eyed for a moment as she watched her nose stretch out from her face. The young Lady tried to scream at this point but seemed to only be able to produce the donkey sound no matter how hard she tried. Within a few moments, she no longer resembled a pretty, freckled young Lady but instead a girl with the head of a very buck-toothed donkey. With tears in her large donkey eyes and a 'Hee-Hah!' on her lips, the girl ran deeper into the hedge maze and was lost from view.

"Now, is there something you would like to call me?" Mary asked Donavan in the same quiet dangerous tone.

Donavan looked very undecided as to what exactly he should do. After a moment he seemed to come to a conclusion, and he ran after the donkey-headed girl and was lost from view. Mary's color quickly changed back to its normal white hue and the fire extinguished behind her eyes. When her appearance had completely returned to normal, she turned and looked at Wendell for a moment before passing out into his arms.

"That was very foolish," Wendell sighed as he stoked her fine straw-colored hair out of her face and then kissed her on the forehead.

40

The knock at the door of Baron Brinswick's apartment was expected, but that didn't make it any less dreadful to Wendell and Marry. One of the Baron's retainers started towards the door, but the Baron halted him with a raised hand and proceeded to open it himself. Beyond the door was a very grim faced nobleman with fiery red hair holding the hand of a girl concealed within an oversized cloak and veal. Behind them Donavan Kellroot glared at Wendell and Mary venomously.

"Viscount Highbreak, please won't you come in," Baron Brinswick bowed as he gestured them into the apartment.

"Baron," The Viscount tilted his head as he led the girl inside. He winced when she released a loud donkey like 'Hee-Hah!' as they stepped over the threshold and immediately fixed Wendell and Mary with an angry glare, "Are these the two who assaulted my daughter?"

"Yes, Milord, it was her," Donavan pointed at Mary accusingly, "She cursed Greta."

"Please, Milord, won't you sit down so we can sort this out? Is their anything my staff can get you?" Baron Brinswick asked as he shut the door behind them.

"No. Thank you, Baron, but you're generous hospitality is not why I've come," the Viscount seemed to be struggling very hard to remain polite and although he walked over towards the sitting room's chairs he didn't take a seat.

"Very well. Please leave us," The Baron sent his staff away with a grim nod just as the veiled young Lady released another frightful 'Hee-Hah!' that made everyone wince.

"We've been to see the Court Magician but he is rather, indisposed at the moment. I myself have tried to do what I can for my daughter, but I must confess to have no real understanding of this type of magic. Therefore, before I must endure the humiliation of calling upon outside aid I've decided to give you the opportunity to put right what you have done young lady. If you do so I shall try to be lenient when I decide what punishment is suitable for this insult upon my family," the Viscount told Mary coldly with a stony grim visage of barely controlled anger. Wendell was shocked to see Donavan smirk at the mention of punishment and had to struggle to hold his anger in check.

"Yes, Milord," Mary answered him quietly as she rose from her seat very slowly.

Mary stepped forward towards the veiled young Lady reaching for her hood, but hesitated when the girl flinched away releasing a frightened 'Hee-Hah!' Mary's countenance soften into a sorrowful look of compassion.

"Its alright, I wont hurt you," Mary assured the girl before she reached for the hood again.

This time the girl didn't flinch away from Mary but her body did begin to shudder. Mary gently pulled back the deep oversized hood then removed the veil to reveal the girl's very bucked-toothed red-haired donkey head. Baron Brinswick made a small sound in his throat before he controlled his shock at the girl's appearance and she immediately turned away from them, hiding her sad tear streaked face in shame. After a moment, Mary gently took the girl's fury cheeks in her hands and turned her head back so she could look her in the eyes. Mary looked deep into those large tear-filled donkey eyes, chewing her lip for a few moments before she began to speak.

"What you called me really hurt my feelings, Greta. I really get angry when I'm hurt like that and well, I don't always react well. I haven't been practicing magic for very long and when you called me that name it just kind of got away from me. Will you please forgive me?" Mary asked quietly as a tear trickled down her left cheek. The donkey-headed girl looked at her for a long moment before she nodded her head and released a sorrowful 'Hee-Hah!' "Thank you, Greta," Mary smiled, and then she leaned forward and kissed the girl on her fuzzy donkey nose.

The kiss's magic reversed Mary's curse almost instantly, causing the girl's donkey-like visage to melt back into her pretty freckly one. The girl gasped in surprise. After touching her freckly face for a moment to reassure herself that it was in fact her face; Greta then threw her arms around Mary's neck sobbing with relief.

"I'm sorry, too. I, I was being horrible to you. I never should have called you that!" Greta apologized between sobs as the two girls hugged.

"You never said anything about calling her names, Donavan," the Viscount glared at the Magician's Apprentice irritably.

Donavan got a very frightened and guilty look under the Viscount's gaze and lowered his eyes before it. He shifted uncomfortably for a moment before he responded, "They had it coming. They were mocking me. All we wanted was to see what kind of magic Wendell could do," Donovan stated quietly.

"Liar! All I did was offer you a piece of candy!" Wendell growled without thinking. Donovan's crystal blue eyes instantly flashed with anger and his pale white visage twisted into an ugly snarl.

"How dare you call my honor into question! I demand satisfaction!" The albino boy growled.

"Think about what you're doing, Boy. Don't be hasty," Baron Brinswick quickly tried to intervene, but Donovan paid him no mind.

"Tomorrow at dawn in the West Court," Donavan growled before he threw open the door and stormed out of the apartment.

Both Viscount Highbreak and Baron Brinswick looked at each other for a moment before turning their grim gazes at Wendell.

"Have you ever dueled before, Wendell?" The Baron asked quietly after he noticed Wendell's confusion.

"No, Sir," Wendell answered quietly as Mary gasped in disbelief.

SECTION 5

41

Wendell took a deep breath and tried to ignore the crowd that was watching him expectantly. The Western Courtyard was quickly filling up and Wendell groaned inwardly when he noticed even the Duke himself had joined the crowd of spectators. It probably wouldn't have been so bad if he had had a chance to speak to his Master, but when Wendell returned to the Magician's Study he'd found both Bergstrom and Reginald floating near the ceiling, locked in an enchanted slumber from which they could not be roused with happy grins across their bearded faces. To make matters worse Aggie had not returned to the Palace that night, so Wendell had gotten no council on dueling whatsoever as well as no sleep.

"Breath, Wendell," Mary commanded as she took his cheeks in her small hands. When she was certain she had his attention she kissed him tenderly then smiled wickedly, "Now go kick the snot out of that half-wit albino buffoon!" Mary growled loud enough for most of the crowd to hear: some gasped; most snickered.

As Mary returned to where Greta, her father, Sir Gawain, and Baron Brinswick waited in the crowd, Wendell looked toward Donavan standing confidently twenty feet before him. The albino Apprentice's face was as polished marble as he glared into Wendell's eyes and worse still he looked well rested. Wendell again tried to go over all the magic he knew wondering what would be the best way to precede but he kept losing his train of thought as he looked into those hate-filled blue eyes.

"Prepare yourselves, Gentlemen," the Duke's Master of Arms declared and the crowd hushed expectantly, "On my mark."

Wendell could feel his heart thundering in his chest as the Master of Arms paused with his hand poised in the peripheral of his vision, "Begin!" The man's arm chopped through the air like an executioner's axe.

Donavan plunged his hand into his pocket like lightning and drew forth three arrows which he hurled towards Wendell with a savage cry. The arrows streaked towards the surprised Apprentice as fast as if they'd been shot from a bow then stopped dead in the air a few feet in front of his chest. Wendell blinked and then noticed it wasn't just the arrows that had stopped but time itself. Donavan was still bent from the hurling of his projectiles and his albino face was stuck between a snarl and a grin. Mary was frozen with one hand over her mouth and the other gripping Greta's shoulder with the dark shadow of fear in her eyes. The crowd at large was frozen in excited surprise as all followed the projectiles' path towards him.

"Ah, there you are, Wendell," Bergstrom stepped out of thin air through the arrows as if they were made of smoke. They quickly reformed behind him but continued to be held suspended in time, "I think it's about time we started your training on the practical applications of magic in combat, don't you?"

Wendell was speechless as the old Wizard approached, put an arm around his shoulder, and turned him into another place and time. After the customary moment of disorientation passed, Wendell found himself and Bergstrom standing on the rim of a deep snakey canyon amidst a blacked and crater-pocked plain. The sky above was completely blanketed by churning black clouds that flashed with the occasional forked bolt of lightning. In the distance just on the edge of Wendell's vision, he could see a meteor shower pummeling the horizon and could hear the thunderous rumbling impacts.

"Where are we, Master?" Wendell asked in awe of the devastated landscape around him.

"We're home," Bergstrom grinned as he amused himself by kicking a stone off the canyon's cliff to watch it fall, "At the end of the world, or at least as close to the end as it's safe to be. Our valley sure has seen better days, aye?"

"What happened?" Wendell asked in shock. There was nothing recognizable or living upon the apocalyptic plane as far as the eye could see.

"Time happened. Nothing lasts forever, Wendell. Anyway I thought this would be the safest place to start you're combat training since if something unforeseen should happen no one will notice," Bergstrom winked as he moved away from the cliff's edge. He chanted off a quick incantation to summon his favorite old leather chair then sat down.

"What happened to all the people?" Wendell asked still trying to come to grips with the idea that this was home.

"Those who could, left for other worlds and the rest died off several hundred years ago. Try not to let it get you down. This old world had a good run. So are you ready?" Bergstrom asked expectantly.

Wendell looked at the old Wizard soberly and nodded. He was instantly hit in the forehead by a flying pebble that stung like the dickens, "Ouch!" Wendell exclaimed as he rubbed the tender spot.

"Apparently not," Bergstrom chuckled. The old Wizard removed his pocket watch and began to wind the magical timepiece, "I guess this is going to take longer than I thought."

42

Wendell stepped back into the present in front of the arrows as time started to sluggishly move foreword again. After a moment's consideration, he decided that despite his new combat skills he should probably take advantage of the situation if for nor other reason than to rattle Donavan and quickly moved around the projectiles so that he was now within ten feet of his opponent. Time reached its normal pace just as the Apprentice stepped into position.

The crowd gasped as the arrows flew on to shatter harmlessly against the Courtyard's wall then roared with excitement as they found Wendell in another spot before them with a mischievous grin plastered across his face. Donavan turned red with rage and conjured more of the deadly projectiles to hurl. This time Wendell just vanished them out of the air with a wave of his hand before they could reach him. That didn't seem to improve the albino Apprentice's mood either as he released a curse of frustration.

The Magician's Apprentice then conjured a flame from his pocket in the palm of his hand. He blew on the flame to send forth a billowing tongue of fire that seemed to envelope Wendell as he chanted an incantation. Mary screamed and tried to rush forward toward her burning lover, but Wendell grabbed her from behind.

"Quite a show, huh?" he whispered in her ear as his illusion continued to burn in his stead. Mary glared up at him with anger mixed with her relief.

"Don't treat this like a game, Wendell! He's dangerous!" Mary growled irritably and smacked him hard in the shoulder. Some of the crowd then noticed his presence and began to howl with laughter.

"Sorry honey, I guess I better get back to it," Wendell kissed her and stepped back out of the crowd as Donavan looked between him and the burnt husk of his illusionary self in confusion, "Sorry Donavan, Mary looked scared so I thought I'd reassure her with a kiss," he taunted the albino as he vanished the illusion and fire so he could take his position once more. The crowd roared even louder.

"Quite being a Jester and fight, fool!" Donavan growled trembling with rage.

"Are you certain?" Wendell asked with a wicked smile as he removed his cloth hat, "It's not too late to walk away from this."

"You're not walking away from anything, Cur!" Donavan bellowed as he conjured a dagger from his sleeve and hurled it towards Wendell.

Wendell was ready for the dagger and caught it neatly in his hat. He Winked at Donavan, then reached into the headwear to conjure not one but four daggers held by the tip of their blades between each of his fingers and thumb like a bladed steel fan. The crowd hushed instantly and Donavan crouched readying for an attack. Wendell tossed the daggers into the air before him where they tumbled once then stopped as if caught by invisible hands. The daggers spun around in a circle while pointing at the Magician's Apprentice, but instead of attacking shot away in different directions around the Courtyard like glimmering missiles with a mind of their own.

Donavan was able to vanish the first dagger that streaked toward him over the heads of the gasping spectators, but the next slashed a large cut in the side of his robe as it flew by low from his other side. The albino Apprentice howled with surprise more than pain as another dagger poked him in the rump then flew away again as he began to twirl around. Donavan vanished another then froze when he found the last two hovering just out of range of his hands. They made a few jabs as if to advance but kept hopping back out of range.

"Go ahead; I've got plenty more where those came from," Wendell called to the albino. The crowd gasped and Donavan's jaw dropped when they saw Wendell had near twenty more daggers hovering over his head all pointed at the Magician's Apprentice. The moment he was distracted, one of the two daggers that had been close to Donavan moved to prod him gently in the small of the back while the other pressed against his throat, "Yield."

"Never!" Donavan hissed stubbornly as his eyes focused in an angry glare upon the dagger at his throat a split second before it burst into flame and melted out of the air. The molten remains of the dagger splashed onto the cobblestones with an angry hiss as Donavan whirled and vanished the dagger at his back, "I'll never yield to a clown like you!"

"Alright then, have it you're way," Wendell shrugged as all twenty daggers spiraled towards Donavan at once.

The Magician's Apprentice destroyed two of the oncoming daggers with angry glares and vanished two more before the others reached him and flew through his body harmlessly as smoke. Donavan blinked with surprise then growled with rage. The sky above began to instantly blacken as thunder rolled. A lightning bolt streaked down towards Wendell like a brilliant spear but before it could strike a hand grasped his collar and yanked him to yet another time and place.

"Hello, Father," the beautiful woman with straw-colored hair greeted him as his disorientation passed.

The woman was at least twenty years his senior and strongly resembled Mary, all save for her eyes. The woman's eyes were his and very sad as they gazed upon him. He knew her instantly even if they had only met when she was but a toddler. He smiled and wiped away the tear that trickled down from her eye gently.

"Hello, Wendy. You look absolutely beautiful," Wendell greeted his future daughter.

"You always say that," she smirked for a moment before it turned into a sorrowful frown, "At least you used to."

"Oh," Wendell stated soberly as he glanced around and saw they were standing in a large cemetery on a familiar hill. Below the hill spread not the village he remembered but a very large thriving town with at least a dozen new towers sprinkled through out it, "I see."

"Mother asked me to fetch you. She over there waiting," Wendy pointed towards the top of the hill where a black-cloaked figure hunched before a very large tombstone, "You must be gentle with her, she's in a lot of pain and she can't do magic anymore. I'll be waiting here to take you back when you're done talking," Wendy wiped her eyes on the sleeve of her strange gown.

Wendell sighed then nodded to his daughter before walking up the hill. As he approached the frail-looking hunched figure he conjured a bouquet of pink roses from his hat.

"Hello, my love," Wendell embraced the future Mary from behind placing the roses before her. She sighed deeply and leaned back against his chest as she took the roses with a near skeletal-withered claw. He looked up at the tombstone before them that was an obelisk shaped from a single piece of crystal near ten feet tall and read his name, "Nice tombstone."

"I knew you'd want something subtle that wouldn't draw attention," Mary whispered with a raspy chuckle, "It was the last bit of magic I had in me."

"You shouldn't have sent Wendy. This, this isn't healthy," Wendell sighed as he squeezed her gently.

"I had no choice. You were taken from me. I, I'm alone," Mary began to weep softly.

"I see to many towers in the valley to believe that, Mary. And Wendy's heart is breaking for you," Wendell whispered, "You have to move on my love."

"I didn't have our daughter bring you here to try to pull me back from my despair, Wendell. You're here so I can ask a final request of you," Mary slowly pulled away and turned.

Wendell was horrified by the appearance of his love as she gazed up at him from the depths of her heavy black cloak. It wasn't that time had withered her into a hallowed skin skeleton that terrified him. It wasn't that her straw-colored hair had changed to thin wisps of gray that clung to her scalp in patches. It wasn't that her beautiful eyes had grown milky with little trace of their former color. What was truly terrifying was that Mary had turned a horrible ashen gray in her despair that made her appear as if she was already more than halfway in her grave.

"What is it you wish of me, Mary?" Wendell asked as he took her hands in his and knelt before her.

"I want you to do something that goes against your nature, Wendell. I want you to kill Donavan Kellroot when you return," Mary rasped as she caressed his cheek gently with a cold gray claw.

"Why would you ask this of me?" Wendell sighed uncomfortably, knowing he wasn't going to like the answer.

"Because you didn't the first time, or the second, or the third, or any of the times he foolishly challenged you. You treated it always as a game humiliating him over and over again. And with each humiliation Donavan became even more bitter and obsessed with destroying you until one day...he succeeded. I want you to kill the man who will murder you so I won't become this. So I won't stand here each day praying to deaf Gods to take my life. So I won't be alone. Do this for me, Wendell. If you love me you'll grant me this final boon," Mary pleaded pathetically before she drew away and began to slowly walk down the hill. Just before she was out of earshot she rasped one finale remark, "Thank you for the roses, they smell divine."

43

"Wait a moment, Wendy. I, I need to think," Wendell stopped his future daughter as she reached for him.

"She asked you to change something, didn't she?" Wendy asked with concern.

"Yes," Wendell sighed.

"Of all the people in my life, I trusted your wisdom more than any other's father," Wendy admitted as she looked down at the town thoughtfully, "So I must trust you're judgment in the choice that lays before you even if it means the future of all my children may be put at risk. Follow you're heart and decide."

"She is my heart," Wendell declared without doubt, "Okay, I'm ready."

"I love you, Father," Wendy smiled as she pushed him away from her and back into the present.

The lightning bolt split the cobblestones of the Courtyard before Wendell close enough to scorch his flesh as thunder deafened his ears. Wendell reached into his hat and drew forth a great swarm of bees that flew towards the Magician's Apprentice as he simultaneously chanted off another incantation. Donavan again conjured fire and blew it towards the advancing swarm. The bees were incinerated in mass before they could reach him.

"Is that the best you can…" Donavan choked on his words as the blade of Wendell's sword erupted from his chest and a great hush fell throughout the Courtyard. Slowly Donavan turned to look at Wendell even as his illusionary counterpart continued to mimic drawing nothing from his hat repeatedly before them. The Magician's Apprentice tried to speak but only a wet gurgle issued from his mouth.

"Forgive me," Wendell whispered before Donavan fell dead at his feet. He ignored the clapping and cheers from the crowd as he strode out of the Courtyard and into the gardens beyond. It had been no victory he thought with despair, for along with Donavan a piece of his soul had been slain by his own blood stained hands.

Mary found Wendell an hour later still sobbing like a child, deep within the hedge maze. As she held his head to her breast he told her all he'd done and experience that had led him to the decision to kill the Magician's Apprentice. He told her of their beautiful future children that now may never be. He told her of the future Mary and her final request that he could not deny. He told her of the terrible hollow in his heart that ached since the moment he watched the life leave Donavan's crystal blue eyes. He told her all and she wept with him.

44

"Wendell, Mary, you must come," Justin spoke gently with a grave look in his eyes when he found them within the hedge maze.

"What's happened now?" Wendell asked wearily as he rose then offered his hand to Mary. He didn't dare to guess how much worse the day could get and it still wasn't even noon.

"Aggie's been arrested for murder," Justin sighed grimly as he led the way back out of the hedge maze, "She killed a barber in the city last night and has been sentenced to execution at dawn tomorrow."

"No. It can't be true. There must be some mistake!" Mary cried but the knight just shook his head.

Baron Brinswick and his escort were already prepared for their departure when they arrived at the Palace. One of the Palace Guards led them to the Barbican where the Witch was being held within its dungeon. Baron Brinswick arranged for them to see Aggie while he and Justin spoke to the Captain of the Watch in the tower above. Wendell and Mary found

Aggie quietly knitting a green and white striped stocking within her dark damp cell with a bright red scarf wrapped around her head.

"What happed to you? You've lost something since yesterday," the Witch narrowed her eyes suspiciously at Wendell as soon as he came through the door. Wendell didn't have a chance to respond because Mary nearly knocked him over as she flew by to embrace the Witch.

"What happened, Aggie?" Mary asked as the Witch paused her wooden knitting needles and allowed her protégée her moment of comfort.

"I killed a barber," Aggie stated bluntly as she continued to stare at Wendell.

"Was it an accident? I'm sure Baron Brinswick can speak on your behalf," Mary suggested as she drew back but continued to hold her Mentor.

"Nope, I hexed his shop to fall on the idiot. You've lost you're innocence," she stated towards Wendell. She paused for a moment then shrugged before continuing her knitting, "Well, suppose it had to happen some time."

"Did he threaten you?" Mary asked taken back a little by Aggie's seemingly unconcerned attitude towards her plight.

"Nope, it was cold blooded murder," Aggie grunted as she tied off the green yarn on the stripe she'd just finished and switched to the white.

"What happened?" Wendell asked quietly though his thoughts were still tumbling around Aggie's assessment of his lost innocence wondering if the mark of Donavan's death was visibly etched upon him.

"Well I went into his shop to get my hair fixed and he ruined it so I refused to pay. As I was leaving he threatened to call the watch and have me arrested, so I turned back and caused his shop to collapse on his head. The watch arrested me and this morning I was sentenced to death by the guillotine tomorrow at dawn in view of the public," Aggie explained as she began to quickly produce a white stripe with her clicking needles.

"What did he do to you're hair?" Mary asked after a moment of dumbfounded shock. The Witch sighed and looked at her.

"If I show you will you promise not to tell Bergstrom? He'd never let me live it down," She shook her head in disgust.

"Of course not, you have my word," Mary swore as she looked back toward Wendell.

"And mine as well," Wendell stated quietly.

"I'll hold you to it," Aggie glared threateningly as she set her knitting upon her lap and removed her scarf. Mary gasped aloud when she saw what the dead barber had done, "He told me it was the latest style amongst woman my age and I agreed because he swore that it would look dignified."

Aggie's hair was now short and blond save for two floppy locks on the sides that looked very much like Dog ears. These locks had been stained a deep burgundy as if dipped in wine. Upon looking at this incredibly ludicrous hair style both Wendell and Mary could sympathize with the elder Witch's impulse to kill the deranged barber. Aggie concealed the abominable hair cut back under her red scarf and returned to her knitting.

"Surely they can't execute you for loosing you're temper after--that!" Mary stumbled unable to call it a haircut, "I'm certain the Baron can get them to reconsider the sentence. We'll go speak to him this instant."

"No, you will not. I committed a crime and I must accept the punishment for it regardless of what noblemen I know. Bergstrom taught me to accept the consequences of my actions a long time ago and I'm not going to stop now. Why I couldn't look him in the eye if I manipulated my way out of this. And what makes you think that I couldn't march right out of here if I was so inclined? It would take more than the Duke's army to hold me if I didn't wish to be held," Aggie muttered irritably as she finished the stocking and tied off the yarn.

"But what will your pride matter if you're without a head, Aggie?" Mary began to weep. The old Witch softened a bit as she looked at her protégée.

"Pride always matters, Dear, without it we're not but beasts. Now make me proud now and dry those eyes so you can help me," Aggie muttered as she withdrew another spool of yarn and two more needles from her shoulder pouch and placed them into Mary's hands, "Bergstrom will be needing at least two more pairs of stockings for the year to come and he's absolute rubbish when it comes to knitting."

"I'm surprised they let you keep those," Wendell commented after watching Mary and Aggie knit for a few minutes.

"Oh they tried to take my bag but decided better of it," Aggie chuckled wickedly, "So who'd you kill Wendell?"

"Donavan Kellroot." Wendell answered after shifting uncomfortably under the Witch's gaze for a moment.

"Oh Bergstrom's going to love hearing that on top of his hangover," Aggie whistled as her knitting needle continued to click away, "Did you enjoy it?"

"No, of course not!" Wendell exclaimed in utter horror at the very thought.

"Good. It would kill him if you went bad. His old heart just couldn't take it," Aggie stated with certainty, "So what happened?"

Wendell couldn't answer so Mary had to tell of yesterday's events after she'd left and this morning's duel. The Witch listened quietly as she finished another stocking in the mean time. When Baron Brinswick and

Justin arrived to tell them it was time to go, Aggie removed six mismatched stockings from her pouch and handed them to Mary.

"Make certain Bergstrom gets those, otherwise he'll likely catch cold come winter. Have to make them all mismatched now so the Brownie won't steal them," Aggie muttered irritably as she hugged Mary and kissed her on the forehead. Then she held the girl at arms length and spoke to her sternly, "I want you two to be at my execution tomorrow. I think it will be nice to have friends witness my demise. Remember what I told you about pride, though. I don't want to see you blubbering like some little girl. You're a Witch now, Mary, if you're going to cry do it in private after they've cut off my head."

Then they departed heading back to the Palace.

45

No one spoke as the column rode back to the Palace, grim faced and depressed. Mary was very upset but seemed determined not to shed tears in public as the imprisoned Witch had instructed. Wendell was still lost in the desolate emptiness that was eating at his heart, though he did his best to comfort her with gentle looks and caresses upon her hand as they rode. Baron Brinswick sympathized with Mary's pain, but upholding the law was deeply ingrained within his character and could not in good conscience justify what Aggie had done--and then there was Sir Gawain.

Wendell and Mary had seen little of the knight since they'd come to the Palace for the Gentry had been taking turns passing him from one social gathering to the next from dawn to well after midnight, all wishing to spend time with the Dragon Slayer. He was the latest highlight within the Court and the subject of most conversations. Lords wish to be seen in his company to improve their status. Ladies wished to seduce him into their beds, even many of the married ones much to Justin's horror. Justin had recounted his battle with the dragon so many times at this point that he physically winced whenever someone asked now. It was taking a heavy toll upon the confused knight and he was falling into a deep depression all his own. His depression broke when a woman screamed down the avenue ahead of them.

Sir Gawain's stallion reared up and kicked at the air for a moment before the woman's scream was even concluded. Wendell and the others saw the cause of the woman's distress lay in a runaway wagon that was thundering down the avenue out of control toward a child who'd wandered into the cobblestone road. It was simply amazing to watch the glittering armored knight and his incredible snow-white stallion in action as they raced towards the child faster than any normal horse could run.

Over a dungy man's wagon and two very surprised tradesmen, Sir Gawain's stallion leapt on the way to the child. Justin leaned over and scooped the small girl up with one hand and deposited her in his lap without slowing. Then Justin raced straight toward the runaway wagon, building up even more speed as his stallion's steel-shodden shoes sparked across the cobblestones. The white stallion let out a majestic neigh as it leaped boldly over the runaway wagon and its terrified horse in the mightiest of bounds. As the stallion flew Justin pushed right off its rump, landing backwards on the wagon's horse far more gently than any plate armored knight should. Justin nimbly turned around upon the terrified horse's back even before his stallion and the very excited toddler had hit the ground. He grabbed the horse's halter and brought it to a halt moments before it would have crashed into the dungy man's wagon. Justin slid down from the horse's back and stroked the scared beast into submission, as its very out of breath and sweaty owner came running up behind to thank him.

"Thank you, Milord! Thank you!" the man wheezed in between gasps for air.

"It was nothing, Sir," Justin smiled as he gave the man a friendly pat on the back before whistling for his stallion.

The white stallion returned with its head and tail held high in a prideful canter. The toddler on its back had the stallion's reigns in her hands with a grin from ear to ear. Justin reached up and lifted the happy child off the saddle, as her terrified mother finally caught up and people in the street began to cheer.

"Horsey!" the toddler giggled happily as Justin placed her back into her mother's arms.

"Milord..." the woman began as she squeezed her daughter to her in a vice-like embrace, but she was far to overcome with emotion as tears of joy rolled down her cheeks. Justin just smiled and nodded to her before climbing back up into his saddle.

"That was a truly heroic act, Sir Gawain," Baron Brinswick tilted his head to the knight as he returned. The Baron's countenance was one of awed disbelief as he leaned over to pat the hero's back.

"It was nothing; Chester here did most of the work," Justin stated as he leaned to rub his stallion's neck. The stallion released a neigh of pleasure that made the knight chuckle. Then he muttered to the horse just quiet enough to be heard by the Baron, Wendell, and Mary thoughtfully, "It did feel good, didn't it, Boy?"

Justin was very introspective for the rest of the ride to the Palace and it didn't surprise Wendell in the least when after they returned to the Baron's apartments he announced that he was leaving.

"Where will you go, Justin?" Baron Brinswick asked as Sir Gawain packed up his meager belongings into his saddle bags.

"Wherever I'm needed," Justin answered after thinking about the question for a moment.

"If you ever need anything please come and find me, Justin. I owe you a great debt," Wendell stated in a reserved sober tone as he offered the knight his hand.

"I think I'm the one who owes you, Wendell. You gave me life. It may be an unnatural and confusing life but it's all that I have and for that I am grateful," Justin clasped his hand warmly with both of his. Then he grew sober once more as he looked Wendell in the eye, "I see your pain, Wendell. Try not to dwell on this morning's act., Donavan was evil and gave you little recourse."

Wendell could find no response so he just nodded to the knight. Justin then turned to Mary who came forward to embrace him.

"Aggie's death may be a very hard blow for you, Mary, but I think her willingness to face the punishment for her deed is very noble," Justin stated as she drew away. Then he drew both Wendell and Mary into another great embrace, "Take care of one another."

"When you need rest from the roads hardships know that you shall be welcome at Castle Brinswick, Justin," Baron Brinswick shook the knight's hand.

All three of them walked Sir Gawain to the western Courtyard and bid him farewell a second time before he mounted his stallion. As fate would have it the sun was setting as he rode towards the western gate. Before Sir Gawain passed out of sight, he turned and his stallion reared as he raised his hand in farewell. It was a moment Wendell thought well deserved to be written in some epic poem as he gazed upon the brilliant silhouette of his friend backed by the beautiful fiery sunset--and then Justin was gone.

"What did he mean when he said his life was an unnatural one?" Baron Brinswick asked thoughtfully as they returned to their apartment.

Wendell could see no harm in it so after having the Baron swear that he would not speak to others on the matter he related the truth of Sir Gawain's origins and his thoughts as to what the knight truly was. When the story was complete the Baron was thoughtful for a long time as they prepared for dinner. Then as they were about to leave the apartment Baron Brinswick stopped and turned to Wendell.

"Such magic is truly beyond my grasp, Wendell, but after thinking upon what you've told me I've concluded that bringing Justin into world is probably the noblest I've ever heard tell of. I think having such a hero walk amongst us is a great blessing and look forward to hearing what becomes of him. I've a strong feeling that wherever he rides and whatever trials he faces shall be the stuff of legend that will inspire all towards something better than we would be otherwise. Thank you," the Baron offered his hand and tilted his head to Wendell.

46

Wendell would have preferred to have dined within the Baron's apartment that evening, but Baron Brinswick had informed him that his presence would be expected and that his absence may even be taken as insulting to the Duke who would certainly wish to congratulate his victorious duel. The Apprentice's fears were confirmed upon entering the great feast hall for most the Lords and Ladies bowed and curtsied before him as if he were one of their own to be acknowledged with honor despite his common blood.

The Palace feast hall was the largest chamber Wendell had ever beheld, though Baron Brinswick had informed him the Ball Room was even larger. This grand chamber was supported by twenty four giant marble pillars adorned with inlays of gold and silver that held a deeply vaulted ceiling above. Six huge bronze chandeliers with crystal inlays and hundreds of candles each hung above three rows of six long feast tables, throwing refracted light around the chamber in diffused rainbow spectrums. Upon the walls between the pillars, great murals of fey creatures at play had been enchanted with simple illusions to seem alive as they danced and frolicked within their Sylvan Woods. It would probably have been the most entertaining of places to eat if not for the fact that every meal was held up by strict and tedious ceremony.

This ceremony began with everyone lining up at the doors in pairs or as individuals to be announced before entering the Feast Hall. Once these individuals or pairs had been announced they were directed to their seats within the hall as determined by their personal status within the Duke's Court and bid to wait standing before their chairs. After all had been sorted to their places along the six great tables they would wait for the Duke and Duchess to arrive. It was customary for the Duke and his wife to keep everyone waiting for at least a few minutes as a sign of their power over the Court. When the Duke and Duchess were finally announced and took their seats at the head of the central table at the far end of the hall, then as one everyone bowed or curtsied to them before taking their seats.

The next part of the ceremony was one of washing. Rows of servants would file into the chamber with large bowls of water and towels, then would line up at the heads of each table before the drawn out chairs while others filed in behind. These expressionless-uniformed servants with white powdered wigs and crisp yellow uniforms would first present the bowls of water to the nobles to rinse their hands and then the towels for drying before moving on to the next down the line. As soon as these washers had cleared out of the way two or more servants, depending on the girth of the noble in question, would pick up and scoot in their chair before moving on.

The third part of the ceremony didn't start until all the washing servants had complete their task and filed back out of the hall. As the last yellow-uniformed servants disappeared through the servant's doors at one side of the hall, a line of green-uniformed servants filed in through the other. As before these servants started at the head of each table and worked their way down the line carefully unrolling each person's large cloth napkin from their silverware and tucking it around their collar before arranging said silverware in the complex pattern around their plate and moving on. As these green-uniformed servants finished their task and exited on came the red-uniformed servants with fancy silver decanters, who worked their way down the table pouring wine into each person's silver goblet. As the red-uniformed servants filed out of the hall on came blue-uniformed servants with the first course of the meal, hidden within large covered silver platters. These platters were placed down the tables exactly four feet apart. When every platter was in place, as one the blue-uniformed servants removed their covers and began to serve up small portions of the steaming breaded meat pudding on each person's plate. When each person had their equal share, once again as one these servants covered the Platters, picked them up, and filed out of the hall. When the last of these blue-uniformed servants disappeared, the final stage of this ceremony could begin.

All eyes would then turn to the Duke as he tapped three times upon a small golden chime held by his personal servant with his fork. After carefully returning his fork to its proper position around his plate, the Duke would raise his golden goblet in the air which was the cue for all others to do the same. The Duke would then toast the good fortune of the land to provide such a plentiful bounty before taking a drink. This would cue everyone else to call out 'All hail his Grace's wisdom,' before taking a drink themselves. When the Duke returned his goblet to the table it was the signal that the meal could begin and the tables immediately erupted with the sounds of conversation and eating as if time had suddenly awoken within the chamber and realized the hour was getting late and it should get onto the business at hand.

To Wendell this whole tedious affair was absolute torture and made him glad he was not born of noble blood. This meal was only beginning however and there were far more tortures yet in store. As Wendell set down his Goblet he immediately looked to Baron Brinswick as had been prearranged so that he may be reminded of which was the proper silverware around his plate to carve into the meat pudding before him. When he had been so subtlety informed, he began to dissect a small bite of the crumbling pie shaped wedge of wonderful smelling food and that's when the next torture was inflicted upon him coming in the form of a fat old Baron who seemed to have little to no interest in eating whatsoever.

"So young Wizard; that was a very impressive showing this morning. Tell me, why did you play with you're opponent so long?" the fat old Baron growled across the table.

"I had hoped that I might scare him into withdrawing his challenge, Milord. Though I found him unpleasant, I in no way wished his death," Wendell lowered his fork back down to his plate as was proper to address the Lord's question.

"I've rarely seen such feats of magical prowess from even our illustrious Court Magician. How much of what we saw was real and how much illusion?" the Baron asked next, waiting just long enough for Wendell to raise his fork halfway to his mouth.

"Forgive me, Milord, but I am forbidden to reveal such secrets by my Master. I will say however that most of what you saw can be quite deadly even if only illusion," Wendell smiled and tilted his head to the Baron. The Baron immediately sucked in breath for his next question but was cut off by a young Lady sitting beside Mary, who had brightened considerably upon mention of Wendell's Master.

"Is it true that Bergstrom fell the Mythandred Serpent with a spell that swallowed it within the earth?" the Lady almost leaned directly into Mary's plate with anticipation.

"I'm uncertain for I have never heard an accounting of that battle from my Master, but I would not be surprised to find such a feat was within his power, Milady," Wendell answered, fidgeting with the fork against his plate.

"Mr. Weatherbee is very enigmatic about his past and has lived a very simple and quite life since moving to our valley, Milady. I would not be surprised to find that all here know more about his exploits than we," Mary explained in an attempt to give Wendell a moment's peace. This information seemed to subdue the Lady's interest just long enough for the fat old Baron to jump back into the conversation.

"How many of those flying knives could you actually maintain at once young Wizard? Such a power would save many lives upon the field of battle," the Baron queried, scratching his beard speculatively.

"Such a power can only take lives not save them, Milord, and I have more blood now upon my hands than I ever wished," Wendell answered soberly, setting down his knife and fork. He had the feeling that he would get no rest from the noble's inquiries during the meal.

"I understand, Son, but one must know one's duty to one's lords. The day may come when you are called upon to use such powers for the good of you're country and I would think an appraisal of such assets should be mandatory if we are to properly defend our great nation," the fat old Baron informed him gruffly. Wendell started to open his mouth, but Baron Brinswick intervened on his behalf.

"You must forgive Baron Grenfork's militant attitude, Wendell. You are too young to know the turbulent border wars in which he and his honorable family defended the Duchy in the years before you were born. As a repercussion of those troubled times, he and many of the other valiant Lords who fought beside him tend to see shadows of war at the best of times when we should be doing not but enjoying our meals and each other's fine company," Baron Brinswick stated elegantly, before tilting his head to the old Baron and raising his glass to his health. The old fat Baron was silent for a moment then broke out into a bout of loud boorish laughter that made many turn their heads and gawk at him.

"I don't think I've ever been called an obnoxious old warmonger with such elegance in my life, Baron Brinswick," Baron Grenfork raised his goblet to his fellow Baron with tears in the corners of his eyes once his mirth had subsided, and many of the surrounding Lords and Ladies laughed as well.

Wendell was just beginning to hope that he could take a bite of the meat pudding in the distraction, but before he could raise his fork the Duke's chime was sounded signaling that it was time for the second course to begin. Immediately all present set down their silverware and sat back in their chairs as the lines of blue-uniformed servants returned to remove their plates. Wendell released an audible sigh as he watched his untested meat pudding taken away. Mary cracked a small smile as she noted his longing for the food now quickly being taken out of reach.

The red-uniformed servants returned to top off everyone's goblets before the blue-uniformed servants brought in the second course of small game hens drenched in a bloody looking sauce. Again all were given their portion and all eyes turned to the Duke. The Duke made no toast, but simply made a show of cutting off a small piece of his hen and taking a bite. This was the cue that the second course had begun and once again the tables erupted in conversation and feasting.

Wendell had hope when he saw Baron Grenfork cut into his game hen finally intent upon his food but before he'd even finished cutting off a single bite someone cleared their throat behind his chair. All present stopped and looked at the Duke's personal servant still holding the ceremonial golden diner chime. Wendell sighed heavily and put down his silverware before he turned in his chair.

"Wendell Glasswright, his Grace request you're presence," the purple-uniformed servant made a slight bow after his announcement, then two yellow-uniformed servants rushed forward to draw back his chair for him.

Wendell rose and was guided between the tables towards the Duke, fully conscious of all the eyes that watched him along the way. He tried very hard to remember all Baron Brinswick's lessons as they marched, but in his nervousness could hardly remember a thing beyond the fact that the Duke was to be referred to as 'Your Grace' rather than 'Milord.' The march into his Grace's presence was one of the most uncomfortable of Wendell's life.

The Duke was a small lean-muscled man of some twenty years. He had neatly trimmed dark hair and a very pale complexion. His features were noble and fair but seemed a bit immature despite his apparent age. He paid Wendell no attention whatsoever as he slowly ate his game hen before the ravenous Apprentice, one tiny mouthwatering bite at a time pausing every so often for a small sip of wine. When the hen had been reduced to all but skeletal remains, he wiped his mouth carefully upon his napkin and turned to examine Wendell closely. Through all this, the beautiful teenaged Duchess slept soundly in her chair with soft gentle snores.

"You're duel was fought honorably, Wizard. Know that I will testify to the Magician that you gave his Apprentice more than one opportunity to withdraw his challenge. That is all," the Duke stated quietly then turned back to his wine goblet, dismissing Wendell completely.

"Thank you, Your Grace," Wendell barely remembered before the purple-uniformed servant motioned him to return to his seat. The Duke didn't acknowledge his gratitude at all as he sipped his wine.

Wendell wasn't even back to his seat before the chime rang out to signal the final course of the evening. He found himself having to walk quickly to stay ahead of the blue-uniformed servants as they whisked the dishes away behind him. He sat back down in his chair and was pushed in by the yellow-uniformed servants just in time to watch his game hen be taken away. Both Mary and Baron Brinswick were smirking at him this time, though they tried to disguise their smiles.

Again the red-uniformed servants filed through to top off the goblets, then the blue-uniformed servants returned to serve desert. This desert was a bite-sized square of fudge toped with a sugar-glazed cherry. As this tiny sweet was set upon Wendell plate, Mary couldn't help but to release a giggle as his shoulders slumped in defeat. As soon as the Duke signaled that desert could begin Wendell grabbed the closest fork within reach, stabbed the tiny piece of fudge, and jammed it into his mouth.

47

Wendell and Mary rose well before dawn for they had gotten little to no sleep. When Baron Brinswick had readied himself, they left the apartment and headed into the city to witness Aggie's execution. It did not take long for them to reach the dreaded square at which Lavittia's justice was carried out.

The Square of Sorrows, as it was commonly referred to by the Lavittians, was unadorned with the embellished stone work that was common through out the city. This square's soul feature was the large guillotine set upon a raised platform against the side wall of the Barbican. Grim-faced watchmen were already about servicing this gruesome device of death when the three arrived with their escort, sharpening its heavy slanted-blade with files and oiling its pulleys. When these men had completed their task, the blade was raised until it locked in place ten feet above the wooden stock. The watchmen then removed a gourd from a burlap sack and placed it within the stock as if it were a human head. Mary winced and grew paler than Wendell would have believed possible when the release cord was pulled and the guillotine's heavy blade fell to slice the gourd neatly in two with the dull shriek of metal sliding over metal. Satisfied that their job was complete, the two watchmen raised the blade once more before they sat down on the edge of the platform to eat their breakfast of the raw sweet gourd.

As the sky began to lighten with the first hint of dawn, people started to slowly trickle into the Square of Sorrows to witness the execution to come. Most were the lowest form of vermin the great city had to offer, who jested with one another with ghoulish anticipation of the execution. These foul folk were very fortunate it was taking every ounce of Mary's will to keep her face in its emotionless stone-like countenance, so she may obey her mentor's command to shed no tears or Aggie may not have been the only Witch to be tried for murder. Some of the crowd were not like these bloodthirsty Ghouls: some looked to be grim-faced public officials and noblemen intent to see justice was done, others wept and were dressed in the black shrouds of mourning that marked them as family of the victimized barber as they huddled together for support. To Wendell's surprise, these mourners seem just as outraged by the Ghoul's behavior as he and one man amongst them even cursed those nearest for their callousness to their pain. After that the Ghouls kept their jests to themselves or in more respectable murmurs.

As true light filtered down upon the Square, the ominous beat of a single drum preceded Aggie's escort as they filed out of the Barbican. These men surrounded the Witch as stern as death itself as they marched towards the guillotine with their swords held unsheathed against their red uniformed shoulders. Aggie looked very small as she shuffled along amidst these large men, muttering under her breath in irritation still holding her shoulder pouch and wearing the bright red scarf tied around her head. One of the mourners spat at her as she passed but shrank away under the Witch's terrifying glare, looking as if he'd just seen his own death in her eyes. Aggie was escorted to the top of the platform and a hush of anticipation fell over the crowd.

"Aggie Hartford, you have been found guilty of murder and sentenced to death by the guillotine. Have you any last words before your sentence is carried out?" a very deep-voiced Magistrate with a long curly powdered wig asked loud enough for all to hear. Aggie looked at the floor of the platform for a moment thoughtfully then shook her head.

"Nope, nothing comes to mind," Aggie grunted irritably.

"Then we shall proceed," the Magistrate nodded to her guard.

Aggie shot a look across the crowd directly at Mary that seemed to reinforce her command that the girl not shed a tear. When she was certain Mary had received the silent message, she gave a slight nod of approval and turned towards the guillotine with determination.

"I can do it myself!" Aggie growled irritably towards the guard -- who moved forward intent upon forcing her head down into the guillotine's stock -- with a glare that caused him to instantly back away.

Aggie paused a moment to give the guillotine a once over before she knelt down and put her neck within the stock's groove to be secured. The same guard approached more respectfully this time and carefully lowered the upper portion of the stock to lock the Witch's head into place. When he'd cleared out of the way, the Magistrate cleared his throat and addressed Aggie once more.

"Aggie Hartford, prepare to meet justice for you're heinous crime," the Magistrate declared grimly.

The drummer began a rolling beat that built along with the crowd's anticipation. Mary watched like a grim statue of a mournful Goddess, betraying no emotion save to squeeze Wendell's hand as tightly as a vice. Aggie looked up as the drum's beat climaxed and grinned wearily just before the Magistrate nodded his head to the executioner and the guillotine's release cord was pulled. The crowd released a gasp of excitement as the dull shriek of metal sliding over metal proceeded

Aggie's severed head tumbling into the wicker basket below. Most cheered the Witch's demise, even amongst the black-shrouded mourners.

The crowd's jubilation was short lived however for a moment later Aggie's headless body stood up, striaghtened her gown, and proceeded to walk around the guillotine to fetch her head. One could have heard a pin drop upon the cobblestones, as Aggie's body leaned over the wicker basket with blood pulsing from its neck and picked up her head in both hands. Aggie's body raised the dead-looking head before her for the entire gasping crowd to see, and then turned to present it to the magistrate and guards. These men backed away quickly from this macabre spectacle and more than one tumbled off the platform to get away from it. After a few moments Aggie's body turned away, walked slowly down the steps, and then presented its horrific trophy to the black-shrouded mourners. These mourners and the surrounding crowed reacted the same way. Many tripped over themselves to get away from the restless corps that seemed to refuse to succumb to death.

Aggie's body then raised her head high above and turned around slowly to give all one final look at it before setting back to its proper place upon her neck. The severed flesh instantly mended as if it had never been marred and within a few seconds the Witch's face returned to a healthy life-like pallor. The crowd winced as Aggie's eyes snapped open and rolled back into place to fix them with an irritated glare. She looked them all over once then gave them a slight nod before turning to march directly towards Wendell and Mary, causing even more people to trip over themselves to get out of her way.

"I don't suppose you two thought to bring along my horse?" Aggie asked accusingly. When they failed to answer she sighed with frustration, "Well, I guess I'll have to ride with you, Mary. Come on, I don't what to miss a moment of tormenting Bergstrom for his overindulgence. Block-headed fool would drink all the time if I didn't remind him just how painful a hang over can really be."

48

"Get up, you lazy old fool!" Aggie cackled as she banged two frying pans together above Bergstrom's head causing both he and Reginald to start awake with cries of pain.

"Hell spawned Witch! What are you trying to do, kill me?" Bergstrom cursed miserably as he held his head. Aggie seemed truly pleased by this reaction and grinned wickedly as she ceased her banging.

"I think I need another drink," Reginald muttered as he rubbed his temples. "Donavan? Where is that blasted boy?"

"Dead," Aggie stated bluntly. Both Bergstrom and Reginald looked at her as if they'd just been kicked in the head, "He challenged Wendell to a duel and was found wanting."

Both Wizards turned slowly and fixed their questioning gazes on Wendell. Wendell had been dreading this moment and found it was far worse than he'd anticipated now that it was here. The Apprentice sighed deeply then approached the Magician as if he were walking towards the gallows. When he stood before the old Wizard he found he couldn't bring himself to look him in the eye so he focused on the floor at his feet.

"Forgive me, Mr. Giles. I wished Donavan no ill but he left me little choice in the matter. I gave him opportunities to withdraw after it became clear that he wasn't up to the challenge but he refused. I took no pleasure in his death and regret that it was necessary," Wendell explained honestly, still looking at his feet.

"You..." Reginald growled dangerously and thunder rolled above the Palace. Wendell looked up into the Magician's eyes and saw them burning with hatred.

"Reginald, control yourself!" Bergstrom was suddenly between them placing his hands upon the Magician's shoulders, "You told me yourself the boy was hot tempered and stubborn."

"I...He..." Reginald sputtered as he tried to come to grips with Donavan's loss. After a moment he stormed toward the door, but stopped in the threshold and glared back at Wendell and then Bergstrom, "You have until nightfall to remove him from Lavittia or I shall do it for you."

Bergstrom winced at the tone the Magician put into his statement. The Magician glared once more at Wendell then stormed out, slamming the door to his Study behind him. Bergstrom's shoulders sagged and Wendell felt his despair at his friend's loss.

"Master I..." Wendell started, but Bergstrom cut him off quietly.

"Go pack your bags, we're leaving. Meet us at the south gate when you're ready," Bergstrom commanded seemingly without feeling.

"Yes, Master," Wendell sighed and started towards the door. Mary quickly followed after him.

"He's been torturing himself enough without you being angry at him, too," Aggie stated after the children were gone, "He isn't like that other boy. Wendell feels what he had to do was wrong and it's been eating him up inside."

"I know, Aggie. I can feel his pain," Bergstrom informed her quietly.

"Then I guess your going to have to decide which is more important to you, the love of that boy or your friendship to that treacherous snake," Aggie growled as she stuffed her frying pans into her palm-sized cauldron with a bazaar warping of their forms.

"There's no decision to be made, Wendell is all that matters," Bergstrom sighed as he finally looked at the Witch.

"Well good," Aggie grunted a little taken back that she wasn't going to get to lecture him further, "I'm glad that's settled. It will be good to get out of here, the cities a pain in the neck."

"Why are your clothes bloody?" Bergstrom asked as he rubbed his temple.

"I got executed this morning, not that you would care what with traipsing around the dream realms with that foolish grin on your face," Aggie glared at him accusingly.

"Again? Who'd you kill this time?" Bergstrom glared at her with blantant disapproval.

"Someone who sorely had it coming," Aggie answered cryptically, "Anyway I'd best get to my packing so we can be off."

"What packing? You keep everything you own in that satchel," Bergstrom growled as she headed towards the door. The door slammed shut before the Witch could make her escape, "You better explain yourself, Aggie. I told you I wouldn't tolerate you returning to your evil ways no matter how much I love you."

"The man caused me great emotional distress then threatened to have me arrested. I didn't mean to kill him, but it happened. I was sentenced and faced my punishment even though I sorely wanted to escape just because you've taught me to be responsible for my actions. So don't start getting all judgmental about what I've done or you'll sorely regret it, Bergstrom," Aggie turned around and shook her finger at the old Wizard defiantly.

"How?" Bergstrom asked placing his hands on his hips.

"How what?" Aggie grunted meeting his stare evenly.

"How did he cause you great emotional distress?" Bergstrom narrowed his eyes at her.

"Oh, that how," Aggie suddenly couldn't seem to meet his eyes.

"Yes, that how," Bergstrom began to tap his foot impatiently.

"Well, he gave me a haircut," Aggie sighed as she glanced around the Study at everything but him.

"A haircut. You killed a man over a haircut?" Bergstrom glared at her with disgust.

"A really bad haircut," Aggie stated sheepishly as she unconsciously put her hand up to her scarf to make certain it was still in place.

"Let me see it," Bergstrom demanded.

"I'd rather you didn't," Aggie stated truthfully.

"Let me see it, Aggie, or we're going to have to settle this the old way," Bergstrom threatened.

"I think that might be preferable," Aggie admitted thoughtfully.

"Aggie..." Bergstrom's tone told her there was no other way out of this. With a heavy sigh, she slowly untied the red scarf and showed him the abominable haircut. Bergstrom was silent for a long time as he stared at her hair, "Alright, he had it coming."

49

"Are you going to be alright, Milord?" Wendell asked as he and Mary said their farewells back at the Baron's apartment, "We never did learn who tried to poison you."

"I think so. I've spread the word throughout the Court that someone attempted to poison me and have made a point of being very visible. I think any further attempts would outrage so many Lords at this point that even the Magician would be reluctant to tempt their wrath," Baron Brinswick smiled wearily.

"What if he tries to frame someone else for the deed? Then it would cost him nothing to kill you," Mary asked furrowing her brow with worry.

"The right people have been informed of my suspicions of the Magician's involvement. I don't think he'll risk it. I'm far more concerned with what he might do to you, Wendell. You don't have a title to protect you and the Magician's reach is long," the Baron warned with concern.

"I'll be alright as long as my Master is around. He won't allow any harm to befall me," Wendell smiled.

"I hope you're right, Wendell. That's enough of such talk. I wish you both a safe journey and bid you to remember my oath. Should you need anything you have but to ask," the Baron tilted his head with respect to the Apprentice.

"Farewell, Baron," Wendell nodded in return.

As they left the Baron's apartment Wendell and Mary met Lady Greta Highbreak in the corridor on her way to see them. After Mary's curse had been lifted, the two young women had become friends of a sort and Mary was glad she was able to see her before they departed. The freckly young Lady was a bit upset as she drew towards them determinedly.

"Oh Mary, I'm glad I caught up with you. I'm afraid my father's been called back home so we'll be leaving within the hour," Greta told them, before realizing their own traveling packs were upon their backs.

"We're leaving as well. What road will you be taking?" Mary asked.

"Northeast towards the Breakgrad Mountains. That's where we live," Greta stated excitedly until she saw Mary's face fall.

"We're headed south," Mary sighed.

"Well then you must promise to write me," Greta conjured a folded parchment from her gown's sleeve and presented it to Mary, "Here is my address."

"But I don't know how to read or write," Mary confessed as she took the parchment.

"Then how are you able to learn magic?" Greta asked in confusion.

"Witchery is different than Wizardry. We feel our way around magic rather than learn it from books," Mary explained.

"Well then have Wendell write for you, or better yet have him teach you. I'd love to hear all about the differences between the two arts,"

Greta smiled, and then she embraced Mary, "I have to go. My father is going to be cross when he discovers I've snuck out while I'm suppose to be packing as it is. Safe journey to you."

"And to you as well, Milady," Wendell smiled and nodded to her before she hurried away.

"I can probably teach you how to read on the journey home," Wendell told Mary as they headed towards the southern Courtyard.

Despite the beauty and splendor of the Palace, both Wendell and Mary were relieved to be leaving it. It was not their place as they had found out all too quickly, and the idea of returning home was very appealing indeed. Wendell found himself thinking about his father's words of wisdom their last night before this journey began and smiled as he realized how the splendors of the Palace seemed like hollow illusions in comparison to the quiet tranquility of their valley home.

"Are you two ready yet?" Aggie growled irritably from behind them as they entered the southern Courtyard. They turned to find the Witch and Bergstrom walking towards them holding hands.

"We just need to fetch the horses from the stable," Wendell answered her noting that both she and his Master were blushing happily.

"Don't bother; they'd only slow us down," Bergstrom stated with amusement as he reached out and grasped both his and Mary's shoulders and turned them about so they were now facing their village from about a quarter mile up the hill from the stone bridge.

"I really wish you'd show me that trick," Wendell smiled as he looked down at home.

"All in good time," Bergstrom chuckled.

"Well, it isn't as bad as I imagined," Aggie stated thoughtfully as she peered down at their village, "Maybe I'll stick around for awhile and see how it feels."

"I told you you'd like it, Aggie," Bergstrom smiled.

"Well, no promises," The old Witch grunted and then without a word of farewell she marched off into the woods.

"Aggie?" Mary called after the Witch and started to follow but Bergstrom held her in place gently and shook his head, "I thought she said she was going to stay?"

"She is, but Aggie doesn't like society all that much on account of she was raised alone in a swamp by a Witch. She'll find a place she likes in the woods somewhere to set up her hut. Give her a few months to warm up to the idea and she might come into town once in awhile. Until then you'll just have to come out here when you want to visit her," Bergstrom explained as they watched Aggie disappear into the trees.

"How will I find her?" Mary asked as the old Wizard started to guide them down the road towards the village.

"I think if you go into the woods intent on finding her she'll find you," Bergstrom chuckled.

"Is that why you've not married, Master?" Wendell asked reluctantly. He'd been feeling Bergstrom's love for the Witch ever since they'd approached from the Palace.

"That, and other reasons. Our relationship is very complex. We long for one another when we're apart and drive each other insane when we're together. I think this trip is likely the most time we've spent together in several decades. But who knows, maybe it's a sign things are changing. We didn't start fighting this time before she left like every other time we've parted," Bergstrom chuckled with the thought.

"She told me to give you these last night," Mary told him as she handed him the six stockings, "She even made them mismatched so the Brownie won't steal them."

"That was very thoughtful of her. Thank you, Mary," Bergstrom stated with a curious expression as he examined the stockings.

Wendell was about to ask his Master what was the matter but at that moment a hand grabbed the back of his robe and yanked him into another place and time. As the disorientation passed, Wendell found he was in a long dark corridor adorned with ugly gargoyle-like sconces and moth-eaten tapestries. He turned to find that he was being held by a future version of himself -- a much darker version of himself.

This future Wendell was perhaps thirty years his senior and held none of the happiness he'd had earlier in his life. The left side of his face was a mass of scar tissue from what looked to be the most horrific of burns while the right was a haggard deeply lined visage of a man who's been dwelling in darkness for many years. His hair and beard were much longer and had lost all color as they hung limply about his head. He was still clothed in midnight blue robes but had a thick black cape draped over his left side that hung down to only about an inch above the uneven flagstone floor. His future self released him, looked into his eyes for a long moment, and then moved to pass him down the corridor.

"Follow me," his future self commanded without emotion as he passed. He walked with a pronounced limp and dragged his left leg with each step making a horrible scraping sound against the flagstones.

"What happened to us?" Wendell ventured more to distract himself from the horrible scraping of the future Wendell's left foot than out of curiosity.

"Reginald Giles," the Future Wendell hissed with a hatred that made Wendell wince. He chose to ask no more questions of himself as they proceeded down the hall.

The Future Wendell led himself to the end of the hall and opened the door before them with a wave of his right hand. The huge square chamber beyond was if anything gloomier for the shutters were all closed over the windows even though sunlight trickled in through the cracks. The central facet of this chamber was the Legacy Tome upon a short table with a bench before it. A sanctuary circle was engraved in the floor around the Tome and bench as well a second circle that Wendell didn't recognize. Before the windows stood two large objects draped with heavy black velvet cloth that had lumpy shapes that defied Wendell's guesses as to what lay underneath. On the other side of the chamber was a large shelf full of spell components as well as a cloth-covered bird cage. As the Future Wendell limped through the two circles, a crow-like squawk erupted from beneath the cage's veil.

The Future Wendell lowered himself onto the bench carefully, using only his right arm for support. During the course of this strenuous exercise, the black cape slid open to reveal the left leg that had scraped so horribly. The Younger Wendell gasped as he saw the left leg was transformed into cracked and fissured stone as it jutted from beneath his robes. The elder Wendell smiled hideously as he drew his cape back over the petrified appendage.

"Not the man we use to be," the elder Wendell stated dryly.

"Why have you brought me here?" Wendell demanded quietly. He didn't like this elder Wendell; he was far too callous and cold as he sat in this dark room. This future Wendell reminded him far too much of Mr. Garroph, or at least what he imagined Mr. Garroph's life had been like.

"No pleasantries? Very well, I'll get straight to the point. I want to teach you some advanced magic so this..." He waved his right hand over his left side while turning his head so the burns could be seen in horrific detail, "Doesn't happen to us."

"I don't think that would be proper. Our Master ..." the younger Wendell began but the future Wendell cut him off angrily.

"Thinks we have time, but we don't! Reginald's vengeance is coming even as we walk down the hill towards the village! We must be prepared for it or else..." the Future Wendell trailed off and his anger melted into a deep sadness. He took a deep breath and let it out heavily. Once he'd regained control of his temper he started again in a cold even tone, "Forgive me; I haven't had much human contact for a very long time. Let's start again shall we? Go and look upon what's under those drapes. When you've seen all you can bear, cover them back up and then open the shutters so you may look upon the valley."

"Don't do it, Wendell!" A bird like voice cawed from the birdcage.

"Be silent, old bird!" Future Wendell barked with annoyance, "Go on, there's no harm in seeing what I would have you prevent is there?"

Wendell wasn't so certain but he wasn't able to resist the macabre curiosity of the two large lumpy covered masses. He went to the larger of the two first and with a shaky hand tugged off the heavy black velvet cloth to reveal the horror that lay beneath. It was his Master locked in a silent scream forever for he'd been petrified into stone. Bergstrom's hands were extended before him as if trying to shield himself from something while his face was turned away locked forever in his last scream of utter terror. Wendell couldn't breathe as he stared into the grey eyes of his master which held far too much detail to have ever been sculpted with an artisan's chisel. He looked at his future self but the elder Wendell was making a point to look away not wishing to see their Master. Wendell covered the statue up again then looked at the other with a deep chilling dread.

"The other is even worse. Prepare yourself," the elder Wendell stated without looking as if he could read his mind.

"W-who is it?" Wendell asked as he found his breath again. He thought he knew the answer but something compelled him to ask anyway.

"You know the answer; now find your courage and look. I wish to never utter her name again," Future Wendell whispered in a voice devoid of emotion.

Wendell approached the statue of his love, but as he reached for the black velvet drape he found he didn't have the will to look into another set of life like stone eyes. Slowly he withdrew until he was leaning against the wall next to one of the large shuttered windows. His breath was coming in short gasps that made him dizzy.

"That's alright. I can't bare to look at her either. When you've gained control once again go ahead and look out the window. The view is terrible but nothing compared to looking upon her," the elder Wendell turned and smiled grimly at his younger self.

When Wendell had calmed himself he did as he'd been instructed and opened the shutters. At first the sunlight was blinding, but as his eyes adjusted to the light he saw the village he remembered resting in the valley below. He was looking down upon the village from Mr. Garroph's tower and at first everything seemed completely normal until he started noticing the details.

The first detail Wendell noticed was the buildings all seemed in very poor repair. Paint had all but been worn away from the cottages. Many roofs had gaping holes in their shingles and some had collapsed completely. Then he noticed the yards around the houses were all overgrown and wild. Why, even the roads were choked with weeds and brush as if they'd not been used in years. And finally he noticed the people. The unnaturally still people, some of whose arms had broken off and lay beneath them in broken shards. Wendell looked as long as he could bear it and then he closed the shutters.

"I brought them up here because I couldn't bear the thought of the elements slowly wearing them away year after year," the elder Wendell confessed as he gestured towards the covered statues as if their very presence was some type of self-inflicted torture.

"Tell me how this came to pass," Wendell demanded of his future self quietly as he approached.

"It happened as we opened the door to our Master's tower coming back from Lavittia. Reginald had set up some kind of magical trap that triggered when the door was opened. There was a flash of blinding grey light and the whole village was cursed in an instant into what you've beheld," Future Wendell explained bitterly as he sagged upon his bench.

"How did we survive it?" Wendell asked curiously. The elder version laughed desolately at the question for a few moments before answering.

"We didn't. For the others the curse was designed to petrify instantly but for us it was designed to work slowly over the years so we could look upon all we loved and despair. That's Reginald's revenge. He watches us and laughs as we slowly turn to stone in his favorite garden surrounded by all we cherished. His curse also compels us to remain here. I can't leave for more than an hour before the compulsion becomes to strong to ignore and I must return. It won't matter; soon too much of my body will be stone to move anyway," the elder Wendell chuckled dryly before casting his gaze to the covered statue Wendell hadn't had the courage to unveil, "Just before I can no longer move I will go to her and embrace her in my arm. I-I think she would like that. Don't you?"

"Take me back," Wendell told the desolate husk of his future self.

"No, you must learn the magic you need to prevent this. If you are as strong as I am then you can defeat him," The elder Wendell told his younger self decisively.

"You've already given me the knowledge to prevent this. You have to trust in our Master as I still do to decide when we're ready for more powerful spells," The younger Wendell told himself, shaking his head with pity for that which he'd become.

"I've given you what you need to prevent this but not what you need to defeat him," the elder Wendell argued.

"Listen to your heart!" the bird squawked as it rattled its cage.

"What is that?" the younger Wendell asked.

"It's Aggie. She wasn't affected by the curse in the woods. She went with me to confront Reginald the first time and that's when we got these burns. She faired worse than I. Her intelligence comes and goes now. I keep her because I don't have anyone else," the elder Wendell explained with a sad sigh.

"Take me back," Wendell demanded again. After searching his own youthful eyes for several moments, the elder Wendell reluctantly nodded.

50

"How many of these jumps in time have you made, Wendell?" Bergstrom asked quietly after Wendell had told him about his latest visit to the future.

"A few," Wendell sighed as he looked down at his own distorted reflection under the stone bridge, "It's getting very confusing trying to keep it all straight in my head."

"I can imagine it is," Bergstrom muttered thoughtfully to himself.

"Well we know the spell trap is there now, so can't you just dispel it, Mr. Weatherbee?" Mary asked sitting on the bridge's rail beside Wendell.

"Possibly, but if Reginald sees that his spell trap has been removed he may just decide to make another. One we'll have no prior knowledge about this time. Leaving it be at the moment seems like a more prudent course to me, at least until we have some idea of what to do," Bergstrom scratched his beard.

"One of my future selves warned me that you have a blind spot when it comes to Mr. Giles, Master. He said that it may very well be your undoing," Wendell stated as he started to pinch his nose between his eyes. A migraine was steadily flaring.

"That may have been true in that Wendell's timeline but not in this one. If he has indeed left a spell trap for us as the cursed Wendell warned then he has gone down a very dark path and likely none of the man I befriended remains," Bergstrom sighed heavily.

"Can you take him, Mr. Weatherbee? In a fight I mean," Mary asked rather reluctantly.

"It's hard to say, Mary. Duels are always dicey affairs at best and we would be very evenly matched. It may come to that but I would prefer to defeat him another way if at all possible," Bergstrom looked at her soberly then at Wendell with concern, "Headache again?"

"Yes, Master. I'll be alright," Wendell hoped aloud. Mary pulled his had to her lips and kissed it. He felt a tingling electrical spark move through his body as her lips touched and his headache began to subside, "Thanks."

"For what?" Mary asked raising one of her eyebrows with interest.

"You made my headache go away," Wendell grinned as he kissed her hand in return. Bergstrom smiled at them. Wendell thought of everything he'd experienced then he ask his Master a new question, "Master, is it normal for Wizards to experience so much travel through time?"

"Absolutely not. I've only met one other Wizard who made mention of similar experiences and he only visualized the other possible timelines. He never actually traveled to them. It's very intriguing and frightening at the same time. It hints that you may have a very extraordinary and dangerous power that has yet to develop, Bergstrom explained.

"But you and our daughter did it as well," Wendell stated, feeling the same remorseful hurt he'd been getting each time he thought of the daughter he may have erased from ever being when he killed Donavan.

"From what you said I used a device to accomplish the act and your daughter may have inherited the power just as you inherited your mother's Third Sight," Bergstrom looked at Wendell curiously, "Let's try a little experiment. I want you to visualize a specific point in time and concentrate upon it."

Wendell closed his eyes and did as he was told. He concentrated upon the day he and Mary fell in love under their old Oak tree within the wood. It was a particularly vivid memory that he often thought about and concentrating upon it wasn't very difficult. A few minutes went by and nothing happened. Finally he gave up and opened his eyes. The world before him distorted for a moment as if he was looking at it through a peace of thick slightly warped glass and then returned to normal.

"Nothing huh? Well it was worth a try," Bergstrom shrugged.

"No, for a moment the world looked strange just as I opened my eyes but then it returned to normal," Wendell scratched his head, disheveling his stocking cap. Mary unconsciously straightened it a moment later.

"Strange how?" Bergstrom asked curiously.

"Like looking through thick glass or still clear water," Wendell described it.

"Forgive me, Mary, but I think I need some time alone with Wendell," Bergstrom told the girl apologetically after thinking on what Wendell had told him for a moment.

"Oh, well I suppose I should go let my parents know I back anyway," Mary smiled. She then hopped down from the rail, gave Wendell a kiss goodbye, and then headed for home.

"Come on," Bergstrom pulled on Wendell's arm when Mary had walked about a hundred feet down the road and took him to a long sandy beach on a tropical island.

The Island's heat hit Wendell like a physical blow and he gasped under the weight of the change in humidity. Despite this the view around him was spectacular for never before had he seen either the sea or tropical plants such as palm trees. Bergstrom smiled at the look of awe upon Wendell's face as he gazed around in wonder.

"Not bad, aye?" Bergstrom asked after letting the boy soak up his surroundings, "One of the ships I traveled on in my youth stopped here to make repairs after a particularly violent storm. I find it to be a very nice place when I need solitude. Much better, I think, than artic mountain ranges, isn't it?"

"It's a shame we couldn't bring Mary, she'd love it," Wendell sighed as he watched the turquoise waves crash out beyond the coral reef.

"Well, perhaps you can bring her here one day by yourself. Today we need to talk about what you've just experienced," Bergstrom chuckled. "What you described sounds very much like what I experience during a teleport and I think perhaps unlocking one power may start with mastering another. So I think that I'm going to show you how to teleport far sooner than I had intended and trust that you have the wisdom to use the power wisely despite your youth."

Wendell couldn't help but grin. The ability to move from one place to another instantly like his Master had been alluring ever since he'd discovered the old Wizard could do it.

"This power like most starts with visualization and is not so very different from scrying. We're going to start by visualizing the end of the beach there," Bergstrom pointed to where the beach curved out of view along the tree line. "Lock the image of it into your mind then visualize moving there in a single step. When you think you've got it, your going to open your eyes and take that step. As you teleport you'll see the world out of focus as you described. It's important that you pay it no mind and just step through the distortion to the end of the beach. That's all there is to it, so whenever your ready go ahead."

Wendell gazed at the end of the beach for nearly a minute, memorizing every detail. He then closed his eyes and visualized stepping to where he'd seen. When Wendell was certain he had it completely worked out in his brain he opened his eyes and stepped forward to teleport for the first time. Bergstrom chuckle with mirth as Wendell reappeared far out to sea above the water with a cry of surprise before he fell in with a great splash. Shaking his head, the old Wizard kicked off his boots and teleported to fetch his drowning Apprentice.

"That was very good, Wendell, you even managed to hold onto your hat," Bergstrom chuckled as he patted the choking and sopping wet Apprentice on the back, "The problem was you were focusing upon the general landscape instead of the spot you wanted to step. It's a common mistake and the reason I chose the beach to practice on."

"You're really enjoying this, aren't you?" Wendell asked glaring with accusation after he'd finished clearing his lungs.

"I don't know what you're talking about?" Bergstrom smirked as he rung the water from his robes, "When you're ready, try it again."

It took several more attempts before Wendell got the hang of teleporting. He missed the beach completely several times and landed on a palm tree once. Despite these setbacks and the painful scratches and lumps, Wendell learned how to teleport.

Once Wendell was comfortably teleporting from one spot to another, he and Bergstrom worked on his speed and accuracy with an exciting game of teleport tag around the Island. While Wendell could not catch his Master, by the end of the game he was only a step behind at any given time. When they were finished, they gathered driftwood and started a large fire on the beach to keep them warm as they talked about different ways the power could be used.

SECTION 6

51

When Wendell awoke the sun was already up and the air was growing warm. He found his Master down the beach, wading barefoot in the sandy shallows gazing out to sea lost in thought. Despite Wendell's first impulse to teleport to his Master, the Apprentice walked to meet the old Wizard. When he drew near it was clear from the bags under his eyes that Bergstrom had not slept. Wendell stopped near his Master's side, waited for a moment, and then cleared his throat quietly to draw attention to himself.

"You should get some rest, Master," Wendell suggested respectfully when the old Wizard turned his gaze upon the boy.

"Perhaps in a bit," Bergstrom smiled wearily, "You should conjure yourself something to eat before we get started today."

"Yes, Master," Wendell acknowledged and then took off his hat to conjure a large sugar frosted pastry. A portion of this pastry ended up being thrown to the large black-striped white Seagulls that were hovering and fishing nearby.

"I want you to focus once more upon a specific point in time, Wendell, but like with teleporting I want you to visualize stepping into that time in a single step. I'm going to be holding onto your robe during this in case you succeed. When you think your ready, open your eyes and take the step. Remember that we are merely observers. I don't want to change things, just see if I'm right about how your power works," Bergstrom instructed.

"What if we're seen, Master? Won't that change things in itself?" Wendell asked.

"You have a point. Wait a moment and I'll conceal us," Bergstrom opened his belt-pouch and fished within until he found a small shard of broken glass. He then used the glass to cast a spell of invisibility over himself and Wendell. Once his casting was completed Bergstrom grasped onto Wendell's sleeve, "Whenever you're ready, Wendell."

Again Wendell focused upon the day he and Mary fell in love. It leaped into his mind with pleasant clarity and he visualized going there in a single step. When he felt he had it, he opened his eyes and took his first step into the past. It wasn't easy or pleasant. The distorted air before him resisted the intrusion like a thick barrier of honey and he felt a painful tugging in his bellybutton, as if he was struggling against an invisible tether. These sensations seemed to last for a long time even though Wendell was only taking a single step. Wendell then burst through.

"Wow, that sounds exciting. I wish I could learn magic. Its way more fun than being a milkmaid," The twelve year old Mary admitted longingly, as she watched the Wendell of the past stuff a handful of acorns into his belt pouch nervously. The future Wendell hadn't realized how much she'd changed over the years and even the sound of her voice seemed strange in comparison with the Mary of his time.

"Master says it isn't all good, some of its very frightening and dangerous," The younger Wendell stated just before his childish features turned from happiness to an introspective look of despair, "And my Apprenticeship didn't come without a heavy price," he stated quietly, full of sadness and gloom.

"How much did your father have to pay? My father has already started saving my dowry in an oak chest he keeps on the mantle. It might be enough to cover an Apprenticeship, that is if Mr. Weatherbee is willing to train girls," the pretty little Mary asked as they stood up and brushed the dirt and twigs from their clothing.

"That isn't the kind of cost I was talking about. As far as money goes my Master paid my father. That's apparently the way of it with Wizards, because even Mr. Garroph tried to pay my father to train me. I think you have to show you have some magical talent first though before their interested," the young Wendell stated looking very sad as he avoided Mary's gaze.

"Oh. So what was the cost you were talking about?" the young Mary asked with concern as she watched him closely.

The young Wendell remained silent for a time before he turned to her with tears welling in his eyes.

"My mother is afraid of magic and the supernatural. And now since the magic has awakened in my blood she's afraid of me, too. I became my Master's Apprentice because she wouldn't come home while I was there," the young Wendell told her quietly as he wiped his eyes on his sleeve.

Little Mary knocked him back a step as she embraced him in a fierce little hug. He stiffed at first, startled and frightened by the contact, but after a few moments embraced her warmly in return. They held each other for a few minutes this way and Future Wendell had to fight the urge to run up and embrace the both of them as he was overcome by his own emotions. Bergstrom silently tugged upon his sleeve, reminding the elder Wendell this was not their time.

"Don't worry, Wendell; I won't abandon you like she has," the crying little Mary promised as Future Wendell closed his eyes and visualized stepping back to the future, "Even, even if we're not meant to be together. I'll always be your friend."

Little Mary's voice echoed hollowly as Wendell stepped through time back to the present and was once again crushed under the tropical island's heat. Bergstrom canceled the invisibility spell with a word just as Wendell swooned with exhaustion and fell down into the sand. The old Wizard pulled from his pocket a glass goblet with a funny little red umbrella that was filled with a light blue liquid and handed it to the Apprentice. The glass goblet was ice cold, but before Wendell tried the colorful beverage he fished out the small bright paper umbrella and looked at the old Wizard questioningly.

"I don't know. That just seems to happen here," Bergstrom shrugged, "The drinks are quiet tasty. Go ahead and try it."

Wendell had to agree with his Master's assessment after he'd sampled the wonderful icy beverage. Its sweet flavor was like nothing he'd ever tried before. It seemed to be made of liquid snow.

"Tell me what the travel was like for you," Bergstrom instructed thoughtfully as Wendell downed the drink greedily and then examined the masterfully crafted goblet with interest.

"It was kind of like pushing through the sanctuary barrier for the first time, though not as exhausting. There was some pain in my belly when we traveled back but the return was far easier. What did it feel like to you?" Wendell asked with interest as he vanished the empty glass goblet with a wave of his hand.

"Disorienting. The world seemed to blur and distort around me and it took a few moments to recover," Bergstrom explained thoughtfully and then he grinned with amused nostalgia, "I had forgotten how cute you and Mary were when you were younger."

"Seeing her and me like that was strange, but pleasant for me as well. I hadn't realized how much we've grown over the last couple years," Wendell grinned, "Now I can understand why most of my future selves, you, and Mary get so nostalgic each time they see me."

"We tend to forget the little things as the years go by," Bergstrom stated quietly as he looked out to sea thoughtfully. After a moment he chuckled and turned back, "I just had a very interesting idea. Why don't you try to scry one of your memories of the past."

Wendell obeyed, excited by the idea as he fished his crystal ball out of his belt-pouch. Quickly he thought of the game of teleport tag they'd played the day before and within seconds the image of the two popping back and forth across the beach appeared within the crystal along with the sounds of their laughter.

"I think that will be far safer to use to lock onto specific memories before you travel through time," Bergstrom suggested after a moment distracting Wendell's concentration so the crystal went blank, "Now try scrying the future."

"I don't know what to visualize?" Wendell started, after staring at the crystal ball for a moment.

"You have a point," Bergstrom looked around thoughtfully for a moment then pointed at a coconut in a nearby tree. "In a minute or two, I'm going to cause that coconut to fall by magic. Try visualizing it."

Wendell closed his eyes for a few moments getting the picture of his Master blasting the coconut down with a bolt of lightning. When he had the image visualized, he opened his eyes and attempted to scry it. The crystal ball remained clear showing nothing but the magnified view of Wendell's palms. After a minute or so of trying he looked up just as his Master caused the coconut to fall simply by waving his hand downward.

"It's no good. The image I visualized was of you using lightning to bring it down," Wendell sighed as he shook his head, "I can't just guess what's going to happen then scry it."

"I thought maybe you'd have foresight along with your other powers over time, but it appears the two powers are unrelated," Bergstrom mused aloud as he sat down beside Wendell, "Well we've seen what you can do, now let's look at the dangers. Already your and my apparent meddling with this power has changed the course of our lives significantly. Any time you go back and alter something you are in fact changing everything from that point on. I've seen the look you get when you mention your daughter Wendy, so I know you have some grasp of what these alterations are jeopardizing. I can't tell you not to use this power at all because clearly its use is saving our lives -- even as we speak -- and even if it weren't I'd have little chance of enforcing the command short of killing you. So let me just say that you must think very carefully before you change anything. At no time should you ever change something on a whim just to see how things turn out. Do you understand?" Bergstrom knitted his bushy eyebrows together as he looked at Wendell. Wendell nodded, "Now the second warning is to how you interact. You've managed to avoid causing a paradox backlash by taking yourself out of phase and just now by being invisible so reality wasn't confronted by the two simultaneously existing Wendells. Make certain you always take such precautions for there really is no way to tell how reality will deal with a blatant paradox. Confronting yourself could very well erase you entirely from existence or something even worse."

"What could be worse than that?" Wendell asked morbidly.

"Never ask that kind of question! The Gods just love to inflict the answer upon you if you do," Bergstrom sighed as he scanned the blue sky above them distrustfully.

"I don't know how to move out of phase, do you?" Wendell asked after a moment.

"No. Can't say as I ever gave the notion much thought," Bergstrom scratched his beard thoughtfully, "But I suppose I'll have to look into it."

Both Bergstrom and Wendell were quiet for a long time, just watching the turquoise waves crash into the beach. Wendell spied a strange armored creature scuttle across the beach sideways but it seemed fairly harmless despite its claws. The Seagulls cried across the water as the day grew warmer.

It was very peaceful on the beach, but Wendell finally decided he had to ask another question that was eating at him, "Master, what are we going to do about Reginald?" Wendell asked with a heavy sigh.

"I don't know, Wendell. I just don't know," Bergstrom whispered as he continued to watch the sea.

52

"Why don't you go spend some time with Mary and your family, Wendell? I think I'm going to go have a chat with Aggie and see how she's settling in," Bergstrom suggested after they teleported back to the stone bridge around noon, "I'll come find you when I've decided what to do."

"Yes, Master," Wendell smiled as the old Wizard turned and headed into the woods. His Master's love for the Witch was warm and pleasant to the Apprentice.

Wendell chose to walk into the village rather than teleport, for he knew such a display would generate even more displeasure towards him. He didn't mind as the warm day was pleasant and nothing as oppressive as the tropical island had been. Neighborly farmers waved to him in the fields as he passed, before returning to their never ending battle to keep their crops weed free. Swallows darted above his head on their way to and from their mud-cemented straw nests that clung to the eves of the cottages and barns. The smell of manure and freshly tilled earth welcomed Wendell home as he made his way first to Mary's cottage.

"Welcome home, Wendell!" Mrs. Miller paused from beating a dusty rug hanging on the clothes line with her broom long enough to embrace him warmly, "Mary went into town near an hour ago to get some vegetables for supper, but I'd bet you're more likely to find her at your brother-in-law's shop than the market. Chores have always been more of a suggestion between socialization to her," Mrs. Miller informed him with a frustrated shake of her head, "After you've seen your family you should come back with her and have dinner with us."

"Thank you, Mrs. Miller. I'm not certain if I'll be able to but the offer is appreciated," Wendell smiled.

"Well you know we always have plenty for one more and you're always welcome," she told him as she pulled her scarf back over her nose and prepared to pummel the rug some more.

Wendell found not only Mary but his father and Wendy chatting in the Tailor's shop, as Fredric was busy sowing the sleeve onto a plain-looking tan tunic. Mary paused from her recounting of the splendors of the Duke's palace so Wendy and his father could welcome Wendell home with warm hugs. Fredric just paused and shot him one of his rare smiles with a nod before returning to his work.

"Mary says you met the Duke! What's he like?" Wendy asked enthusiastically once she'd released him.

"He's very neat and eats ponderously slow," Wendell answered after reflecting upon the question for a moment.

"You've got to tell us everything! Absolutely everything about your journey!" Wendy was so excited Wendell began to fear she was going to go into premature labor at any moment.

"I will, but only if you calm down and have a seat so I don't have to worry about my nephew plopping out on the floor too soon," Wendell smiled as he directed her back to her stool.

"What if it's a niece?" Mr. Glasswright asked with a chuckle.

"I don't think so," Wendell answered after a moment of contemplation. He didn't know how or why but he just sensed Wendy was having a boy.

"Do you hear that, Honey? Wendell says it's going to be a boy!" Wendy exclaimed as she took her seat. Fredric just nodded without turning from his work.

The next hour and a half was spent telling the edited version of their travels to Wendell's family. Both he and Mary took turns relating the story, leaving out only little portions such as Wendell's time travel and such things that would only confuse or worry their otherwise peaceful lives. Mary had to show them the bottled universe she'd created before they'd believe she now could do magic. She had tied a leather thong around the small bottleneck and taken to wearing it as a necklace concealed under her clothes. Wendell believed that the inhabitants of the tiny universe must be the happiest in existence from where they sat against her flesh and got smacked hard by Mary in the shoulder when he made mention of it.

Further evidence was required when the accounting of the dragon's attack was told, so Wendell removed his crystal ball and showed them his memory of the events. This got even Fredric to put down his work to come see the wonders of the Sir Gawain's battle. He had them all swear they'd not relate his noble friend's origins for he did not want to take the chance the rumor would spread and cause Justin undue pain. Further memories were brought forth of the journey's many highlights all save the duel with the Magician's Apprentice. Donavan's death was still to recent and painful for Wendell to view it again and they understood.

When the storey was all told both Wendy and his father hugged Wendell again for they could see what a heavy toll the events had taken on him. Mr. Glasswright mentioned he'd noticed Wendell looked older somehow when he'd come in and now he understood why. The next few minutes were spent hearing what had been going on in the valley and Wendell was happy to hear that not much had changed.

The biggest news was the aftermath of the family's confrontation with his mother over Wendell. Apparently Maggie was now shunning all who'd opposed her decision to treat Wendell as if he were dead. Even Vernon and his wife had admitted that his mother's behavior was a bit excessive and had secretly related such to the rest of the family though their opinion of Wendell hadn't softened any. Still Wendell thought that there might be some hope for him and his older brother someday, if Vernon was recognizing the unnatural level of hatred his mother bore him. The rest of them weren't as optimistic, but they chose not to share this with the boy.

The day progressed and the shadows lengthened as they talked on trivial matters until a happy squeak interrupted them, as Squeaker ran forward to reunite with her two favorite humans with a very plump pregnant belly.

"Squeaker, you're a girl!" Wendell exclaimed in surprise as she jumped into his palm.

"You mean you didn't know?" Mary asked with a giggle as the Brownie placed her hands on her hips and gave him a perturbed whistle.

"Well I guess I just never gave it much thought," Wendell admitted as he handed the annoyed Brownie a candy in apology.

"I figured it out when I saw the male that lives here in the Tailor shop," Mary stated smugly as if it had been very obvious.

"Oh," he conjured another piece of candy as he saw the male Brownie approaching and handed it to him, "Well, I guess congratulations are in order."

Squeaker and the male whistled, that Wendell took as thanks.

53

"Now what's got you and Mary so worried, Son?" Wendell's father asked as soon as they were out of the Tailor's shop. He'd asked Wendell to walk him home as dinner approached so that Wendell could help him lift some new windows into his wagon, but now the Apprentice saw that it was just a ruse to get him alone, "Come on, out with it."

"It's the Master of the Apprentice I killed in the duel. He's left a trap for us at the tower that would curse the whole village if it went off just so he could have vengeance against me," Wendell sighed, knowing he didn't have the heart to lie to his father, "Master is trying to decide what to do about it as we speak."

"Is this Wizard powerful?" Mr. Glasswright asked bluntly as they walked towards his cottage.

"Master says they'd be evenly matched if it comes down to a fight, but we're hoping to avoid that," Wendell waved to Trevor as they passed the smithy and was happy to see the Smith's son was using the dye he'd made for him.

"Is there anything that I or anyone else in the village can do?" Mr. Glaswright asked grimly, knowing the answer already.

"No, this Wizard is beyond us. I still have faith in my Master though, he'll think of something," Wendell smiled wearily.

"Well if anyone could it would be Mr. Weatherbee. He plays the fool often enough but after watching him these past three years I know that's just a show. He is definitely clever in ways that puts the rest of us simple folk to shame," Mr. Glaswright smiled and disheveled Wendell's hat lovingly, "Go on and get back to Mary, I think I can remember the way home from here."

"There's nothing simple about you!" Wendell grinned, "I love you."

"I love you, too, Son, and I'm glad you're home safe," Mr. Glasswright embraced Wendell tightly then started for home.

Mary was just coming out of the Tailor's shop as Wendell returned with her nearly forgotten vegetable basket looped around her arm. They took each other's hand without a word and started towards Mary's house. As they crossed the deserted market square she looked around and let out a heavy sigh.

"It really is quite small, the village I mean. I never noticed it before but I have been since we got back," she smiled and laughed merrily, "I'm not complaining mind you, but it doesn't even have a name."

"Yes, it does," Wendell stated, gazing at her beautiful face as she turned back to him and raised a questioning straw colored eyebrow, "It's Home; and I can think of no better name in the whole world."

"I love you, Wendell," she smiled again and leaned over and kissed him tenderly.

"I love you, too, Mary," he answered as she drew away.

"Last night was horrible," she pouted as they walked on, "We've been sleeping together for so long I kept waking up and wondering where you had gone."

"We don't have much longer. Be patient my love," Wendell squeezed her hand.

"I thought we'd be of age by the time we got back, but then Mr. Weatherbee just whisked us back in an instant. The next few weeks are going to be torture," she shook her head with disgust.

"I nearly forgot, there's something I want you to see," Wendell grinned mischievously as he looked around to make certain no one was watching, "Close your eyes."

"Alright," Mary smiled happily, she always liked his surprises. In a moment, it got much warmer and the smell of the air changed completely. "What are you up to, Wendell?" Mary asked, wrinkling her beautiful freckly nose at the salty air.

"Have a look for yourself," Wendell chuckled as he embraced her from behind.

"Oh!" Was all Mary could say as she opened her eyes to find the sea before her just as the sun was setting brilliantly. Tears of wonder and joy welled in her eyes as she beheld the sight of waves reflecting the fiery rays of the setting sun as they rolled into the sandy shore. After a few minutes, she sighed heavily and whispered in a voice choked with emotion, "I never thought I'd see it. I'd heard stories but I never dreamed..."

"Master taught me how to teleport. We can come and see it whenever you like," Wendell whispered in her ear before kissing her gently on the neck. She sighed happily and leaned back against him, Wendell grinned and said, "We'd better get back, though. Your mother will be wanting those vegetables. I just couldn't wait to show you."

"Alright, but I think she'd forgive me once she knew the reason," Mary sighed as she tried to memorize every detail of the sea.

"Close your eyes again," Wendell instructed before transporting them back to the road in front of Mary's cottage. They quickly went inside.

"You're late!" Mrs. Miller accused crossly, drawing a pan of rolls from the oven as Wendell and Mary came in. Mr. Miller was already sitting at the dining room table dozing as he waited for dinner.

"Sorry, Mother, but you'll never guess what Wendell just showed me!" Mary apologized far too excitedly to be sincere.

"Well you can tell me all about it as you chop up those vegetables for the soup. Hello again, Wendell, are you staying for dinner?" Mrs. Miller asked hopefully.

"Sure, Mrs. Miller. I'm waiting for my Master to return anyway. Is there something I can help with?" Wendell offered.

"Yes. You can go in and keep my husband awake until the food is ready. He has to wake up so early to milk the cows he'll fall asleep without supper if we let him," Mrs. Miller glared at her husband as she fanned a towel over the rolls.

"I was just resting my eyes. Hello there, Wendell," Mr. Miller greeted him groggily, blinking his eyes to bring the world back into focus.

"Hello, Mr. Miller. Sorry, it's my fault your dinner is going to be late. I wanted to show Mary something before we came back," Wendell apologized as he took the seat opposite his future father-in-law.

"Oh, and what was that?" Mr. Miller asked curiously.

"He showed me the sea, Father! It was so beautiful I cried!" Mary blurted excitedly before Wendell could even open his mouth.

"The sea? But that's hundreds of miles from here," Mr. Miller raised his eyebrows in surprise.

"Actually where I took Mary is a lot farther than that. Would you and Mrs. Miller like to see it? We wouldn't have to go there," Wendell said and grinned.

"Alright, Wendell," Mr. Miller accepted, giving his wife a skeptical look as she came around the counter.

"This will only be my memory of what we saw. The real thing is far more impressive," Wendell explained as he fished his crystal ball out of his pouch, but before he called up the memories image he had a better idea, "You know, I think this would be better if I showed you on Mary's mirror. Hold on and I'll go fetch it."

Both the senior Miller's watched with interest as Wendell brought the large mirror his father had made Mary for her fifteenth birthday and propped it up in his chair. Then he hesitated again before readjusting it so it set horizontally across the arms of the chair. Wendell then stepped away and conjured his memory of the sea at sunset that he and Mary had just watched. Both of the Millers were struck speechless by the view they'd never would have had a chance to see otherwise. Wendell held the memory as long as he could and by the time it faded from the mirror's surface, Mrs. Miller was weeping just as her daughter had done.

"That was truly amazing, Wendell. It's a shame you can't keep the image like a painting. I think people all over would pay to see that," Mr. Miller sighed, "It's definitely worth having a late dinner."

"I'm glad you liked it, Sir," Wendell smiled just before Mrs. Miller nearly knocked him down with a fierce embrace.

"Thank you, Wendell. I've never seen anything so beautiful," Mrs. Miller whispered before kissing him on the cheek.

"You're welcome, Mrs. Miller," Wendell stated awkwardly as she continued to hold him for a few more moments in her crushing embrace. After she finally released him, Wendell couldn't help but ask Mr. Miller a question in a hushed tone as he rubbed his shoulders, "Are all the women on her side of the family so freakishly strong?"

"Yep," Mr. Miller answered with a nod.

"I heard that, you two," Mrs. Miller barked from within the kitchen as she was wiping her eyes dry. Mr. Miller winced reflexively.

Wendell and the Millers ate dinner slowly and enjoyed one another's company, but before they had finished the meal was interrupted by a knock at the door. Mr. Miller opened it to reveal Bergstrom and invited the old Wizard inside to share desert with them. Though he was tired, Bergstrom entertained the Millers with some simple tricks while Mary and Wendell served up the blackberry pie Mrs. Miller had baked earlier that day. It was a delicious homemade pie that they enjoyed far more than any waferthin cherry-topped fudge the world had to offer. When the pie was consumed, Bergstrom and Wendell said their farewells to the Millers and went on their way.

54

"Have you decided what we're going to do, Master?" Wendell asked as they started down the road towards the village.

"Yes Wendell, we're going to fight," Bergstrom stated soberly, "I've discussed the situation with Aggie and she agrees that the only way to ensure the valley's safety is to put Reginald down. She's preparing as we speak, but we have a few tasks to do and plans to make of our own before we return to her hut."

"Aggie's going to fight with you?" Wendell asked feeling a whole lot better knowing the old Witch was on their side. Bergstrom chuckled at the question.

"If Aggie could teleport she'd have been in Lavittia already challenging Reginald by herself after I told her what had happen in the future where that spell trap went off. She's become very fond of you and Mary, though she probably wouldn't admit it to you. As a Witch she's got to regard men as fools just on general principle, and male Wizards doubly so. Mary, on the other hand, is her protégée and Witches get downright nasty when someone threatens their heirs. Aggie will fight alright, and you'll likely have nightmares because of it."

"I'm going to be there?" Wendell asked in surprise.

"We'll talk about that when we're within Aggie's sanctuary, so there's no chance of being overheard. Right now we're going to go fetch something from my tower and then have a look around Mr. Garroph's to see if he's left anything behind that may help us." Bergstrom explained as they turned off the main road onto the path that led up to the tower.

The Master and Apprentice walked the rest of the way in silence towards the round tower's shadowy form. As they entered the gate they both slowed going up the path because for the first time ever the tower felt nothing like home. It had a menacing feel to it though to the casual eye nothing seemed out of place. At the bottom of the steps Bergstrom stopped Wendell with a hand on his shoulder and just stood gazing at the door in silence for several minutes.

"It's a very tricky bit of magic," Bergstrom admitted aloud after his contemplation of the door was complete. "Had you not warned us I would never have detected it. The trap is set to go off when the door is opened and I don't think I want to risk trying to dispel it while Reginald still lives."

"Then can't we just teleport in Master?" Wendell asked as he squinted at the door trying to detect what Bergstrom had without success.

"Normally yes, but the Tower is magically sealed. When a place is sealed all within becomes frozen in time otherwise decay would ruin many our belongings. If you teleport into a sealed dwelling you automatically become frozen in time along with everything else until it is unsealed. In this way a Wizard may be assured his dwelling is secured against magical theft as well," Bergstrom explained. "Let me think on this for a moment."

Wendell remained quiet as Bergstrom scratched his grey beard in thought for a few more minutes, obviously trying to figure out how to enter the sealed tower without setting off the spell trap. As he grew bored, Wendell began to look around. He first looked down at the spot where Mr. Garroph's remains had been when he'd left several weeks ago. No trace of the evil Wizard remained accept for a crack in the step where the heavy gargoyle Churchill had crushed him. Wendell assumed the future Bergstrom had vanished the unpleasant mess when he'd returned to seal the tower. Then as he continued to look around, he noticed a new addition to the tower's yard in the form of a large tombstone that had been hidden from view on their approach by one of his Master's bee-hives.

Curious, Wendell walked over to the tombstone to investigate. It was a rather plain rectangular slab of granite with 'Garroph' chiseled upon its face in deep blocky letters. What Wendell at first took for a large stone resting on top of the slab was revealed to be the sheared-off visage of Churchill still locked in its last ugly toothy grin. Wendell didn't notice that right away however for a parchment envelope slid from beneath the gargoyle's remains when they were moved and fell heavily to the grass below.

Wendell picked the envelope up and felt something hard within and saw it was sealed with red wax bearing his Master's sigil. He turned it over to find his own name neatly printed in his Master's style of writing. Wendell looked up at his Master but Bergstrom was still looking at the tower's door scratching his bushy beard, so Wendell set the stone on the ground and open the letter to find a large brass key and the following message from the future Bergstrom Weatherbee:

Dear Wendell,

Here is the key to your new tower. I know you and Mary will be very happy there when you're not hexing each other or some other nonsense. Now go over and tell me I should unseal the tower from the key hole or I'll be still standing there scratching my beard when the sun rises tomorrow. Best of luck to you in the battle ahead (You're going to need it).

B.W.

"Master!" Wendell yelled as he ran back to the steps holding the letter and key excitedly. "You've got to see this!"

"Where did you get this?" Bergstrom asked after he'd read the letter, bemused.

"From under the stone on top of Mr. Garroph's tombstone," Wendell pointed.

Bergstrom walked over and examined Mr. Garroph's grave and while doing so Wendell noticed that the stone was in fact Churchill's face. The old Wizard seemed amused as he picked up the Gargoyle's remains and set it back on top of the tombstone. He then read the letter a second time before stuffing it in his pocket with a smirk.

"I'm going to need the book," Bergstrom stated as he guided Wendell back to the stairs. Wendell immediately fished the palm-sized Legacy Tome out of his belt-pouch and handed it to the old Wizard as they headed up the stairs, "I really am quite clever sometimes," the old Wizard muttered as he squinted at the keyhole.

Bergstrom sat down cross-legged before the door and conjured a lit candle with a brass stand from his pocket that he set beside him. He then spoke three words of power that caused the Tome to return to its original size and grunted as the weight of the thing crushed down upon his bony lap.

"Show me the spell to reduce one's size," Bergstrom commanded and the tome immediately flipped to only a half-dozen pages before the end. Bergstrom caressed the page reverently with a heavy sigh, "This was one of my Master's," he told Wendell quietly, before scanning the pages contents silently while moving his lips.

After carefully reading the spell, Bergstrom remained perfectly still for a few minutes as if waiting for something. Wendell thought he might be mentally preparing for the magic at hand, but then all of a sudden his reached out like lightning and snatched a moth from the air that had been drawn by the candle's flame. He winked at Wendell after examining his catch for a moment, held by its dusty wings.

"Needed a bug," the Wizard explained. He then read through the spell a second time before shrinking the tome back down again and handing it to Wendell, "You better keep holding on to that."

Bergstrom stood up, vanished the candle, and then recited the Spell of Shrinking from memory. It didn't seem as if they shrank so much as the world around them grew, very quickly. When this very humbling spell was finished, Bergstrom and Wendell were about the size of your average flea standing before a door so awesome they couldn't see the top.

"Come on," Bergstrom grasped Wendell's arm and teleported them into the large cave of the door's keyhole, "I'm really glad I thought of this, the other idea I had was far more risky."

"You are very clever, Master," Wendell stated, wondering how you learn something from yourself that you didn't know to begin with.

At the far end of the keyhole was a wall of shimmering light that Bergstrom approached and raised his hand before. He closed his eye and concentrated for a moment then the light flashed and disappeared to reveal the entrance hall stretching out before them.

"There, now we can teleport to my room," Bergstrom nodded before he grabbed Wendell's shoulder again and they were away. They appeared on top of the old foot locker that Wendell had retrieved the Pouch of Needful Things from, "And now we wait."

"Wait for what, Master?" Wendell asked curiously.

"For this spell to wear..." Bergstrom froze and turned deathly pale in mid-sentence. He didn't have any clue why he was suddenly so terrified but some sixth sense had warned the old Wizard that something truly horrific was right behind him. Slowly he turned around and looked at the colossal spider that had been silently creeping up behind them.

Now Wendell had learned long ago that his Master had a phobia of spiders, though the old Wizard didn't like to talk about it. After many years of fighting this unnatural fear Bergstrom had gotten to the point where he could, after struggling with his primal instinct to flee for a minute or two, squish a spider with something large and heavy like an old boot. All this progress went straight out the window, unfortunately, when the old Wizard was confronted by a spider large enough to squish him with said boot. As his Master's face twisted into the horrific aspect of a scream that produced nothing but a high-pitched child like whine, Wendell got the distinct impression that he might have to be the one to deal with the colossal monster spider.

Wendell stepped before the gargantuan arachnid and quickly cast his flash spell before its eight huge black orb eyes, blinding the beast. As the spider rubbed its eyes with several of its hairy brown and black legs, Wendell calmly walked up to it and pushed upon its leg to teleport it away. Wendell then walked calmly back to his Master and patted him on the back reassuringly.

"W-w-where d-d-did y-y-you s-send it?" Bergstrom stuttered after a minute or two still trembling with fear.

"Those artic mountains," Wendell smiled.

"I-I I-I-love y-you, B-Boy," Bergstrom stuttered, after letting Wendell's answer sink in for a moment.

"I know, Master," Wendell smiled smugly.

55

By the time the shrinking spell had worn off, Bergstrom was more or less back to his normal self though still a bit jumpy. After carefully scanning the surrounding area for any more intruding arachnids, he opened the trunk distrustfully and peered inside. The old Wizard sighed with relief when all he found within the heavy wood chest was the worn pair of boots with a hole in one toe and the twisted oak wand. Carefully he picked up the wand at arms length as if it was something dreadful and then fixed Wendell with a serious look.

"I wish to take a moment to instruct you on the finer points of wand safety, Wendell. Wands are very dangerous weapons and should always be handled with the utmost care. Never point them at yourself or anyone else you do not wish to see come to a gruesome end for you never know if a wand is loaded or not. Never store them in your pockets, belt, or sleeves unless you've grown tired of the surrounding appendages. Never run with them for if you fall they may go off or poke out your eye. Do you got all that?" Bergstrom asked seriously, knitting his bushy eyebrows together sternly.

"Yes, Master," Wendell nodded as he stared at the wand with respectful interest.

"Good!" Bergstrom grunted before walking towards his wardrobe with the wand still held before him pointed at the ceiling. He opened the wardrobe door, revealing nearly twenty identical tan robes that hung within and then looked down at Wendell as if accessing him for the first time before he presented the wand to him, "Hold this just as I have done and be certain not to look at anything with ill intent."

Wendell hesitantly took the twisted oak wand from his Master's grasp and instantly felt the vast and frightening power it contained. He'd felt this kind of power only twice before; once during the Oath of Apprenticeship and then when he'd lost control of his anger and summoned lightning down upon Trevor. The wand was different, however, for the vast power that had been concentrated within its seemingly frail wood form seemed to want to be released as he held it in his sweaty grasp. Wendell had no doubt whatsoever that the wand's power would come in an instant if he wished anything harm for it was weapon specifically designed to unleash great destruction upon anything that had offended its wielder.

Once Bergstrom seemed satisfied that Wendell wasn't about to blow the roof off the tower, he turned back to the wardrobe's door and proceeded to pull a heavy leather belt off one of the pegs where it had hung next to four identical acorn-shaped hats and one well-used linen night cap. This belt was reminiscent of a sword belt save for a few differences: around the left hand side of the belt were several small leather pouches in two rows -- one on top of the other -- for storing individual spell components a Wizard might need in the heat of battle. The right-hand side of the belt had a polished leather sheath for the wand, held by a lower secondary leather strap so that it would hold the weapon at an angle away from the Wizard's leg to prevent accidents. Bergstrom buckled the wand belt over his normal one, and as he reached to retrieve the wand from Wendell, the Apprentice noticed the buckle itself for the first time. It was a large square buckle of tarnished silver adorned with a protruding skull and crossbones motif. Two glittering rubies had been placed within the skull's sockets under its sinister-angled brow, so that the buckle appeared to be glaring forward angrily.

Bergstrom slid the wand home in its sheath then proceeded to transfer the components he'd need for combat from his normal belt pouch to those of the wand belt's with methodical thoughtfulness. Once this sorting was complete, the old Wizard unbuckled his normal belt and hung it from the same peg the wand belt had previously occupied. After that, Bergstrom opened the second door of the wardrobe to admire himself in the mirror. After a quick appraisal his reflection, he shook its head and pointed towards the wardrobe's interior.

"Oh, I had forgotten that," Bergstrom snapped his fingers causing a flash of light to go off before his eyes.

Once the blindness had passed, Bergstrom withdrew a short black velvet cape from deeper within the wardrobe's shadowy interior. He pinned the cape around his neck with a silver skull clasp that matched that of his belt buckle, then twisted it so that it sat roguishly covering his left side just above the wand. Thusly adorned, he gazed into the mirror once more and was very pleased when his reflection gave him the thumbs up with a wink. Wendell did his very best not to giggle, but it escaped him nonetheless.

"Come on!" Bergstrom growled irritably, as he grabbed the boy's shoulder and transported them to the gates of Mr. Garroph's tower.

It was Wendell's first time to the square tower that had loomed infamously above the village all his life and he found himself wishing that they'd chosen any time to explore its mysteries other than now under the light of the bright sickle moon. The iron fence and gates around the tower's yard were uniformed rows of bars that had been toped with twisted spear-like heads. The yard itself seemed to be an orderly rock garden choked with weeds that were pleasant but lacked imagination or style. A path of square-cut stones led straight back to the short staircase up to the tower's door. Two serpentine dragon statues flanked either side of this staircase, locked in identical fearsome snarls made far more menacing by the moonlight.

Bergstrom pushed upon the iron gate and it opened with a nerve-grating creak that sent shivers down Wendell's spine. The old Wizard then hesitated for a moment, scanning the yard cautiously before he stepped through the portal. As soon as he'd placed his foot upon the stone path the dragon statues released menacing growls as they came to life. The stone dragons' eyes began to burn with a hateful fire, as they turned their heads towards the Wizard and gnashed weather eroded stone fangs with a sound of cracking stone. They reared back their frightening reptilian heads and let out short breaths of billowing orange flames.

"Oh Scott, for all your cunning you really had very little imagination," Bergstrom muttered shaking his bearded head. Then he beckoned to Wendell without taking his eyes off the scaly stone guardians, "Show them the key."

Wendell drew the large brass key from his pocket and held it up as he stepped forward into the yard. The dragons immediately turned their fiery gazes upon him and ceased breathing fire. Their stone tails swished behind as the dragons leaned forward as if to get a better look at the Apprentice.

"Now claim the tower as your own and command them to rest," Bergstrom instructed quietly from the boy's side. Wendell cleared his very dry throat before he made his declaration.

"I, Wendell Glasswright, claim ownership of this tower and command you to rest," Wendell called out in what he sincerely hoped was an authoritative voice.

The dragon statues instantly tilted their thorny heads in acknowledgement of Wendell's command, before returning to the menacing stance they had held when the Wizard and Apprentice had first arrived. Within seconds the fire in the dragon's eyes extinguished, and they appeared to be nothing more than inanimate statues. Bergstrom cautiously approached the stairs eyeing the statues distrustfully, but when he saw there was no reaction from the scaly sentries he turned to Wendell with a smile.

"Well done, Wendell. I'm glad that we didn't have to resort to violence. If we get through this you should take the time to talk to these two and befriend them. It will do wonders to improve their dispositions," Bergstrom suggested before heading up the stairs.

"So are they alive, Master?" Wendell followed the old Wizard's lead eyeing the statues distrustfully.

"Not really, but like magic they get imprinted with the emotions of their Master and develop personalities of their own because of it. I'm guessing that Scott was rather neglectful to them and that's why they're so cranky. A loyal guardian statue will go out of its way to please a caring Master. That's why Churchill started to sing for me and killed Scott when you were threatened even though I'd given him no order to attack. With a little time and attention, I think you'll find these two dragons will become more than just the fearsome guardians you just saw," Bergstrom explained, as he examined the formidable iron studded door before him.

"Good boys!" Wendell told the statues after a moment's consideration of his Master's explanation. The statues made no indication that they'd heard their new Master's praise, but Bergstrom smiled at him.

"Well I don't see anymore wards. Why don't you open her up so we can have a look inside?" Bergstrom instructed as he stepped to the side to let Wendell at the door's lock.

Wendell was hesitant as he approached for he still felt insecure with the idea that the menacing tower was really his. Slowly he placed the large brass key within the lock and turned it until its tumblers clicked loudly three times and the door opened a crack. He withdrew the key and placed it in his pocket before pulling open the loud creaking door by its large ornate brass handle. The portal opened to reveal the shimmering wall of the future Bergstrom's seal.

"Ah, allow me," Bergstrom stepped forward and placed his hand before the shimmering wall. After a few moments of concentration, the old Wizard caused the seal to disappear, revealing before them a huge dusty cobweb-choked corridor that disappeared into the darkness within.

56

"Hah!" Bergstrom yelled as he blasted a spider out of its web with an arc of lightning from his wand. The old Wizard seemed to take just as much sadistic pleasure from the outrageous overkill as he had from the first six spiders they'd encountered since entering Mr. Garroph's tower.

"You're going to bring the roof down on our heads if you keep that up, Master," Wendell sighed as the elder Wizard sheathed his wand after a satisfying twirl.

"I'll help you repair any damage I cause," Bergstrom promised after eyeing the burnt crater the wand had left in the ceiling for a moment. He opened the next door along the corridor that's hinges creaked in protest. Bergstrom shook his head in disgust, "Would it have killed you to oil some of these, Scott?"

"I can't see me ever wanting to live here," Wendell stated as he peered around the neglected dusty bedchamber with disgust. Everything was moth-eaten, cobweb-choked, and depressively grim in appearance.

Bergstrom let out a low chuckle. Wendell looked at him, confused.

"Don't worry about a thing. The first thing women do when they move in is rearrange everything to their liking and vanish what they don't. Otherwise they just can't consider a place home. Trust me, as soon as Mary takes a look at this place all you'll have to do is make yourself scarce until she needs something moved and this old tower will be homey in no time!" Bergstrom explained as they did a short search of the room.

Most of Mr. Garroph's tower seemed to have been abandoned decades ago to all but the spiders and moths. Bergstrom and Wendell had already gone through all but this final top floor and had found nothing of interest. The bedchamber they were currently searching was proving to be just as fruitless but they went about the task none the less. When it was done they came back out into the hall and Wendell gazed down at the door that had led to the cursed future Wendell's laboratory with apprehension for it was the only door left unopened.

"I can do it alone if you're afraid," Bergstrom stated as he walked towards the door.

"No, I'll be alright. It won't contain what it did the last time I was here," Wendell shivered with the memory of looking upon the horrific statue of his petrified Master.

"Are you certain?" Bergstrom paused with his hand upon the dusty and rusty doorknob.

"Yes, Master," Wendell smiled grimly.

Bergstrom nodded to him before opening the portal and the corridor was flooded with an eerie green light. Within, the chamber looked much as it had in the future except for some minor changes and the room's dimensions were smaller. Where the Legacy Tome had rested before the cursed Wendell's bench, now sat a large black iron cauldron ornamented with grinning skulls that held iron rings in their teeth. This cauldron was the source of the unwholesome green light which bled from within it in a thick bright beam to the ceiling above. Beyond the cauldron the large shelves of spell components still remained, but the covered birdcage was absent. In its place was a small desk of red-stained oak with a black leather tome and a candle atop a human skull resting on top. The bench upon which the cursed Wendell had sat was against the wall opposite the large shuttered windows and had several bottles resting upon it in a small display. Underneath the windows, a small cot with a disheveled blanket and pillow had been placed next to a small oak chest of drawers.

Bergstrom walked up to the cauldron cautiously and peered within and Wendell could feel the sickening evil of the thing as he followed his Master's lead. Within the bright cauldron's depths was a shimmering green liquid that boiled even though it rested above no fire. Shadowy skeletal visages peered up from the liquid's depths, shoving one another in contest to look out of the cauldron. As soon as these wraiths from the beyond spied Bergstrom and Wendell, they cried out in haunting voices as they tried to reach up with their shadowy skeletal hands. Their cries drowned out one another in a roar of desperation that filled Wendell's heart with dread.

"What on earth were you up to, Scott?" Bergstrom asked under his breath and instantly the cauldron's liquid began to swirl quickly while its light intensified.

Bergstrom yanked Wendell by the arm behind him as they backed away from the agitated cauldron cautiously. Within moments a shadowy skeleton rose out of the cauldron's depths radiating the same unnatural light as it fixed it eyeless gaze upon them until it was waist-high above the cauldron's rim. The roar of the other netherworld skeletons subsided and then the shadowy horror opened its jaws and spoke with the voice of Scott Garroph.

"A curse upon you and the boy Bergstrom! My only pleasure beyond the grave was knowing that you'd be forever trapped within that bottle and now you summon me forth to crush that last pleasure. Very well, have your vengeance and ask what you will so I may return to my damnation," the dammed spirit of Scott Garroph hissed with unearthly malice dripping off of each word.

"What is the purpose of this cauldron, Scott?" Bergstrom asked after considering the shade for a moment. Scott laughed at him before he answered the old Wizard.

"Isn't it obvious, Old Fool? It is a device for accumulating knowledge from the dammed. I made it to ferret out those secrets lost to the grave. Within our dark prison it casts an irresistible light to draw us, and when our name is called we may rise up into that light to answer the questions of those who summoned us. The accumulation of knowledge is the purpose of the cauldron, nothing more," Scott's voice hissed impatiently when his desolate mirth had subsided.

"We intend to challenge Reginald Giles. Is there anything within your tower that can aid us towards that end?" Bergstrom asked after considering what the wraith had told him.

"One dark Wizard down and on to the next, aye, Bergstrom? I hope Reginald finds an especially cruel curse to afflict you with and if he possessed this cauldron I'd be happy to suggest a few. If you have my tower then you possess my spellbook. The knowledge within its pages would aid you far more than any trinket I possessed. But would the great Bergstrom dare to delve into such dark mysteries even when faced with a powerful foe such as Giles? Could he tempt the shadows he has always sworn to fight against? I think not, but should I be wrong I would save a place for you by my side within the darkness to remind you throughout eternity what a self-righteous insufferable fool you've always been," the skeletal shade hissed with venomous spite.

"Return to your place, Scott, and may your hatred keep you warm within the dark," Bergstrom sighed and shook his head as he watched the shade sink back into the cauldron's depths, screeching with fury.

Bergstrom considered the cauldron for a few moments as someone who is considering an open grave with a blank headstone. Then slowly he turned his gaze to the book that rested upon the desk beyond it as if tempted to dare the shadows held within its black leather cover. Almost mechanically, the old Wizard approached the book and slowly reached out and vanished it without turning a single page. Wendell was proud of his Master and wondered if he would have had the strength of character to do the same as Bergstrom turned back to the cauldron.

"I must consider what is to be done with this device very carefully," Bergstrom muttered to himself thoughtfully. Then he reached out and touched the cauldron to teleport it away, "Though it was created for an evil purpose some good may still yet come of it."

"Where did you send it?" Wendell asked curiously as their attention was drawn to the bottles on display. The light of the cauldron had been drowning out the bottles soft glow but with its disappearance theirs' was the only light left within the chamber.

"To my tower's basement," Bergstrom answered absently as he approached the bottles.

"Your tower has a basement? I never saw a way to it," Wendell furrowed his eyebrows as he to approached the bottles.

"There's a lot of that old tower you've never seen, and I imagine there's a lot more to this one as well. But we haven't the time now to explore such mysteries," Bergstrom stated as he knelt before the bottles.

There were four bottles of various sizes on display atop of the bench that the Wizard and Apprentice beheld in wonder. The largest of which lay on its side and contained a three-mast galley in full sail upon rolling ocean waves. The tiny crew of this ship in a bottle appeared very much alive as they went about their nautical tasks, seemingly oblivious to the fact that they were not really at sea. At the helm of this ship stood a well-muscled handsome captain, gazing to the non-existent horizon ahead with determination that closely resembled that which Wendell had seen in Justin's eyes every time he was about some heroic act. The Apprentice noted this, but didn't make mention of it to his Master at once for there were three other bottles with wonders of their own.

The second largest bottle was the rather plain type, used for containing strong spirits such as Dwarf whisky. Within the whisky bottle, however, was not liquor but a small Unicorn grazing in a wooded field. Like the Mariners aboard the ship, the Unicorn seemed completely oblivious to the fact that it was not within its natural woodland home. After a moment the Unicorn seemed to tire of the patch of grass it had been diligently mowing and moved to another. Although the Unicorn had just moved from one side of its bottled habitat to the other, the illusionary terrain around it shifted dramatically as if it had moved across a meadow to a large patch of inviting clovers. This appeared to explain why the Mariners had not seen them looming over their glassy prison, for to them they were moving across the sea.

The third largest bottle was a short and rounded jar, save for where it tapered to a stout-corked neck. Within this bottle was not but two small human skeletons hunched against the back wall of the glass. No illusions surrounded the skeletons, and Wendell had the horrible hunch that Mr. Garroph had just left them there to slowly die of starvation.

The smallest bottle was an ornate affair whose neck and stopper were embellished with gold and small pearls. Within the bottle seemed to be nothing but a billowing scarlet smoke, but after a few moments of examining it, the smoke seemed to condense within itself to form a scantly-clad veiled-woman with dark skin and slanted eyes. This woman was very aware of Bergstrom and Wendell's presence and immediately began to bang upon the inside of her bottle begging to be freed.

"Shouldn't we let her out, Master?" Wendell asked after watching her for a moment.

"I'm not certain. She's obviously some kind of Genie and such creatures are rarely trustworthy," Bergstrom stated as he watched her.

The Genie's shoulder's sagged as she sank down to her knees and began to weep. Bergstrom grumbled something into his beard that Wendell didn't quite catch then he addressed the Genie directly, "How about if we make you a deal? I don't like seeing any creature in captivity so I'll set you free on the condition you give me your word that you'll return these other captives safely to wherever they came from. But I warn you, Little Lady, any misbehavior and you'll wish I'd never let you out of that bottle. Do we have a deal?"

The Genie smiled and shook her head vigorously while weeping tears of joy. Bergstrom -- still muttering into his beard -- took hold of the bottle and pulled off the stopper. The Genie instantly returned to her gaseous state and flowed out of the bottle with joyous laughter. She reformed human-sized a moment later beside them and instantly fell to her knees and began to kiss Bergstrom's feet.

"Thank you, Kind Wizard. May the Angels smile upon you the rest of your days. May your greatest desires all come true. May your lands and women flourish. May your…" there's no telling where these blessings would have ended if Bergstrom hadn't interrupted the grateful Genie.

"I get the idea," Bergstrom sighed as he leaned over and grasped her naked shoulders to help her rise, "Just take care of those in the other bottles and we'll call it square."

"As you wish," The Genie bowed, but before she snapped her fingers to cause herself and the other captives within the bottles to disappear, she brushed her veil aside, leaned up, and kissed the old Wizard passionately upon the lips for several seconds.

As the Genie disappeared, Bergstrom was red as a radish and grinning from ear to ear. The old Wizard seemed to be lost in some kind of very pleasant trance and after a moment Wendell noticed that he wasn't even breathing. Worried, Wendell tugged on his Master's robes.

"Are you okay, Master?" Wendell asked fearfully. Bergstrom let out a long sigh after which he appeared to breathe again.

"Yes, I just need a moment or two," Bergstrom stated dreamily as he continued to gaze ahead at nothing with a large foolish grin. Wendell waited almost five minutes before he interrupted his Master's trance.

"Shouldn't we be going to meet up with Aggie now Master?" Wendell asked hopefully. Bergstrom let out another long sigh before he answered him.

"I suppose. Best not to tell Aggie about this though, otherwise she might put that wonderful creature right back in her bottle or worse," Bergstrom stated. Then he grasped Wendell's shoulder and transported them to Aggie's hut.

57

Wendell was surprise to find that Aggie had chosen to 'unpack' her hut in the same glade where his and Mary's old Oak tree still held his Fairy Lure tied upon the high branch. The lure wasn't active right now for there wasn't any sunshine to power it, but as they waited for the old Witch to answer the door Wendell couldn't help but smile as small spheres of colored light flew about the trees and bird-like chirps could be heard in the canopy above. The place he'd fallen in love had become a Fairy Haven and he knew Mary would be thrilled.

"What happened to you?" Aggie grunted at Bergstrom suspiciously the moment she opened the door and gazed upon the tired but euphoric old Wizard.

"Nothing, Dearest," Bergstrom lied as he more drifted than walked into the hut.

"What happened to him?" Aggie asked suspiciously as Wendell entered behind the Wizard. Wendell just shrugged as if he didn't know what she was talking about.

"Why did you choose to set up your hut here, Aggie?" Wendell couldn't help asking as the Witch continued to glare at Bergstrom with narrowed and distrustful eyes.

"What? Oh, well there's strong magic here and since you hung that lure in the tree it's bound to just keep getting stronger," Aggie answered as she shuffled back to her cauldrons still watching Bergstrom like a hawk, "Besides, I kind of like Fairies once you've taught them they'll not get away with any foolish pranks."

"This is the glade where Mary and I fell in love," Wendell told her as he walked over to examine the bubbling black liquid she was stirring.

"Yeah, I figured as much. You've left your imprint all over it. Who knows, you two might have started the magic here," Aggie mumbled thoughtfully, "Now back up before you disrupt what I'm trying to do."

"I could help stir for you?" Wendell offered, but the Witch just released an amused cackle at the notion.

"Wizard magic and Witchery rarely mix well, but thank you for the offer," Aggie grunted as she raced to her second cauldron and began to stir the foamy bright yellow liquid within.

"Aren't all potions the same?" Wendell asked after moving back a respectful distance.

"No, we could use the same ingredients and always come up with very different results from the Witch's. Their magic is just different from ours. If you went over there and stirred that cauldron you'd disrupt the flow of the magic she's channeling into it. At best you'd just ruin the potion, at worst it would explode into wild magic and cause untold mayhem," Bergstrom explained as he mimicked waltzing with and imaginary partner in the center of the hut.

"All right, what's going on? You never dance without your dancing shoes!" Aggie glared at Bergstrom menacingly. Then she sniffed the air and her eyes narrowed into deadly looking slits, "Have you been kissing another woman?"

"No, Dearest. I just took a potion of bliss to calm my nerves. You're probably smelling the sweat of a maiden, its one of the main essences," Bergstrom lied happily as he continued his waltz. Aggie didn't seem convinced, but she held her tongue as she continued to stir the potion before her.

"So are you going to tell me the plan now, Master?" Wendell asked in an attempt to change the subject.

"Right, the plan," Bergstrom sighed as he stopped waltzing and walked over to Wendell, "Despite the preparations we're making there are no guarantees that we can beat Reginald. He's very intelligent and plans ahead for several different outcomes to everything so Aggie and I have decided to incorporate a secret weapon into our strategy that should drastically tip the odds in our favor and that's you. You are going to have two roles in this plan. The first is I'm going to have you deliver our challenge to Reginald at lunch time tomorrow in the Duke's feast hall. This will infuriate the Magician to no end and there'll be too many witnesses present for him to lay a hand on you.

"The second part of your involvement is going to take far more courage and has a lot more risk, I'm afraid," Bergstrom sighed heavily and rested his hands on Wendell's shoulders, "I'm going to cast an invisibility spell upon you and have you watch the battle from what I hope will be a safe distance. If it becomes clear that we are losing, I want you to travel back in time to a few minutes from now when I'll send you outside the hut for five minutes. Once you get back here you must quickly tell what you witnessed before the five minutes are up and must return to your present. Hopefully that will give us the edge we need to take Reginald out the next time around. Do you understand?"

"Yes, Master," Wendell acknowledged. It seemed like a good plan...or at least he could think of nothing better.

"All right then, go outside and get some air for five minutes or more," Bergstrom smiled and patted his shoulder. Wendell went outside and watched the Fairy lights for ten.

58

Wendell took a deep breath and stepped into the Duke's feast hall, just as the Duke was about to take a bite of what looked like roast Quail covered in gravy. Nobles gasped all around at the Apprentice's sudden appearance and the Duke's guards quickly raised their harquebus. The Duke calmly raised his hand to halt his guards and then set down his fork carefully upon his plate.

"Please forgive me, Your Grace, for interrupting your meal," Wendell stated as he bowed before the Duke in what he hope was a graceful manner.

"What is the nature of this interruption, Wizard, so I may decide if it is appropriate that forgiveness be granted?" the Duke asked calmly after wiping the corners of his mouth with his silk napkin.

"Due to the fact that upon our return home, we found that your Magician had placed a magical trap upon our tower that not only threatened our lives but all the lives within our village, my Master has asked me to deliver a formal challenge to Reginald Giles and thought it would be prudent for my safety to have all here be witnesses to that delivery. My Master realizes that this is hardly proper etiquette and sends both his apologies to Your Grace as well as his assurances that he does not believe you ordered this attack upon us or the loyal subjects of our peaceful little valley," Wendell declared loud enough for most of the hall to hear and was very pleased to see many present send disgusted glares the Magician's way.

"Very well, proceed," the Duke tilted his head to Wendell with the faintest trace of a smile upon his pale lips.

"Thank you, Your Grace," Wendell bowed once more to the Duke before turning his gaze upon the silent red-faced Magician. Wendell took a deep breath and as he had been carefully coached, smiled and tilted his head at the furious Magician before issuing Bergstrom's challenge, "Reginald Giles, it has become clear to my Master from your underhanded and dishonorable conduct that you are now to be counted as an enemy to not only himself but all good people across the land. Therefore, my Master has decided to give you the chance to retain whatever small amount of honor you may still possess and meet him within the Burning Plains of the great Eastern Wastelands in one hour, so your differences may be settled without threat to the public."

"Tell your Master my Magician accepts his challenge to honorable combat and will meet him in one hour," the Duke proclaimed loud enough for most of the hall to hear and before the Magician had the chance to respond of his own accord.

"Your Grace?" Reginald blurted out angrily with veins protruding from his forehead in a very ugly manner.

"I wasn't finished!" the Duke snapped at the Magician, though his features still remained slightly amused. Many of the nobles gasped in disbelief and Reginald snapped his mouth shut, glaring at the Duke with open hatred. The Duke smiled before his Magician's rage and then continued, "I would also have you tell you're Master that should he be successful in dispatching my most dishonorable and rude Magician, I would have him present himself to me as soon as he is fit to do so."

"As you will, Your Grace," Wendell smiled and bowed as mummers erupted throughout the nobles across the feast hall.

"You are excused, Wizard," the Duke dismissed Wendell as he picked up his fork. As the Magician began to rise, the Duke turned to him smiling wickedly, "You are not, however."

Wendell was grinning from ear to ear as he stepped back to the glade before Aggie's hut.

59

Wendell was sweating profusely under the sweltering sun of the Burning Plains Desert. He stood invisible nearly two hundred yards from where Bergstrom and Aggie waited patiently for the Magician's arrival. And even though he was not to participate in the duel to come, his nerves were thin as a razor's blade as he scanned the seemingly endless plain of cracked dry ashy earth about them.

The Magician appeared before them suddenly, only 50 feet from the Elder Witch and Wizard. Wendell was pleased to see that in his haste he'd forgotten to remove the napkin tucked around his neck from lunch. It was clear to the Apprentice that the Magician was still angry, but he was in a bit more control of his rage than he'd been within the Feast Hall. He glared at Bergstrom and Aggie for a few moments, then threw back his head and laughed merrily.

"So was this your great plan, Bergstrom? To fight me two against one? Did you think I wouldn't anticipate Aggie's involvement after she left her beloved swamp and traveled half the Duchy to get you out of that bottle?" Reginald chuckled with mirth.

"I'm really very disappointed in you, Old Friend," a second Reginald appeared about fifty feet to the right of the Elder Witch and Wizard, chuckling in unison with the first.

"You bring my honor into question before the entire court and then show up to a duel with your Mistress. Shame on you, Bergstrom," a third Reginald appeared fifty feet behind them shaking his head in mock disapproval and clucking under his breath.

"Do these odds seem more fitting, Old Friend?" all the Reginald's asked together as a fourth appeared fifty feet to the left of them, "They do to us."

"Alright Aggie, you take those three and I'll take this one," Bergstrom chuckled as he tapped the butt of his wand lightly with his fingertips.

"And they say chivalry is dead," Aggie smiled wickedly, a split second before she threw a yellow potion between her feet and was quickly enveloped in yellow smoke.

All four Reginald's began chanting at once but before any spell went off, Bergstrom had drawn his wand and incinerated one of their number with an arc of lightning. The old Wizard then disappeared while Aggie began to quickly outgrow her smoky concealment until she was near fifty feet tall. Two of the fireballs the Reginalds had been casting struck her in the chest and side, exploding with thunderous booms that made Aggie roar with pain. The third fireball flew straight over the spot that Bergstrom had vacated a second before and far out into the wasteland beyond the battlefield.

Bergstrom reappeared in between two of the Reginalds and raised his wand threateningly. The Reginalds conjured a half-dozen daggers from each sleeve to hurl at the Wizard but as they closed in he teleported away again. The two Reginalds had to vanish their own daggers a split second before they would have killed one another.

Meanwhile Aggie had tossed a now giant-sized black potion at the third Reginald, who quickly teleported out of the way while laughing mockingly. His laughter died quickly, after shattering upon the ground the tar-like potion formed into a crude man-like creature that reached for him with stretching and whipping arms. He tried to blast the Tar Creature with a lightning spell but the electrical attack passed right through it, leaving a gaping hole that quickly healed just as its sticky whips wrapped around the Magician. The Magician tried to teleport out of the Tar Creature's sticky grip but found himself unable to do so. Reginald screamed just as Aggie's giant leather shoe came down upon his head and squished him like a bug.

The remaining two Reginalds -- seeing their number halved -- quickly cast the spell to copy themselves again. The two old Reginalds then teleported to either side of Aggie, while the two new ones cast the spell to copy themselves yet again. Bergstrom appeared behind one of the Reginalds surrounding Aggie and incinerated him with his wand, but it was becoming apparent that they would quickly outnumber the Witch and Wizard within seconds. Desperate as he shot off another arc of lightning towards the pack of six new Reginalds, Bergstrom called out to Wendell with his mind.

'Go now!' Bergstrom's mental command speared into Wendell's head like a fiery lance, just as Aggie petrified a Reginald with a truly horrid grin on her giant face.

Wendell concentrated upon the point in time he was outside Aggie's hut, watching the Fairy Lights but before he could step into the past a hand grasped his robe and yanked him into the future. Wendell found himself looking at a nearly identical version of himself save for he had a bandage wrapped around his right hand. They were standing in the same desert amongst blackened craters from the battle of the past.

"It doesn't work no matter how many times we loop back to warn them, but I think I've thought of something that will. I'm sorry but we've got to move quickly," the wounded Future Wendell stated before setting the Wendell of the present's mind on fire with the specifics of his daring and dangerous plan.

As soon as Wendell returned to the present, he teleported right in front of the nearest Reginald and kicked him as hard as he could right between the legs. The fat old Wizard immediately buckled into the fetal position with a breathless wheeze of pain at Wendell's feet. The Apprentice grabbed the incapacitated Magician's robes and quickly stepped into the past. Wendell and the Magician arrived a split second before the first Magician appeared before Bergstrom and Aggie. Reginald teleport into the desert to find his own crumpled form laying at his feet. By then the invisible future Wendell had already stepped back to his own time that would now never happen.

The two Reginalds looked upon one another for a moment in confusion before reality decided to correct the blatant paradox of their simultaneous existence. The Reginald upon the ground imploded into nothingness with a loud popping sound. The Reginald standing above transformed into a very confused chicken with a frightened squawk. What happened to the three other copied Magicians is anyone's guess, for they were not seen or heard from ever again.

"Well there's something you don't see everyday," Bergstrom stated, scratching his beard in bewilderment.

"Did we just win?" Aggie asked in equal confusion.

"I have no idea," Bergstrom shrugged.

"How does roast chicken sound for dinner?" Aggie asked after a moment, grinning wickedly at the bewildered bird.

"You wouldn't," Bergstrom looked at the Witch, wondering if she'd returned to the wicked ways of her youth.

"It would be far more humane than leaving it here to die from heatstroke," the Witch looked at him as the picture of innocence.

"Wendell! I think you can come back now. I almost certain it's over," Bergstrom called out to his invisible Apprentice while trying to ignore the Witch.

"I'm right here, Master," Wendell stated from beside them, causing both the Witch and Wizard to jump.

"Don't do that!" Bergstrom growled irritably.

"Sorry, Master," Wendell apologized, thankful that the invisibility was concealing his grin.

"Going to have to tie a cow bell around that boy's neck," Aggie growled, holding a hand to her heart.

"Yeah right, that wouldn't be the least bit counter productive would it?" Bergstrom asked her sarcastically as he canceled the invisibility spell with a word of power and a wave of his hand.

"Don't get ornery with me or you won't get any chicken," Aggie growled before she started towards the chicken, making clucking noises with her hand extended as if offering it food. The chicken looked at her dubiously for a moment before it ran for it.

"See that Aggie gets home when she finally catches dinner. I'm going to go see what the Duke wants," Bergstrom told Wendell as they watched Aggie chase the chicken across the desert cursing. Reginald made a very quick chicken, despite his weight.

60

"So what did the Duke want?" Aggie asked the Old Wizard, while still chewing on her chicken.

"He Knighted me," Bergstrom smirked smugly as Aggie's jaw dropped open revealing her half-chewed chicken, "I am now Sir Bergstrom Weatherbee, defender of the southern territories. The Duke was very pleased to be out from under Reginald's shadow."

"Of all the blockheaded things to do! You're going to be positively insufferable from now on!" Aggie growled irritably.

"Since you are my love I guess you don't have to refer to me as Milord or Sir," Bergstrom chuckled with eyes twinkling delightedly.

"I have a few other titles in mind for you," Aggie grinned wickedly before tearing another bite off her drumstick.

"So is Wendell off to see Mary?" Bergstrom inquired as he peered around the Witch's hut.

"Yep, he couldn't wait to tell her the good news," Aggie replied in between chewing, "This is really good. Are you certain you don't want some?"

"Quite sure," Bergstrom grimaced as he looked at what was left of Reginald spitted above the fire. He grew thoughtful after a moment then looked at Aggie with a conspiratorial twinkle in his eyes, "So we'll probably not be bothered for hours…"

"Why, did you have something in mind to pass the time, Sir Weatherbee?" Aggie asked, after wiping her mouth on her sleeve and tossing the stripped chicken bone into the fire's coals. The Witch was smirking as well.

61

"I can't believe you three left me behind!" Mary growled with a false pretense of being angry as she and Wendell walked down the sandy beach barefooted holding hands, "If you had died, I would have never known what became of you."

"I wanted to tell you but our plans just kind of took off and there wasn't much time. I'm sorry!" Wendell apologized again. Mary playfully hit him in the shoulder. "Ouch! I said I was sorry!" Wendell exclaimed as he rubbed his tender shoulder.

"Apology accepted, now kiss me," Mary commanded with the noble air befitting a Queen.

"Yes, Your Majesty," Wendell gave her a mock bow before taking her into his arms and following her command with pleasure. They kissed for a long time then parted again with frustration. They walked some more in silence as the sun started to set lazily behind the horizon, "I now own Mr. Garroph's tower. We went up there last night to look around. It's going to take weeks to make livable, but I can't think of anything better to do while we're waiting for our birthdays."

"What's it like?" Mary asked and Wendell couldn't help but see the twinkle of excitement in her eyes.

"Do you want to go have a look? I've got the key right here, somewhere," Wendell stopped and fished in his pocket but instead of the key he pulled out a bouquet of pink roses. He smirked and handed the flowers over.

"Maybe after the sun sets," Mary smiled after placing the roses under her freckly nose.

"You sure? The place really doesn't improve in the dark," Wendell asked as he embraced her from behind.

"I'm never afraid when you're with me," she sighed, leaning back against him with her roses still tucked under her cute nose. They watched the fiery sunset in silence.

62

The next eight weeks were the longest of Wendell and Mary's lives as they counted the days, hours, and sometimes even the minutes until Mary's birthday. They spent most of this time making the old square tower on the eastern hill habitable. True to Bergstrom's word, Mary took charge of this operation calling Wendell only when she needed some large piece of furniture animated to another location. When Mary wasn't supervising the clean up, she was at Aggie's learning the secrets of Witchery. Wendell spent these times either at Bergstrom's tower helping design a magic clock he couldn't tell the elder Wizard was destined to fail or working in his own tower's garden talking to the dragon statues.

Wendell took Mary shopping in Lavittia for her birthday, subtly conjuring coins and small gems for all she desired. By the time she was finished, Wendell had a migraine from teleporting back and forth so many times to deliver her purchases to the tower. He told her he was glad that it would continue to grow throughout their lives or else it would be filled before the end of the week. She just smiled and laughed before moving on to the next shop.

Three days later, Wendell and Mary were wed. Most of the village gathered for this service that Baron Brinswick honored them to preside over. Wendell had teleported the Baron from his castle that morning as well as Lady Greta Highbreak and her father who had been amidst negotiations for the Baron and Greta's betrothal. Apparently Baron Brinswick had been quite taken with the girl and had been quietly waiting for her birthday as well, before making overtures for her hand. Greta seemed to be quite taken with him as well and turned bright red beneath her freckles every time she caught him staring at her. The Noble's presence of course turned the wedding into a celebration that would outshine Yule, for never before had any bothered to stop in the tiny farming community let alone join in the simple folk's merriment.

The service was held within Wendell's garden under an oak tree he'd grown with magic from one of the acorns from the lover's oak within the wood. All present swore that Mary made the most beautiful bride the village had ever seen, within her elegant white gown and Baron Brinswick commissioned a gown from Fredric for Greta as soon as he saw it. The Baron fastened their hands with a lace of golden silk, then the villagers cheered as the two kissed and Bergstrom conjured a whole flock of snow white doves from his pocket. Even Aggie smiled, before she remembered that such things weren't becoming of a Witch. And then they feasted as only simple folk can properly do. No drawn out protocols or strict etiquette intruded upon this feast; just lots of fingerlicking and belches of happiness and contentment.

When all had had their fill of food, those so musically inclined produced their instruments and the dancing began. Wendell had to laugh as Bergstrom swept Aggie into the dance before she could protest, wearing a familiar pair of worn old boots with one large toe protruding from a hole. Another surprise came when Suzy Ingrum pulled Trevor into the dance. Apparently looks weren't as important to the girl as muscles, and they saw her caressing the Apprentice Smith's throughout the night thereafter with a happy little smirk of approval. After a few minutes of watching them twirl about happily, Mary quietly threatened Wendell's life if he didn't take her dancing as well. Wendell obeyed after an audible gulp and the two were quickly herded into the center of their friends and family as they awkwardly twirled. Then as Wendell started to relax a bit and have some fun, all the dancers began to float several feet off the ground much to the villager's amazement. Bergstrom still swears he had nothing to do with it as he smiles with a twinkle of mirth in his eyes.

ABOUT THE AUTHOR

Dave Cox was born in 1976 in Tacoma, Washington and grew up in several foster homes. He is known for his whimsical personality and blunt honesty, and his favoring of chaos over order for the entertainment value. Dave admits to being a sappy romantic who values family and friendship most in the world and tries to embrace the spiritual rather than the material. When he is not writing, Dave Cox enjoys making jewelry, dolls and other artistic crafts. Dave has been writing since a young age and spent most of his adulthood as an artist and writer. He suffers with insomnia and often uses this time to work on his writing. His daughter inspired several of his earlier works and he is proud she is following in his footsteps and writing her own work today. Dave's characters are collages of the people he has met in this strange journey called life that often make him laugh and cry with their antics and he hopes you enjoy their stories as much as he has writing them. He has completed several science fiction series over the years: Keeper of Dragons, Savage Heart Trilogy, Secret Wars. Dave is currently working a sequel to Wizard Pox.

.

www.ingramcontent.com/pod-product-compliance
Lightning Source LLC
Chambersburg PA
CBHW062003170626
46813CB00001B/15